LIFE FORCE

Richard McKay

ISBN: 978-1-916954-86-1

Dedication

For Mike Hodson.
My best friend in any time period.

Acknowledgment

Mike Hodson for writing the prologue.
My wife and sons for their endless reading and generating ideas.

About the Author

Richard McKay lives with his wife in Utah. They have two married children with one grandson. He enjoys boating, camping, and spending time with his family. Richard holds degrees in Mechanical Engineering and Mathematics.

Prologue

David Merrill noticed that the sun had just set as he moved quickly down the darkening street. He was so focused on the task at hand that he hadn't been paying attention to the time. How ironic, he thought. He was walking fast but not too fast. To the few people he passed by, it looked as if he maintained a brisk walking pace. It was the visual effect he was going for. He knew he couldn't start running. He needed the men following him to think they were doing so undetected. It would be the only way he could surprise them if and when he needed to.

A light rain was falling, which was starting to soak through his pork pie hat and the shoulders of his wool overcoat. Of course, it was not enough that it was cold, he wryly thought, but it had to be wet as well. It was early October, and he could not figure out how people survived here when it got really cold, especially with the basic clothing these people had to choose from.

David Merrill was a young looking 38-year-old with a tall, athletically slender build. He was in excellent physical shape. He ran six miles every other day, and on the days he didn't run, he rode his touring bicycle several miles or swam. Back home, he loved to compete in local triathlons, master swim meets, and marathons. Growing up, he had always been competitive, but as he grew older, he developed an insatiable competitive drive that propelled him in everything.

It was this drive that pushed him through his schooling. After graduating from high school, he attended George Mason University in Virginia, and by the age of 22, he obtained his master's degree in mathematics. David then moved on to receive a doctorate in physics by the age of 24.

He knew going into his schooling that he would never teach for a profession. He instead had his sights set on doing business. After graduating, he unsuccessfully tried to start a business with a mathematics colleague he met in grad school. His business partner did not possess half of the drive that David did.

The business partnership turned ugly, with David demanding a buyout from his partner. David's partner could not afford to have David leave the company, knowing full well that the software they were developing had all been written by David. It was during buyout negotiations that David learned that his partner had been skimming money for personal use from the one and only venture capitalist that David had found and convinced to invest with the company. David sued to take full control of the company, won, and ejected his partner. Once this mess was taken care of, David drove forward to finish the software he had set out to develop.

David's software was truly revolutionary. By using very complicated physics algorithms, his software allowed an individual to view, on a computer screen, the physical effects of what happens to a three-dimensional object when it is hit with any outside force. If an object was hit, bumped, or dropped by the operator's virtual hand, the object reacted as it would in a real three-dimensional environment, complete with appropriate gravitational forces, accelerations, and velocities. Shoot an object with a virtual gun, and the object moves or explodes depending on what it was hit with. The software was originally designed for military applications to show what would happen to targets based on the use of different ordinances but was soon adopted by the video gaming industry for first-person shooter games. No one had seen anything like it, and David's company became an unbelievable success. This success provided his rapidly growing company the resources it needed to create software so advanced that the military deemed it top secret. The company was near the top of the digital mountain, and they weren't looking back.

The cold brought David back into focus on what he needed to do. He chided himself for losing his concentration, even for a few seconds. He continued walking quickly towards his destination. He turned right and came around a large building which put him two blocks away from the entrance to the Charles Bridge.

He had been to Prague once, three years ago, with his girlfriend. Although they were no longer together, he really liked her. She was beautiful and smart but could not understand his unwavering drive. He would work ridiculously long hours and be frequently distracted while out on dates and even during sex. Once he latched on to an idea, he had a hard time letting it go. She suggested the trip to Prague, which seemed obscure to him, but that was her point in choosing the city for their vacation.

She had brought him to the Charles Bridge, which was a popular tourist destination. The bridge was commissioned by the Czech King and Holy Roman Emperor Charles IV in 1357. It spanned the Vltava River, once called the Moulau River, and connected people from Old Town on one side to Malá Strana on the other. People entered through a large tower on either end of the bridge to then be greeted by 30 baroque statues of saints, kings, and other religious figures - all mounted to the balustrade.

St. John of Nepomuk was the name that kept running through David's head. It was the most popular of the statues on the bridge. There was a plaque on the statue, which local legend says, when touched, brings good luck and ensures the person's return to Prague. David remembered someone saying that St. John was a martyr, executed during the reign of King Wenceslas IV.

David entered through the tower on the Old Town side. It was fully dark now, with the faint lights on the wide bridge offering more shadows than light. This is where David felt like he could run. He knew he needed to reach the statue, retrieve what was left for him, and get out of the area quickly. David knew the people following him didn't know exactly where he was going, but he knew if he was spotted retrieving the item, he would have to move fast and be smart. There were very few people on the bridge due to the weather and the hour. He wished it was broad daylight when the bridge is usually crowded with people, but he knew he didn't have a choice. He broke into a sprint.

The statue was located in the middle of the bridge, and if David remembered correctly, the bridge was about 560 yards long. This is where he would surprise his followers and create some much-needed distance. He would need the extra few minutes because, just as with the other destination points, David would have no idea where the item was on the statue. The only thing he had was a note from his last destination point, which read: "An object not of the time of this creation." To David, this meant not of the time of the statue's creation. He reached the statue, and for the first time during his trip through the city, he allowed himself a glance back. He saw no one on the bridge yet, but he did see three figures just coming around the same building that David had. All three were looking around. He saw one figure point to the bridge, and they headed toward the tower entrance. David didn't think they had spotted him yet.

The statue was larger than he remembered it. This may take some time, he thought, as he quickly ducked into the shadows of the statue, looking for a likely hiding place for the object. He knew the containers that held the objects were small, about the size and shape of a pencil box. Still hidden, David climbed up on the balustrade, which allowed him to look around the back of the statue where St. John's robes draped onto the statue's pedestal. He felt slowly around the back of the pedestal, then up to the base of the robe hem. There it was! He knew the object as soon as he touched it. It was the same size and shape as the other objects he had collected at different destination points across the world in the last two exhausting weeks. He immediately forced the thought out of his mind that the object in his hands was the last token of this crazy quest. David refused to let his mind allow his body to relax. The last thing he needed was an overzealous sense of relief, which could dull his senses in any way. He had one last destination point to go before he could allow any such release to occur.

He quickly hopped off of the statue and broke into a run for the opposite end of the bridge. He had already proven previously that if he ran, people following him could lose him easily. He was much faster and in much better shape. These thugs relied on guns and luck. He was nearing the far gate tower when he heard the first shot. The few people on the bridge dropped to the ground, but David didn't slow down one bit. More shots rang out as David reached the far tower. He cleared the entrance quickly, almost running a young couple over. He sidestepped them and continued on. He looked back to see three figures running towards him, then a sharp flash as he rounded the corner.

Once around the building, he ran across a small plaza and cut through a café's patio, which was closed at this time of year. David moved at a good pace through the city for about a mile. He then slowed to a brisk walk again, confident that he had lost his pursuers. What he really needed now was a taxi, but the streets were quiet. He reoriented himself and headed back to the predetermined destination given to him last night. As he walked, he opened the small container. In the past, the containers held paper with clues to what he was to do and where he was to go next. This one held only a small piece of paper that said simply FINISH! He was confused. There was no clue, instruction, or destination point. Just finish?

He threw the container in a trash can and put the paper in the inside pocket of his overcoat. He was fully sweating now and, due to the rain, was wet to the bone, but he didn't feel cold. He was actually surprised to feel so content. He tried to force the feeling of relief and relaxation out of his mind, but he didn't try too hard this time. "I'm only about a mile and a half from my goal; maybe that was why I felt so good," he told himself. Something started to gnaw at David's feeling of contentment, something he missed he thought. He went through every step, every moment of the last 24 hours. No, he told himself, he didn't miss anything. David was not the type to miss things. He was too thorough and complete. It's how he lived his life, and it's why he was a success in school, in business, and in this ridiculous Alice in Wonderland task.

David made another turn which pointed him directly to where he needed to be. He needed to cross a small park then he was home. As he was entering the sparsely lit park entrance, it hit him. He was still breathing hard, he was still warm, and he was bleeding. As he continued into the park, he looked down at the hand that had put the piece of paper in his coat; it was covered in blood. David reached back in under his coat. He felt around and felt a distinct depression just below his left breast on his rib cage. How? How did he not feel that? He figured it was the adrenaline or the fact that he was in shock. The bullet had missed his ribs and exited his body but had punctured his left lung. David didn't know his lung was punctured, but he did know that he was losing blood at a high rate. He thought that would account for the contentment, allowing himself a slight grin. He slowly turned to look back to the route he took into the park. There was a trail of blood. He was leading them right to it! He knew if they reached the destination point before he did, he would lose. Losing was unacceptable! Not because of his drive and determination but because David's existence depended on it. He was almost to the other side of the park. He was almost there. David coughed, bringing the unmistakable coppery taste of blood to his consciousness. He could see the street about four hundred yards ahead, but he noticed that he didn't care as much as he did about this test. He was moving slower now, like a man running in deep dry sand. He stumbled but maintained his balance and kept going. Two hundred yards left. He could do that with no problem. He looked ahead and saw a familiar figure wearing a similar fedora hat and heavy wool coat. There's Jonah, he thought loudly to himself. He saw Jonah lift his arm in what David thought was a greeting. Jonah was not saying hello; he was trying to warn David. At that moment, it wasn't the sound but the thud of the bullet in his upper back that resonated with him the most as he fell to the wet ground. David managed to roll to his side to try and get up, but he couldn't move. The last thought that crossed his mind as his life left his body was how strange it was that he would die here in Prague in 1935.

Chapter 1

March 2016

Ryan White had seen dead bodies before. And not just one or two bodies either, but hundreds of bodies in all kinds of conditions. The bodies of the old and sick, the bodies of the young and healthy, the bodies of those involved in car and industrial accidents, homicide victims, as well as the bodies of children, much too young to die. Then there were the bodies of those who chose to end it all. The suicide victims were the strangest. The logic that some of these individuals used regarding the method of how to carry out their final act always escaped Ryan. Some of the suicide bodies were totally without blemish, while some were horribly mangled. The worst were the folks who felt that the only way suicide would be effective would be to use a twelve-gauge shotgun to the face. The effectiveness was total and gruesome.

Ryan had worked for a mortuary when he was in college. Digging graves, washing hearses and limos, mowing the grass, delivering flowers to grave sites, and any other odd job that needed to be done. So this shouldn't be anything new. But, for some reason, the man lying in the casket seemed different to him than the others he had seen before.

He stood staring at his father. The cosmeticians at the mortuary had done a very good job in presenting him for the viewing. What Ryan couldn't quite get over was the fact that he actually looked much better now than he had a few days before, which was the last time he saw him alive.

His father was 86 and had been very sick for quite a while. The cancer he had suffered from was merciless in its painful attack but patient in its finality. Frankly, Ryan and his siblings weren't sure how he hung on for so long. There were a number of theories, but it was finally concluded that he was just a stubborn old goat and wasn't going to leave until he was good and ready. He died as he lived. On his own terms.

Ryan wasn't with him when he died. For a few months before his father died, he and his brother and three sisters had been taking turns sleeping over at their parent's home to help their mom with their father during the night. The night before he died was Ryan's turn. The cancer was slowly destroying his body. Something else entirely was ravaging his mind. The doctors had never settled on Alzheimer's or Parkinson's. It really didn't matter. It was a foregone conclusion that the cancer would kill him long before the neurological disease he had been battling on another front. However, there were brief moments when he was quite lucid and able to carry on a conversation. Miraculously, that night was one of those times. Ryan and his father talked about everyday stuff. Politics, books, football, normally boring things like that. But there was nothing boring about that night. It was a night he would always remember and treasure. It was the simple pleasure of hanging out and talking with his dad like he had done, not nearly enough, in the past.

Ryan was called out of town on business the next day. His brother called him about 10:30 pm that night on his way from the airport to the hotel to tell him that their father had died. Surprisingly, Ryan didn't cry. He felt more relieved than sad. His father had endured a great amount of pain and suffering over the last couple of years, and he was ready and blessed to move on.

In fact, he didn't cry until he was standing there staring at his father in the casket. He was a wonderful father, and Ryan knew that he would be with him again someday. Maybe not in this life but certainly in the life to follow.

Chapter 2

September 2016

"Time out!!" Ryan called his team over to the sideline. "Alright, we've got two yards to go, you guys," he said as his players jogged over and took a knee. They were down by four points. It was fourth down, and there was just under a minute left in the game. They were on their own 40-yard line so those two yards seemed like a very long way to go. "This is our last time out guys, so we need to do this right the first time, got it? We just need two yards, but you have to get those yards and get out of bounds to stop the clock. Let's focus! You all know your assignments. We're only down by four points! If we play smart and get to the sideline, we should have enough time to get in three plays to score! Are you with me?!" Ryan asked his exhausted players. "Yeah," they all called out in unison. He looked at all of them in turn. They were sweating and breathing hard, but their energy was unbelievable. Ryan had been the coach of this team since they first started at age eight. Now, at fourteen, they were an incredible bunch of kids. He had told his wife, Michele, many times that he'd be a little league coach full-time if it paid better. Or paid anything at all, for that matter. Ryan's 14-year-old son, Jackson, was one of the stars on the team. Or, more appropriately, one of the "studs," as they are usually referred to. He's a great athlete despite only weighing a hundred five pounds, dripping wet. His athletic ability had enabled him to play just about every position on the field other than lineman. He understood the game as well or better than Ryan did. Many times, they drew plays together at night and he would 'correct' his father when he came up with something that just wouldn't work. Right now, the coaches are using him as a wide-out receiver since he is their fastest player and has the best hands on the team.

Ryan and Michele have two sons. Jackson is the oldest at fourteen, and his little brother Colton is the younger at eight years old. The young parents had always been puzzled at both their sons' athletic abilities. In each of their age groups, the two boys are recognized for their great athleticism. Neither Ryan nor Michele had ever played organized sports when they were young. Ryan was very active as a kid participating in every sport under the sun, but usually only in neighborhood pick-up games.

"Okay guys, we're going to run a 24 fake, bootleg right on two," Ryan said, looking around at the kids in their sideline huddle. The play is designed to fake a handoff to the fullback who would run up the middle, hopefully drawing one or more of the linebackers to him at the center of the line. The quarterback would then run to the right side of the line getting the two yards they needed and running out of bounds to stop the clock. This play would only work if the tight end and receiver made their lead blocks. Blocking properly was one of the most difficult things to teach, but over the years they had all learned to make excellent blocks. Most of the time. Jackson was up against a much bigger cornerback and would have his hands full. So far, he'd been able to burn him on routes but wasn't having great success in blocking him. The referee blew his whistle, and the team ran back to the field to get set.

"Down...Set!" the quarterback called out loudly looking both right and left.

"Hut, hut!" The ball was snapped, and it looked like the fake was working perfectly, but as the quarterback rolled to his right, he slipped on the wet grass and almost went down. In the league they were playing, if the player's knee touched the ground, the play was over. Ryan realized right then that there was no way he was going to make the two yards they needed for the first down. Jackson had made his block perfectly and turned just in time to see the quarterback slip and almost fall and get caught in the backfield. Jackson then left his man and took off down the field and raised his hand calling for the quarterback to pass the ball. At 14 years old, the quarterback had a decent arm but not great. Just before a 200 lb. defensive tackle annihilated him, he threw the ball as hard as he could toward Jackson, racing down the field. The quarterback's pass was high, well over Jackson's head. Jackson timed his leap perfectly and was able to just tip the ball with his fingers to slow it down, allowing him to grasp and pull the ball in while still running towards the end zone 50 yards away. The whole team, coaches included, all began running down the sidelines with him, screaming as they went. A defensive safety was quickly cutting across the field on a collision course. 20, 15, 10, Jackson was sprinting for the end zone. As he dove head first for the goal line, the safety stretched out and grabbed for the only thing he could bring Jackson down before he crossed the line. What the defensive player had a hold of was Jackson's face mask. The defensive player fell while still holding the face mask which caused Jackson's neck to turn sharply to the side while his body was slammed violently to the ground. The tackle happened in a split second and ended just two feet inside the end zone. The force of Jackson's body hitting the ground caused the ball to bounce off of his chest pads and roll out of bounds. But it didn't matter. The ball had crossed the plane of the end zone while he had possession of the ball. Ryan looked at the game clock. There were ten seconds left. He looked at the referee just in time to see his arms go up, signaling a touchdown. They were up by two points. The sideline and the fans went crazy. The whole team was now in the endzone, but Ryan couldn't see Jackson. He was straining to see his son through the celebration. He was already thinking about the extra point play when one lof the players yelled, "Coach, coach, Jackson's hurt." Ryan ran down the field to the end zone and saw Jackson lying on his back, players from both teams surrounding him. He wasn't moving. Over the years, Michele had her husband promise that whenever one of the players went down, he would hold his hand up when he got to them to let her know they were okay. Ryan's hand didn't go up. He knelt down over Jackson. He had seen his son scared before, but the fear he saw in his eyes left him nearly speechless.

"Jackson, you're okay. Where does it hurt?"

He looked into his father's eyes and cried, "I can't move my legs, dad."

Chapter 3

July 2163

Mary Bainbridge stared at the stack of papers on her desk. She was supposed to file them but didn't really feel like it. Even though 'filing them' simply meant lifting them from her desk and placing them in the filer. The filer was fully automatic and would do everything for her. She absentmindedly placed her hand in the PerfectNails 2200. When she removed her hand, each finger was perfectly manicured, and each nail was painted a different color. Mary was bored but content. Although she wasn't aware of it, she was the poster child of what the human race had become. Bored but content. Too content.

Mary worked at the Life Force Institute. She is the executive secretary for Darius Ramsey. Darius is the CEO and President of the Life Force Institute. On the outside, the Life Force Institute is a non-profit organization committed to environmental conservation and wilderness protection. On the inside, however, a very different mission statement had been formed. Darius' father, Alexander Ramsey, had formed the institute around the turn of the 22nd century. Alexander was a brilliant man with a flair for the dramatic, and he was committed to changing the world. One person at a time, if necessary. When Alexander began the Life Force Institute, he could see that the world was changing, and not for the better. His goal was to somehow re-invigorate the human race to bring back creativity, ingenuity, and excitement. Bring back entrepreneurship and risk-taking. It had been a long time since the human race had shown those characteristics.

In September 2026, twenty-five years after the devastating 9/11 attack in New York City, Washington, D.C., and Pennsylvania, a series of twenty coordinated biological terrorist attacks were carried out worldwide. Los Angeles, New York, and Chicago were attacked in the United States. London, Paris, Berlin, and Madrid were hit as part of the European Union. Cities in Asia, Africa, Mexico, Argentina, and Australia were also included in the attack. More than one Islamic Fundamentalist cells had claimed responsibility, but it had never been confirmed which one. The initial casualties were horrendous. Within a week, over 250,000 were killed worldwide, but what followed was much, much worse. The virus used in the attacks quickly mutated and became airborne. Possibly even the terrorists had not planned this level of destruction. Ground zero for the mutation was Central Africa. Entire populations were wiped out. Mass graves were filled until, finally, cremation was universally accepted to prevent further disease. The virulent strain moved into Europe, where it was slowed but not stopped. In February 2027, the first case of the airborne strain showed up in the United States. Although international travel had been shut down, somehow, the virus made its way to the Americas. The Centers for Disease Control worked quickly to quarantine outbreaks, but the disease still spread. By 2028, virologists had been able to develop and distribute a vaccine throughout the world. But the damage had been done. The number of lives lost was staggering. Estimates ranged from 750 million to over 1 billion worldwide. The total number was never accurately tabulated. The political and social fabric of the entire planet had been irreversibly altered.

In late 2028, the United Nations was dissolved. A New Global Union was proposed. Against heavy protest from the citizenry, especially in middle America, the United States joined the NGU. The United States economy had virtually collapsed. The current administration in power at the time felt that the only solution was complete government control. Over the next decade, the United States went from a capitalist country to a completely socialist, nearly communistic, society. The dream of the founding fathers had turned into a nightmare. The government controlled the airline industry, the automobile industry, banking, farming, manufacturing, housing, healthcare, pharmaceuticals, and even the dairy industry. Everything was socialized. In order to pay for everything, the government tax structure went through the roof. Anyone making over $100,000 per year was taxed above 75%. Karl Marx's utopia 'From each according to his ability, to each according to his need,' had become a reality.

At first, things seemed to be working. But as any historian will tell you, any time a group of people is given what they need and don't need to work for it, the end result will be negative. There was no motivation to succeed. No entrepreneurs. Nobody was willing to take a risk. For what? If you succeeded, the government would take everything away from you. By the time Alexander Ramsey was born, a generation of Americans had been under this socialist regime, and the effects were nearly unimaginable. But very real

Chapter 4

September 2016

"Don't move," Ryan said. "We need an ambulance!" He held Jackson's head steady, leaned close to his head, and whispered into his helmet, "Stay still, son. Don't try to move. Everything's gonna be okay." Suddenly, Michele was there.

"What's wrong?" she cried.

"He's going to be fine. We need to get a stretcher, though." Jackson was miraculously calm. He was either too scared or in shock. The rest of the team was a different story. Ryan heard a commotion behind him. He turned to look and saw half his team squaring off with the other team trying to get at the player who had face-masked Jackson. He could hear a lot of profanity and yelling from parents and players but figured he'd let the other coaches handle that. People from the stands had even started to filter down onto the field. In the far recesses of Ryan's mind, he was thinking about the extra-point play. But he figured he'd let the other coaches handle that as well. Suddenly, winning the game didn't matter that much.

It only took the ambulance about three minutes to get there. But it felt like an hour. There was always an ambulance at every game. The EMTs on the weekend assignment were probably excited to have something to do. Ryan didn't share in their excitement. The two paramedics looked like they could have played for the team, they were so young. But they at least had some training. "What've we got, coach?" the wiry paramedic asked as he set down the backboard and pulled his penlight out. "His neck got wrenched and he says he can't feel his legs," Ryan said with a little quiver in his voice. The medic looked at Ryan with new concern in his eyes then knelt down and checked

Jackson's pupils. Ryan held his son's head while the other paramedic secured a collar around his neck. The collar was much smaller than usual since they kept his helmet on. Michele had arranged for a friend to take their other son, Colton, to the hospital. Ryan looked over at Colton and saw him crying. He was only eight, and even though they fought like cats and dogs, he knew he loved his brother very much and looked up to him. This all must have been pretty scary for him, as well. He called him over and gave him a hug and told him everything was going to be okay.

They were taking Jackson to Mountainside Medical Center. But Ryan wasn't about to follow in his car. Both he and his wife got in the ambulance with Jackson. "I'm sorry, sir. You can't ride back here," one of the paramedics tried to tell them. Ryan just looked at him and then slowly looked back at Jackson. The paramedic sighed and closed the door.

There's nothing worse than emergency room waiting rooms, Ryan thought as they arrived at the hospital. There's nothing to do and you can't get any information from anyone. "We'll let you know when we hear something," or "You'll have to wait to speak to the doctor." Bullshit like that just pissed Ryan off. He didn't know what he expected them to say but it wasn't helping. Michele was on the phone with her mom. "He can't feel his legs, Mom," he heard her say as she paced back and forth. She hung up and went over and put her head in her husband's chest and sobbed, "What are we going to do? Tell me he's going to be okay."

"He will be," Ryan said unconvincingly.

"What the hell was that stupid-ass kid thinking, anyway? Yanking his neck around like that," she asked. She had been bouncing between being pissed and being scared ever since the ambulance arrived and Jackson had been wheeled into the emergency room.

"I don't know. If it was up to me, he'd be thrown out of the league," Ryan said.

"That kind of flagrant foul is way over the line." He knew deep down that in a game situation like that, the kid probably didn't try to hurt Jackson. But he was still pissed.

The rest of the team and their parents started showing up. Steve Simmons, one of the other coaches, approached Ryan slowly.

"How's he doing?"

"We don't know yet."

"Well, when you see him, you can tell him he won the game," Steve said, somewhat sheepishly. He knew the coach didn't care but he also knew Jackson would. "We scored the extra point. We kicked off, and our boys destroyed them. They didn't even gain a yard," he explained. "That's good," Ryan said somewhat absentmindedly and turned back to Michele. He wasn't trying to be rude, but at that moment, he didn't care at all about the damn football game. He appreciated Steve for letting him know, though.

"Ryan White?" a nurse called from the front desk. Michele and Ryan rushed over.

"How is he?"

"The doctor's ready to see you. Please follow me," she said rather coldly. The two nervously followed her down the sterile, antiseptic hall with all those 'wonderful' hospital smells. Something akin to urine mixed with alcohol and a bleach chaser. Dr. Valenteen introduced himself and shook Ryan and Michele's hands. "Your son is a very lucky young man. His third and fourth vertebrae were strained but his spinal cord was not penetrated or compromised," he explained. Michele heard the word vertebrae and gasped and started crying again. "His temporary paralysis was caused by the swelling. He'll need a lot of rest, but all our tests show that he should make a full recovery."

"Can we see him?" Ryan asked as he breathed a silent relief.

"Of course, follow me," the doctor said.

"Hey, bud," Ryan said as they walked into his room. He looked tired but surprisingly not too bad.

"Hey, Dad. Hi Mom," Jackson replied quietly.

"Jackson." Michele was crying again.

She went to the other side of the bed and kissed his cheek. Jackson gave a little smile and said "Dad, I can't remember. Did I make it?"

"You sure did, you won the game," Ryan said with a smile.

"What happened?" he asked.

"The safety tried to twist your head off. I guess he wanted it for a souvenir," his dad joked but got no laugh. Just a somewhat dirty look from his wife. "But the doctor says you're going to be just fine."

"You need to get some rest, though," Michele said.

"I'll go talk to the doctor and see when we can go home," Ryan said. He held his fist up to Jackson and he gave him 'knuckles.' At 14, he was too old for a kiss from his old man. Ryan started to leave, but stopped. 'To hell with it,' he thought. He went back over to Jackson's bed and bent down and gave him a kiss on the forehead. He didn't seem to mind too much.

The doctor said they wanted to keep him for a day or two, just to be sure. The relieved father gave the news to his son and wife and then walked back to the waiting room to tell the rest of the team the good news. When he got back out, he was shocked at what he saw. The place was packed. Their whole team was there. Their parents were there. And, about half of the other team was there with their parents. There must have been over 50 people standing around.

The receptionist looked at Ryan coldly and said, "I'm going to have to ask these people to leave. This isn't a social hall!"

"Just give me a minute," he asked. All of a sudden, Sean came over. "How is he?" he asked.

"He's going to be okay. He was pretty lucky."

Sean Jensen and Ryan had been best friends since they were 7 years old. What puzzled Ryan was how Sean had even found out. "What are you doing here?" he asked.

"Michele's mom called me," he said. Ryan nodded. He felt kind of bad for not calling him but with everything that had happened, he figured he'd understand.

"Can I have everyone's attention?" Ryan raised his arms and his voice. "The doctor said that Jackson was very lucky. His neck was strained, and he temporarily lost feeling in his legs. But he should be fine," he explained. A cheer went up in the waiting room. A glance at the receptionist showed she was not happy. From the back of the crowd, a young player from the other team approached Ryan, still wearing his pads and jersey. He had obviously been crying. And it took a lot to get a 14-year-old to cry these days. The coach didn't recognize him with his helmet off, but he remembered his number. "I'm really sorry for hurting your son, coach," he said sorrowfully with his head down. "I didn't mean to."

"I know you didn't, and so does Jackson." He knew he was being sincere and kind of felt bad for being so mad. "Thanks for coming to make sure he was okay. That means a lot." He put his hand on the player's shoulder and noticed a tear hit the floor. It wasn't his. It was Ryan's. He wiped his eyes and looked back at the crowd.

"That goes for everyone," he raised his voice again. "Thanks for coming. But I've been told we need to clear out or we'll all be sedated and given rectal exams," he joked. A chuckle went through the crowd as people started to leave. He stole a glance over at the receptionist, but she had already returned to her stack of exciting paperwork. But he did notice a slight grin on her face. Not so cold after all, he thought.

Chapter 5

July 2163

"Mary, please send him in," Darius called to his secretary.

"Mr. Ramsey will see you now."

The old man stood and walked into the director's office. The office was enormous. The ceiling was at least 75' high. It was decorated in the 'Old World' style. It had a mariner's theme. A complete 40' sailboat hung from the impossibly high ceiling. The old man was sure that one of these times it was going to fall on him. Those cables could not possibly hold on forever. He had always wondered how the hell they got that boat in here in the first place! They must have built the room around it, he figured. As always, he walked around the edge of the office so as not to travel directly beneath the boat. There were several model ships placed around the office. A wooden steering wheel from an old sailboat was mounted on the wall behind Darius' desk. A large world globe sat alone in the center of the room on top of a two-dimensional map of the world. Several large projection screens were mounted in a circle around the room. No expense had been spared in creating this fortress of an office. Darius sat behind a large antique mahogany desk, perfectly restored with nothing but one single blank sheet of paper on top.

"Ah, there you are, my friend," Darius said cheerfully. "Please, sit down. Make yourself comfortable." Darius actually came out from behind his desk and pulled a chair from the corner of the office so it sat in front of his desk.

"Thank you," the old man said quietly as he sat down. Darius sat down next to him. The old man was actually shaking. Not with fear necessarily. Just apprehension. He had worked for Darius for years. Actually, he had started out working for

Darius' father, Alexander. When he first started, he and Alexander had been quite close friends and had known each other since they were boys. They were roughly the same age and had gone through many of the same trials and tribulations. As Alexander grew the company, he had not elevated his friend at the same rate. But, he was always fair with him and was loyal. Darius had carried on the treatment but the old man never felt completely comfortable around him. There was no real reason, just something unsettling about the man.

"The reason I've asked to see you is, I have a small problem," Darius started out.

"Surely you are aware of my efforts in our genetic engineering lab? Well, of course, you are, that's where you spend most of your time, isn't it?"

The old man nodded, but didn't look directly at his boss.

"Yes, well. As you know, our genetics team has, how should I say, failed miserably. This sheet of paper on my desk is the sum total of all the information we have been able to glean so far from our experiments," Darius reached for the paper, held it up and let it drift from his hand onto the floor next to his desk.

"Well, th...that's not entirely true," the old man stammered. "We've been able to gather a significant amount of data from each experiment, save for the last one. We have data on intelligence, physical stamina..."

"Yes, yes," Darius interrupted and stood up. "I'm familiar with the minute amount of data that you 'think' you have. But I'm not sure you completely understand the big picture," as he held his hands up above the globe in the center of the room. Always the showman. The old man leaned up in his chair so he could watch Darius' performance. "The very problem we're trying to solve is causing our biggest failure. It's like the alchemists of old. Trying to get gold from iron. Our test subjects are too afflicted with the disease we're trying to rid them of."

The old man furrowed his brow in confusion.

"Let me put it this way," Darius continued as he sat back down in his chair, "we've gone as far as we can with our current pool of volunteers."

"Well, we can broaden our search. Even beyond our borders," the old man suggested meekly.

"No, no. You still don't understand, my friend. We cannot use any human test subjects from today," Darius stood up and walked behind the old man and put his hands on his shoulders.

"I'm not sure what you mean, sir," the old man said quietly as he seemingly shrunk under Darius' hands.

Darius put his mouth just inches from the old man's ear. "We're going to need to go back. Before the plague. Before the government turned us into slaves. Back when people still had their freedom and could hold their heads high. That's where we'll find what we need. And you're going to lead the effort!"

The old man closed his eyes. "Sir, if you're talking about using the orb, you know what happened last time," the old man said sadly.

The orb technology that made time travel possible was developed near the end of the 21st century. However, the technology had not been refined and due to serious health effects and several tragic experiments gone wrong, the implementation of any time travel or time travel experimentation was made illegal worldwide with severe penalties for violators. Not to mention the fact that experimentation in this realm was extremely expensive. Plus, the very real problem of altering the past and thus altering the future was not completely understood but genuinely feared by most scientists. After the devastation in 2026, not many individuals or even companies had the resources to conduct widespread test campaigns. Some had reported minimal success recently. But they conveniently disappeared, along with their labs, with no explanation or inquiry. Scientists from around the world had thrown up their hands in defeat and the technology development had ceased. Most of those with adequate resources had been thwarted by the moral implications of time travel. As with other ventures, however, Darius Ramsey was not deterred by the threat of 'penalties' and was not affected at all by moral or ethical issues. He had formed a team inside the Life Force Institute that had managed to solve the enormous engineering complexities needed to not only perfect time travel but also make it technically safe. At least so far. Very little effort had been expended toward the problem of the space-time continuum. A term that had lasted from 20th century Hollywood but was actually very accurate in its definition. In fact, the first successful time travel experiment was conducted in a laboratory named Enterprise. Very few people beyond the scientific community understood the implied humor.

Darius had taken his father's vision and modified the parameters, to say the least. Darius was not interested in changing people's behavior or in social engineering. He had come to the conclusion that his father's quest had failed. Darius' intent, as he had explained it to his staff, was to change the very essence of the human body and spirit. Or more to the point, to create the perfect human. His new vision and the major project at the Life Force Institute was genetic engineering. Over the previous hundred years or so, significant advances have been realized in the arena of genetic engineering. The entire genetic code had been completely mapped around 2075. It was this basis that Darius had started with. To create humans with the intelligence of Einstein, Mayer, or Southwick and the strength and physical prowess of top athletes. These traits had been relatively easy to quantify and isolate. What was missing were other, less tangible characteristics such as loyalty, compassion, willingness to take risks, cunning, bravery, or even love. People of Darius' time were sorely lacking in these areas. In order to attempt to quantify these aspects of humanity, the Life Force Institute would select teams to participate in various competitions. These competitions were meant to physically and mentally push the participants and force them to make sometimes very difficult choices and then use that experience in an effort to instill those traits back into Darius' improved society. Some of these competitions had little or no reward for the participants. Some offered very elaborate and lavish gifts. In nearly all these competitions, however, neither team had the fortitude or endurance to complete the task. They almost always ended in some sort of tie, or one or both teams would simply quit or lose interest. Meaningful data was difficult to decipher.

Darius quickly realized that it was going to be impossible to genetically engineer the types of characteristics he was looking for with the currently available pool of participants. He needed to find test subjects that had not been affected by The Incident in 2026, as it had come to be known. Darius' first attempts to gather contestants from past generations had ended quite badly. Fortitude and endurance were not the problem. Both teams selected had completed the task and one team was victorious. The subjects in the first test were taken from the year 2017 and sent back in time to the year 1935. The jump back in time, he had explained, was meant to add another factor, confusion of the subjects and disorientation, to the mix. But something went seriously wrong with the time travel device and both teams had been tragically killed. Several members of each team had families. As far as their families knew, their loved ones had simply disappeared overnight, with no explanation or closure to the mystery. At that point, attempts at time travel had been temporarily halted, as far as the old man knew. Now, Darius was suggesting to resume the tests with subjects from the past and that thought terrified the old man.

"I do know what happened last time," Darius replied. "But, as you know, the new travel orb has been perfected and there is very little chance of malfunction. In addition, we will be able to utilize the consciousness transfer technology we recently perfected."

The consciousness transfer Darius spoke of was not time travel, per se. The consciousness (their mind, memories, self-awareness) of an individual could be transferred to that same individual in an earlier time frame. So, time travel was necessary for an 'Institute Handler' to initiate and complete the transfer but the participant would not actually travel through time. Their consciousness would simply be transferred to an earlier version of themselves. It was groundbreaking technology that belonged solely to the Life Force Institute. It was well guarded and nobody outside the Institute knew of its existence. Many attempts had been made to transfer the consciousness of one individual to another person, but it was soon discovered that a neural signature existed that prevented such a transfer. Attempts had been made to go around this neural signature, but all had failed. Therefore, a person's consciousness, including memories and experiences, could only be transferred to a younger version of that same person. The technology worked both ways. At a given time, the transferred consciousness could be 'erased', and the individual in question would return to their normal 'self.' Of course, this imposed some obvious limitations. Obviously, a person's consciousness could only go back as far as that person's life permitted. There also were limitations with age. Before approximately age 12, the transfer did not work. Physicists at the Institute eventually threw up their hands and could not adequately explain the age boundary. The best explanation was that the brain had not sufficiently matured enough to handle the transfer.

"Yes, sir. I am aware. But we have not had any research teams in the field. We don't have any suitable teams selected. It could be months or even years before we're ready," the old man said, hoping that this could possibly deter Darius' intentions.

"Don't worry about that. I have already selected the teams and have completed the necessary research," Darius said with finality.

The old man didn't have anything else he could say. He had to admit that he was curious how Darius had managed to complete all the necessary research and fieldwork to select two suitable teams. Something deep inside him was making him very nervous about what was about to happen.

"If I'm right," Darius continued, "this could be the final test needed. Gather your team and assemble in the atrium for the briefing."

Darius returned to his desk, sat down, and turned away from his guest. The old man sat still for a moment. Then got up slowly and walked out of the office, unaware, or at least not caring, that he was walking directly beneath the ship that hung from the ceiling. It wasn't the time travel he was most concerned about or even the consciousness transfer. It was the disruption of lives and families that bothered him. He was committed to the cause, as he understood it, and felt it could ultimately better humanity. But lately, Darius was becoming less and less concerned with human life and more concerned with the 'mission.' This is what made the old man tremble as he left.

Chapter 6

2016

A few weeks after Jackson's close call, the White family had been invited over to Sean's house for a barbeque. While the rest of his family had gone ahead, Ryan had a few things to catch up on. As he headed out towards Sean's house to join them, he started thinking again how close they had come to real tragedy. He'd been doing a lot of that kind of thinking lately. If Jackson had been paralyzed, their lives would have been completely changed. He thanked God in a silent prayer for watching out for Jackson and bringing him back to them in one piece. One working piece, he thought.

As he drove, he thought about how lucky he truly was. He had two handsome and healthy sons that were well-behaved most of the time. He had a beautiful, loving wife who was a great mother and his best friend. He had a good-paying job that he didn't hate. They had plenty of friends and family close by. As he drove along patting himself on the back, he came to a stop light. It was about 6:30 pm, and it had started to get dark. As he waited for the light to turn, a lone man was walking across the street in the crosswalk in front of his car. He was dressed in a dark gray raincoat and a fedora hat. He was holding what looked like a small basketball in his hands. His hat was pulled down so Ryan couldn't really see his face in the dusk light. As he crossed in front of the car, he stopped and turned towards Ryan, and looked directly into his eyes. Ryan raised his eyebrows and his hands as if to ask 'What?' He was about to roll down the window and ask what his problem was but the man turned and continued across the street. 'Well that was weird,' Ryan thought out loud. The light turned green and he proceeded through the intersection. He looked in his rearview mirror and could see the entire corner sidewalk where the man had been headed. He was gone! Simply vanished. Unless he had sprinted once he hit the corner, there was nowhere he could have gone. There was no way to turn around or go back so Ryan just went on.

When he got to Sean's house, the barbeque was in full swing. Sean had bested him in the kidlet department by one. He had a 15-year-old son, Mark, a 10 year old son, Mike, and a little 4 year old girl, Elizabeth. His wife, Cindy, was carrying a plate of burgers to the backyard when Ryan pulled up.

"Let me help you," he offered.

"Thanks. That's the third plate of burgers I've brought out. You'd think nobody had eaten for days," she sighed. Cindy was great. She and Michele got along really well which always helped when he and Sean wanted a golf day or wanted to play 'Call of Duty' in his basement.

Ryan walked out back with the plate of burgers and gave them to the official cook, Sean's dad, Sean Sr... "Thanks," he said. "They'll be ready in a minute."

Sean had invested a bunch of money in lighting for his backyard. It looked like it was high noon and the backyard was pretty full. Sean came from a big family. As far as Ryan could tell, they were all there. Kids everywhere. He always thought of Sean's brothers and sisters as the little twerps they had to babysit now and then when they were in high school. Now they were all grown up and had kids of their own. 'Man, I'm old,' he thought.

Sean and Michele were over spotting kids on the tramp. Funny, he thought. When they were kids, they never had anyone spotting them. More than once, one of them had gone through the springs or fell clean off. They just picked themselves up and got back on.

"So, if one of these kids goes shooting off here, you're actually going to catch them?" Ryan asked Sean as he approached the trampoline.

"Hell, no," he said. "I'll just volleyball spike 'em over the fence, so the neighbors will have to deal with them," he joked.

"Hey, I gotta talk to you about something when you have a minute," Ryan said.

Michele came over to their side of the tramp. "What, did you find a new girlfriend to replace me?" she asked quizzically.

"Yea, she was about 70 years old and looked a lot like an old man," he retorted back.

"What the heck are you talking about?" she asked.

"Yea, dude, that was pretty random," Sean added.

"It seemed anything but random to me," he said. He proceeded to tell them about the experience with the man in the crosswalk.

"Just some confused old blue hair," Sean said. "I wouldn't worry about it."

"I'm not worried, just a little freaked," he said with more than a little apprehension in his voice. "If you could have seen his eyes. They seemed to look right through me into the back seat. It was weird, to say the least."

"Burgers are ready," Sean Sr. announced.

"Let's eat," they all said in unison.

Ryan had managed to forget about his experience with the old man in the crosswalk for the rest of the party. On the way home, the kids fell asleep almost immediately.

"So what was up with that old guy, do you think?" Michele asked.

"I have no idea," Ryan said. "It wouldn't have been so weird if he hadn't disappeared like he did."

Michele was doubtful. "He couldn't have just disappeared, Ryan. Maybe you just didn't see which way he went."

"No way, Michele, I could see the whole corner, in both directions for 20 feet or so. There was no place for him to go," he argued.

"Didn't you say it was already getting dark? Maybe he just blended in. You did say he was wearing a dark grey coat," she countered.

"Yea, maybe you're right," he said more to himself than to her. "In any event, I doubt I'll ever see him again, so let's just forget about it."

"That sounds like a good idea," she said. Then she put her head back and fell asleep for the remainder of the ride home.

After they got the kids to bed, they flopped on their California king, totally exhausted. They'd had the bed for nearly 10 years, and it still felt great. As they got into bed, Ryan turned to Michele and said, "Earlier tonight I was thinking how lucky I am."

"What do you mean?" she asked.

"Well, it's just that compared to a lot of alternatives, we've got it pretty good. I mean, we're not rich but we're not hurting. Our kids are healthy, thank goodness." he pointed his eyes toward Jackson's room. "And we still love each other after 19 years of marriage which is pretty rare these days," he said, kind of mushy-like.

She gave him a strange look and rolled on top of him. "Yea, I guess I can put up with you for a few more years," she said with a smile. Ryan rolled her nightgown off her shoulders and reached over, and turned off the light. "I love you, honey," he whispered in the dark. Sleep would have to wait a little while tonight.

Chapter 7

2016

Even though Ryan's wife and best friend didn't think much of his 'encounter' with the old man in the crosswalk, he couldn't get it out of his mind. The thing that bothered him the most was the way the old man looked at him. It wasn't just that he was looking him in the eye but it felt like the old man was looking right through him.

Ryan was driving through downtown Salt Lake City taking care of some honey-do's he had been 'assigned.' It was hard getting around with so much construction going on. It always seemed like a building was either coming down or going up. He supposed that was good news for the local economy, but it was a pain to navigate around. As he drove up State Street looking for his next errand destination, he looked at one of the new buildings going up. If he hadn't gone into chemical engineering, Ryan thought he would have chosen structural engineering. It was amazing to him to see how quickly these huge buildings went up. He slowed and stopped at a red light. He watched as one crane lifted another crane onto a higher level. The amount of weight involved was staggering. As he watched where the new crane was going, he noticed something that took his breath away and made the hair on the back of his neck stand straight up. Standing on the steel beam directly above where the crane was going was the same old man in the grey coat and fedora hat! Ryan was sure it was him. The light turned green but he didn't drive through the intersection. Instead, he quickly pulled over and looked up. The man was still there. He couldn't see him very well at this distance, then he remembered something. A couple of weeks ago, he had gone to a basketball game with his family. Still trying to keep his eyes on the old man, he reached back with his arm and searched blindly for a small black case. There it was. He grabbed the case and pulled out a pair of binoculars. He looked up through them and adjusted the focus. Just as he thought. Or just as he feared, it was more like it. The guy was looking right at him! He pulled the binoculars away and stared up at the man as he slowly started to walk along the beam moving out of view. Ryan looked through the binoculars again but couldn't see him. He didn't know what to think.

Something was going on but he couldn't imagine what it was. How did an old man get up on a steel beam at least 100 feet up in the air without being noticed or stopped by the construction crew?

Ryan jammed his truck into gear and pulled across the street into the construction yard. There were all kinds of signs saying 'Stay Out' or 'Authorized Personnel Only.' He ignored them all, threw his truck into park, and jumped out. He grabbed the first guy in a hard hat and asked where the foreman was. The construction worker pointed to a white trailer about 50' away. Ryan started to walk toward the trailer when the guy he'd been talking to yelled, "Hey, you need a hard hat in here!" Ryan ignored him and kept going. 'They could arrest me for all I care,' he thought to himself. He had to know how that old man got up on that beam.

Ryan walked up to the trailer and pulled the door open a little too hard. It slammed into the railing with a loud "whack." All heads turned toward the sound. The inside of the trailer had a conference room in the middle with small offices around the outside. The conference room was completely full of construction workers sitting around a large table and scattered around the room on single chairs. The room fell completely silent as Ryan stood awkwardly in the doorway. "You looking for anyone in particular, mister?" the only person in a suit asked. He was sitting at the head of the table with a set of blueprints in front of him and was obviously running the meeting.

"I'd like to talk to the foreman," Ryan said rather sheepishly, not knowing exactly who he should be talking to.

"Well, he's sittin' right over there but you're going to have to wait. We'll be done in about an hour," the same guy said rather rudely. He turned back to the table and restarted the meeting. In the back of his mind, Ryan started to think about how his question about the old man on the steel beam was going to sound. Especially in front of all these hardened construction workers, he was sure he'd get laughed out of the trailer. So, instead, he said something like "fine" or "okay" and walked back out. He heard somebody say something as he turned and the entire room erupted in laughter.

Ryan walked slowly and with much less bravado back to his truck. He got in and as he began to back up, he looked in the rearview mirror. There was the old man! He was standing at the entrance to the construction site, which was about 50 feet behind Ryan's truck. He was holding something in his hands. It looked like a bowling ball but smaller. Ryan jumped out of his truck and started half-jogging, half-running towards him. As he did so, the old man began walking down the sidewalk out of view. Ryan yelled "Hey" a couple of times to try and slow the old man down but when he reached the entrance to the construction site, he looked in the direction the old man had walked. He was gone. Again, simply vanished. The protective fence they had installed at the edge of the site ran for at least 100 yards in the direction he had gone. Unless he was an Olympic track star, there was no way he could have reached the end by the time Ryan got there. Ryan stood, dumbfounded. He was starting to seriously consider that he was losing his mind and was seeing things.

He walked slowly back toward his truck. He'd left it running with the door open. As he neared it, one of the construction crew met him at the truck. "Sir, I'm the safety officer for this site. I'm going to have to ask you to vacate these premises immediately. This area is for authorized personnel only. You're going to have to get you and your vehicle out of here, now!" he said sternly. Again, Ryan considered asking him the question about the old man but seriously doubted if he would get any answer. Without a word, he got in his truck and backed out.

As he got back out on the road, he grabbed his cell phone and called his wife. "You'll never guess what I just saw downtown," He said before even saying hello.

Hello to you too," his wife said.

"Sorry, hello, but I think I'm going a little insane. Remember that old guy I saw the other day before the barbeque?" Ryan asked.

"Yea, the guy that looked 'through' you," she said emphasizing the 'through'.

"That's right. Well, I just saw him again. But he wasn't walking through the intersection. He was standing on a beam about 100' up on the new hotel being built on State Street."

"What the heck are you talking about?" Michele asked.

"I'm telling you. He was there. He was standing on the beam and was looking right at me! I watched him for like 2 minutes. Then he just walked back on the beam and out of sight. It's really freaky. Something's going on," he said, rather exasperated. "So, I drove over to the construction site but they wouldn't talk to me. Then, I saw him again when I was leaving. I ran after him but he disappeared." Ryan told her in a little more detail about the ball the old man was holding and how there was no way a guy that age could have moved that fast.

"You drove onto the construction site?! You're not supposed to do that," she said as if that was the worst part of the story. Michele used to work for a construction company and knew all the ins and outs.

"You're not listening to me," Ryan said too loudly. "The guy was on a steel beam 100' up in the air and then he was standing at the entrance to the construction site and just disappeared when I ran after him. Haven't you heard a word I've said?" He was losing his patience, if not his mind.

"Well, that's weird, I'll give you that. You need to stop screaming, though. I'm not the bad guy here. Maybe you just thought it was him. It was probably just an old construction worker."

"No, I looked at him through my binoculars. I still had them from the game we went to. It was him. And I saw him much closer when I saw him behind the truck."

"Well, I don't know what to say, Ryan. Why is an old man following you?" she asked.

"I have no idea. I'm coming home. I want to talk about this some more," Ryan said and hung up.

The whole drive home he racked his brain, trying to think of any reason why this guy was following him. Actually, the old man wasn't following him. He just kept showing up in the same places Ryan did. And how in the hell did he get up on that building in the middle of a construction site? Ryan was almost home and turned into his subdivision. His house was located in a bedroom community surrounded by a golf course and a lake. He turned down toward the clubhouse which was his normal route home. As he rounded the bend, he looked across the lake and slammed on his brakes. There he was!! What in the hell was going on? The old man was standing on the bridge that went across from the clubhouse to the first tee. Ryan didn't even pull to the side of the road. He jammed his car into park and jumped out and sprinted toward the clubhouse. He was about 100' from the clubhouse and had to go around it to get to the bridge. As he came around the building and could see the bridge, the old man was gone. Of course! Ryan bent over and put his hands on his knees. "Wow, I am severely out of shape," he thought to himself. He ran across the bridge and looked out over the 1st fairway but couldn't see the old man anywhere. Ryan heard honking and looked back and realized that his car was blocking the narrow road that passed in front of the clubhouse. He ran back to his car and said sorry to the 5 or so cars that had backed up behind him. He drove on with his mind running about a million miles an hour. Something was seriously wrong. There was no way the old man could have beaten him home. Unless the guy was parked right at the construction site and somehow beat Ryan onto the freeway. It was impossible and Ryan knew it. Even if the old man beat him out here to the golf course, he still disappeared from there. Now he was giving serious consideration to the possibility that he may be losing his mind. He was actually scared. He was sure he had never seen the old man before.

"What the hell is going on?" he yelled in frustration.

When Ryan got home, he went inside and Michele was picking up the family room.

"Hey," she said.

"Hey...can I talk to you for a minute?" Ryan asked as he sat down and put his face in his hands. She came in and he told her what had just happened. Now she had a look of concern on her face.

"If he's here, Ryan, that means he probably knows where we live," she said, obviously rattled.

"I know. That's what concerns me," he said. Just then the phone rang. Ryan grabbed the cordless on the couch. "Hello?" he said. It was Sean.

"Hey, I think I saw your geezer buddy," he said.

"What? Where?!" Ryan asked, a little too fast.

"Whoa, settle down. I just saw him over at the soccer field at Mike's game."

"When?" Ryan asked.

"About 10 minutes ago. It was your guy, all right. Just like you said, he was wearing a grey raincoat and a brown fedora. I wasn't very close, but I could tell he was old and he walked away as soon as I saw him. The weird thing was he was staring right at me. Kind of gave me the creeps."

"That's impossible!" Ryan said. "I just saw him about 15 minutes ago on the bridge at our clubhouse."

"Well, unless he can fly and fly fast, he couldn't have been the same guy. Maybe you have twin stalkers," Sean said with a laugh.

"It's not funny, Sean. He knows where I live. Plus, I also saw him downtown today. He was standing on a beam at the Embassy Suites construction site," Ryan said.

"Okay, okay. Sorry for laughing. What the hell is going on, man?" Sean said, now with some apprehension in his voice.

"I have no idea. But this has gone way past a prank. I'm going to take a rain check on Monday Night Football tonight, okay?" Ryan said.

"Yea, me too. Well, let's talk tomorrow. Are you going to call the police or what?"

"No. Yes. I don't know. He hasn't actually done anything. Except freak us out. I think we're just going to hang here tonight and keep an eye out. I'm going to go drive around the neighborhood to see if I can see him. I'll tell you one thing. If I find him, I'm going to pin his bony ass down and demand he tell me why he's following us. I'll call you tomorrow."

"Alright, see ya," and he hung up.

Michele and Ryan drove the neighborhood for over an hour but didn't see any sign of him. They picked up their kids from a friend's house and went home. They decided not to say anything to the kids because there was no reason to worry them. Ryan did decide to stay home from work the next day just to be safe. He had already decided he would call the police in the morning just to file a report if nothing else. He and Michele put the kids down and got into bed. Ryan kissed his wife goodnight and told her not to worry. Everything would be okay. Ryan's dad used to say that everything looks different in the morning and his dad was usually right.

Chapter 8

September 1982

"Time to get up," a voice said. The light flashed on and off twice. Ryan put the pillow over his head.

"What's with the light, Michele?" As he lay there with his face on the mattress, something was very different and very wrong. The mattress was moving.

"What the hell?" It was completely dark in the room. He looked over to Michele's side of the bed but there was no one there. He pushed his hands into the mattress and they sank several inches. It was a damn waterbed!! He threw the covers off and rolled off the bed onto the floor. Wham!! The floor was hard as a rock. He grabbed his knee. It felt like his kneecap had shattered. When the stars cleared, Ryan opened his eyes and tried to adjust to the dark. There was a sliver of light coming from the door, but the door was in the wrong place. It was all very familiar and very foreign at the same time. He just stood there trying to gather his thoughts. He looked down and realized he was only wearing what looked like a pair of boxers and no shirt. He hadn't worn boxers in years. He didn't even own a pair. Looking back at the light coming from the doorway, he finally realized where he was standing. But it was impossible. He sat back down on the bed. Being a waterbed, it didn't support his weight and he rolled backward and fell off the bed again. Wham!! Same knee, same place. "Holy Crap!"

He hobbled up and approached the door. In his mind, he knew where he was, but it was how he got there that had him puzzled. He'd stopped drinking years ago so he knew he hadn't driven here by accident instead of going home. Suddenly, it hit him. He had been home, and he and Michele had gone to bed, in THEIR bed, just a few hours ago after looking around the neighborhood for that weird guy. What in the hell was going on? He was standing in the middle of his old basement bedroom at his parent's house!!

His eyes were now fully adjusted to the dark. He could see the waterbed, the weight bench, and the dresser and could just make out the stereo on the shelf in the wall. A dream. It had to be a dream. He took a step and smashed it!! He grabbed his toe. He'd run right into a 45 lb. plate lying in the middle of the floor. "Aaahhh!" He guessed it wasn't a dream. The pain proved that. He hobbled over to the door, peeked out, and sure enough, he was at the bottom of his Mom and Dad's basement stairs. He had absolutely no idea what he was doing there.

Suddenly, his mom's voice rang out from the top of the stairs, "Ryan, you better get up or you're going to be late." He ducked down almost like the voice scared him. The stairs turned 90° halfway up so she couldn't see him from where she was standing. He didn't know what to do. He put his hands on top of his head. What the... he had hair!! He had been shaving his head ever since he'd started losing his hair 10 years ago or so. He felt around his head and, sure enough, had a full head of hair. He pulled on it, and it was his, alright. Now he was even more confused and a little scared. Something was going on, and he had to find out what. So he half crawled, half walked up the stairs one at a time. He peeked around the 90° turn towards the top but nobody was there. As he started to ascend the stairs, he looked down again. He was thin! He only had a baby roll hanging over his boxer shorts. Lately, he had gained some weight and his kids were always making fun of his gut. That gut was gone!

He got to the top of the stairs and just stopped and listened. The only sound was the sound of newspaper pages being turned in the living room. The foyer was dark but the living room light was on. He couldn't see into the living room from his vantage point, so he stepped slowly forward and peeked around the corner. What he saw nearly stopped his heart and literally took his breath away. He pulled back into the foyer and realized he was hyperventilating. He put his hands on his knees and put his head down, which is probably not what you're supposed to do if you're hyperventilating but it was all he could think of. He stood up again and put his hand on the wall to steady his legs. He slowly edged his way back to the entrance to the living room and looked in again. There was someone sitting on the couch reading the newspaper. It was Bill White, his dad!

Chapter 9

September 1982

"Hey, you better hurry and jump in the shower or you're going to be late," his dad said without looking up from the paper. Ryan walked in and sat down hard in the chair facing the couch on the other side of the room. He just stared at him. His dad lowered the paper and gave him a quizzical look over his glasses. "So what's with you?" he asked.

Ryan couldn't form any words. Finally he managed, "Dad?" Now his father put the paper down and leaned forward.

"Yes?"

He didn't know what to say. He squeaked out, "What are you doing?" It didn't make any sense, he knew.

"What's wrong with you?" his dad asked.

"Nothing," Ryan said too quickly. "I'm just surprised... or glad... or I don't know. I guess I'm just tired."

"Well, if you'd start going to bed at a decent time, you wouldn't feel so tired in the morning," he told him in his fatherly tone. He picked up the paper again. "You better jump in the shower before your brother or sister beats you to it."

Ryan's brother, Mason, was seven years younger than he was. He was married and had four kids. His younger sister, Britney, was ten years younger than he was. She was married, had three children and lived in Hawaii! He had two older sisters but he couldn't possibly mean them. He just sat there in silence. His dad was sitting in front of him, reading the newspaper. He looked great. And very much alive!

"Are you going to take a shower or not?" his father asked.

"Uh, yea. I mean, no. I mean, yea, sure," he muttered. He got up and walked toward the foyer. From there, he could see into the kitchen, his mom was fixing breakfast for his dad. His mom and dad were old school. She fixed the meals and he made the money. She was fine with it and so was he. Ryan never questioned it. It was just the way it always was. He slowly walked into the kitchen.

"Hi, honey. Do you want some cereal and toast?" his mom asked. He didn't say anything. "Are you okay, dear? You look a little pale. You should probably get in the shower before Mason does," she warned. Again, he didn't say anything. Just stared at her. She looked great, too. No grey hair and so thin. "Seriously, what's wrong, honey. Don't you feel well?" she asked as she came over and very motherly put her hand on his forehead.

"I'm...fine. Just a little tired," was all he could think of saying.

"Well, go take a shower, and I'll have your breakfast ready for you so you won't be late for school."

School??!! What school? What the hell was she talking about? Suddenly, everything started to fall into place, and it nearly knocked him over. He sat down hard at the kitchen table.

"Mom, what's the date today?" he asked slowly.

"It's the 9th, no, the 10th," she corrected herself.

He got up from the table and went back into the living room. He didn't get too close to his dad. It still felt weird that he was sitting there. Ryan grabbed one of the pieces of newspaper that his dad hadn't gotten to yet. "Hey, I haven't read that yet. You're suddenly interested in the Opinion section?" he asked.

"No. I just want to check something," Ryan mumbled. He quickly scanned the top of the paper looking for the date. When he saw it, he dropped the paper and sat back down in the same chair he had recently vacated. His mind was trying to cope with what he saw but was failing miserably. The date on the paper was September 10, 1982!!

Chapter 10

2100 – 2120

When the Life Force Institute was first created around 2100, Alexander Ramsey had a vision. His great-grandfather had spoken many times of his country as it once was. A place where men and women could pursue their dreams. Where government was controlled by the people and for the people, not the other way around. Alexander dreamed of such a country and he was confident that it could once again be like it was. However, he knew that it would not be easy. Several generations had been raised in the socialist-controlled environment that now existed.

At first, there were great upheavals and rebellions by those who knew what the death of capitalism and the free market system meant. But those voices were easily silenced over time. The majority of the populace was naïve. Men and women were working again. The low-paying jobs were at least jobs. Parents could again feed their children.

Students of history could point to another man, Adolf Hitler, who at first was a Godsend to the German people. He was able to put the people back to work building the infrastructure of Germany and the Autobahn. But the history books were replete detailing the tragic end of that experiment. Now, with the socialization of America, the motivation to succeed and reach for unseen levels of prosperity has been taken away. Men and women were no longer creative. There were no risk-takers. There was no need. Everyone got what they needed to survive...barely. Poverty had not been eliminated, it had simply been redefined. Never in the history of mankind had the ideals of socialism or communism been successful. By the time that became evident, it was too late. The damage had been done.

There were a few citizens left who had studied history and realized the futility of the current policies. Alexander was one of those citizens, and he had the resources to pursue his dreams. His father and grandfather had amassed a fortune in gold, in secret. The US dollar was worthless. The New Global Union had developed a worldwide currency that was the only thing of any value. People were paid in units. Units of currency. These would be exchanged for food, clothing, and other necessities. Vehicles and homes were given out by need. Luxury items such as boats or RVs were virtually nonexistent. Anyone who was observed to have excess supplies or 'fancy items' was investigated thoroughly. Usually, the excess was promptly taken away and re-distributed. Amendments to the constitution had been swiftly passed to allow this. The remaining document barely resembled what the Founding Fathers had fought and, in many cases, died for.

Therefore, Alexander had been very careful about hiding his fortune from the government. He did this by forming the Life Force Institute. It was located in Montana, one of the last states with wide open spaces. His family had owned thousands of acres for generations and it was the perfect place to locate. The environmentalists working for the White House were very welcoming of any environmental protection company. They pretty much left him alone as long as the annual audits didn't show anything out of the ordinary.

Alexander Ramsey was a genius both in business dealings and social engineering. His original plan was social re-engineering. Recover his country from the people up. This had proved to be a daunting task. He was able to recruit a number of followers but since secrecy was of utmost concern, he had to be very discretionary regarding who he involved. By 2110, his organization numbered only in the hundreds. They were spread out across the country in tightly knit groups who had been sworn to secrecy and were extremely loyal to the cause.

Alexander's aim was to spread the ideals of capitalism and free market trade across the country. There were underground meetings where liberty and freedom were the main topics of conversation. The work was slow and tedious, and the progress even slower. The communistic government was so ingrained in people's minds that the very idea of a completely free society was incomprehensible to most people.

Two months after Darius was born in July 2125, Alexander was giving a rare speech at an underground meeting in New Jersey. It was being held at a member's house. The home was located in the previously upper-class town of Alpine, just across the Hudson River from Manhattan. Years ago, Alpine had been one of the richest, most exclusive towns in the country. Now, it resembled much of the rest of the country with broken-down homes, burned-out cars and garbage strewn about the streets. Most of the residents had left when many of their belongings were seized by the government and redistributed to the less fortunate. It was a classic and sad reminder to Alexander and the others of the state the country had fallen into. About 100 people were in attendance. This particular house was not very large but was located on a full acre so the meeting was being held outside. A dangerous place to hold this type of meeting. Alexander wanted to start well after dark to minimize the risk of being discovered. But a nationwide curfew of 10:30 pm for all non-essential personnel had been enacted. This meant the meeting must be completed by 9:30 pm in order for everyone to make it home on time. In July, the sun was only beginning to go down by 8:00 pm. Alexander decided to go ahead with the meeting anyway. A few speakers started out with accolades for the freedom movement. Alexander's name and the name of the Life Force Institute were forbidden to be mentioned in remote meetings such as this, for obvious reasons. Alexander was the final speaker. He stepped to the podium. He was not a tall man, only about 6,' but he held himself with such grace and stature that he seemed much larger than he was. He gave an eloquent speech about liberty and freedom. About his dream that the United States of America could once again be free of tyranny and oppression. He spoke not of capitalism and money but of the God given gift of the human spirit and the blessings of democracy. In keeping with protocol, applause was kept to a minimum but there was a palpable feeling of well-being and hope, as there often was at these types of gatherings. As Alexander finished and was shaking hands and exchanging hugs with the organizers, a shot rang out from behind the crowd. The back of Alexander's head exploded with the impact of the bullet. Blood and brain matter sprayed everyone near him. Alexander Ramsey spun around and fell. He was dead before he hit the ground. Then all Hell broke loose. People were screaming and running for cover. Automatic gunfire broke out from behind them. There was nowhere for the audience to run but back into the house and out onto the street in front where they were met with more gunfire. By the time the shooting was over, 45 people lay dead or wounded on the lawn. The remaining survivors barely escaped with their lives. It would never be proven who the gunmen were or who they were working for. All the dead were claimed by relatives. Alexander's wife identified his body and he was buried in a secret ceremony on his property in Montana. Investigations into the shooting went nowhere, obviously. Luckily, very little was made of the incident or the meeting and its intent. All media was controlled and the story was written as a mass murder/suicide of a crazed cult. But the Life Force Institute was left without a leader, and Alexander's quest for freedom and liberty had been crushed.

Alexander's wife ran the institute for the next fifteen years. There were weak attempts at maintaining Alexander's work, but without a passionate leader, the movement all but died. The institute became more of a scientific research center, as it had been portrayed all along. When Darius was old enough to take over, the Life Force Institute was a shadow of its former self. But Darius had inherited his father's passionate and outgoing character, in addition to his fortune. It was his intent to reinstate Alexander's original plans, and more.

Chapter 11

September 1982

"Liz?" Ryan's Dad yelled. "Will you come in here, please?" his mother came in while drying her hands on a dishtowel.

"What is it, dear?" she asked.

"Ryan, do you want to tell us what's going on? Why are you acting so strange?" his dad asked. Ryan's mom came over and put her hand on his forehead again.

"You don't have a fever," she declared. "Do you feel sick to your stomach?" I sure do, he thought to himself.

"No. I just don't feel well. Maybe I should go back and lie down," He said half under his breath.

"I don't know if it's such a good idea for you to miss school so early in the year," his dad said. School! There it was again. What school?! Ryan started to put the date he'd seen in the newspaper in perspective. 1982. He would be starting his junior year in high school. If the date was correct, he would be sixteen, almost seventeen. He was trying to process all of this surreal information. He needed to think, and this certainly wasn't the time or the place.

"Is it okay if I take a bath upstairs?" he asked.

"I suppose your brother doesn't need to shower," his mom said. "Go ahead. Are you sure you're okay?" she asked.

"Yea, I'm fine. I just need to take a bath," he lied as he started to move up the stairs. He could hear his dad rustle the newspaper again.

Ryan was trying desperately to get a mental handle on what was going on. He continued climbing the stairs with the same pounding thought in his head. 1982. 1982. How the hell was it 1982? A few hours ago, he had been in bed with his wife and it was 2016. Suddenly 30 years went away. No, 34 years! Where were Michele and Jackson and Colton? Why was this happening? And how?

He reached the second floor and walked down the hall past his little sister's room which was in the front of the house. He peeked in and saw her sleeping. Yep. There was a six-year-old Britney. As he turned to leave her room, he glanced out the front window. There he was! The same man in the dark grey raincoat and hat was standing on the front walk looking up at Brit's window. It was the same man Ryan had seen on his way to the barbeque and downtown and then near his house. He was sure of it. He didn't know what to do. He instantly fell to the ground, his heart pounding in his ears. He crawled over to the window. For a moment, he couldn't bring himself to look. Then, after a few seconds, he slowly looked out over the window sill but the street and sidewalk were empty. Nobody was there. A lady was walking her dog on the other side of the street, but the old man in the coat wasn't anywhere. Had Ryan imagined him? No, he couldn't have. Ryan went downstairs and was going to go outside when he realized he was still in nothing but boxers. He went to the foyer and looked out the front window. Nobody. Ryan went back upstairs to run the bath. At this point, he was sure he was losing his mind.

As the water slowly filled the tub, Ryan looked at himself in the bathroom mirror. The reflection was certainly not what he saw yesterday morning before he shaved. The reflection he was staring at was like looking at his yearbook picture 30 years ago. This can't be happening! Ryan thought while staring at his young face. He had always thought how great it would be to travel back in time and live his life again, especially his high school years. He had daydreamed about what he would do differently and so on. He should be exhilarated and excited but instead, he was filled with dread. Ryan realized that traveling back in time would only be great if he didn't stand to lose so much. All he could think about was his wife and kids. What if he lost them? What if he couldn't get back to where or when he belonged? Where would that leave him? The whole situation suddenly hit him in full force. Ryan broke down and started to cry. Not sniffling crying, but with uncontrollable heaving sobs. It was an emotional expression of the deep fear and frustration that he felt at that moment. Ryan was not accustomed to this type of release. Even at his father's passing he had not fully let go. He had told himself he had to be the strong, responsible man that people had come to count on in a crisis. No, this reaction was due to the fact that he was clearly not in control of this situation. After a couple of minutes, he was able to compose himself enough to notice that the bathtub was finally full. Ryan turned the water off, got into the water, and sunk in up to his neck letting the warm water relax his body and mind. He remained motionless for a moment slowing his heart rate and collecting his thoughts. He started to pull the facts of his situation together. His father was alive, so this was no practical joke. Ryan also had a full head of hair as well as his high school physique. The newspaper was dated Monday, September 10th, 1982. His little sister was little again. Somehow, some way, he had gone back in time 34 years. But that was impossible, right? Of course it was. But Ryan couldn't disregard the facts.

Ryan heard the phone ring. He could hear the tones of his mother's voice as she answered it, but he couldn't make out what she was saying. He heard a pause, then footsteps on the stairs. There was a knock on the bathroom door. "Ryan, Sean's on the phone." His mom called out. He says he needs to talk to you right now. It sounds urgent. What do you want me to tell him?"

Sean. Sean. Could it possibly be...?

Chapter 12

"Hello?" Ryan said somewhat tentatively. "Hello?" No response. "Hello, Sean?"

"Who is this?" was the response.

"This is Ryan. Is this Sean?" he asked.

"Yea," Sean said quietly.

"How's, uh, it going?" Ryan asked. No response. He thought he'd take a chance. "Dude, did it happen to you, too?"

"I think so. I don't know what's going on, man." Sean said with a definite quiver in his voice.

"Alright. We need to meet. NOW," Ryan demanded.

"Where?" Sean asked.

"Meet me at Meatballs in a half hour," Ryan said. "Oh and Sean, bring your backpack and make sure you've got some paper and something to write with," he said.

"Why?" he asked.

"Just do it," Ryan said.

"Wait," he said. "Do you know what's going on?"

"No, I don't. Meatballs in a half hour," and Ryan hung up.

Ryan moved quickly downstairs still in his towel. His father was walking out the front door. He must still be practicing, Ryan thought. His dad was an orthodontist. If memory served, he didn't retire until well into the 90's.

"Feeling better, I see," his father said.

"Uh, yea, a little better," Ryan answered. It was still so weird to talk to him, considering.

"Well, see you tonight," his dad said as he kissed Ryan's mom and left. Ryan went down to his room and looked around for some clothes. He spotted a pair of Levis draped over his weight bench. He looked at the tag on the back of the jeans, it said 30" waist. Right! Ryan thought as he pulled on the jeans. Sure enough they fit, and they were actually loose. Amazing! Ryan threw on a shirt and shoes. As he was leaving his room, he glanced over at the nightstand. There was a motorcycle helmet. He tried to think back to when he sold his bike. If memory served, he was eighteen. Ryan grabbed the helmet and ran upstairs.

"Don't you want something to eat?" his mom asked.

"Uh, no thanks. I'm not really hungry," he lied. Actually, Ryan was starving. This struck Ryan as strange because he had stuffed himself last night after being freaked out by the experience with the old man. Ryan had to remind himself that his current physical existence dictated several different facts. It may have been last night in his present mind but it wasn't his fifty-year-old body that ate all of that food.

"Call me if it starts raining, and I'll come get you. I don't want you riding that thing on wet streets," his mom called to him as he went out the door.

There it was, his Honda 650L. Ryan smiled remembering the day he bought it. It had taken months to convince his parents to let him actually own a motorcycle. Ryan's mom had all the statistics of death and mutilation that would certainly follow if they allowed him to buy it. It took everything he had saved, which wasn't much, for the down payment, and then he had to work his butt off to make the monthly payments. It was worth it. He sadly remembered now why he had to sell it. It was either partying and girls or paying for the motorcycle. Ryan had opted for the former and had regretted it ever since. He strapped the helmet on his head, turned the key, and fired the motorcycle up. He loved the deep throaty sound and the thrum of power in the handlebar grips. This bike had some serious balls! He pulled out of his driveway and raced towards the golf course to meet Sean.

No one really knew how Meatballs got its name. It was just a little abandoned gatehouse at the opening of the municipal golf course. It was sort of a central meeting point they'd used when they were young. Sean lived just down the street so Ryan figured he might already be there. He pulled up but didn't see Sean anywhere. Ryan habitually started feeling around his pockets for his cell phone but then snapped back to what year he was in. Cell phones were still a number of years off. At least the compact phones you could stick in your pocket.

"Hey!" someone yelled from down the street. Ryan turned and immediately recognized Sean coming towards him. Sean actually didn't look that different. He hadn't ever shaved his head, so he looked pretty much the same; just smaller and skinnier. Sean had always been a pretty big guy, but like Ryan, he'd gained some weight over the years.

Ryan didn't know what to expect. Sean came right up to Ryan and gave him a huge hug. Ryan and Sean never hugged. "Yea, I'm glad to see you too," Ryan said with a laugh.

"What in THE hell is going on, Ryan?" Sean asked as they both sat down on the bench by the gatehouse. "I have no idea, but we're going to find out," Ryan said adamantly. "Before we compare notes," Ryan said, holding his hands up in imaginary quotes, "tell me exactly what you remember since last night."

"Okay, we were talking about seeing that old guy all over the valley, at the same time. Then you said you were going to drive around and call me today. Then I went to bed and woke up in my sixteen-year-old body!" he finished.

"Right," Ryan confirmed.

Sean closed his eyes to concentrate and went on. "I remember I woke up in the middle of the night to take a leak. Nothing seemed wrong. Then I woke up in my old room in my mom and dad's house." He hadn't opened his eyes yet. "I didn't know where I was at first when I woke up. When I realized where I was, I went upstairs and kind of freaked out." He opened his eyes and looked at me. "My dad thought I was on drugs or something. I finally calmed down and figured the only thing I could do was call you to see if you had experienced the same thing." He looked over at me and said, "That's it. Here we are, so now what?"

"That's pretty much what happened to me, too," Ryan said. "Except for one thing."

"What's that," Sean asked.

Ryan looked at Sean and said,, "I saw him again."

"Who?" Sean asked.

"The old guy in the raincoat and hat," Ryan answered. "The same freak I saw yesterday and a couple of weeks ago before your barbeque."

"Where, when?"

"This morning. I was in my little sister's room. Britney. Oh, and by the way, she's six. It's weird. Anyway, I was in her room, and I looked out the front window and he was standing on our sidewalk looking right at her window. I dropped to the floor and crawled over to the window. But when I looked out, he was gone." Ryan stood up and walked around. He couldn't sit anymore. "Sean, my dad is alive! I talked to him this morning,"

Ryan said. "I sat in my living room and talked to my dad! Plus, do you know what today's date is?" Ryan asked Sean.

"Yea," Sean said. "I saw a newspaper and nearly passed out."

"Me too," Ryan agreed. "1982. Unbelievable. Did you tell anybody?" Ryan asked.

"Hell no!" Sean said. "If I had, they would've taken me to a shrink. Why? Did you tell anyone?"

"No," Ryan said. "But they thought I was sick or something. I guess I was acting pretty weird."

"So what do we do now," he asked.

"I'm not sure, but I want to do something. Did you bring some paper and a pen?"

"Yea, why?" he seemed puzzled.

"I think we should write down everything we can about our lives, as they were yesterday, or whatever. You write down everything you know about me and I'll write down everything I know about you. Okay?" Ryan said.

"What for?" Sean asked, still looking puzzled.

"Look, I don't know what's going on. But I do know that I don't want to forget anything about where or when, we came from. We need to read and re-read these notes every day." Ryan said.

"Every day???" Sean exclaimed. "Exactly how long do you think we're going to be here?" he asked.

"How the hell should I know," Ryan said. "Let's just do it. It will make me feel better."

"Alright," Sean said as he pulled his backpack off, reached in, and got some paper and two pens. He handed a pen and a piece of paper to Ryan. They spent the next 20 minutes or so writing down everything they could remember, names, addresses, nephews, nieces, brothers, sisters, friends, jobs, hobbies, everything. When they had finished their lists they handed them to each other so some of the gaps could be filled in.

"Well, what now?" Ryan asked out loud.

"I guess we go to school," Sean said with a smile.

"Go to school," he repeated in a bewildered tone. "Yeah, I guess so. At least we won't be in trouble with our parents," Ryan smiled. "Plus, we can see if anyone else is 'acting weird,'" he said. "Maybe this happened to more than just me and you."

As they got up to go Ryan looked out across the golf course. There he was!! Standing on the 16th tee, about 150 yards away. "Look!" Ryan yelled and pointed. "It's him. Let's go!" Sean said something but Ryan was already in a full sprint toward the man in the gray raincoat that he saw this morning on his sidewalk. As he ran full speed, Ryan held his eyes on the figure of the old man. Ryan didn't look away once. He was determined not to lose this guy again. As soon as Ryan started running towards him, the old man quickly turned and started walking down the hill toward the 15th green. Sean was pretty far back. He'd never been known for his speed, but amazingly he caught up just as Ryan was cresting the hill past the 16th tee. "What the hell?" Ryan said, out of breath. "Where did he go?" The 15th green was at the bottom of two hills. It was bordered on one side by a highway and on the other side by some very dense brush. There was no way the old coot could have gotten back up the other hill by the time they got there.

"You saw him, right?" Ryan asked.

"Yea, I saw him," Sean confirmed. "Who is he? Where did he go?" he asked as he spun around looking in all directions.

"I don't know, but I'm sure he knows something about why we're here," Ryan said.

"How do you know that?" Sean asked.

"Because I've seen him here, and I've seen him 34 years from now, three times, that's how." They turned and started walking slowly back toward Meatballs.

Ryan looked at his watch. It was already 9:35 am so they were already pretty late. Sean jumped on the back of Ryan's bike, and they took off towards good ol' Lakeside High School. A place they were both very familiar with but in a time they wanted nothing to do with.

Chapter 13

Ryan and Sean pulled into the student parking lot and headed toward the front door of the school. In the years since they graduated from high school, the entire school had been torn down and rebuilt, completely different. This was the old Lakeside High. Just more proof that they were actually where, or when, they thought they were.

"Wait," Sean said as he stopped. "We don't even know what classes we're in or where our lockers are or what our locker combinations are." He was right. They couldn't exactly walk in and ask where they're supposed to go and where their lockers are and, oh by the way, "what is our locker combination?" Not with school, having been in session for at least 2 weeks. And neither of them could remember all that information from over 30 years ago.

After thinking for a minute, Ryan said "Look in your backpack. I always kept my class schedule and locker stuff for a few weeks. School just started a couple of weeks ago. Maybe we still have it." They both set their backpacks down and started pulling out books and papers.

"Here's mine," Ryan said. His class schedule was there, and his locker location and combination were stapled to it.

"I can't find mine," Sean said.

"Look through your books. Maybe it's in there," Ryan suggested. He started to leaf through each book. He only had two. His English book and his Math book. As he turned his Math book upside down and flipped through the pages, a piece of paper fell out. "That's it," he said. He grabbed his class schedule. But no locker info.

"What do I do now? I can't go in there and say I forgot where my locker is," he exclaimed.

"Alright, we'll just go to the office and say you forgot your combination. It happens all the time. The locker location will hopefully be on the slip they give you."

They walked in the front door. Both boys just stood there in silence. They'd spent four years here a lifetime ago. It was very surreal to once again be standing there as students. They went into the office and explained Sean's predicament. Luckily, as they had hoped, his locker location was listed along with his combination. Ryan was a Junior. Sean was a Sophomore. So their lockers were on different floors. Just then the bell rang and a flood of students filled the halls. The third period started in 10 minutes. Ryan had Chemistry. Sean had English. They both should remember where the rooms were. "I guess we go to our classes," Ryan said. "Meet me for lunch. Remember to keep an eye out for any strange behavior or anyone talking about 'time travel,'" he reminded Sean. Ryan went to his locker and opened it on his first try. He seemed to remember always having to try two or three times before it finally opened. Looking in his locker, there wasn't much in there. Some papers and books. A jacket he'd left there and a bag of gym clothes. He vaguely remembered that jacket. Weird, he thought.

"Hey, where have you been?" Ryan turned and saw Lisa Strand walking toward him. He suddenly remembered he had dated her for a while. He couldn't remember when, though. Was he dating her now? Oh boy, he thought with a definite sense of dread. She came up and kissed him full on the mouth. That certainly answered his question.

"Why are you so late?" she asked.

"Um, I just slept in by accident," he managed.

"Why didn't you call me back last night?" she asked. "You said you were going to. I waited up forever."

"I know. Um. I'm sorry. I got really tired and went to bed early," he said.

"Well, remember you said you'd give me a ride home after school," she said. "See ya at lunch," she leaned up and kissed him again and bounced down the hall. He felt really weird kissing another girl. He hadn't kissed anyone but Michele for over 19 years. He felt guilty even though he knew he hadn't initiated it. 'Oh well,' he thought. "That will certainly be interesting to deal with." He grabbed his Chemistry book and headed off to Doc Brown's classroom. He remembered it well. Having gone through years of engineering chemistry in college, he shouldn't have too much problem with high school chemistry. Even though he wasn't planning on sticking around for finals.

On another floor, Sean had found his locker and opened it on his third try. He was about ready to go back to the office when it finally opened. Looking in his locker, he didn't see much. Some books. A pair of pants (what for he had no idea). He was pulling out his English book when he was about knocked over by a girl jumping on his back.

"Hey you," she squealed.

"Gina?! How's it, um, going?" he stammered. Gina Whitton had been Sean's on-again, off-again girlfriend since their freshman year. Apparently, it was on again, he concluded.

"Where have you been? I was worried because you weren't here and I didn't know where you were. I thought maybe you were sick or just slept in. I told Lisa..." She kept talking but Sean wasn't really listening. He just stood and watched her mouth move. She never stopped talking. It was as if she didn't even need to breathe. Just continuous word after word… That much he clearly remembered.

Unfortunately, Gina and Lisa were best friends which made things tough when either relationship soured. This would definitely make things interesting.

"Um, well I was late because I overslept and my alarm didn't go off," he lied convincingly.

"Well, you better meet me for lunch or else," she said and sauntered down the hall. She looked over her shoulder at him and gave him a little wave. He waved back somewhat sheepishly and looked around to see if anyone saw him. How had he EVER liked that girl? She was cute but was about the most annoying thing he'd ever encountered. He walked slowly to Mr. Wilson's English class. Mr. Wilson was a very effeminate homosexual who didn't like girls and, as Sean recalled, didn't like him much either. 'This should be fun,' he thought.

Chemistry class did prove to be quite boring. Very basic stuff. Ryan couldn't remember what kind of grade he had gotten, but if it was anything but an A, he should be ashamed. Both of the boys saw a bunch of old friends. They tried to stay as low-key as possible. They still had no idea why they were there and didn't want to start any weird rumors. They both knew how fast news traveled in a high school. At lunch, they had to endure the entire 40 minutes with Lisa and Gina going on and on about the party they were planning for Friday night. Tonight!

"Ryan, remember you promised you and Sean would get the keg," Lisa said.

"Keg?" he asked.

"Yea, you said you could get one," she said with some force. He looked at Sean. He shrugged his shoulders, "Yea, we could probably locate one," he said, saving the day. Neither Sean nor Ryan had had a drink in years. They had both become fairly active in their church and their church sort of frowned on drinking, to say the least. So, they would definitely have a problem if they stayed here for very long.

Finally, the girls bee-bopped off, and Sean and Ryan could talk. "What the hell were we thinking?" he asked.

Sean shrugged his shoulders. "I have no idea," he said. "Were they always that annoying?"

"I don't know. I think I must have blocked most of that out," Ryan replied. "So, did you notice anything about anyone?"

"No. Nothing," he said.

"Yea, me neither."

"So, maybe it's just us."

"Yea, but we still don't know why or how or anything," Ryan said, somewhat exasperated. "Plus, Lisa says I promised to give her a ride home after school," he said.

"Can you get out of it?"

"I'm going to have to. We've got to figure this out," he said with resolve. "I'll just tell her that you and I have to...have to...go downtown...and...what?" he asked. They thought for a minute.

"We have to go down to my dad's store to help him with inventory," Sean came up with.

"Alright, that's pretty good."

"Where should we actually go?" Sean asked.

"Maybe we'll just go back to meatballs and try to figure this out. I know one thing for sure. All this has something to do with our mystery man in a fedora. Meet me at my locker right after school, and we'll try to get out without being seen," and they both left for class.

Ryan didn't really pay much attention in class for the rest of the day. He just kept racking his brain as to why or how this happened. Time travel was just in the movies, right? From a physics standpoint, it's theoretically possible, or so he heard once. But it would require speeds and distances that simply aren't attainable. Especially overnight in his bed. But someway, somehow, it had happened and they weren't any closer to figuring it out now than they were this morning. As he sat in Civics class, he pulled out the sheet that they'd filled out this morning about their lives. He read slowly through the names and dates and other things Sean had written down about his life. Sean knew him as well as he knew himself. And vice-versa. Ryan had to hold back his tears as he read the names and ages of his two boys. He wasn't sure if he had it in him to deal with all this. But he also realized he didn't have much choice. He put the paper away and went back to ignoring the teacher as much as possible.

The final bell rang, and Ryan hurried to his locker. He wanted to avoid Lisa if at all possible. He'd told her earlier he couldn't give her a ride home, but he was sure she was going to try again. Sean was already at his locker by the time he got there.

"How did you get here so fast?" Ryan asked.

"I ran. I wanted to avoid Gina," he said while breathing hard.

"Yea, let's get outta here," he said, while slamming his locker and heading downstairs. The halls were full of students. As they approached the front door, Lisa and Gina came bouncing toward them. How could they possibly have that much energy at the end of the day?

"Oh no," Ryan said.

"Hi, guys. Where'ya goin'?" Gina asked in that ridiculous valley girl voice.

"We've gotta go help my dad with inventory in his store. He's paying us, so we need to be on time," Sean said.

"Why can't we come? We'll help out," Lisa chimed in.

Ryan blurted out, "You can't...because you have to be bonded...to take inventory. It's a federal law. Because of all the audits." Sean looked at him like he was crazy. And he was. It was a complete lie, not to mention ridiculous, but it was all he could think of.

"Well, that sucks," Gina said. "Oh well, talk to you tonight. Don't forget about the party. Be at my house at 8 sharp. And don't forget about the keg," Lisa threw in. They bought it! No big surprise. Ryan had forgotten all about the keg. Where the hell were they going to get a keg? No matter. They didn't plan on being here that long and they definitely weren't going to the damn party.

By now, a lot of the students had left, and the front of the school was emptying out pretty quick. As Sean and Ryan went out the front door and approached the top of the steps, they looked down and stopped cold. There he was. Same grey coat. Same fedora hat. He was standing at the bottom of the steps and he was staring right at them!

Chapter 14

He didn't say anything. Sean and Ryan didn't say anything. He just stood there, looking at them. Both boys didn't know why they felt scared, but they were. He looked like he was about 70 years old and only weighed maybe 140 pounds. But he was tall. Probably about 6'4." He didn't look mad or sad or happy or anything. He had zero expression. His eyes were either gray or light blue. And, like before, they seemed to look right through the two boys staring down at him. "Holy shit," Sean whispered. "Yea," was all Ryan could manage. They slowly walked down the steps and stood on the first step so they were at his level. Ryan was about 6'2", and Sean was pushing 5'10."

"Master White. Master Jensen," he said in a deep voice with some weird Euro accent, looking at them in turn.

"Who the hell are you?" Ryan asked, not very authoritatively.

"My name is Maxwell. I assume you gentlemen have some questions," he said.

"You could say that," Sean said with a little more bravado in his voice. "For instance...," Sean started but the man put his hands up and said, "Not here. Not now. Meet me where you were this morning, and we'll talk there. In one of your...in one hour." He turned and walked away. He stopped, but didn't turn around. He held his finger in the air and said, "By the way, gentlemen, you must tell no one of your experience. Not yet." And he continued on.

The boys both just stood there. Dumbfounded. Ryan wanted to chase after him, but he had given them a meeting place and time. Ryan looked at Sean. Sean looked at Ryan. "What the hell was that?" Ryan asked quietly. "I guess it's back to meatballs,"

Sean said, shrugging his shoulders. They both started running toward the student parking lot. Neither of them was sure why they were running. It just seemed like the right thing to do. It would only take them 2 or 3 minutes on Ryan's motorcycle to get there.

"Wait," Ryan said. He put his arm out to stop Sean. "Do you think we should take anything with us?"

"Like what?" Sean asked. "A gun or a baseball bat? We could blow this guy over with one punch."

"Yea, but something tells me there's more to this guy than meets the eye. But I guess it doesn't matter. I get the distinct feeling that whatever happens is 'going' to happen, no matter what. Let's just go."

They got to Ryan's motorcycle and started up toward meatballs.

"Hey, let's go by my house real quick," Sean yelled from the backseat.

"Why?" Ryan asked over the wind.

"Cause it's damn cold back here and I don't even have a jacket," he said. He was right. Neither of them was wearing more than a t-shirt. It was getting cold and it would just get colder as the sun set.

They pulled up to Sean's house. There were a bunch of kids playing in the front yard. Ryan recognized most of them as Sean's little brothers and sisters. They were all just kids! Just a couple of weeks ago, he'd been at a barbeque with them, and they were chasing kids of their own. It seemed like a lifetime ago.

"Get me a jacket, too. I don't want to go to my house right now," Ryan yelled as Sean ran inside.

"Alright," he said and disappeared into his house. One of Sean's little sisters went over to where Ryan was sitting on his motorcycle. It was Terri.

"Hi, Terri," Ryan said.

"Hi, Ryan. Can you take me on a ride?" she asked.

"Sorry, but I don't think your mom would let me," he apologized and she made a little groan and ran off. Besides, he was still getting over the shock of seeing her this young. It had been a long time.

Watching the kids play, he started to think about his own kids, Jackson and Colton. What were they doing right now? Did they even know he was gone? Then he realized that they didn't even exist right now. He felt a drop hit his arm. It wasn't raining. IIe then realized he was crying. He wiped his face. He didn't know why this was happening, but he told himself to sack up and face whatever came and to quit crying.

Sean came back out with two coats, his helmet, and a couple of golf clubs.

"Here, take one," and he threw Ryan a club. He then went into his garage and came out on his motorcycle. He had a Yamaha YZ 450. Definitely not street-legal.

"You're taking a chance," Ryan said over the noise of his engine, "if your mom sees you, or hears you, you're history."

"I don't plan on being here long enough to care. Let's just go." He took off down his driveway and Ryan followed behind. Sean was technically a better rider than Ryan was. He'd been in a couple of races and had done pretty well. Ryan was probably better on the trail and in the open desert, though. As Ryan followed behind Sean, it brought back memories of doing this exact thing 30 years ago. They would often sneak his motorcycle out of the garage and ride the nearby canyons. He got caught a few times but always seemed to squirm out of it.

It brought back a particular memory for Ryan that happened about this time of year, probably around 1984. He couldn't remember, for sure. One afternoon, they pushed Sean's bike out of the garage and took off toward Middle Creek Canyon, which was just a few minutes away from his house. As soon as they crossed the highway, a sheriff in a Suburban pulled in behind them and flipped on his lights. They both knew why he was pulling them over. Although Ryan's bike was 'street legal' because it had a light and signals, the knobby tires were definitely not legal and it wasn't licensed. Plus, Sean's bike was totally not 'street legal.' Being stupid teenagers, they decided to run for it. They had talked about this many times before and knew exactly what they would do. They both gunned their bikes and headed toward the opening of the golf course. As they did so, they both could hear the sheriff rev his engine as he flipped on his siren. Of course, their motorcycles had much faster acceleration than his car, so they were pretty far ahead of him by the time they hit the parking lot. Their plan (as they'd rehearsed it before) would be to take off across the golf course, where he wouldn't be able to follow. Or so they thought. It was pretty cold that day, so there were only a few diehard golfers out on the course. Without even slowing down, they transitioned from the parking lot to the 9th fairway and took off toward the other side. There was a pretty steep hill that led from the parking lot to the fairway, but it was all grass so it wasn't hard to navigate. As they did so, they looked back, and, much to their chagrin, the sheriff did the same thing. Tearing up grass as he pulled in behind them. At this point, Ryan thought they'd had it. He pulled up next to Sean and yelled over the engines, "What now?" He looked back and, as his eyes got bigger seeing the sheriff behind them, he yelled, "Let's go!" and he floored his bike across the fairway and into the rough where his Suburban might have some trouble. No luck. It didn't even slow him down. At that point, they only had one chance of getting away. If they could get to the 8th hole tee box, there was a small bridge that went across to the 7th green. He wouldn't be able to follow, and it would take him a good 5 minutes to go around. As they headed toward the 8th hole, he came on his P.A. and yelled, "Don't try it, boys!" They figured they would be in about the same amount of trouble if they got caught now or if they got caught later, so they decided to go for it. They hit the bridge and sailed across. Ryan almost lost it near the far side when his handlebar hit the railing but he held it together, barely. As if to rub it in, Sean stopped on the other side and looked back at the sheriff, who had stopped before the tee box. They both waved like the little smart-asses they were and took off around the bend. They were laughing as they came around the other side when they ran straight into three sheriffs waiting for them. Another one came out from behind them and blocked them in. They were trapped!

Needless to say, neither of them was allowed to ride their motorcycles for quite a long time after that. Actually, looking back on it, Ryan felt he was lucky that his parents didn't sell his motorcycle. They ended up having to do about 100 hours of community service. Mostly repairing the grass at the golf course that their bikes and the sheriff's Suburban had torn up. They were both amazed that so many police officers had been involved in the chase. And that the sheriff had been so aggressive as to follow them onto the golf course. The reason became clear a little later. Apparently, there had been a rash of kids riding on the golf course and had even injured a player. The local pro was friends with the sheriff and he had convinced him to increase his patrols. Ironically, it hadn't even been Ryan or Sean that had caused the damage prior to that day. They played golf there and didn't like the grass being torn up any better than the pro did. But an example had to be made and they were perfect for it. A couple of upper middle-class kids causing problems at the local golf course. Made for a great story in the local paper. Much to their parents' embarrassment.

As Ryan rode behind Sean, he couldn't help but smile, remembering that day so long ago. It was pretty typical of those two. They weren't bad kids. They were just mischievous and they pushed the envelope quite a bit.

As they approached the meatballs, Ryan started to get more and more nervous. The trepidation he felt was not really fear but anxiety as to what he was about to find out. They arrived in just a few minutes, with only about 30 minutes elapsing from the time they had left school. They figured they had some time to kill. They parked their bikes right next to the gazebo so nobody would hit them on their way in or out of the golf course. There were a lot of golfers that would play until the first snow fell, and there were still a lot of cars in the parking lot.

They looked around but didn't see any sign of him. "I guess we just wait," Sean said. They sat in silence for about 5 minutes before Sean finally said, "I've been thinking about my kids a lot today."

"Yea, me too," Ryan agreed.

"It's weird. Right now, they don't even exist. But last night, we were tucking them into their beds. I don't know if I can handle this, man," he said dejectedly.

"It would appear we don't have any choice but to handle this," Ryan said, equally dejected. No more words were spoken. They sat there for what seemed like hours but it was only about 15 minutes. Ryan looked up across the 17th fairway.

"There he is," he said and pointed where he was looking. The old man was walking toward them very slowly.

"So, did he walk all the way from the school?" Sean asked.

"I don't know. He seems to get around pretty well."

He stepped up into the gazebo. The boys stayed sitting down. He sat down on the bench across from them.

"Gentlemen, I trust I didn't keep you waiting long?" They didn't respond. What followed was a very awkward silence. Finally, Ryan spoke up.

"So, are you going to answer our questions?"

"Possibly," he said. "My answer would depend on the nature of the question."

Sean and Ryan looked at each other.

"What the hell does that mean?" Sean asked.

"It means, gentlemen, that I can only answer certain questions. There are some questions that I can answer now and some questions that I can answer later. There are still other questions that I cannot answer," he said in his weird accent. The two looked at each other again.

"Well, let's start with an easy one," Ryan said. "Why did we travel back in time 34 years for no apparent reason?"

"Ah, but there is a reason," the old man said. "And technically you didn't travel back in time. But I will explain that later. For now, yes you traveled back in time 34 years."

"That's not an answer," Sean said.

"Maybe I didn't like the question," the man said with a small smirk. The first real emotion he had shown.

"This isn't a fucking game show!!!" Ryan screamed and stood up. "WHY ARE WE HERE?!" Ryan was as shocked as everyone else at his outburst. He wasn't a monk by any means, but he rarely dropped the f-bomb. He always thought it made the person saying it sound ignorant.

"There's no reason for profanity, Master White," the old man said calmly. Even though Ryan was essentially 'in his face,' he remained perfectly at ease. Ryan had a pretty toned body at this age and at 6'2," he was fairly imposing, but the old man didn't even flinch. Ryan exasperated, turned, ran his hand through his hair, and sat back down.

"I'm sorry," Ryan said. "But it has been an extremely confusing day. Can you at least understand that?!"

"Of course I can. And I will make every effort to explain as much as I am able to," he said in return.

"Okay, then," Sean said. "Why don't you just explain what you can and we'll have a little Q&A afterward. How's that?"

"A splendid idea, Master Jensen," he said. "But I must warn you that much of what you are about to hear is going to be somewhat difficult to accept."

"That much I'm sure of," Sean agreed.

"I can tell you one thing," Maxwell looked them both in the eye, "in a way, you both brought this on yourselves."

Chapter 15

December 1998

Ryan was exhausted. He could barely keep his eyes open as he sat on the shuttle taking him to his car in the long-term parking lot. He had just arrived back from a long and tedious business trip to Atlanta. He was the lead engineer on a project his company was completing in Bangladesh. He was overjoyed that he hadn't been asked to fly to the site again. He had already made two trips overseas and was glad that the project management team had agreed to meet in Atlanta. Still, he had been gone for a week and was looking forward to a kiss from his wife, and a long hot bath.

The shuttle pulled up to his stop and he slowly climbed down from the bus and started walking toward his car. As he approached his car from behind, he noticed it was leaning to one side. "That can't be good," he thought. Much to his dismay, when he got closer, he noticed that both tires on the driver's side were flat. Right to the rims. "What the hell?" Ryan asked out loud as he set his bags down and stared at the tires. As if staring at them long enough would magically make them fill with air and he could be on his way. "Well, this is just great," he thought. "A crappy end to a crappy week." He pulled out his cell phone and dialed his wife. He'd only gotten the phone a month ago and hadn't used it very much. It cost an arm and a leg, but luckily, his company picked up the bill. As it dialed through to his house, he glanced over at the pay phone at the shuttle stop and realized there was no handset. Just a bare wire hanging down. Thank heaven for '90s technology, he thought.

"Hello," Michele answered, sounding rather tired herself.

"Hi, honey. I just got in and you won't believe what I found when I got to my car," Ryan said with the requisite amount of sadness in his voice. He knew she wouldn't hesitate to come get him, but it would be easier if she also felt bad for him. Little tricks husbands learn, he thought to himself. "I don't know how it happened, but both tires on the driver's side are completely flat. I must have run over something as I came into the airport on Monday. I've only got one spare. So..."

"So, you need me to come get you??" Michele asked the obvious.

"Could you?"

"Okay, I guess I cou... Wait, no, I can't! I don't have a car, Ryan. Remember my mom borrowed it until tomorrow. I'm sorry, honey, but I have no way of getting over there," Michele explained honestly and genuinely sorrowfully.

"Damn, I forgot. Alright, well, I'll either call a cab or see if Sean's got nothing better to do on a Friday night. I'll see you soon. I missed you. Love you."

"Love you, too, hon. Sorry. I'd really rather not have you pay for a cab. If Sean can't come, let me know and I'll see if I can borrow Cynthia's car."

"Alright, I'll let you know. See ya." Ryan hung up and wearily thought about his next move. He felt a drop on his head and looked up. It was late in the afternoon but already getting dark, mostly from the clouds. It looked like they were in for another rare rainstorm in early December. There had been a sudden warming trend from a southern jetstream that temporarily caused it to rain instead of snow. But as the sun set and the temperature dropped, the rain was freezing as it fell, turning the storm into an icy nightmare. The roads would be a mess. He moved quickly into the hut at the shuttle stop and dialed Sean's number.

"Hey, you get lost on your way home from Atlanta?" Sean answered, seeing his friend's new cell phone pop up on his caller id.

"No, I made it. But I obviously ran over something last week when I got here. Both tires on the driver's side are flat, and Michele's without her car. I figured with your boring life, you wouldn't have anything better to do than come pick me up? Right?" Ryan said jokingly.

"Well, Cindy's still gone with the baby and I've got my girlfriend over, and we were just getting started," Sean said with a smile in his voice.

"Yea, right. If you were just getting started, you never would have answered the phone. Get your hands out of your pants and get your ass over here. It's freezing."

"Alright. Give me a half hour. What stop are you at?" Sean listened as Ryan told him where he was in the enormous airport parking lot.

By the time Sean arrived, the sprinkle had turned into a full downpour. And the temperature was dropping rapidly. Ryan ran from the hut into Sean's car and they headed for home.

Around 5:30 pm, Marianne Thomas was driving home on Mountain View Road with her two children, Taz and Janey. Taz was a four-year-old boy who refused to sit in a car seat but agreed to a booster seat. Even though he complained every time his mother strapped him in. Janey was his six-year-old sister, who also sat in a booster seat. Although Janey told Taz she only sat in the seat so she could help Mommy look out for potholes. The family had hit one a few weeks before and now she was always on the lookout. Both children were sitting in the back of their family's Jeep Cherokee playing 'Who can make the most annoying noise?' game, much to Marianne's dismay. As the rain turned to ice, car tires everywhere were beginning to lose traction on the slippery asphalt. As Marianne drove through the driving rain/ice, even her wipers at full speed could not give her the visibility she needed. She switched the Jeep into four-wheel drive but she knew that wouldn't help much on ice. She approached a signal light and could barely see that the light was green. She slowed down and proceeded through the intersection.

She saw the truck out of the corner of her eye. But it was too late. She slammed on her brakes but even with anti-lock brakes, she barely slowed down. Then everything went black.

A few minutes before, nineteen-year-old Bobby Levenson was late for work. If he didn't make it on time tonight, there was a good chance he'd be at the unemployment office the next day. It was one of those months when everything seemed to go wrong and his boss was losing his patience. The driving rain was smashing his windshield. His wipers barely cleared a drizzle on a good day, let alone an onslaught like this. As he approached the intersection, he couldn't see that his light was red. He thought as long as his F-350 truck was in 4-wheel drive, he was invincible. He was wrong. As he entered the intersection going at least 45 miles per hour (in a 30 mph zone), his truck slammed broadside into Marianne's Cherokee. He didn't even get a chance to touch his brakes. The truck drove the Jeep across the intersection, down an embankment and into the ice-cold, swollen river below. At this particular location, the slow-moving river was over 15 feet deep. The impact immediately knocked Marianne unconscious. The two children in the backseat were dazed but miraculously unharmed, physically. The booster seats had performed exactly as advertised. Mentally, however, they were both frozen with fear as their Jeep began to sink and they were too scared to scream or yell for help.

Unfortunately, Bobby truly thought he was invincible and hadn't even bothered to put his seat belt on. It was the last mistake he would ever make. He was thrown through his windshield and was run over by his own truck as it pushed the Cherokee into the river. His neck broke from the impact of the windshield. He was killed instantly.

Three cars that were in or around the intersection immediately stopped and their occupants jumped out. One of those cars was Sean Jensen's. "Holy shit!" Sean yelled as he slammed on his brakes. Both men immediately jumped out and ran towards the river as the Cherokee began to sink. Neither one hesitated. They both jumped in and swam toward the sinking vehicle. The cold water took their breath away. However, neither of them thought about retreating. Sean yelled above the noise of the storm, "Ryan, go on the passenger side. See if you can get a door open." They split up. Sean swam toward the driver's side and Ryan toward the opposite side. Ryan remembered thinking that the Jeep wasn't sinking nearly as fast as he thought it would. As it tipped forward with the weight of the engine, the water had only reached halfway up the hood. People had gathered on the riverbank but nobody was about to jump into the frigid water to help. Finally, one man jumped in and swam toward Sean. Together they were able to open Marianne's door and pull her unconscious body from the vehicle. Neither man noticed the two nearly catatonic children sitting in the backseat, clinging to each other with their eyes closed. But Ryan did. "Sean," he yelled. "There're two kids in the back!" But Sean couldn't hear him. He was helping pull Marianne to the shore. As he got close, several people jumped in and grabbed Marianne and pulled her out of the icy water. Sean could barely feel his legs. The water couldn't be much warmer than 40 degrees. As he pulled himself out of the river, he looked back but couldn't see Ryan. "Ryan!" "Ryan!" He looked but couldn't see anything on the other side of the Jeep.

Ryan could clearly see the kids. They were struggling with their booster seats, trying to get free. He could hear the sirens in the distance but knew they wouldn't get there in time. Now that the driver's door had been opened, the vehicle began to sink much faster. Ryan reached down but couldn't reach the back door. Finally, he reached lower and grabbed the handle. It was locked! As fast as he could, he swam around the Jeep as it continued to quickly sink. He dove down and began swimming towards the driver's side door that was still hanging open. It was nearly impossible to see, but remarkably the headlights were still on and helped to illuminate the immediate area. Ryan's heart sank. The Jeep was now completely underwater. As Ryan headed for the driver's side door, suddenly, another light appeared inside the truck. It was near the back. Nice going, kids! They must have been able to get out of their seats and climbed in the back. They had found an air pocket and turned on the rear light. Nearly out of breath, Ryan swam through the driver's door, over the front and back seats and popped up in the back and came face to face with two very scared little kids. The air pocket was fairly large. Thanks to those dedicated engineers in Detroit, the Jeep was sealed tightly and the water didn't seem to be rising too quickly. But Ryan knew the water was too cold to survive in. If they didn't drown, they'd die of hypothermia before the vehicle could get pulled out. As Ryan popped his head up out of the water, both kids screamed and jumped to the other side of the truck. All Ryan could think of to say was "Hi." Both kids' lips were turning blue. Ryan knew that hypothermia was very close for all three of them. He had to get them out now.

"Hey, my name's Ryan. I'm going to help get you guys out, okay?" Ryan could barely speak. He was so cold and his mouth didn't want to form his words very well. He and the children were shivering uncontrollably. "What're your n...names?" Ryan asked. "T...T...Taz and J...Jan...Janey," Janey said slowly.

"Well, Taz and Janey, your m...mom is already outside. She really wants to see you g...guys so I need you to do me a favor. We need to s...s...swim out of here so we can see your mom and get out of this c...cold water. Do you think you can do that for me?" Neither child moved or made any indication that they had even heard Ryan, let alone understand what he was asking them to do. He could see them clearly since the light was still miraculously lit. Finally, Taz said, "I can d...do it. Can y...yo...you do it, J...J...Janey?" Janey nodded. "Ok...Okay," Ryan said, "we're going to have to g...go one at a time. Taz, since you're b...being so brave, do you think you could g...go first?" Taz nodded.

Just then, Ryan felt something slide by his leg. Sean's head popped up. Both kids screamed again and backed away. Sean coughed and gagged but managed a "Hey guys."

"What took you so l...long?" Ryan said as his lips began to turn blue, as well.

"Hey, sue me, okay?"

"Guys, this is my good friend, Sean. He's g...going to help us get out, alright?"

Ryan turned to Sean. "Sean, this is Taz, and this is Jan...Janey. Taz is being really brave and is going to s...swim with you out of here, okay?"

"Alright, T...Taz. You ready?" Sean asked but could barely get the words out.

Taz nodded his head and literally jumped into Sean's arms. "Okay, take a deep breath and hold on," Sean said. What neither Ryan nor Sean knew was that, at age four, Taz held the neighborhood record for holding his breath and swimming underwater. The problem was that that record had been set in a swimming pool in July, not in a freezing river during a

December ice storm. While Ryan and Sean had been talking to them, Ryan had been able to open the back passenger door with his foot. So there was barely two feet between the top of the water and the door. Then it was a clear shot to the surface. "Back door's open. G...Get him out and don't come b...back," he managed to say to Sean. Sean nodded. "Okay, 1...2...3," Taz took a big breath and closed his eyes. Sean grabbed him and pulled him under the water and pushed him through the open door. He could see him kicking towards the surface. Thank heaven for swimming lessons, he thought.

Ryan turned to Janey. "O...O...Okay, J...Jan...Janey. Are you ready?" Janey's eyes were starting to close. Ryan smacked her lightly on the cheek and she opened her eyes. "Stay with me, honey," he said. It was now or never. Either he gets this girl out of here now or she was dead. Her eyes began to close again and she started to sink into the water. He slapped her face harder but she was not responding to him at all. Ryan didn't have much choice. He grabbed her limp body and dragged her under the water and pushed her out the door and toward the surface. As soon as she took her first gulp of water, she began thrashing and fighting him. Luckily, the little bit of strength he had left was slightly more than what she had left. They both broke through the surface. She was coughing spastically. Ryan grabbed her and pulled her toward the side of the river. He could see that Taz had been pulled out and was being looked at. Sean was lying on the side of the river but was out of the water. Just as Janey and Ryan popped out of the water, the first fire engine had pulled up. It had been nearly fifteen minutes since the Jeep had entered the water. As they neared the shore, the last ounce of energy suddenly left Ryan's body like an hourglass-draining sand. It was gone. He pushed Janey towards outstretched hands on the side of the river and sank back under the water. He had nothing left. He couldn't move his legs or his arms. Yet he felt strangely peaceful and calm. He no longer felt cold. He just wanted to fall asleep. Suddenly, two strong pairs of arms grabbed him and pulled him out. The last thing Ryan saw was a fireman looking down at him and yelling something about a blanket. Then everything went black.

Ryan woke up to his wife's pretty but tear-stained face in the hospital. He would later find out that he had been in an advanced state of hypothermia and it was a miracle that he had survived. Sean wasn't much better but hadn't been in the water as long as Ryan. He had been treated at the scene and released. Marianne, Taz, and Janey were all going to be fine. The mayor of Salt Lake City awarded Sean and Ryan the Hero of the Year award for their bravery and selflessness. They both hated the publicity. Everyone from Leno to Letterman to the Today Show wanted interviews. They begrudgingly agreed. Luckily, the hype died down as quickly as it had come and life returned to normal.

Taz Thomas was born in 1994. He went on to marry and have several children. One of Taz's sons was born in 2031. Taz's son's daughter was born in 2064. Taz's son's daughter's son was born in 2105. And Taz's son's daughter's son's son was born in 2125. That son's name was Gerald Senyer. The great-great-great grandson of Taz Thomas. Who, without Ryan White and Sean Jensen, would certainly have died in December of 1998. Gerald Senyer's best friend while growing up and into adulthood was Darius Ramsey. When Darius was nine years old, he and Gerald and two other boys had built a fort in a pine tree behind the Life Force Institute. This was a time when the institute was barely staffed and it was easy to get bored running through the nearly empty halls. One day, while in their 'fort' under the pine tree, Darius had the great idea to build a signal fire. Needless to say, the fire immediately caught the rest of the tree on fire. As the screaming boys ran to exit the fort, Darius tripped and hit his head on a root sticking out of the ground. He was knocked unconscious. When Gerald and the other boys got out and looked for Darius, Gerald realized he was still inside. He ran back through the burning pine tree into the fort and dragged Darius out just seconds before the fort collapsed and the tree exploded into flames. Gerald was burned badly on his neck and back from a burning branch that fell on him. Darius was dazed from smoke inhalation but was otherwise fine. If not for Gerald Senyer, Darius would have never had a 10th birthday.

The story of the underwater rescue had been embellished and passed on from generation to generation. By the time it was told to Darius Ramsey, Ryan White, and Sean Jensen were made out to be some sort of superheroes. It was this story that drove Darius to find Ryan and Sean, study them, and ultimately use them as participants in one of his final tests. Darius knew that he had to choose his participants wisely, and the personal risk was enticing. If Ryan or Sean died or was seriously injured, Darius' best friend's very existence and his own would almost certainly be in doubt. However, as was the case with countless men like Darius throughout history, his drive for success and perfection had become an obsession. He no longer thought clearly about consequences. Only results. What had started as a noble venture to improve mankind had turned into a maniacal quest for power and glory. Darius had become truly dangerous.

Chapter 16

September 1982

"What do you mean, we brought this on ourselves?" Ryan asked.

"All in good time, Master White." Maxwell stood up and turned his back to the boys. It seemed as if he was looking out over the golf course, whose trees were now casting long shadows across the faded green fairway. "It certainly is beautiful here," he said to nobody in particular. He turned back around and cast his face to the ceiling of the gazebo as he began to speak. "As I stated previously, my name is Maxwell. I have been assigned as your guide, assistant or handler might better describe my function. The two of you have been brought here, in this time, to compete in a...a contest," he started. It was as if the contest wasn't the right word but just the best he could come up with. "I will explain the nature of this contest later. But before I can explain exactly what this contest is, I must delineate the choices that you have at your disposal."

Sean and Ryan looked at each other as if to say in unison, 'What the hell...???'

He went on, "We know virtually everything there is to know about each of you. At least everything that is pertinent to this situation. For reasons that I cannot divulge to you at this time, you two have been chosen. The choice has been made, and it is final. Now, as to the choices I have been authorized to present to you. Once I've given you these options, you will be given three days to make your decision." He turned and sat back down on the bench across from them. He leaned forward and put out one of his long, bony fingers. "Each of you may 1) decline the challenge to compete or," now he put up two fingers, "2) accept the challenge to compete," he said.

"Wow, slow down so I can write this down," Ryan said with the requisite sarcasm.

"It is not the choices that you must remember, Master White, but the eventual effects and consequences of those choices," he said with significant emphasis on the word 'consequences.'

"What 'effects and consequences'?" Sean asked with similar emphasis.

Maxwell looked to Sean and continued, "If you choose to decline the challenge, you will remain in this time and will live out the remainder of your life. You will have no memory of this situation nor will you have any memory of the life you have led from this time moving forward. In other words, any memory of your life in and up to 2016, from whence you came. Certainly, there is a remote possibility that you will meet and marry the same girls and then possibly have the same children. However, I must emphasize that the probability of that occurring is statistically zero." He paused, obviously to let this sink in. "Alternatively, if you choose to accept the challenge to compete in this 'contest,' and you emerge victorious, you will be returned to your families at the exact moment you left them. They, nor you, will have suffered any deleterious effects and will have no knowledge that you ever left. On the other hand, if you fail to successfully complete the challenge, you will remain in this time and, as before, have no memory of these occurrences. And the last 'effect,'" he stood up, "if you are to be killed during this contest, your children will obviously cease to exist since there will be no chance of your eventual meeting with their mother." Maxwell was back to showing no emotion. But it was obvious that he did not enjoy delivering this information. He also deliberately left out the part of the consciousness transfer vs. actual time travel. But the eventualities remained the same.

Ryan's mind was racing. He was trying to comprehend what Maxwell had just told them. He looked over at Sean. His head was in his hands. Ryan stood up and slowly walked to the edge of the gazebo. Maxwell said, "As I said before, you have three days to..."

"I don't need three days, you son of a bitch!!!" Ryan screamed at him. "How about another choice? I rip your heart out of your chest and shove it down your goddamn throat!!," Ryan yelled as he grabbed him and threw him up against the wall of the gazebo. He hit the wall so hard that dust fell down from the rafters.

As calmly as if he was ordering a side of French fries, Maxwell replied, "That would be an unwise choice, Master White. As I stated before, I am here to help you, not hinder you."

"Help?!" Ryan said. "You just gave us only one chance out of three of returning to our families and told us we might DIE in the process." He let him down hard on the bench.

"I understand your frustration, but..."

"Do you, do you really??!!" Ryan sneered. "I don't think so. I think this is a big game for you and whoever you work for. What, are you going to put us in some big coliseum fighting lions and shit, while you and your buddies get ready for the thumbs up or thumbs down? Look, I'll do whatever I can to get back to my family. But don't sit there and tell me you understand our frustration. It's not like you have anything riding on this," he sat down next to Sean, who still had his head in his hands.

"On the contrary, Master White, I have my very existence dependent on the outcome of this 'contest,'" he said.

It was Ryan's turn to put his head in his hands. He was suddenly very tired and didn't want to hear anymore.

"So what is this 'contest,' anyway?" Sean asked quietly from the other side of the gazebo, much calmer.

Maxwell cleared his throat and straightened his raincoat. "It's actually more of a…a quest. In the beginning, you will be given one clue. This clue will direct you to a second clue which will lead you to a third clue and then to a fourth and final clue. If you are able to retrieve all three subsequent clues, you will then be faced with finding the final object of your quest. This object will facilitate your return to your family. Quite simple, really."

"Yea, and what's the dangerous part? You said we might get killed during this so-called 'contest'?" Sean pointed out.

Maxwell looked at them with the first hint of emotion. Ryan could only classify it as a sort of sadness or at least sorrowful apprehension. "You will not be the only ones looking for these clues," he said slowly. "There will be another team working toward the same end but for a very different reward. As you will be competing for the right to return to your families, they will be competing for, how should I say, more temporal rewards."

"Who is this other team?" Sean asked.

"I can't tell you who they are. However, if you accept the challenge, I expect you will meet them soon enough," he said. "I can tell you, although, that the deck is stacked somewhat against you. This was not my choice nor my wish. You see, there are four of them and they are, as your society says, 'bad seeds'. They are criminals. All of them. From your time in the future. They range in age from 21 to 23, in this time. They have also been brought back to compete. They will be competing for 2 million dollars each, if successful. Plus, a complete pardon of their crimes, of course," he stated matter of factly.

"Well, that's just great!" Ryan said. "We're up against four dirtbag criminals who would kill us just as soon as spit on us."

"You're right, Master White, they are quite ruthless and without conscience and your quest will not be without its challenges. However, you and Master Jensen were chosen for a reason. You see, we believe friendship, trust, and love of family are much more powerful weapons than hatred, jealousy, and love of money. I should add that you will also be given a number of 'assets,' shall I say, that will assist you," Maxwell said.

"What kind of assets?" the boys asked, almost in unison. Maxwell took the next several minutes to describe what each team will be supplied with. When he was through, he gave each of them a small black bag with a tie string.

Maxwell turned to leave. "Remember," he said, "you have three days to make your final choice." He looked briefly at Ryan as if to say 'I know...you probably won't need three days'. "In the meantime, you have also been offered an additional asset if you choose to take it."

"What's that?"

"The other team has been barred from explaining their situation or telling anyone of this 'contest.' If they do, they will immediately be disqualified. You two, on the other hand, have been given the option of telling your immediate families. And ONLY your immediate families," he stressed. "Your family, if you can convince them you are being truthful, can assist you in deciphering clues but under no circumstance can they accompany you or assist you in the retrieval of the clues and final object. I will warn you, however, that trying to explain your situation to your family will not be an easy task. We've seen unfavorable results with this tactic in the past," he explained.

"You mean you've done this before?!" Ryan asked incredulously.

"I'm not allowed, at this time, to elaborate," he explained. "But," holding up his hand to stop Ryan's next outburst, "there will come a time that I can explain in greater detail. This may help in your discussions with your families." He reached into his raincoat pocket and tossed them a folded-up sheet of paper.

Maxwell turned to walk away. "Hey, Max!" Ryan called to him. He turned with his eyebrows raised. He obviously didn't appreciate the shortening of his name. "You said your very existence depended on the outcome of this 'contest'? What does that mean exactly?"

He stared at them and simply said, "Three days, gentlemen. Three days." And walked away.

Sean and Ryan looked at each other. "What do we do now?" Sean asked.

"I guess we figure out how to tell our families," Ryan said. "They might not believe us, but it would be nice to have someone else to bounce ideas off of."

"So we're going to accept?" Sean asked.

"You know we are," Ryan said.

"Yea, I know."

Chapter 17

The two boys walked their motorcycles down to Sean's house. They needed time to talk. It was about 6:30 pm and they figured they should get home. It was amazing how quickly they were returning to their teenage years. They hadn't had to be "home for dinner" for quite some time, at least not for their parents.

Ryan left Sean at his house. They agreed that they had no choice but to accept the challenge in order for a chance to return home. They also agreed that they would spend the next 24 hours trying to figure out a way to tell their families (in this time) what was going on and how they needed their help.

Ryan rode his motorcycle the rest of the way to his mom and dad's house. He figured it was also his house for the time being. He walked in the back door and was greeted with the smell of his mom's cooking. That was something he could remember very well. Ryan's mom was a great cook. Although cooking for seven people sometimes resulted in pancakes for dinner or leftovers from Sunday or 'fend for yourself night.' It didn't matter. He was hungry enough to welcome anything tonight.

"Where have you been?" his mom asked as he walked through the kitchen. It always seemed like his mom was either in the kitchen or walking around the house picking up clothes and toys. He rarely saw her just sit down and relax. He had to smile to himself. He and Michele would often just leave the dishes in the sink and go lie down on their bed and watch NCIS or Criminal Minds or some other waste of time. He'd give anything to waste some time with Michele right now.

"I was just hanging out over at Sean's house," he said.

"If you're going to be past six, you know I would appreciate a call," she said with raised eyebrows, although not upset. "Your father has something to talk to you about. He's in the living room," she said and went back to what she had been doing before Ryan came in. From the scent in the house, it smelled like French toast. He remembered some of his friends couldn't figure out why they sometimes had breakfast food for dinner. He always thought it was pretty cool.

Ryan went to the living room. His dad was sitting on the couch reading a novel. He read more than anyone Ryan had ever met. He figured that was a lot better than what some other fathers were doing. Getting drunk and playing punching bag with their wives and kids. He had had more than one friend that had to live through that Hell growing up.

"Hi, Dad," Ryan said as he sat down in the same chair that he had sat in when this whole odyssey started this morning. He still felt a little weird talking to the man he had buried just a few short months ago.

"How was school, Ryan?" he asked quietly. Ryan knew something was up. He could always tell when his dad spoke quietly and acted like nothing was going on.

"Fine," he replied.

Then his mom came in, drying her hands on a dish towel as she sat down next to his dad. So his suspicion was right. Something was up. His mom spoke first. It always intrigued him how his mom would say that his dad had something to talk to him about but he rarely did much talking. It was always his mom that got right to the point.

"We got a call from the school today, Ryan. They said that you didn't show up until 3rd period. Anything you want to tell us?" she started.

He didn't really know what to say. It had been so long since he'd had to lie to his parents that he was a little out of practice. But it came back pretty quick.

"Oh, well, Sean was having some problems with his mom and dad, so we went up to the golf course to talk about it," he said. It wasn't really a lie since Sean had told him that his parents had thought he was on drugs when he had 'freaked out' this morning.

Out of character, his dad spoke up. "Why did you have to go to the golf course to talk?" he asked.

"No reason, really. It's just a place we go sometimes to hang out. You know the little gazebo-type thing at the entrance? It's just a meeting place we have since a lot of my friends live on the other side of the course," Ryan explained, not really expecting them to understand.

"Well, it's not acceptable to us that you were two hours late for school. Especially when it's only a couple weeks into the year," his mom said.

"Sorry."

"Well, we've talked about it and we think you can take the bus to school for the rest of the week. You can leave your motorcycle at home," she said. Ryan was sure they expected him to protest, but he was still reeling from the day's events, so he just said, "Okay, fine."

"Don't let it happen again, Ryan," his dad said. "It would be nice for you to get a scholarship for college and missing class isn't the way to get it." He picked up his novel again and his mom went back to the kitchen. Ryan looked at his dad. He couldn't believe that he was sitting there, alive and well. So weird.

Just then, his little sister, Britney, walked by on her way to the family room. Probably to watch TV or something. Ryan got up and followed her. "Hey, Brit," he said a little too excitedly. He didn't see her very often in "his time." She lived in Hawaii and only came to visit once or twice a year. Now she was a skinny little six-year-old kid with ponytails.

"Hey," she said without turning around.

"Where's Mason?" he asked. He couldn't wait to see his little brother. They were eight years apart in age and had only become 'friends' when they were adults.

"I don't know. In his room, I guess," she said and turned back to Barney and Friends.

Ryan went upstairs to Mason's room. He was sitting at his study desk doing some homework.

"What's up, little man?" Ryan asked.

"Nothin' much," he said without turning around. He was nine, so he hadn't become a jerk yet.

"Whatcha working on?" Ryan asked as he sat down on his brother's bed.

"I have to write sentences with my vocabulary words," he said. Ryan just looked at him while he worked. He couldn't believe he was so young. About a week ago, Ryan had helped him move into his new house with his wife and three kids. As he remembered that day, his two sons had come with him to help. His youngest, Colton, was the same age as Mason's daughter. They got along really well. It was the only place Ryan and Michele would let him sleep over at (their rule was they had to be 10 before they let them sleep over at a friend's house). Ryan started to feel sad again. Ironically, he had just helped his eight-year-old with vocabulary words two nights ago.

"Do you want any help?" Ryan asked.

"I'm almost done. What does holocaust mean?" he asked. He pronounced it totally wrong.

"It means a big fire or an immense conflagration," which is the way Alan Alda's character defined the holocaust in an old episode of M.A.S.H., Ryan remembered. He had seen every episode multiple times and committed most of them to memory. It had become a ritual during college. He'd always rush home from the campus in time to catch M.A.S.H. at 10:30 pm, Magnum P.I. at 11:00 pm, and then get back to the books. Sleep was something he often did without during college.

Ryan continued, since Mason wrinkled his brow at the word 'conflagration,' "It usually refers to what Hitler did to the Jews in World War II," he clarified.

"Oh yea, we talked about that," Mason said. "Didn't he kill like a thousand people?" he asked.

"More like 6 million," Ryan corrected him.

"Whoa, that's a lot," he said.

"It sure was. He was a pretty bad guy. What kind of a sentence are you going to write for the holocaust?"

"How about 'The holocaust was really hot'?" he asked.

"I think you can do better than that. How about 'Hitler slaughtered 6 million Jews during the Holocaust in World War II,'" Ryan suggested.

"Cool," he said while he wrote. He spelled slaughtered as 'slotered,' but Ryan figured his teacher would get the point.

"See you later, buddy," Ryan said as he left his room. Except for the fact that he wouldn't see his family again, the thought of staying in this time was not a horrible one, in and of itself. Ryan had had a wonderful childhood. Sure, they had problems like every family but all in all, it was a great life. He never considered them wealthy but in comparison and hindsight, he guessed they got along pretty well. They lived in a great upper-middle-class neighborhood. Not too snooty, not too trailerish. It was a great time and a great place to be a kid. But that kid had grown up and had kids of his own. And he wasn't going to lose all that. Not now. Not ever.

Ryan started to go through the status of his family at this time. One of his older sisters, Jessica, had already gotten married and moved out. He was trying to remember. He thought she had like one kid or maybe two at this point. His other sister, Debby, was still living at home. But he didn't think she was home. Her bedroom was dark. She was in college and didn't spend too much time at home, if his memory served.

Ryan went downstairs to his room to think. Maxwell had said that they could tell their immediate family. That meant brothers and sisters, too. How was he going to tell them what had happened to him? Just then, he remembered the black bag and the folded piece of paper Maxwell had given to them. He ran back upstairs and got his backpack and went back down to his room. He couldn't believe that he and Sean hadn't thought to open them together. He slowly pulled out the black bag. It was made of silk or something similar. It was really soft and had a weird design on the outside, kind of like a logo or something. It was basically a blue sphere with the words Life Force on it. 'Weird,' Ryan thought.

He opened it up and poured the contents onto the bed. There was a card that looked like a driver's license. It had his picture on it, his address, his social security number, his height and weight, and his hair and eye color. At the top, it said 'Federal Identification.' Whatever that meant. All the information was correct. There was a passport with all his information inside and there were several pages of stamps from various countries. Mostly in Europe, although he had never traveled outside the United States, up to that point in time. There was also another card that looked like an ATM card. Then he pulled out the folded piece of paper. It simply had three dates on it with what looked like headlines next to the dates. There was also a short paragraph below two of the headlines. The dates were the next three days; September 11th, 12th, and 13th. Maxwell had said that this might help them with their 'proof.' Ryan supposed they could use these events to prove that they had indeed come from the future or at least give them some credibility.

He looked at his bed. Not very inviting. No warm body to sleep next to. He deeply missed his wife. So much had happened today. It felt like it had been days since he was home. When, in actuality, he had gone to bed just last night with his wife in his own bed in his own home. Ryan's mind was still reeling from what Maxwell had told them. He still hadn't fully processed what it all meant. But he knew one thing for sure. They would accept the challenge and they would win the challenge and he would see his family again. Or he would die trying.

Chapter 18

Since it was Saturday morning, Ryan slept a little late. His mom finally turned on his light and left it on. A little trick she sometimes played when he wouldn't get out of bed to help with the Saturday chores. He lay in bed for a few more minutes. His brain was still struggling with everything that had happened but he had also begun to form some resolve to get through it. If it weren't for some irrefutable facts, such as the man outside raking the lawn instead of being six feet under it, he wouldn't believe any of it was true. He really wished he could bounce this one off his wife for her take. As he pulled himself out of bed, he realized that he and Sean had totally forgotten about Lisa and Gina's party last night. And the keg they were supposed to get. He figured he'd be getting a call anytime now. Oh well. No great loss.

Ryan helped around the house as much as he could. He called Sean and reminded him about the party they'd missed. Gina had already called him and they had promptly split up again. Good. Maybe Lisa wouldn't call him, Ryan thought. So much the better. He and Sean agreed to meet later to discuss how they were going to tell their respective families about their "situation." They decided tomorrow would be the day.

Sean and Ryan got together and spent the rest of the day driving around in Sean's mom's grey station wagon. Minivans hadn't come around yet, so enormous gas-guzzling station wagons were the first choice for hauling kids around. They called it "the boat" because it handled about as well as his dad's 20' Stingray. Their main mission was to see if Maxwell had been telling the truth about some of their 'assets' contained in the black bag. There wasn't really any reason to doubt him, given the other obvious signs of their situation. But it couldn't hurt to check. Maxwell had told them that they would have a significant financial advantage over the other team, but hadn't elaborated as to how or how much. They figured it had something to do with the card that was in the bag he gave them. The one that looked like an ATM card.

They pulled up to the first bank they came to, got out, and walked up to the ATM machine.

"Hey, isn't it going to ask us for a PIN?" Sean asked.

"I guess so," Ryan said, "but I don't remember Maxwell ever telling us any code."

"Me neither," Sean agreed.

Ryan pulled out his card and looked at it more closely. It had the VISA symbol on the front and the letters LFI as a hologram behind the same symbol that was on the black bag. His name was printed as Ryan White but the back was completely blank. Only a place for his signature and the magnetic strip.

"Well, here goes nothing," he said as he slid the card into the slot in the ATM. The screen went black for a minute and then, sure enough, a screen popped up with: "Enter Personal Identification Number:"

"Great, now what?" Sean asked. "Why would he give us ATM cards but not tell us how to use them?"

"I don't know," Ryan said. "Maybe we should just try some obvious numbers." They started trying birthdays, first names, last names, birth years, 2016, 1982, and even their pets' names without any luck.

"Well, this isn't getting us anywhere," Sean said as he hit cancel and pulled Ryan's card back out. They started to walk back to the car when Ryan stopped.

"Hey, didn't Maxwell say that they knew everything about us? At least everything that pertained to this situation?"

"Yea, so what?" Sean asked.

"So, if they know everything about us, wouldn't they know our PIN numbers in our time in 2016?"

"I guess it's worth a shot," Sean agreed.

They walked back to the ATM and slid Ryan's card in again. Even though they've been told all their lives to make up some random PIN, especially for bank accounts, Ryan always used the same one. It was the number on a telephone keypad that corresponded with the first letters of his family's first names; Ryan, Michele, Jackson, and Colton. 7652. He punched it in.

"Bingo, nice going, Sherlock."

The screen changed and gave several options, including "Current Balance." Ryan punched the button and the screen went black for a few seconds. At first, he thought it was going to give them an error, but then the screen came back on. They both stood in silence at what they saw on the screen:

"Available Balance: $125,000."

"No way," Ryan said quietly. He looked around as if they were doing something wrong or illegal.

"Hit cancel. I want to try my card," Sean said eagerly. They repeated the steps using Sean's PIN from his 2016 bank account. He had the same balance on his card.

"Well, I would say that Maxwell was right. Financially we shouldn't have any problems," Ryan said as they pulled Sean's card out of the machine. "The true test will be if we can access the money. What do you say?" he asked Sean with a slight grin.

"Alright, I guess. What's the worst that can happen?" Sean asked.

"We can get arrested for fraud and put in jail," Ryan replied.

"Why?! The accounts are in each of our names. We have the cards and our ID. There's nothing illegal about it," Sean argued.

"Yea, I guess you're right. Let's go."

The bank was about ready to close. They walked in, and there was a small line. As they waited in line, Ryan asked Sean "So, how much?"

"I dunno. How about a hundred bucks?"

"Dude, we each have $125,000! You get what you want. I want to test this thing. I'm getting ten grand."

"Ten grand!? Are you crazy?!" Sean asked in a loud whisper.

"Hey, we want to see if this account is for real, right? If I walk out of here with ten thousand dollars, I think we can assume that it's for real," he said as the next teller became available. He was trying to think if he had ever withdrawn ten thousand dollars at once before. There had never really been a need. He remembered withdrawing five thousand dollars once. He had to transfer money from one bank to another for a four-wheeler he and his wife were buying. He remembered they had asked him if he wanted a certified check but he wanted to see what 50 hundred dollar bills felt like. That was a pretty scary drive across town to the other bank.

Ryan walked up to the teller. "Hi, I'd like to make a withdrawal but I don't have my account number on me," he said to the frizzy-haired blond behind the window. Early eighties hairstyles were hilarious. But at the time, they were cool.

"That's okay. I just need to see some ID," she said as he handed her the Federal Identification card that had also been included in Maxwell's bag of goodies. "And how much did you want to withdraw today, Mr. White?"

"Ten thousand, please in hundred dollar denominations," he said matter of factly. She looked at him and it was then that he realized that he wasn't a 50-year-old, slightly out-of-shape businessman but a seventeen-year-old punk with a hole in his levis and crappy tennis shoes.

"One minute, Mr. White," she said as she took his ID and went over to what must have been her supervisor. An extremely large, round woman with a serious-looking face, bouffant hairdo, and from what Ryan could see, a pretty healthy mustache. "Oh crap," he thought. The teller pointed at him, and the fat supervisor looked at him very unapprovingly. He gave her a slight smile. The supervisor punched in some numbers on a keyboard and then waddled over to the window. "Mr. White, do you have any other form of ID?" she asked bitterly.

"Why? Isn't that ID sufficient?" he asked. He had his passport, but he was curious as to why the Federal ID wasn't working.

"This ID is valid, but for withdrawals over five thousand dollars, we require two forms of ID," she said with a sickly grin expecting him to fold and slink out.

"Well, I have my passport. Will that do?" he asked. The grin disappeared from her face.

"That should be fine. Go ahead, Bridget," and she handed his ID back to the teller. Bridget, who was actually very pretty, started counting out 100 hundred dollar bills. "Are you sure you don't want a money order or bank check, Mr. White?"

"I'm sure. Thank you," he said as he walked away from the counter and waited for Sean. Sean had wimped out and only gotten five hundred dollars. He didn't run into any problem with the round Nazi supervisor.

"You got it?" Sean asked once they were outside.

"Yep. And fatty behind the desk even punched it up on her computer, and it checked out. So I think we can assume that these accounts are for real," he said as they high-fived each other and walked back to the car.

Chapter 19

It was Sunday. Ryan's family always ate Sunday dinner around 1:00 pm or so. They usually had everyone together, including his sister Jessica and her professor husband John, and two kids. Both boys. Ryan's next oldest sister was Debbie, who still lived at home but, if memory served, he thought she moved out sometime this year. Or maybe next year. He couldn't remember exactly.

He had hinted to his mom that he wanted to talk to her and his dad and the older children (as they were collectively called) after dinner. She asked what it was about, but Ryan dodged the question and changed the subject. He still was seriously concerned about how this was all going to be received and if they were making the right decision. He and Sean had agreed that they would tell Ryan's family first and then tell Sean's parents. Ryan told Sean to come over around 2:00 pm unless he called first.

A few minutes after 2:00 pm, the doorbell rang, and Sean came in. The Whites always had a ring first, then enter policy at their house for close friends. Ryan guessed he remembered because he didn't wait for someone to open the door for him. They were just serving dessert and Ryan's mom asked Sean if he wanted some. He said, "No thanks," but, of course, his mom said, "nonsense," and pretty soon Sean was eating his boysenberry cobbler with the rest of them.

"So, where are you two off to?" Ryan's mom asked.

"Um, nowhere. Actually, Sean and I both wanted to talk to you and Dad and Jessica, and Debbie. And John, too, if they have time," he said.

"What's this about, Ryan?" his mom asked.

"I'll explain it all when we get together. Can we meet in the living room for a minute?" They spent the next several minutes getting all the kids corralled in the family room in front of a movie. Then they got everyone else into the living room. Ryan couldn't remember when he'd ever been so nervous. He had absolutely no idea how his family would react to what he was about to tell them. He and Sean had gone through several scenarios of elaborate lies that would explain their odd behavior and possible trips that they might have to soon take. But, in the end, they figured the truth would probably have just as much of a chance as any lie they could come up with. They had both agreed that Maxwell was right. If they could get their families on board, their help would be invaluable. But that was a big 'if.'

Everyone had settled down, and all eyes were on Ryan. His mom and dad, Jessica and John, and Debbie. He hadn't invited the younger ones for obvious reasons. Not only would they not be much help, but he was sure they would blab to the world if he told them.

Ryan stood up in front of everyone and in his mind, figured, 'just start at the top'. He felt like he was in an Agatha Christie novel and was about to expose the murderer. "I'm sure you're wondering why Sean and I asked you to stay after dinner for a little while. To put it bluntly, we need your help. But it's going to require you to open your minds a little...or a lot, listen to what I'm saying, and consider it carefully before disregarding it as nonsense. I want to start off by saying that we haven't been drinking, we're not on any drugs and we haven't taken up with any comet-chasing cult. We're both completely sane and in complete control of our faculties. We don't really expect you to believe what I'm about to tell you, at first. But I would ask that you bear with us and give us a chance to fully explain before you ask any questions or object." Confused faces were all he saw. But at least he had gotten their attention.

He took a deep breath and started, "Last Thursday night, I went home to MY house, tucked in MY two kids, and got in MY bed with MY wife of nearly 20 years and fell asleep in the year 2016. I woke up the next morning in my old bed in my old room in my old house in my 17-year-old body." He paused. Not for effect but just to see the initial reaction. More confused faces. His sister Jessica smiled as if to say, 'Nice one, Ryan.' He went on. "Mom and Dad," he looked directly at them on the couch, "you remember how I was acting on Friday morning? I wasn't exactly acting like myself, right?"

His dad slowly said, "No...not really."

"In fact, I was pretty much in shock," he continued, "I had no idea what was happening. I went to bed in 2016 and woke up in 1982. I knew it wasn't a joke. I'd already seen proof of that. What I didn't understand was how...or why. I didn't know what to do or who to talk to or anything. I decided to go upstairs to take a bath. Remember, mom?" She nodded slowly, with a deer in-the-headlights expression. "When I got upstairs, I went into Britney's room. Even though I'd already seen proof of what had happened, I needed to see more. I looked in at Brit sleeping. Sure enough, there she was. Six-year-old Britney. A couple of weeks ago, I talked to her on the phone. She lives in Hawaii with her husband and three children. As I left her room, I glanced out her window and saw him."

"Saw who?" Debbie asked, somewhat incredulously.

He paced for a few seconds. "Before Sean and I got sent back here, I had three encounters with a man. He wore a dark grey raincoat and a brown fedora hat. He looked like he was about 70 years old. The first time was at a stop light in my car. He walked in front of my car. He stopped and turned and looked right at me. Then he kept going. As I went through the intersection and looked in my mirror, he was gone. The next time I saw him was downtown. I was driving along State Street and looked up and saw him standing on a high rise that was being built. He was standing on a beam about 100 feet up and just standing there staring at me. Then, I saw him again near my house that night."

"Wait a minute," Jessica said, "Ryan, I have no idea what you're talking about, but there aren't any buildings going up downtown, let alone high rises."

"That's right," he said. "There aren't any right now. This happened a week ago, but it wasn't 1982," he clarified.

She rolled her eyes and said, "Okay, go on. Next you were kidnapped by aliens and taken to their home planet, right?" He could see he wasn't being very convincing. He held up his hand as if to say, 'Just wait a minute.'

"When I looked out Britney's window, that same guy wearing the same coat and hat was standing on our front sidewalk looking up at her window. Looking right at me. I dropped to the ground and crawled to the window but when I looked out again, he was gone. Just Mrs. Thrombello walking her annoying little poodle down the street. So, I got in the bath and that's when Sean called. Mom, remember you said it sounded 'urgent'?"

Again, she nodded slowly as if in some sort of trance but didn't look up at him.

He knew he was going too fast, but didn't know any other way.

"After some initial confusion and Sean sounding like he was 'losing it,' we figured out that what had happened to me had also happened to him. When I left for school, I didn't go to school. As you guys later found out when the high school called. I had, in fact, gone to the golf course like I said. But I specifically went there to meet Sean and try and figure out what was going on." Again he paused. There was serious doubt on everyone's face.

"Sean and I met at Meatballs. That's what we call that little gazebo near the entrance to the golf course. You know what I'm talking about, right John?" John was an avid golfer and knew the course almost as well as Ryan and Sean did.

"Yea, I know where it is," he said.

"We sat and 'compared notes.' As we did, I looked across the 17th fairway and I saw him again. The same guy I had seen on our sidewalk out front. He was standing on the 16th tee. We took off running toward him. As soon as we started running, he started walking away towards the 15th green. By the time we got there, he was gone."

"So, who is this guy?" John asked. Jessica looked at John as if to say, 'You're believing this??!!'.

"I'll get to that," Ryan said.

He continued, "We didn't know what to do. So we figured we'd go to school and try to see if there was anything or anyone else 'out of place,' so to speak. But nothing seemed different. Just the same old Lakeside High School. By the way, it gets torn down and rebuilt in a few years." he threw in. More confused faces and rolling of the eyes. He heard Jessica say something about bullshit under her breath. He didn't care. He had to get through it. He figured the worst that could happen was they don't believe them and they're on their own. He had to try, though.

"As Sean and I were leaving the school through the front entrance at the end of the day, we were at the top of the stairs when we looked down and there he was. Standing at the bottom of the stairs staring right at us. We walked down the stairs and he said, what was it, Sean, something like 'I suppose you gentlemen have some questions?' or something like that. Of course, we said yes. He said to meet him at the golf course where we saw him that morning. And he left. So, we went to meet him at the golf course."

"You're serious?!" Jessica blurted out. "Some strange old guy asks two good-looking teenagers to meet him and you said okay?!? He could have been some psychopath or pedophile," she exclaimed.

"Jessica, I'd seen this guy multiple times in two different time periods, and he claimed to have answers to multiple questions. Of course, I was going to meet him."

She went on. "You know, Ryan, this is a little too weird for me. I have no idea what you're telling us but if this is some sort of joke, it's gone too far. You're making mom cry!" She stood up and turned to leave. "Let's go home, John." He looked over at his mom and there were tears rolling down her face. He felt bad, but he had to finish. He knew she'd start crying eventually. It was just a little earlier than he had estimated.

"Please! Wait! I understand it's a lot to take in. But it's no joke, and I'm begging you to please listen until I'm done. Then you can ask questions or leave or call me the world's biggest liar or have me committed...or whatever," he said.

She stared at him for a few seconds. "Fine, finish your fantasy. But there's no way I'm going to believe your 'from the future,' Ryan," she put up her hands in surrender and sat back down. Ryan was kind of surprised. He had figured that Jessica would ask the most questions but he didn't figure she would be the first to completely discount what he was saying.

"So, we met him, this guy, at the gazebo at the golf course." he was going to say they had brought golf clubs for protection but in his head, it sounded really stupid. Which it probably was. "Turns out his name is Maxwell. He said he couldn't tell us where (or when) he came from. But he did say he was sent to help us. He told us that we had been sent back in time to compete in a contest. Or a quest, as he called it. He said he couldn't tell us why we had been chosen. Believe me, we asked. He said he might be able to tell us more soon. In any event, he gave us essentially two choices. One, is to accept the challenge to compete in this contest. Or two, to refuse to compete."

Now it was his mom's turn to speak up. "Honey, I'm very confused and scared. I can't even begin to understand what you're trying to tell us. You're saying you're you but you're not you. That you've somehow been sent back in time to run a race? How can we be expected to even begin to understand?"

Ryan walked slowly over to her and knelt down in front of her. He took her hand and said, "Look in my eyes, Mom." She did, through a lot of tears. "I'm your son. I've always been your son and I will always be your son. I completely understand that this is scary and confusing. Sean and I are very scared, confused, disoriented, and feel very alone. The only thing we have to cling to right now is family. I don't have all the answers. In fact, I have more questions than answers. But I do know that we are going to need your help if we're going to get through this. So, please, let me finish, and then we'll talk more about trying to understand all this together." He let go of her hand. It was shaking and she had begun to cry again. He almost lost it then. He hated to see his mom cry and he had always been somewhat of a sympathetic cryer. But somehow, he held it together.

He went on, "So, this Maxwell, as he likes to be called, told us that we had been chosen to compete in a contest. As I said, we only had essentially two options. If we accepted the challenge and won, we would be sent back to our families at the exact time that we had left. If we refused to compete, our memories of this experience and our 'former lives' would be erased and we would continue on in this time as if nothing had occurred. Of course, there is the remote possibility that we would meet the same girls and get married and have the same children, but the chance of that happening is statistically impossible. In other words, we would lose our families. Everyone in this room has children. Except you, Debbie. But you will. And sooner than you probably think."

She raised her eyebrows and shook her head. "Not me. Not for a long time."

Ryan smiled. She got married during her freshman year in college and had four kids before she graduated.

"I don't believe any of you could stand the thought of losing your families. Sean and I, of course, can't either. Therefore, we're obviously going to accept the challenge to compete. It's the only way we will ever see our wives and children again."

He sat back down and took a deep breath. "If it's okay with everyone, I'm going to go grab a quick drink of water. I'll be right back." Sean shot him a look like 'you're leaving me here alone???'. He walked out of the living room and quickly into the kitchen. He could just imagine the conversations that would start if he was gone very long. As he was filling up a glass of water, Debbie came in.

"So, time travel, huh?" she said, smiling.

He looked at her and eked out a small smile. "Out of everyone in that room, I figured you were the only one that would at least give it a chance," he said. Debbie was the most practical of his siblings and the smartest, except maybe for Britney, who went on to get a doctorate at MIT in BioMechanical Engineering. But for weird stuff like this, Debbie was it.

When he and Sean had 'drifted off course' in their youth, Debbie was the only one he could talk to about hangovers, girls and such. "I'm not sure what to think, Deb. Nothing in my life could have prepared me for what's going on." They both started to head back to the living room.

She stopped him just outside the kitchen. "Hey, you said that on the first morning when you 'came back,'" she held her fingers up in quotes, "you said you had already seen proof. What did you mean?" she asked.

"I meant I saw dad...alive," he said and walked past her back to the living room.

He expected everyone to be talking or maybe even getting their coats on to leave. But everyone was where he had left them, completely silent. "Sorry about that, my throat was getting dry," he said as he sat back down.

"Back to the contest. If you thought everything up 'til now was confusing, just wait. Sean and I are both still in a quandary about this next part. This contest, or quest, or whatever, is essentially a treasure hunt of sorts. We will be faced with the challenge of finding three clues. Each one will lead to the next. These clues will be used to complete the final task of finding the location of an orb." He put his hands up as if holding a small ball. "Maxwell told us that this orb is about the size of a cantaloupe and it is the object that will enable us to go 'back to the future.'" he smiled. "It makes me think of a movie that will be coming out in about three years." Sean chuckled.

"There are several caveats, however," he said. "One is that we're not the only ones competing. There is another team. This is where it gets a little scary. The other team is composed of four men. They are criminals, taken from the same year we were. They range in age, now, between 21 and 23. In 2016, they were all serving life sentences for various crimes. Rather than playing for the right to return to their families, they are playing for money and freedom. If they are successful, they will be given

$2,000,000 each and granted full pardons. I'm not sure how this would be achieved but we all got sent 34 years back in time. So I'm guessing it can be done. Now, I know what you're thinking. I don't like the odds, either. However, we've been given a couple of advantages. The first and most important is that we've been given permission to tell all of you about this. The other team cannot tell anyone or solicit help from anyone. Also," he dug in his pocket, "we've been given these." He dumped out his passport, ID, and bank card on the table. "Both Sean and I have been given passports and ID. The ID puts me at 21 years old and Sean at 19 years old. Go ahead. Take a look," he said and tossed the passport to his Dad and the ID to Debbie.

"What's that?" his mom asked, pointing to the bank card with a shaky finger.

He picked it up. "We were each given one of these. It's an ATM card that works in every bank in the world. Each has an account balance of $125,000. It's true. We've checked it out in about ten ATMs around the city. The money's there. Here's some of it." He tossed the card to his mom and put the envelope with the ten thousand dollars on the table and turned it upside down so the bills spilled out on the table. She looked at the card briefly and put it back down like it was 'uncomfortable' to hold. She then looked at the money on the table. "God in Heaven, Ryan," she said, "where did you get all that?"

"I told you, Mom. Maxwell gave us the cards and we had to verify that the accounts were real." He thought he probably should have held off on dumping the money on the table.

"So, just for grins, let's say all of this is somehow true, which it's not," Jessica said. "What happens if you don't win?" she asked.

"Well, that's the bad part," he said. "If we don't find the orb before the other team does, we suffer the same fate as if we hadn't accepted the challenge in the first place. Our memories will be erased and we live out our lives from this point and never see our wives and children again." Nobody spoke. A very eerie silence ensued. It seemed everyone was trying to process everything.

John broke the silence, "Does this other team know about you? I mean, who you are, where you live, that sort of thing?" he asked.

"I truly don't know, John," Ryan answered. "But I'm assuming that since we were told about them, they were at least told about us. But nothing specific. We don't know who they are or what they look like or where they are. We do know, however, that they have only been given $5,000 each. If this quest goes international, that could be a big plus."

International??!!" his mom asked as if he just told her he'd contracted a terminal illness. "You expect me to just let you fly all over creation looking for some damn ball while criminals are trying to kill you??!!" she started really sobbing now.

"Mom, I didn't say they were going to be trying to kill us," although the thought had crossed his mind. "I don't know how this is going to play out. But I do know that we have to try!" he said. He was beginning to lose his patience, but he also knew he had to stay calm if this was going to work.

Debbie finally spoke up. She had been pretty much quiet this whole time, as was typical. "Okay, hypothetically, let's just say everything you just told us is true. What can we do?" she asked and motioned to everyone around her.

"It's good that you asked that. This is very important. We've been given permission to tell our immediate families, and NO ONE ELSE. It's imperative that you don't tell anyone about what you've heard today. Outside of the people in this room. And, of course, Sean's parents who we have yet to talk to." Ryan looked at Sean, and he suddenly realized that they still had to do this with his parents, as well. "Plus," he continued, "your role in this is to help us decipher the clues. You can, in no way, accompany us or assist us in retrieving the clues," he said.

"So we just tell you where to go and wait for a call from some Sheriff's department in some corner of the world who tells us you've been gunned down in cold blood??!!" his mom said, still sobbing. He ignored her for the time being. He had just remembered the historical facts that Maxwell had given him. He just hoped they were for real. He could remember them happening but couldn't remember if the dates were correct.

"There's one more thing," he said as he pulled out the sheet of paper from his pocket. "We really need your help on this. I truly don't think we'll be able to do it alone, even though I don't even know yet what we're faced with. But to prove I'm telling you the truth, I have a couple of facts that might help persuade you to believe me." He flattened the piece of paper on his leg.

"You all know Grace Kelly, the actress and Princess of Monaco?" he asked. Everyone nodded their heads. "Tomorrow, September 13th, she will be in a car crash with her daughter Stephanie. On Tuesday, September 14th, she will die from her injuries. Princess Stephanie will survive. Apparently, her mother has a stroke while she is driving." A lot of 'what's' and 'oh my gosh's' sounded throughout the room. "On Wednesday, September 15th, a national newspaper called USA Today will be published for the first time. It will eventually come to be one of the most circulated newspapers in the country. And, between September 16th and 18th, Israeli and allied forces will attack two Palestinian refugee camps, Sabra and Shatila. Thousands of men, women, and children will be massacred. There's nothing we can or should do to stop these things from happening. They happen. It's history. I'm simply telling you this to help prove my story. There's no way I could know about these things. Sean and I need your help. We need you to believe us." Debbie looked at him as if to tell him there was another fact he was forgetting. Their Dad. But he softly shook his head and she nodded in agreement. Especially since he wouldn't die for another 34 years. It would be simply cruel to unleash that information. He even regretted telling Debbie, but he knew she would keep it quiet.

Debbie, again being the pragmatist, asked, "So what happens now? Where do these 'clues' come from?"

"I'm not sure," he said. "We're going to meet with Maxwell again tomorrow. He gave us three days to decide. Tomorrow is the third day." He looked at Sean. "Where and when are we supposed to meet him, anyway?"

"I guess we should go to Meatballs tomorrow morning and see if he shows up," he suggested.

"Well, this is a lot to take in, Ryan," Jessica said. "I can't say that I totally believe you, but if you are telling the truth and these things did happen to you, what's 2016 like?" she asked, somewhat sarcastically.

"Not that different than today," he said. "We're not all teleporting around or using hovercraft or anything like that. There's a lot of new technology, but everything's pretty much like it is now. There's a lot more crime, especially terrorism. There are a couple of really bad things that happen but I don't think it's a good idea that I tell you about them.

There's not really any point. Suffice it to say that the world's much smaller and everything affects everyone."

"Who's the president in 2016?" John asked.

"A guy named Barack Obama. He's the first black president, which is pretty cool. He won in a landslide. Personally, I think he borders on being a socialist, but he's very popular." he looked at Sean. Sean's wife is pretty liberal and thought Barack Obama was the best thing since sliced bread. He just rolled his eyes. He was more of a conservative, like Ryan.

"Any other questions?" Ryan asked.

"Just one," John said. "Sorry to be the one to ask this, but what if you're killed, or Sean?" His mom let out a little gasp.

"Honestly, John, I don't know. I'm assuming that if one of us doesn't make it, the other one still has a shot. But I can't say that for sure," he said softly as he looked at Sean. He was looking at the ground, obviously considering that same possibility.

"I'd like to thank you all for listening. Again, I know you have your doubts. But we really need your help with this. If you don't want to help, I totally understand and I won't hold it against you in any way," he said. "But if you do want to help, we're going to meet here tomorrow night after Sean and I meet with Maxwell. Hopefully, we'll have a few more answers as to where we go from here," he finished. They all said they'd be there.

Everyone got their coats and left. He could just imagine the conversations on the way home. Ryan's mom and dad hadn't left the couch. His mom was still red-eyed but had stopped crying, for the moment. He asked Sean to wait outside.

He knelt down in front of them. "Mom? Dad? Can you tell me what you're thinking?" he asked.

His dad looked at him with tears in his eyes. That did it for Ryan. He had only seen his dad cry once in his life, at his grandma's funeral. Ryan started crying and put his head on his mom's lap. She stroked his hair but didn't say anything. He stood up and sat down next to them and held his mom's hand.

"I didn't ask for this to happen, you know," he said.

"We know that dear," his mom said. "We're just confused and scared. We don't know what to believe."

"I'm confused and scared, too. We don't know how this happened or why. But I do know one thing. It's something I learned from the two of you. Family is the most important thing in a person's life. Even though it's hard for you to understand or believe, I have a beautiful, loving wife and two wonderful boys. I have to get back to them. I need you two and the others to help me do that. I don't know what's going to happen. We might make it. We might not. But I know for a fact that if you were in my shoes, you would do anything, even give up your life, for your children. I have to do the same. I don't have a choice. You understand that, right?"

"Yes, of course," his dad said. "It's just you're asking us to believe a lot, Ryan."

"I know I am."

"I'll tell you what," Ryan stood. "If Grace Kelly is alive on Wednesday, I'll drop this whole thing. I won't mention it again. Fair enough? I have to go now. We need to tell Sean's parents. I suspect you'll be getting a call from them later."

He grabbed his coat and walked outside to meet Sean. They decided to walk to his house. "So, that went pretty well, considering," Ryan said.

"Yea, I guess. I'm not sure my parents are going to be quite that accepting," he said.

"I wouldn't exactly classify what we just heard as 'accepting.'"

"Yea, but at least they're not hauling us off to a loony farm or calling a priest or anything," Sean said.

They kept walking. It was a perfect Autumn afternoon. Fall had always been Ryan's favorite time of year. It was a little cool but not cold. The leaves had turned and were starting to fall. Football had started. It was an awesome season. As they walked in silence, he thought about his childhood. He knew this neighborhood so well. He saw people that had either died or moved away. They'd wave at them just like they used to. A small part of him wanted to stay. It was a time when their biggest worry was how to cover up a hickey or where they were going to get 10 bucks for the arcade. There was no worry about a job or a mortgage they couldn't afford or how they were going to send their kids to college. A lot of people would give anything to go back and do it again. But then he thought about his wife and boys. He suddenly realized, maybe for the first time with real clarity, that he might never see them again. He stopped. He suddenly felt sick and bent over and took a couple of deep breaths.

"What's wrong," Sean asked.

Ryan didn't say anything for several seconds. He stood up straight and went over and sat down on a small cinder block wall. "I just had this sudden realization that I might never see my family again," he said. "Why the hell did this happen to us?"

Sean sat down next to him. "I don't know, man. Last night I had the same thoughts and ended up crying myself to sleep. Go figure. I'm 48 years old and I cried like a baby."

"I don't think there's any shame in crying, at this point," Ryan said. "You know," he looked at Sean, "we might not get out of this. We're up against four criminals who would probably shoot us on sight in order to get back to money and freedom. I don't want to wait until tomorrow. I get the feeling that Maxwell is very aware of where we are pretty much all the time. After we talk to your parents, let's go up to Meatballs just to see if he shows up," he suggested.

"I agree," Sean said. They walked the rest of the way to his house in silence.

All of Sean's siblings were too young to hear their story. So they pretty much went through the same routine with his parents as they had with Ryan's family. Neither of them thought Sean's parents believed a word of it. But, in the end, Sean's mom was crying and his dad was mad and convinced they were on something, but they at least got them to agree to join them tomorrow night for their 'kick-off' meeting as they'd come to call it.

Afterward, they walked up to Meatballs. It was about 7:00 pm, and it was already dark. They sat for about an hour. Just as they were getting ready to leave, they looked across the golf course, as much as they could see, and saw Maxwell walking toward them. What, does he live in the damn bushes?!

"Hello, gentlemen," Maxwell said as he stepped up into the gazebo. "It would appear you are early."

"Yea, well, we've made our decision and want to get started," Ryan said.

"Very well, what have you decided? Are you going to accept the challenge?" he asked.

"Yes. We are. But I think you already knew that."

"Splendid. Then here is the first clue." He handed Ryan what looked like a leather envelope. "I cannot say much about these clues. But, for this first one, I can say that it is quite close. As for the others, I hope neither of you gets airsick. By the way, there is only one rule for gathering the next three clues. You can take a picture or copy the information, but once you find the clue, you cannot take it with you. You must leave it as you found it. And I will give you one more piece of advice. Make sure you read each clue carefully and take note of ALL the information given.

And above all, keep all the clues until the final task is achieved. Good luck! I'll stay in touch." He simply stood up and walked back across the 17th fairway and out of sight. What he handed them was, in fact, more like leather parchment, for lack of a better description. It was folded in thirds and sealed with wax on the front. It had the same logo and markings as on the pouch he had given us earlier. It was now completely dark. Ryan grabbed a small flashlight when they left Sean's house. They broke the wax seal and read the first clue. They suddenly realized they were in big trouble.

Chapter 20

"So, do we know who these little pricks are?" Jerry asked the group. Jerry Stillwell was the self-appointed leader of the group. He was 55 years old (in 2016) and was incarcerated for attempted rape, assault, attempted murder, murder and drug possession.

"No, but we have an idea where they live. We know they go to Lakeside High School, which is on the upper east side. Other than that, not much," answered Dirk Bendar. Dirk was 54 years old (in 2016) and was in jail for assault, robbery, rape, aggravated rape, kidnapping, breaking and entering, and drug possession. His little brother Willy Bendar had also been 'sent back.' He was 50 years old and up for murder, attempted murder, assault with a deadly weapon, and possession with intent to distribute. The fourth and final member of the team was Jose Alvarez, age 49: aggravated rape, kidnapping, assault with a deadly weapon, attempted murder. All were serving life sentences. None of them were exactly choir boys, but Willy was especially dangerous and unstable. He was known, among his friends, for having zero conscience and would kill for the sheer excitement of it. He loved to kill and he loved to watch people die.

"We've got to figure out who they are and where they live. I don't know about the rest of you, but I don't plan on staying here when there's 2 mil back home and a free ticket," Jerry said. "It's simple. We'll let them figure out where the clues are and follow them. Willy, don't get any fancy ideas about offing these kids before they lead us to the clues."

"Yea, yea. Don't worry about me. But when that final clue is in, I get to slit their throats," Willy said with a dirty smile. He held up a knife with a curved 10" blade. The four of them had been brought back together. In other words, they didn't have to find each other. They had all been held in the Utah Federal Penitentiary. So they knew each other or at least knew of each other. Their handler, Maxwell's counterpart, was named Tyler. He had laid out the plan and the potential reward and they all had eagerly accepted. Dirk just about killed Tyler when he first met the team. It was Jerry that had pulled him off before he strangled the poor man to death.

They were staying in a hotel in downtown Salt Lake City. In addition to the $5,000, they had also been given IDs and passports, which would allow them to travel freely. Under threat, Tyler had divulged Ryan's and Sean's names and where they went to school but he told them, honestly, that he didn't know where they lived. It would just be a matter of time and a few questions around the school to find out that information.

Monday morning, Jerry and Dirk paid a visit to Lakeside High School. Jerry's first thought was to pose as an uncle in order to get personal information on Ryan and Sean from the office. However, after thinking it through, he realized it would be more than suspicious for an uncle to not know where his nephew lived. Therefore, they hung around until lunchtime, when the students would be roaming the halls. At 24 and 20, Jerry and Dirk didn't look completely out of place. They went in through a back entrance and started asking students at random, "Do you know Ryan and Sean?" They didn't have last names, so most of the answers they got were "Ryan who" or "Sean who." They disregarded these and kept asking. Finally, they came across Steve Brandt and Lisa Strand. They were walking to their next class. "Excuse me, do you know Ryan and Sean?" Jerry asked.

"Yea, and you can tell that dickhead Ryan that we're through," Lisa said with the requisite amount of teenage venom. "My party was totally lame because of him." Lisa was never shy about her extracurricular activities. For all she knew, Jerry and Dirk could have been friends of Ryan's parents. But she really didn't care.

"Well, that sucks. I'll make sure and tell him when I see him," Jerry said. "But the reason I'm asking is that Ryan and Sean did some work for my dad a couple of weeks ago and we need to find them so we can hire them back. But my dumbass dad didn't keep their last names or their phone numbers. You wouldn't happen to know what Ryan's phone number is, do you?" Jerry asked.

"Yea, it's 572-0893. But I wouldn't hire them. They probably won't show up. They're good at that," Lisa said.

"Well, I'll make sure and tell my dad that. Hey, you wouldn't happen to know where he lives, do you?" Jerry pressed his luck.

"I know how to get there, but I don't know his address. He's probably at home, though, 'cause I haven't seen either of them today, thank goodness!" Lisa stomped down the hall after Steve.

"Hey, I know his address," came a voice from behind where Jerry and Dirk were standing. It was Eric Daniels. The school know-it-all. Eric was about 5 years ahead of everyone academically and 5 years behind everyone socially. He was the kind of kid that you could only stand to be around long enough to get answers to the English test. "It's 2025 Longview Avenue," Eric told them. "And Lisa's right. Neither of them is here today. I heard they both called in sick. I'll bet they're playing golf, though. Or just riding around on Ryan's stupid motorcycle. He thinks he's such hotshit because he has a motorcycle. Big deal. I could get one if I wanted," and Eric strutted off toward class, thinking he had really let Ryan have it. What he didn't know was he had a piece of toilet paper stuck to his shoe. Typical Eric. Eric hadn't liked Ryan ever since he got a better grade on an Algebra test. Nobody ever did better than Eric, and he hadn't gotten over it. The fact that Ryan rubbed it in afterward hadn't helped matters much.

"That's it," Dirk said. "Now we stake out the house and wait for them to move. Let's find out where Longview Avenue is and get the others."

"Wait a minute, Dirk," Jerry said. "How are we going to keep a leash on your crazy brother? We can't have him taking shots at these kids until they've led us to the clues."

"Don't worry. I'll keep him in line," Dirk said. And they went back out the way they had come in.

Chapter 21

Monday morning...

"Is there any way you can come now? We have the first clue. But there's a problem. We could use your help." Ryan asked Jessica. "Everyone else is on their way over." He had been able to get a hold of everyone except Debbie, who was at work and couldn't break away. Sean's parents showed up around 9:00 am. They were in the living room talking with Ryan's mom and dad. He had a good idea of how that conversation was going.

Once everyone got there, except Debbie and John, they all gathered in the living room. Before he could start talking, Jessica spoke up.

"I have something to say before we get into this," she started. "I've thought a lot about what you said yesterday, Ryan, and I simply can't believe it. I don't know about the rest of you, but it goes against everything I believe in and everything I can even comprehend. I'm sorry. Ryan, I love you but I'm not sure I can go along with this little game anymore." She actually started to tear up, and her voice started to quiver. Ryan felt bad. He had a feeling Jessica might have a hard time with this. And he wanted to give her a way out.

"Jessica. I understand that you have doubts. I really do. And, like I said yesterday, I won't hold it against anyone if they don't want to participate. You guys need to understand something. This isn't just something that Sean and I dreamed up and thought it would be fun to put you all through. Without the irrefutable proof that I've already seen, I would have already made an appointment for both of us in the nut house. But unless both of us are completely out of our minds, this has happened. However improbable or impossible it seems."

"What is this irrefutable proof that you've seen?" Jessica asked.

Ryan looked at Sean. He shook his head slightly. "Well, being new to the whole 'time travel thing,' I'm not really up on all the protocols. But I'm pretty sure that there are some things about your future you shouldn't know about. I'll just say that 34 years is a long time and a lot of things can happen." He paused. "How about this," he glanced at Sean, "like I said to you yesterday, Dad. If Princess Grace doesn't get in an automobile accident today, I'll forget the whole thing. I'll never bring it up again. Does that sound fair, Jessica?" Sean looked at him as if he'd lost his mind. How the hell did he know if the information Maxwell gave him was accurate? But he had to take a chance. He had nothing else.

It was Ryan's dad that ended the argument. "I think we should all listen to Ryan, Jessica. Monaco is eight hours ahead of us. This morning on the news they said that Princess Grace was in an automobile accident with her daughter Stephanie. The princess is in intensive care. They think she had a stroke while driving. She lost control, and the car flipped. Stephanie will most likely be okay. Princess Grace has not regained consciousness and has slipped into a deep coma. She's not expected to survive." His dad said all this as though he was reading a headline. And he was obviously very sad. Princess Grace and he had been born in the same year, 1929, and he had always admired her life and career. His dad continued, "So, at least for now, Ryan, your 'evidence' seems to be accurate. Although I don't think I needed the evidence. Your mother and I agree. We can see it in your eyes. You're telling us the truth or at least telling us what you honestly believe to be the truth."

The rest of the group was stunned, including Sean and Ryan. Jessica spoke first, through tears. "Ryan, I'm sorry I doubted you. If what Dad says is true, your claim that Princess Grace dies tomorrow appears to be right. So, I guess I'm in," she said sincerely and sat back down slowly.

Ryan stood up and gave her a hug. "Thanks, Jessica. And thanks to everyone else. Sean and I took a big chance telling you what had happened. We honestly didn't know what to expect. Sean and I are still trying to comprehend the reality of it all. Very few of our questions have been answered. Both of us have cried like babies over the situation. In our minds, we're grown men in our 50s with wives and children and mortgages and belly fat. Yet here we stand, in teenage bodies with only one hope of returning to our families. We have to find this orb before the other team does. We're out-numbered and very likely out-gunned. But what we do have is a more powerful weapon than any gun. We have the love and support of all of you. You can't come with us to retrieve the clues but you can help us figure out where to go. My offer still stands. Anyone who wants out, say so. I won't hold it against you at all." He waited. Nobody moved or raised their hand. "Okay," he said, "let's get going." And he pulled the leather envelope from his pocket and laid it on the table.

Chapter 22

First, Ryan explained how they had received it. Folded and sealed with wax. He also showed everyone the logo or design on the outside. He then turned it over and everyone looked at the clue. It was written in some sort of fancy script and was centered on the page. At the top of the page in the center was the number 17 and then in the center of the left margin was the number 5 and in the center of the right margin was the number 23. The numbers were in a much smaller font than the text in the middle. It was the text that had them perplexed.

Hwnrxts rjxf nx ymj ittw

Qttp mnlm ytbfwix ymj xpd

Tshj ts ytu qttp itbs gjqtb

Gjybjjs ybt lnfsyx dtz rzxy lj

"Now you see our problem," Ryan said.

"I don't get it," Jessica said. "It's not in English. Does anyone know what language that is?"

"It's hard to read," Ryan said, "read me the letters, and I'll write them larger." He grabbed a blank sheet of paper and re-wrote the clue as Debbie read it out loud. She and John had just arrived. John had given her a ride from her job. Normally, Debbie took the bus everywhere she went. But she had called John for a ride so she could make it home faster. She was the most excited of the group. The letters now covered a complete sheet of paper.

Hwnrxts rjxf nx ymj ittw

Qttp mnlm ytbfwix ymj xpd

Tshj ts ytu qttp itbs gjqtb

Gjybjjs ybt lnfsyx dtz rzxy lj

"I don't think this is any language," John said as he stared at the paper. "If it's what I think it is, it IS in English. I think it's a cryptogram."

"A what?" Jessica asked.

"A cryptogram," Debbie said excitedly. "It's a puzzle. Each letter is replaced with another letter from the alphabet. Sometimes, you need a special password or key that will help you solve it. Remember when you were a kid and there were those clues on the back of cereal boxes. You had to substitute a letter for each number and it spelled out a sentence? This is the same thing. We just need to figure out the key. I love doing these in the Sunday paper," she said as she sat down at the coffee table and grabbed the sheet of paper to study it closer.

"And how exactly do we do that?" Sean asked.

"Easy," Debbie said. "You just start substituting letters that you think fit. Then you see if it starts making sense." We all gathered around and watched Debbie as she started writing letters above the other letters. Ryan had an idea where she was going. She explained that she always started with single letters since they can only be an 'a' or an 'i'. Since there were no single letters, she then looked for three-letter words since often a three-letter word is thes word 'the.' There were two three-letter words that repeated in the first two sentences. She kept working and after ten or fifteen minutes, it seemed to be taking shape. She filled in the last few letters. "Voila!" Debbie exclaimed and handed Ryan the paper. He laid it down on the coffee table, and they all stared at the clue.

Crimson Mesa is the Door

Look High Towards the Sky

Once on Top, Look Down Below

Between Two Giants You Must Go

They all mumbled the clue to themselves, trying to make sense of it. Ryan was focusing on Crimson Mesa. For some reason, that sounded familiar to him. But he had no idea why. "The only hint we got from Maxwell was that this first clue is local. He made it sound like the next clues would require some air travel. Let's look at this one line at a time," he said. " 'Crimson Mesa is the Door.' Crimson is a color. Red. Mesa is what, a hill, right? And 'Door' is an entrance or entry? What do you think?" he asked.

"A mesa is a hill, but a mesa has a flat top. So another word for crimson is red but what's another word for mesa?" Jessica asked.

"What about butte?" Sean Sr. said. Everyone turned to look at Sean's dad. "Red Butte. Crimson Mesa could mean Red Butte Canyon."

"If it's local, that would make sense," Sean agreed. Red Butte Canyon is located at the base of the Wasatch Mountains near the University of Utah, very close to where Ryan's mom and dad (and he, for now) live. He and Sean were very familiar with this area since they spent a lot of time in and around that area when they were growing up.

"Okay, so 'door' could mean a starting point," John pointed out. "If you look up towards the sky using Red Butte as the starting point, what do you see?"

"Not much. Just the side of the mountain." Sean said. "Let's look at the next line. Once on top, look down below. What's on top of that mountain?"

"The beacon," John said. "You know, the old airport beacon. We used to have to hike to it once a week when I was in graduate school. And down from there are the two microwave repeaters," John pointed out. "Those could be the two giants."

"Yea, we've been up there before. Remember Sean? We scratched our names into the old metal box at the base of the beacon." Ryan said.

"I remember. But I don't think we hiked. Isn't there an old road that leads up there? I remember we went with Alex and Jeremy in Alex's blazer." Sean looked kind of sad when he brought up the memory. Ryan understood why.

Alex and Jeremy were their friends from high school. The four of them were inseparable. Alex had this old Ford blazer that they took everywhere. It got horrible gas mileage and broke down about every half hour but they had some great times in that truck. And one terrible time that none of them would ever forget. During their senior year, they were exploring the desert west of Salt Lake City. They'd spent a lot of time out in the desert since Alex had gotten his truck the year before. It was a great place to get away. They stopped to set up camp. Jeremy, Sean, and Ryan got out to set up the tents. Alex was going to drive around and look for firewood. An hour later when he hadn't come back, the other three started to get worried. They split up and headed out in different directions from their campsite. They all had .22 rifles since there were a lot of rattlesnakes that time of year. It was starting to get dark when a shot rang out about 300 yards away from where Ryan was walking. He ran toward the shot. What he saw he'll never forget. He came up to the edge of a shallow gorge. It was about 25 feet deep and about 30 feet across. It had obviously been formed by rain and flash floods. The narrow road that ran alongside had given way. Alex's blazer was at the bottom, flipped upside down. Jeremy was already trying to make his way down to the truck. Ryan put his rifle down and started sliding down the unstable wall of the gorge toward Jeremy. By the time they got there, Alex was gone. They found out later he had died instantly. He had always been the "safety Nazi" as they called him. He always wore his seat belt and chastised the others if they didn't wear theirs. He even saved up for an entire year for a roll bar for just this kind of accident. Ironically, when he left the campsite, he hadn't put his seat belt back on. After all, he was just driving around looking for firewood. When the blazer slid into the gorge and flipped, Alex had been thrown out and crushed. It was, up to that point, the worst day of any of their lives. Obviously, in 1983, none of them had cell phones. Sean stayed behind to keep predators away from Alex's body. Jeremy and Ryan had to walk for 2 hours to the nearest highway to flag down a ride. By the time they got back with the sheriff and their parents, it was nearly morning. Alex's parents were obviously devastated. Alex had just applied and been accepted to Stanford. He was the smart one of the bunch. It affected Jeremy the worst. He went a little "psycho." From that point on, he would always try dangerous things and never seemed to care about his own safety or that of others. It definitely changed him and not in a good way. He eventually moved away when his dad got a new job in Ohio. For whatever reason, they never heard from him again. Ryan often thought of trying to find him to catch up but never did. He always found it interesting how Alex's death affected each of them differently. He and Sean seemed, in time, to deal with it internally and move on. Unfortunately, Jeremy wasn't able to.

As Ryan remembered that fateful night, he was also remembering how they got to the beacon in the blazer. "There is a road. It starts further up the canyon and winds back towards the top," he said. He didn't think it could possibly be that easy. He grabbed his coat and walked out on their front lawn. Everyone else did the same. From their front lawn, they could see the beacon clearly. The old airport beacon hadn't been used for years but was still there. And, like John said, just below the beacon were two large billboard-size microwave repeaters that passed radio and television transmissions to the east. 'Those must be the 'giants' mentioned in the clue,' Ryan thought to himself.

"Well, if it's that easy, won't the other team know where it is, too? And quick?" Sean Sr. asked.

"Yea, you're right," Ryan said and started to walk back inside. As he walked toward the house, he looked down the street and saw a dark blue or black Suburban about 4 houses down. He couldn't tell who was inside but he could tell it was two adult males in the front seat. As they were all walking, he nudged Sean and said, "Don't stare but check out the Suburban down the street. Have you ever seen it before?"

"No, I haven't. You don't think...shit!" Sean said. "Do you think it's them? How did they find us so fast?"

"I don't know. Maybe their 'Maxwell' told 'em. If it is them. For now, don't say anything to anyone...yet," Ryan said.

They all got back inside, and everyone agreed that the beacon made the most sense. It fit every part of the clue. One of the trails to the top started near Red Butte Canyon. Crimson Mesa could mean Red Butte, as Sean Sr. had suggested. The beacon is at the top, so "Look Toward the Top" made sense. The microwave repeaters were down from the beacon, so "Once on Top, Look Down Below" made sense. And the 'Giants' would be the billboard-like repeaters. "Well, I think we all agree the first clue's going to be somewhere around the repeaters down from the beacon," Ryan said.

"Great, it's a pretty hard hike to get up there," Sean said.

"I don't plan on hiking up," Ryan said as they all sat back down. "We'll take the bikes and approach from the rear. We'll have to go all the way up the canyon but once we're up there, we can get up to the ridge and the trail on top leads all the way back to the beacon. It's the original access road they used to get everything up there. It should be easy on two wheels."

"Sounds good to me. It's a lot better than hiking it," Sean said. "And we should probably go soon. But we need something before we go."

"Like what, a gun?" Jessica asked, kind of joking. Then she said, "I was kind of kidding, but it begs the question, what are you going to do about protecting yourself against this other team?"

"Well, we don't have concealed weapons permits, so we can't carry a gun legally," Ryan said.

"I don't like the idea of you boys carrying a gun, anyway," Sean's mom said.

"I agree," Ryan's mom said.

Luckily Sean's dad stood up for both of them. "Look, it's not my first choice, but if this other team is out there, it's only a matter of time before they meet up. And from the description the boys got from this Maxwell character, it's a foregone conclusion that these guys will certainly have guns with them. I think Ryan and Sean should have some protection with them." Way to go, Dad, Sean thought.

"Okay, so where do we get a gun?" Ryan asked.

"I've got one," Sean Sr. said. "It's a Glock 9mm. It's clean and I have plenty of ammunition."

"We've got a handgun, don't we, John?" Jessica asked.

"Yea, it's a .380. Not a lot of stopping power, but it would certainly slow someone down," John said.

"Alright, we'll take both of them. We can stop by and get them on the way. The other thing we need is a Polaroid camera. Maxwell told us we couldn't take the clue with us. We can either copy it down verbatim or take a picture of it. I don't want to have to wait to get the film developed. Does anyone have a Polaroid?"

"I do," Debbie said. "Question is, can I find it? I haven't used it in years. I'll go see if it's in my room," and she went upstairs. John and Sean Sr. left to gather the guns. There was some commotion, with everyone talking about guns and the beacon. Ryan went over to the window and looked down the street. The Suburban was still there. He could tell it was idling. It was parked in front of the Anderton's house. Leslie and Heber Anderton were about 150 years old and never left the house. He highly doubted they'd have company idling their car out front. Something was up and it made him nervous.

They quickly put together a backpack with a few supplies. Basically, a first aid kit, some water, the two guns and ammunition, a small camping shovel, and the camera that Debbie finally found stuffed under her bed. Luckily she still had some film. They tested the camera to make sure the film was good. It worked fine. After getting his gun, Sean's Dad had ridden Sean's motorcycle and brought his helmet back over to the house. Amazingly, neither Sean's dad nor his mom said anything about the bike not being street-legal. At this point, it didn't seem like that big of a deal.

"Alright, let's hope it's there. See ya soon," Ryan said. He walked out back to where his motorcycle was and Sean got on his in front. Ryan had always loved his bike. It was a Honda

650L. It was what they used to call an Enduro. That meant it was a dirt bike but had a light, turn signals, and a mirror so it was street-legal. But the knobby tires he had on it certainly weren't street-legal. Some people would say it was the best of both worlds (on-road and off-road). Some people would say it was the worst of both worlds. In any case, it was fast, and it was powerful. So, if the guys down the street were planning on following them, they better be ready. Sean's bike was plenty fast as well, and he was a good rider. Ryan pulled around to the front of the house to where Sean was.

"You ready?" Ryan asked Sean.

"I guess. As ready as I'll ever be. If that Suburban down the street is carrying our competition, I expect we might have to lose them before we head to the canyon," Sean said.

"Shouldn't be too hard," Ryan replied. "Just head across the golf course. Remember? We've done it before." Ryan smiled, remembering their past experiences cutting across the course. "We might get chased by Crandall (the head pro at the golf course), but we can lose him easy enough. At the top of the golf course, we're only seconds from the canyon. They won't be able to follow us across the course."

"Perfect," Sean said. They both started their bikes and slowly rode down the driveway. Once they could see down the street, they both saw the Suburban was still there. Ryan hit the gas, and Sean was close behind.

Ryan went through the gears as fast as he could, only downshifting to make the turns. Sean stayed right with him. They only had about 2 miles to the golf course. Sean yelled that the Suburban was coming fast. But they were accelerating much faster than the large truck. They got to the golf course entrance before the suburban rounded the last curve. But it was clear they saw where the two boys had gone. Ryan couldn't hear their engine above the sound of the bike's engine. Normally, they wouldn't even think of riding across the golf course during the day. The head pro, Chuck Crandall, was always out in his Jeep, trolling for kids in the gulleys looking for balls or just causing trouble. Ryan and Sean were usually those kids (or had been). The only way to get across the course from the front side was either right off the 1st tee or right off the 10th tee. To go off the 10th tee, you had to cross a bridge. That might cause some trouble. So, against Ryan's better judgment, he gunned the bike up through the parking lot, raced by the clubhouse (with a lot of "Hey's" and "Get the hell out of here's" being yelled), went right over a small hedge and flew off the 1st tee. The tee box sat elevated above the fairway. Sean went off right next to him. By the time they hit the fairway, they must have been doing close to 40 mph which felt really fast on slippery grass. Ryan almost lost control but put both feet down at one point and then gunned it up the slope. He brought the bike to a stop and looked back. Crandall was shaking his fist at them and yelling something that Ryan was sure started with an 'f.' Their tires had cut the tee box up pretty well. Both boys felt kind of bad about that but under the circumstances...

From their vantage point, they couldn't see the parking lot and couldn't tell what had happened to the Suburban.

"Hey," Sean said, "didn't Max say these guys were local?"

"Yea, at least they were all in the Utah Federal Pen," Ryan replied.

"Well, then they probably know where the top part of this course leads to. Let's get out of here before they come around and find us," Sean said rather excitedly. In order to get from the golf course parking lot to the top of the course, you had to meander through a couple of neighborhoods. But it wouldn't take more than a few minutes if you knew the way. Ryan could see Chuck running for his Jeep so he knew it was time to get going. He gunned the engine again, and they raced up the fairway. There weren't many golfers. Luckily there hadn't been anyone on the 1st tee when they flew off of it. They got to the top of the course in less than a minute. At the top, there was a road that led to the canyon. They would need to go to the top of the canyon to access the road that went along the ridge back to the beacon. They started up the canyon but kept a lookout behind. So far, nobody was following.

They got to the top of the canyon. The access road was hidden, for obvious reasons. The canyon developers and police didn't want a lot of people finding the way up to the top of the ridge. It would be a perfect place for beer drinking and other illicit activities far away from the canyon patrols. Ryan and Sean had found the road a couple of years ago. If his memory was right, Ryan was about 15. So Sean would have been 14. Sean had an old beat-up trail bike and they found the road one day by accident and followed it all the way across the mountain range to the beacon. So they found it again pretty quickly. There was an old gate but the lock and chain had long since disappeared. They opened the gate and rode through. Sean jumped off his bike and closed the gate behind them and spread some pine boughs out to cover their tracks the best he could. They sat there for a few minutes but no sign of the Suburban. Satisfied, they took off toward the top.

After riding the top of the mountain range all the way back to the front, they finally reached the beacon and got off. The view was incredible. They could see the entire Salt Lake Valley. It was clear as a bell but cold as hell. They were standing at about 11,000 ft., and the temperature had to be in the 20's. But the sun was shining, and they had hats and gloves, so it wasn't too bad.

"Well, according to the first clue, the next clue is somewhere between the two "giants,"" Sean said and pointed down the hill.

The two passive microwave repeaters sat about 100 feet down the slope from the beacon. They could barely see two trails that came from directly below. One of those trails started at the mouth of Red Butte Canyon. A shorter distance than the way they had come but much steeper and much harder. It would have been nearly impossible on their motorcycles.

They slowly rode down the hill to the large repeaters. They looked like two huge billboards facing each other. There was a lot of graffiti sprayed on them from past visitors. It was probably for that reason that the parks department had put up a 10' chain link fence around the perimeter of the dishes. On top of the chain link was razor wire.

"Wow, somebody was serious about keeping people out of here," Ryan said once Sean got down to where he was.

"Yea, how are we going to get in?" he asked. They walked around the perimeter of the fence and came to a gate. The gate was secured with a heavy chain and a combination lock.

"Great," Ryan said, "it's locked. And look," He pointed to a small patch of dirt about halfway between the two dishes that had obviously been recently dug up and re-buried.

"We've got to get in," Sean said as he rattled and pulled on the lock.

"If we go over the top, we'll be cut to shreds, and we can't go under because of the cement," Ryan said. Directly under the chain link fence was a cement barrier that the chain link poles were secured to. The cement went all the way around so they couldn't tunnel under the fence.

Then Ryan had a thought. "Hey, did you bring the first clue?" he asked.

"Yea. I think we stuck it in the backpack. Just a sec," Sean said as he took the backpack off and started looking through it. "Yep. Here it is," he said and pulled it out.

"Remember, there were those three numbers? One at the top and one on each side. Read them to me?" Ryan asked.

"17's on the top, 5's on the left, and 23's on the right," Sean said. Ryan went over to the lock. He tried 17, 5, and 23 and pulled on the lock. Nothing. It didn't open. Then he tried 5, 17, 23. Nothing. He tried a couple more and began thinking he was wrong. When he tried 23, 17, and 5 and pulled on the lock and 'pop,' it opened.

"No way," Sean said.

"That Maxwell thinks of everything, huh?" Ryan said. They got the chain off and went inside, then immediately over to the disturbed portion of the ground. Sean had forgotten the shovel, so he went back to the backpack. Ryan looked back at him and saw him staring up the hill toward the canyon. He pointed and said, "Oh shit. We've got company." Ryan jumped up and looked where he was pointing. He could see a cloud of dust from way up the canyon. But there weren't any other roads. It was obvious whoever it was, was coming along the road they had come in on.

"Can you tell what kind of car it is?" Ryan asked.

"No. It's too far. But I say we don't hang around and wait," Sean said as he ran back with the shovel. They figured they had about 10 minutes at the outside before whoever it was got to the beacon. From there, they were sitting ducks. There was no real cover, and the road out would be behind whoever was coming. And they were coming fast! Ryan grabbed the shovel and began digging. It wasn't very deep. He hit something on the 4th or 5th shovel full. He cleared the dirt away from a small box. The box had the same logo that was on the first clue they had been given.

So he knew they had found it. The box had a latch on the side. Ryan flipped up the latch and pulled out the next clue. It was the same sort of leather envelope and it was also sealed with wax. He broke the wax seal and laid the clue out flat. He didn't even read it. Sean handed him the Polaroid and he took five quick pictures just to make sure he got them all. Sean quickly scanned the clue as Ryan handed him the pictures but he was too nervous and didn't remember much. Plus, it again looked like just a jumble of letters. Per Maxwell's instructions, Ryan put the envelope back in the box and closed the box.

"Go get your bike started," Ryan told Sean. He put the box back in the hole the best he could and covered it with dirt, and then picked up the backpack and ran toward the gate. Ryan pulled the gate shut and wrapped the chain around the pole, locked the chain together, and ran toward his bike. Sean had gotten his started and was standing next to it. Suddenly, Ryan felt a searing hot pain shoot through his right arm, then heard a loud bang and was thrown to the ground. He found himself face down with a mouthful of dirt. Once he realized what had happened, he accurately concluded they had obviously underestimated the amount of time they had. Ryan got to his feet and looked up the hill toward the beacon and saw the Suburban sitting at the top of the hill. Whoever had fired the shot was hurriedly getting back in and the Suburban spun its tires and started down the hill. Luckily there wasn't a road down the hill, and the truck had to slow down to navigate the rocks. Ryan hobbled onto his bike. He grabbed his right arm with his left hand and his hand came away bloody. How bad it was, he didn't know. He could still steer the bike, though, so he yelled at Sean, "Let's go!"

It was obvious to both of them what they were going to have to do. There were three ways off the mountain. The road they came in on, was now out of the question since they'd have to go past the guys that had just shot Ryan. Plus, there were two other hiking trails leading down the mountain. From past hikes up there, they knew the one farther to the north was less steep. But that would mean they'd have to pass fairly close to where the Suburban was coming from. The other trail was steeper and less defined, but it had two advantages. It started away from where they were and it was steep, so it got them out of sight and out of range faster. Plus, if memory served, Ryan remembered it was far too steep and narrow for a truck to navigate. Ryan looked at Sean. Sean knew the mountain, as well as Ryan, did. Sean said, "We have no choice." So they both gunned their engines and headed for the trail on the other side of the repeater dishes. They reached the top of the trail just as the Suburban came roaring around the fence around the perimeter of the dishes. They had to slow down slightly or they never would have made the turn onto the trail. Ryan and Sean heard another shot, but by then, they had descended probably 20 or 30 yards and were out of view. As Ryan had suspected, there was no way a vehicle could get down this slope so they slowed down and very gingerly made their way down between the rocks. After they had gone about 100 yards or so, they stopped the bikes and killed the engines. They both jumped off and looked back up the slope. They couldn't see the Suburban or even the dishes from where they were. Ryan could feel the blood running down his right arm.

"How bad is it?"

"I don't know. It hurts like a mother, though." And it did hurt. As carefully as he could, Ryan took off his jacket and ripped his shirt to expose the wound. He couldn't see it very well, so Sean had to play doctor. Ryan kept an eye on the trail but didn't see anyone on foot coming down. Sean got the first aid kit out of the backpack.

"It doesn't look like the bullet went in. As far as I can tell, you have a nasty gash. It looks like you just got grazed."

"It feels like one hell of a graze," Ryan said through clenched teeth.

"Well, this won't feel very good then. You want something to bite on? I'd rather not have you scream, considering our position," Sean said as he pulled out the bottle of alcohol.

"No, just do it but...shiiiiittttt," Ryan clenched his fists and closed his eyes as Sean poured the alcohol down his arm.

"Thanks for the warning, douchebag!" Ryan said as Sean gave him a little smile and put the gauze bandage on and secured it with some tape.

"Aahh, it's good for you. Now let's get off this damn mountain."

Ryan put his coat back on, and they kept going down the hill. It was too steep and the turns were too tight to ride, in parts, so they had to walk alongside the bikes and make their way down. It was slow going, but it was much better than the alternative, the two boys thought as they went. They got near the bottom and the terrain leveled out. They both got on and rode the rest of the way to the bottom. They had no idea where the other team was, but they knew for sure they hadn't been followed down the trail. They could only assume that they had either figured out the combination or shot their way in. But they would certainly have the first clue by now. And Ryan and Sean had led them right to it.

"Should we drive by the hospital to get your arm checked out?" Sean asked as they got back near civilization. Sean had smirked at Ryan when he was bandaging his arm on the mountain but he knew it was pretty deep and could easily get infected.

"No," Ryan yelled over the wind. "They might be able to tell it's a gunshot wound and they would have to call the police.

Debbie had some first-aid training. Let's get back and we'll bandage it up at the house." Then a frightening thought occurred to him. Ryan slowed down and stopped. He looked at Sean. "Dude, they know where I live," he said.

"Yea, but assuming they have a clue, they're going to go figure it out and try to get a head start," Sean said.

"Either that or come back and stake out my house again and wait for us to lead them to it," Ryan said as he started his bike and started going again toward his house. Sean followed behind, thinking about what Ryan had said. Either way, they had to get back to better bandage his arm and start to figure out the clue. If the other team was going to use them to figure out the clues, it didn't make sense that they would shoot at them. Then, Sean remembered something. When he looked up at the guy getting back in the Suburban after Ryan got shot, he was carrying a rifle with a scope. Assuming he was at least a half-decent shot, if he had wanted Ryan dead, Sean was sure they'd still be up on top of that mountain with a bullet in one or both of their heads. He wasn't trying to kill Ryan. They were just sending a message. They could kill Ryan, Sean, or any member of their families any time they wanted. Sean briefly closed his eyes, shook his head, and drove on.

Chapter 23

As they continued on toward Ryan's house, Ryan was trying to put together in his head how he was going to explain this to his mom. She'd be the one that was going to fly off the handle after her 'baby' was shot. Ryan decided to be straight and tell everyone what happened. He figured if they were going to be helping them with this 'quest,' as it had come to be called, they needed to know everything.

Sean and Ryan pulled their motorcycles into Ryan's driveway and drove around back. Ryan's arm was killing him. It felt like it was on fire. It was good that the ride had been short. He was starting to lose feeling in his fingers and could barely work the gas, let alone the front brake. Sean grabbed the backpack and they went inside. Not surprisingly, everyone was there. The two boys walked in and sat down at the kitchen table.

"How'd it go?" Ryan's dad asked.

"Okay. We ran into a little bit of trouble, though," Ryan grunted as he peeled off his jacket. The field dressing Sean had put on had stemmed the bleeding but had not stopped it. Ryan's arm looked like a bloody mess. 'Great,' Ryan thought as he looked at his arm. 'This should send my mom right over the edge.'

"Oh my Lord, you're hurt!" his mom screamed as she ran over to his side. Ryan had only heard his mom say 'Oh my lord' twice in his life. Once when he brought a five-foot king snake into the house and today.

"It's not as bad as it looks," Ryan said, not very convincingly. "I got knicked by a bullet." As soon as he said it, he wished he hadn't. He hadn't thought ahead but now realized what was going to happen.

"A bullet!" several people said at once.

Debbie came over to his side. "Let me see it," she said. "Jessica, get me some warm water and some towels. Also, some alcohol if you can find any." Jessica ran upstairs to get the towels. Ryan's mom came over and started checking the rest of him out for more injuries. He didn't know why but she felt his head. Why do moms always feel your head?

"I'm fine Mom," he said.

"Tell me what happened," his dad asked. He told them about finding the clue and using the numbers on the first clue to open the lock. Then how the other team showed up and started shooting.

"I saw the gun," Sean interjected, "It was a high-powered rifle with a scope. If he wanted either of us dead, we wouldn't be sitting here right now. I'm sure of that." Sean opened the backpack and pulled out the Polaroids. They looked pretty good. They could clearly see the clue.

"You could probably use a couple of stitches, Ryan. Unless you want an ugly scar," she said.

"Does it look like a bullet wound, Deb? Cause if it does, I don't want to have to start answering a bunch of questions from the police."

She looked at it and tilted her head and said, "Not really. You could have easily gotten this a number of ways."

"Okay, a couple of stitches. Do you think you could put them in?" Ryan asked, not sure he wanted to go through that without anesthesia.

"I'm not a doctor, Ryan. I've stitched up a dog before but never a person. Plus, it's going to hurt like hell," she said, glancing at her mom. Ryan's mom didn't like swearing in the house. She didn't seem to care this time. Any time an animal got hurt in the neighborhood, they'd always bring them to Debbie before going to the vet. Half the time, she could fix the problem.

"Alright, if it stops bleeding completely, I'll just take the scar. Anyone got a couple Advil?"

"What's an Advil?" Jessica asked. Oh yea, Ryan thought. He almost forgot what year it was. Advil must not have been marketed yet.

"Nevermind. How about a few aspirin?"

"I've got something better upstairs," his dad said. He came back down with two codeine tablets. "This will help with the pain. You might get sleepy, but you could probably use the rest," he said. Debbie had finished with Ryan's arm. It had stopped bleeding. She put a fresh bandage on.

"The thing I don't understand is how they found us. We lost them a long way before we even headed into the canyon," Sean said. "They could have seen us heading up to the top from the road. But they would have had to have known where the turnoff was."

"Maybe they knew the canyon better than you thought," Jessica said. "Heck, I've gone hiking up there a bunch of times. I even know how to get there."

"Yea, I guess," Ryan said. "The thing that worries me the most is that they are apparently going to use us to find these clues for them."

"That's good. It makes you valuable to them. But when they find the last clue, they won't need you anymore," John threw in for good measure.

"Right," Sean said.

"Well, let's look at the second clue. The first one was so easy once we figured out the cryptogram. I glanced at it when I took the pictures, and I think we have another cryptogram to work on. I'm guessing they're going to get harder," Ryan said.

They all went into the living room where this adventure had started. They gathered around the coffee table and Sean laid out the pictures. They had taken five. Two of them were either overdeveloped or something had gone wrong. They were totally black. The other three, however, were pretty good and showed the entire sheet. This time, there were no letters, just numbers.

15 22 25 26 23 19   9 22 23 13 3 14 24 13   1 22 23 11 10 11

6 24 3 3 10 4   6 4 23 3 10 11   3 1 14 3   20 22 13 20 10 14 19

25 22 23 4   13 10 16 3   4 22 23 3 10   3 1 4 22 23 7 1

20 22 13 26 23 11 24 22 13

"Great!" Sean said, "How are we supposed to figure this out?"

"This one might be too tough for me," Debbie said. "There aren't any repeating words."

Debbie worked on it for a few minutes but wasn't getting anywhere. The codes were getting harder. And Ryan and Sean were guessing the retrieval of the next clue wouldn't be as easy as the first one.

As Debbie kept working on the clue, Ryan noticed something else. "There are more numbers on the edges of the page," he said. As in the first clue, there were numbers posted around the page. Now, however, there was more than the first clue. There was a number in the top left corner (33), one in the top middle (48), one in the top right corner (37), one in the middle on the right (-117), one in the bottom right corner (55), and one in the bottom middle of the page (8). They all stared at the numbers but they didn't make any sense. They weren't multiples of each other and the negative 117 meant it wasn't a combination of any kind, like in the first clue.

"The numbers in the first clue were the combination to the lock on the gate at the beacon. These numbers don't make any sense," Sean said. Ryan went into the kitchen and grabbed a blank sheet of scrap paper and a pen from the junk drawer. He always was amazed at their junk drawer. His mom would actually organize it. Which kind of ruined the whole "junk drawer" idea. Oh well, in this case, it helped. He walked back in with the paper and pen.

"Read me the numbers. Starting from the number in the top left." Debby read the numbers and Ryan wrote them down in a column on the paper. 33, 48, 37, -117, 55, 8. It didn't help much. The numbers still didn't make any sense. Ryan wrote them in numerical order. Highest to lowest, lowest to highest. Split into pairs and a number of other combinations. Nothing jumped out at anyone.

Just then, Mason walked by. "Mom, I'm going to scouts. See ya," he shouted as he headed out the door. "Just a minute, young man," his mom said. "Get your coat, and when will you be back?"

"I don't know. We have to do some stupid map thing," he said. When he said map, a bell rang inside Ryan's head. "What kind of map thing, Mas?" he asked his very twitchy little brother.

"We have to find stuff on a map. We have two groups. We have to find where things are. Mr. Andrew gives us altidutes and longidutes, and the first group to find it wins."

"You mean latitudes and longitudes?" Ryan asked.

"Yea, that's it," he said and was out the door in a flash.

"That's it!" Ryan said.

"What's it?" Sean asked.

"These numbers. They're latitudes and longitudes. I think latitudes and longitudes are given with 3 sets of numbers; degrees, minutes, and seconds. The first set would be the latitude. The second set would be the longitude. My first thought would be to google it. But that won't exactly work, will it?" Ryan said rather dejectedly.

"What's a google," his dad asked.

"It won't matter for about 15 years. It's a computer thing," Ryan replied.

"My next thought would be, 'Let's go be cub scouts for a little while,'" Ryan said with a smile.

"You want us to have a bunch of 9-year-olds find our next clue?" Sean asked incredulously.

"Do you have a better idea? I know what latitudes and longitudes are but I can't remember how to find things on a map with them."

Jessica had gone into the other room and now returned with one of their trusty Britannica encyclopedias. She read out loud. "Any location on Earth is described by two numbers—its latitude and its longitude. If a pilot or a ship's captain wants to specify a position on a map, these are the "coordinates" they would use. The latitude and longitude are two angles, measured in degrees, 'minutes of arc' and 'seconds of arc.' For example, 35° 43' 9,'"" the minutes and seconds are one apostrophe and two apostrophes, she explained, "means an angle of 35 degrees, 43 minutes and 9 seconds. A degree contains 60 minutes of arc and a minute contains 60 seconds of arc." "There's a lot more but it looks pretty complicated," she said.

"So, without the internet, we either hit the library or go ask the 9 year old geeks," Ryan said.

"And what exactly is an internet? Another computer thing?" his dad asked again with a grin.

"Yea, Dad. Another computer thing. Just so you all know. Right now, the 'internet' is only being used by universities and the military. It's basically a bunch of computers that are hooked together mainly being used for research and communication. In about ten years, though, it will become more widely used by everyone. By 2016, nearly every household in America will have access to the internet. You can pretty much find everything on anything. But for now, we're going to have to do things the hard way. I say we go give the scouts a new project to work on. Unless someone has a better idea?" Nobody said anything. "Let's go," Sean said and grabbed his jacket. Ryan was close behind.

"Debbie, any luck on the cryptogram?" Ryan asked as he got ready to leave.

"No such luck," she said "I'm not getting anywhere with it."

Just then, John spoke up. "You know, the math department is near my building at the U. I have a friend who's into these kinds of things. Maybe he could help us out with this crypto-whatever."

"Alright," Ryan said "can you call him and see if he'll help? Remember, we can't tell him what we're doing or what it's for."

"Yeah, I'll give him a call and see if he has a few minutes to help," John said and went to make the call.

"We'll be back in a little while," Ryan said as they walked out the door.

Mr. Andrew lived a couple of blocks away. Debbie wanted to go along. She'd pretty much given up on the cryptogram. They decided to walk. Ryan looked up and down their street but didn't see any SUVs sitting watching them. He figured they'd be back. But not yet.

They walked in silence for a few steps and then Debby asked, "Ryan, can I ask you a question?"

"Sure, I guess."

"When you were telling us your 'story' yesterday, you said that a really bad thing happens in the future. What were you talking about exactly?" she asked. He looked at Sean, who shook his head slightly. Ryan knew that he shouldn't say anything about 9/11 but he figured it couldn't hurt. No matter how this turned out, she wouldn't remember any of it anyway. He stopped walking and turned toward Debbie and lowered his voice as he spoke.

"In September of 2001, four airliners were hijacked by Islamic extremists. Terrorists. They fly two of them into the World Trade Center towers in New York City. They fly another one into the Pentagon. The fourth was headed for the White House, but some passengers on board overtook the terrorists. Unfortunately, the plane crashed in Pennsylvania. But those passengers saved a lot of people," Ryan explained slowly and quietly. "Over 3000 people were killed. Both towers came down from the heat generated by the fire from the collision. A lot of people jumped rather than being burned alive. It was a nightmare, Deb. We went to war after that. The initial war had ended by 2016, but the fight against terrorism was still going on. That's the problem. We are at war with terrorists. They don't have a country we can just bomb and move on. It's pretty bad." They started walking again. Debbie didn't say anything. He'd laid a lot on her. He still didn't know if he'd done the right thing.

This whole experience had taught him one thing. It's definitely not a good thing to know what your future holds. Good or bad.

Chapter 24

Ryan, Sean, and Debbie could hear the kids inside the house before they even got to the doorstep. Debbie rang the bell. Melanie Andrew, Scott Andrew's wife, answered the door. Melanie was a 38-year-old babe, to say the least. Ryan remembered having more than one 'not too appropriate' thoughts about her in his teens. He felt kind of embarrassed but quickly came to his senses.

"Hi guys, how's it going?" she asked.

"Fine, Melanie. Mason told me that you guys were working on map coordinates. Latitudes and longitudes and such?" Ryan asked.

"Yea, we're just getting started. It's kind of like herding cats, though. The kids are pretty excited. They always are. Come on in," she said as she went back inside. They followed her inside. The Andrews had set up two large world maps on opposite walls of their living room.

"What's goin' on, Ryan?" asked Scott Andrew.

"Hey, Scott. We were just wondering if we could get your scouts to help us out? We have a latitude and longitude and we need to find out where it is. What do ya think?" Ryan asked.

"Well, we already had some locations picked out, but I guess we can use yours. What are they?" he asked as he moved over to one of the maps. Scott was not only the cub scout leader but also the geography teacher at Bryant Junior High School. So he knew his stuff about maps.

"I think the first three are the latitude and the last three are the longitude. But it might be the other way around. I'm not sure," Ryan said as he handed him the list of numbers as he had written them down.

"Actually, the second set of numbers couldn't be a latitude. So you must have them right as you've written them," Scott said.

"Okay, guys. Gather around," Scott said as the kids slowly settled down. "Last week, we talked about latitudes and longitudes. Does everyone remember?"

"Yes," they all said in semi-unison.

"Okay, so we're going to split up into two teams. I'll give each team a latitude and longitude and the first one to correctly find it wins."

"What do we win," Mason, the extravert, asked jubilantly.

"Each member of the winning team gets a full-size Nestle Crunch. Each member of the other team gets a smaller candy bar," Melanie said as she held up a bowl of candy bars.

"Yeaaaa!!" all the scouts yelled.

Scott gave each team the list of numbers separated into latitude and longitude. The latitude is 33°, 48,' 37." The longitude is -117°, 55,' 8." Each team scrambled to their respective maps and started arguing about who was in charge. "If you need any help, just let me know," Scott said as he walked to each team to check their progress. Ryan walked over to Mason.

"So, you really know what you're doing, bud?" he asked.

"Yea, it's easy," he replied. As they started working on the coordinates, it all started coming back.

"Hey Scott, so refresh my memory on latitudes and longitudes. I vaguely remember doing this but I can't remember the specifics," Sean said rather sheepishly.

"It's actually pretty easy," Scott said. "Latitude, shown as the horizontal line on the map, is the angular distance, in degrees, minutes, and seconds of a point north or south of the Equator. Lines of latitude are often referred to as parallels. Longitude, shown as the vertical line, is the angular distance, in degrees, minutes, and seconds, of a point east or west of the Prime Meridian. The prime meridian is located in Greenwich, England. Lines of longitude are often referred to as meridians. The distance between the lines is approximately 69 miles except for the longitude lines. The distance gets shorter as you move toward the poles. The minutes and seconds more precisely pinpoint where you are looking. There are 60 minutes in each degree. Each minute is divided into 60 seconds. Seconds can be further divided into tenths, hundredths, or even thousandths. We've given the boys a little cheat sheet to help them with this part," he explained. Both Sean and Ryan remembered more and more as he described it. Mason's team seemed to be better organized. They sounded like they were almost done. Ryan walked over to the map. They were concentrating their efforts on the western United States. Suddenly Mason yelled, "We got it!" and he stuck a piece of paper with tape on the back to the map. Sean and Ryan walked over to his map. He had stuck the paper to Southern California.

"You got it," Scott said and the team erupted into cheers. The other team dejectedly sighed and started accusing the other team of cheating.

"Nobody cheated," Melanie said as she handed out the candy bars.

"So, exactly where is it?" Ryan asked Scott.

"Well, they didn't get it exactly, but they were pretty darn close. Your coordinates put you in Anaheim, California. I can't get a more exact location on this map, but it's definitely Anaheim."

Anaheim?! Why Anaheim? "Thanks, Scott."

"What's in Anaheim?" Ryan asked Sean and Debbie.

"Disneyland, Knotts Berry, a bunch of tourist stuff," Sean said.

"I know. We've got to figure out that cryptogram." They left the scouts to their chocolate and walked back home. Or more like running back home.

"Well, we know what city it's in but not exactly where," Debbie said as they went back into the house. The group had dispersed throughout the house in their absence but quickly gathered back in the living room. As soon as everyone was there, Ryan said, "I don't know why, but the coordinates put the next clue in Anaheim. Which means there're a lot of possibilities. Did John get ahold of his professor friend?"

"Yea. He's in his office right now, and he's pretty excited to see what we have," John said.

"Alright," Ryan said, "let's go."

Chapter 25

John drove while Jessica, Debbie, Sean and Ryan discussed Anaheim and the huge number of possibilities. Without a more detailed clue, they didn't stand a chance.

The University of Utah is a large campus near the foothills of the Wasatch Mountains. As they neared the math building, a flood of memories came back to Ryan. He had spent 5 long years at the U in engineering and taken a lot of math classes here. Although it was hard, he loved the time that he spent there. It was safe in school. No major job responsibilities, no family to feed, just lots of studying and hanging out with friends. He had ridden his mountain bike everywhere he went. He even had a secret route that he would take home at night after studying at the Union Building. He could make it home in 11 minutes if he really pushed it.

"Dr. Peterson's office is on the second floor," John said as they all got out and started walking toward the building. Ryan had re-written the cryptogram since Debbie had made a mess trying to figure it out. As they neared the building, Ryan was getting a little antsy about what they were going to tell the professor. They had all decided that they would tell Dr. Peterson that it was an assignment for Ryan's math class in high school but that he had been given permission to get help from others to solve it. It sounded a little weak, though.

Just as they were about to go inside, Ryan glanced back toward the parking lot just in time to see the same black suburban pull in. He nudged Sean. "Looks like our competition's right on our tail," he said as he pointed in the suburban's direction.

"You think that's them?"

"I know it. I'm not about to forget that truck. It looks like we guessed right. We're going to do all the work and they're just going to ride in after us," Ryan said as they went inside.

"Yea, until they don't need us anymore," Sean stated the obvious that had been brought up before. Ryan had been thinking about that. One of his favorite movies of all time is 'National Treasure' with Nicolas Cage and that hot blond girl. A similar thing happened in that movie. The bad guys were using Nicolas Cage to find all the clues. Near the end, Cage's father said that they would only be safe as long as the status quo didn't change...or change in their favor. The status quo for them right now was finding these clues and letting them follow. But that was going to need to be changed pretty soon or they might run out of time and out of luck.

"John, so good to see you," Dr. Peterson said with a British accent and gave John a big hug. It would appear they were good friends after all.

"Wayne, you know my wife, Jessica. This is Ryan, my brother-in-law and my sister-in-law Debbie and Ryan's friend Sean," John said as they all shook hands and sat down around a large circular table in his office. Dr. Peterson's office was a mess. Or so it seemed. There were stacks of paper everywhere and textbooks of all different sizes scattered about. Surprisingly, though, the table was clear.

"So, what have you brought me?" Dr. Peterson asked enthusiastically. He looked like an eight-year-old on Christmas morning.

Ryan laid the paper out in front of him. "I'm taking a linear algebra class at Lakeside and this was part of one of our assignments. My teacher encouraged us to get help on it. We were wondering if you could help us figure it out," Ryan said rather tentatively. "Eventually, we're going to be working on writing a program to solve cryptograms such as this, but so far, everyone's stumped."

"Well, let's take a look," Dr. Peterson said as he put his glasses on and pulled the paper closer. "Do any of you know the history behind cryptograms?" he asked as he studied the page.

"No, not really," John said. He looked at Ryan and rolled his eyes slightly. John had told them on the way over that it wasn't a good idea to ask Dr. Peterson any historical questions because you would probably need a good half hour to hear the answer.

Dr. Peterson went on. "Well, cryptograms are secret codes, and were first used for secure wartime communications. One of the oldest versions known was a strip of paper wrapped around a stick. This was used by the Spartan Army over two thousand years ago. A strip of paper was wrapped around the stick edge-to-edge without overlapping, and the message was written vertically. To read it, the receiver had to wrap the paper strip around a stick of the exact same diameter as the one used to create the message, so the letters would line up correctly. The receiver knew what diameter stick to use, of course. Meanwhile, any messages intercepted would take some time to be decoded because even if the enemy knew to use a stick, he had to find one of the right diameter. Quite brilliant, actually.

Cryptograms are used primarily for entertainment now, though. They are usually created using a simple substitution cipher, in which each letter is replaced by another letter or number. The Caesar Cipher, invented by Julius Caesar, may have been the first of this type. These secret codes have been used as entertaining puzzles for over a thousand years.

Solving a cryptogram is usually done using "frequency analysis." This involves looking for the coded letters which are most frequent in a message, and substituting the real letters which occur most often in common usage. In English, the most common letter used is "e," followed by "t" and "a." You also look for one-letter words since these typically can only be "a" or "i,"" Dr. Peterson was certainly enjoying himself. Getting quite animated with his description. As John feared, he wasn't finished. Although the others in the room found it quite interesting.

He continued. "A Caesar Cipher is a simple "shift cipher." You simply substitute for each letter another letter that is a fixed number of positions away in the alphabet. For example, if you were to use a "shift" of five letters, the letter "a" would be represented by "f," "b" would be represented by "g," and so on. As you can imagine, any cryptogram as simple as this can be easily broken. Since there are only 26 "shifts" possible in English, you could break such a code quickly by trial and error.

A computer program could try all 26 in seconds, then display the 26 versions, and the viewer, or a computer in this case, would immediately recognize which was readable. This is why simple substitution ciphers, while used for entertaining puzzles, are not used by themselves for truly secret messages. They may be used as a start, however. The Vigenère cipher, for example, uses a shift but shifts again at different points in a message, the shift value determined by a repeating keyword. There are also multiple ciphers and rotating ciphers. The list goes on and on."

"So, what do you know about cryptograms, Ryan?" Dr. Peterson asked.

"Not a lot," Ryan said. "Certainly nowhere close to what you know. I know the basics. As you said, the letters have been substituted with these numbers. Normally, you would look for repeating words and just start guessing. Right?"

"Well, if it's a simple substitution cipher, yes. But if it was created using other methods, it might take longer to solve.

However, we have the distinct advantage of the computer age," Dr. Peterson smiled as he stood up and sat back down behind his desk at his computer. "I've developed a rather smart little program, if I do say so myself. Essentially, what this program does is methodically try every possibility until a readable and sensible solution is found. With only one or two words, there could be a number of possibilities that make sense. But with this many words, the computer will try to identify when the entire collection is readable." He started putting the numbers into his computer. They all sat silent, waiting for the solution. "Normally, this would take hours to try each possibility, even with a short cryptogram such as this. However, once I've entered it into my computer, it should take just a few seconds," he said rather proudly.

As promised, no more than a minute went by before Dr. Peterson proclaimed, "Aha! Here is your message." He turned his monitor on his desk so they could all read the clue.

As Sean and Ryan read the clue, they looked at each other's confused faces. Nothing jumped out at them as in the first clue.

"I'm still not sure where we're going," Ryan said to no one in particular.

Dr. Peterson looked a little perplexed at his comment.

"Where are you going?" he asked.

Ryan thought quickly and said, "Oh, my teacher said that the cryptogram has something to do with our class trip at the end of the year." It sounded a lot better in his head but the professor seemed to buy it. They thanked him and left.

As they drove back home, Jessica read the clue out loud several times.

JOYFUL MOUNTAIN HOUSES

BITTER BRUTES THAT CONCEAL

YOUR NEXT ROUTE THROUGH CONFUSION

The message was confusing but for some reason, every time Jessica repeated it, something nagged at Ryan's mind but was just out of reach. It was like waking from a dream and remembering the dream but not remembering the dream. The harder you concentrated on it, the further away the memory retreated.

When they arrived back home, everyone was where they had left them, waiting. It looked like both moms had been crying again. Ryan ignored it for the time being. He figured there would be a lot more crying in the near future. Jessica brought the clue in and set it on the table.

"Well, here it is," Jessica said and sat down. She read it out loud for everyone to hear.

"I guess we should take it one line at a time," Debbie said as she stared at the paper on the table. "We know that it's somewhere in Anaheim. The two biggest attractions there are Knott's Berry Farm and Disneyland, right?"

"It's Disneyland," Ryan said rather suddenly.

"How do you know that?" Sean asked.

"I don't know. But for some reason, it just makes me think of Disneyland."

"Okay, let's assume it's Disneyland," Debbie said. "What part of the clue fits Disneyland?"

"Well, it's supposed to be the happiest place on earth. That fits with the joyful," Jessica said.

"Is there a mountain near Disneyland?" Sean's dad asked.

"No, but there's a mountain inside Disneyland," Sean said. "What's that ride that goes up and around that mountain?"

"That's it!" Ryan shouted. "That's what I kept thinking. I just couldn't put my finger on it. The bitter brutes must be the abominable snowmen, or whatever they're called, that's part of the ride. I think there's three monsters inside the Matterhorn. One for each of the two sides of the ride and another one at the start. There are also a couple of red eyes that flash when the car goes by. Along with some scary growling," Ryan said excitedly.

"So, how do you know so much about the Matterhorn?" Jessica asked.

"It's my son's favorite ride." As soon as he said it, he wished he hadn't. It had suddenly brought back the whole 'weirdness' of why they were there. They all had said they were behind him but he still had the feeling that some of them still doubted him. His mom looked sad and got up and left the room. He started to follow, but Debbie stopped him. "She's still having a hard time with this whole thing. She just needs some time. We probably all do."

"Well, Sean and I don't," Ryan said as he came back to the center of the room.

"But the fact is that it is my son's favorite ride. We've gone to Disneyland for the last several years. Well, in my time, anyway. So I know Disneyland like the back of my hand."

"So how are we supposed to get to this monster that's part of the ride?" Sean asked. It was a good question. "I have no idea," Ryan said. "There are actually three 'monsters.' The first one is seen in both tracks. The other two are seen by each track and are set about halfway through the ride, and the bobsleds pass them going pretty fast. There would be no way we could get off the ride at that point. Plus, they are about halfway up the mountain. There's way too much security to try and sneak into the mountain and crawl around speeding bobsleds. We'd get cut in half. Plus, there are climbers who climb on the mountain all day long."

"Unless you do it at night," Sean's mom, Linda, said from the corner of the room. Everyone turned to look at her. She had been pretty quiet throughout this whole thing. She was pretty quiet to begin with but she was pretty smart, so Ryan was counting on her to come up with good ideas. He didn't think this was one of them.

"I've never been at Disneyland after hours, but I'm guessing the security is pretty tight," Ryan said.

"Well, the ride would be shut down. If you could get inside and somehow hide, you could wait until the park closes and then look for the clue," she said, trying to justify her idea. Sean Sr. looked at her quizzically. He didn't think she would be giving advice that was illegal. But he smiled and was proud of her for supporting Sean.

"It might be the only way, Ryan," Sean said.

"Yea, well if we get caught, we're going to have a hell of a time explaining ourselves," he said and sat down with a sigh. He put his hands on top of his head (having hair felt so good), closed his eyes, and tried to picture the area around the Matterhorn. As he formed a mental picture, he remembered it was located between Tomorrowland and Fantasyland. There were a lot of rides around it. With the climbers and all the workers, it would be nearly impossible to sneak inside and hide.

"Well, there's not much more we can do here," he said. "I guess the next step is to go to Disneyland and check it out."

"Your mom's not going to like you going alone," Ryan's dad said.

"Sorry, Dad. Sean and I can't have any help. You know that. If any of you even travel with us, Maxwell will know. And then we're screwed. We'll take a ride to the airport, though."

"There's something you need to think about," John said. "Those guys that followed you earlier today are probably going to try and follow you again."

"He's right," Sean said.

"Yea, how can we be sure that they don't follow us? It's a good guess that those idiots haven't figured out what we have so far. But there's no guarantee. How can we get to the airport and get on a plane without them noticing?" Ryan asked.

"We could go on separate planes," Sean said.

"No. They'd just split up and then we'd be more vulnerable."

Debbie spoke up, "Well, you lost 'em once on your motorcycles. Maybe you can do it again?"

"That's not a bad idea," Sean said. "If we leave early and go through the golf course again, we could loop around some side streets and head for the airport after we lose 'em. It might actually work."

"What if they have two cars this time?" John asked.

"If we can't lose them, we can't lose them. We'll have a lot more chances once we land," Ryan said.

"At least they won't be able to bring their guns on the plane, right?" Jessica said. "Not necessarily. They can just put them in their checked bags," Sean said.

"Which is exactly what we're going to do," Ryan said.

"Isn't that illegal?" Debbie asked.

"Maybe, technically, but chances are they won't be found. They don't x-ray luggage in 1982 like they do in 2016."

"Why are you so insistent on them having a gun?!" Jessica was getting pretty worked up. John fired back, "Because your brother was shot a few hours ago, Jessica. That's why."

"Alright, settle down you two," Ryan said as he stood up. "The fact is. I agree with John. We need some protection. Hopefully, we won't need to use it. But I'll feel better if we have it. Chances are they won't try anything before we get the clue, anyway. So, we'll have some time to plan."

"Well, I guess you at least know where you're going. I've got to tell you, though. Even with everything we've seen, it's going to take some convincing to get your mother to go along with this, Ryan," his dad said matter of factly.

"I know, Dad. And I respect her authority in this. And yours. But, I don't honestly see any other way. We've got to go," Ryan said somewhat sadly, knowing that, at his "current" age, he had no right to tell his mom and dad what he was going to do. But he also knew that they had to go.

Sean left with his parents. They agreed to meet the following morning and leave as early as possible.

After everyone had left, Ryan sat in the darkened living room alone. He couldn't believe that just a few short days ago, he had been happily married in the year 2016 to a wonderful girl who had given him two beautiful children. Why did this happen to him? What had he done to deserve this? He was just a normal guy living a normal life with a normal job and normal friends. What made him stand out? And what made Sean stand out? He fell asleep on the couch with those questions weighing heavily on his mind.

Chapter 26

July 2163

"Maxwell, my old friend, please come in," Darius said as Maxwell walked slowly into his office.

"Would you like a drink?" Darius asked as he walked to the bar.

"Um, yes, please," Maxwell replied as he sat down, after walking around the ship hanging from the ceiling. Darius poured them both a glass of scotch. He handed Maxwell his glass and sat down behind his desk.

"So, how is our test proceeding?" he asked. Maxwell took a sip of his drink and cleared his throat. "Both teams are in place, and the competition is underway. I am pleased to report that your suspicions were correct, sir. The second team has relied entirely upon the first team's intelligence in finding the clues. However, they wounded one of the members of the first team," Maxwell reported.

"How badly?!" Darius asked quickly and sat up straight in his chair. The color had faded from Darius' face.

"It was a superficial wound and the boy appears to be okay," Maxwell replied.

Darius sighed with relief. "Maxwell, as is the case with all our contestants, it is imperative that no deaths occur. But in this case, it is very important that neither of these two boys are killed. If it becomes necessary to sacrifice any team members, it must be from the second team," Darius said coldly and without hesitation.

"Sir, I don't think it will be necessary to sacrifice anyone," Maxwell said nervously, emphasizing the word 'sacrifice.'

"I hope you're right, my friend. But, as you are aware, this test is more important than any one person. I'm sure you will see to it that Ryan and Sean are protected to whatever extent possible. But the completion of the test is our first concern," Darius said as he poured himself another drink. Maxwell sat still. His mind was reeling. Darius was becoming more and more unstable. This 'test' was consuming him, and Maxwell was frightened not only for his team but for himself. If he were to fail, he was certain that Darius would not hesitate to eliminate him, permanently.

Darius sat back down at his desk and leaned back in his chair. "So, how is our second team doing?" he asked.

"Well, as I said, they are relying heavily on the first team to find the clues. Then they simply go in after and retrieve them. I expect this will become more difficult with the second and third clues. I fear that their violence may escalate, however. They have secured several weapons and certainly have the ability and willingness to use them," Maxwell said.

"I would expect that," Darius said. "They are criminals, after all, Maxwell. You know that. One of the reasons we selected them was the knowledge that they would use whatever means necessary to secure their freedom and reward. It is up to Ryan and Sean to figure out how to deal with that aspect. You need to return now, Maxwell. Keep me apprised of the situation as it develops." Darius turned away from Maxwell and stared out the window as he took another drink.

Maxwell sat still for several seconds. Then stood slowly and left Darius' office. He walked toward the far end of the Life Force Institute to the Travel Section. It was an amusing title, The Travel Section. To an auditor, the Travel Section was simply the department responsible for arranging tickets and itineraries for business travel. When, in fact, very few members of the institute traveled anywhere. The only ones that traveled were handlers. And they didn't just travel to locations. They traveled to times. The scientists at the institute had not only worked out the bugs in time travel. They had perfected it. So far, no deleterious effects have been observed. At least not recently. During the perfection process, there were several tragic 'accidents.' Seventeen people died while the process was being refined. A small price to pay, Darius had said. Certainly, the families of those killed would have thought differently.

The process was quite simple, in theory. A travel orb had been developed. The orb was wirelessly linked to the mainframe time network located deep underground beneath the Travel Section. The mainframe computer system demanded an exorbitant amount of energy and required significant cooling due to the heat generated during the time travel process. The entire mainframe was encircled by an underground lake that absorbed the heat. Similar to a nuclear reactor. The orb could transport up to two people at a time. Technicians running the mainframe entered the time and location coordinates into the orb. This information was saved in the orb's memory and could not be altered by anyone other than the technicians. Although handlers had access to alter their location within a specific time period. That is how Maxwell had been able to move so quickly from one place to another in 1982. The traveler or travelers simply placed one hand on the orb and initiated the operating system by entering the activation code. This code was a sequence of seven numbers. Each orb had a unique code. If the code was entered incorrectly, the orb was neutralized and had to be reset locally at the institute. This was a security requirement that could have disastrous results since the institute was located in Montana in 2163. If a time traveler entered the wrong code, he or she would be stuck wherever (or whenever) they were until located by another institute member. Depending on the situation, this might never occur and they would remain in that time for the rest of their natural lives. There were protocols in place to send someone to find a handler if they had not checked back in at the designated time. So far, this protocol has only been put into place one time.

Several years prior to this current 'test,' a disgruntled member of the institute's engineering staff had decided he wanted out. A wish that was not granted very often by Darius, for security reasons. Scott Simpson brilliantly planned his 'escape.' He secured an orb during a planned outage of the system. Since most technicians and other personnel were busy with maintenance, it was fairly easy for an engineer with security clearance to get his hands on one of the orbs. Normally, they are protected by several heavily armed guards. As soon as the system was back up, the team began running tests. Scott volunteered for one of the tests, which was not out of the ordinary. But he substituted his orb for the one reserved for his test. What he didn't realize was that part of the maintenance outage included the implementation of a tracking device for any orb used. Prior to this, they were only tracking orbs that had been reserved. Scott was found in 1921 in South America. He was summarily executed, and the orb was brought back. His 'disappearance' was explained away as a tragic accident during the time travel process. Only Darius and a few others, including Maxwell, knew the truth. Darius had given the order to execute Scott. Maxwell and two other technicians had pleaded for leniency but it had fallen on deaf ears. Although the official explanation was an accident, most people guessed the real reason Scott was killed. Nobody since that event had ever tried to leave the institute again.

Recently, a brilliant young scientist by the name of Jeffrey Hollander had been brought on by Darius to perfect the time travel process even further. Or, more accurately, to add a new feature that before now had not been possible. Jeffrey had written several papers on the theoretical possibility of transferring the consciousness of an individual to an earlier version of that same individual. This consciousness transfer had been used with Ryan, Sean, and the other team. Although there were limitations, utilizing a consciousness transfer was much safer than actually sending someone back in time. If a 45-year-old person was sent back in time, they would still be 45 in the earlier time. The consciousness transfer offered the possibility of that same 45-year-old person's memories and experiences being transferred to a younger version of themselves. A fascinating twist that would add to the experimental data.

Of course, the physics and mechanics behind the process were carefully guarded and nobody but Darius and Jeffrey had a complete knowledge of how it worked. In addition to consciousness transfer, the process also offered the added bonus of being able to modify the subjects' memory. Once the experiment was over, the memory of all those involved could be manipulated and essentially erased. As far as the subject and anyone else involved knew, that period of time became simply a blank. A cruel result that Darius didn't seem to care about.

Maxwell entered the Travel Section by scanning his identity badge. The Travel Section's lobby looked quite innocuous. There were several couches and chairs that looked more like a doctor's office than a time portal. The outside foyer had three doors. One was the door Maxwell had just come through. Another door led to a series of offices with personnel posing as travel agents making arrangements for business travel. The third door didn't have a handle and could only be opened via a keypad. Once inside the foyer, Maxwell was required to enter his travel authorization code and was then granted access to the third door.

Inside the third door, there was only one room. In the center of the room was a single orb resting on a pedestal. A computer screen sat next to the orb. Maxwell entered his desired location and time on the screen and waited while his activation code was authorized and returned. The 7-digit code appeared on the screen. 7-5-13-11-29-37-53. All activation codes were comprised entirely of prime numbers. Maxwell didn't know the significance of the prime numbers. He had asked one of the technicians about this once but was treated with a blank stare. Since then, he hadn't cared to ask again. He wrote down the code in his notebook and committed it to memory, as always. This would be his code for the duration of his "excursion," as these trips had come to be known. He then placed his hand on the orb and entered the code. The orb gently vibrated and the entire room went black. Complete lack of visible light. Maxwell felt a rush of warm air, then nothing. Slowly, light began to return. Maxwell found himself standing in the middle of his hotel room in downtown Salt Lake City. 1982 Salt Lake City.

The actual process was a well-guarded secret that even Maxwell had not been read into. He had picked up bits and pieces over the years. Something to do with space-time continuum or light-speed accelerations or something like that. It was well beyond his level of understanding. Suffice it to say, it worked and it worked quite well. Darius and an elite group of technicians were the only ones who truly understood exactly how it worked. Maxwell and the other handlers had accepted that fact and had stopped asking questions since the answers would not be understood anyway.

The only thing he felt while the process was underway was a feeling of weightlessness and, oddly enough, an almost uncontrollable need to urinate. Several times he had been unable to control his bladder and he 'landed' with an embarrassing stain on his pants. Since then, he always tried to remember to completely empty his bladder before traveling. It was still an uncomfortable feeling and posed obvious problems if he were to land in a public area.

He looked around his hotel room. Just as he had left it. He sat down on the bed and put his head in his hands. He couldn't help thinking that things were starting to spin out of control. Darius was obviously unbalanced but he possessed total control. It wasn't as if Maxwell could call the authorities and have Darius investigated. He would be instantly found out and killed. Plus, the authorities, if they could be called that, had long since been paid off by the institute to look the other way when anything suspicious was found by auditors. Maxwell was stuck, and he knew it. He longed for the days when he and Alexander would sit and talk for hours about the America they hoped to restore. Alexander was a good man with good intentions. Often, Maxwell had wished he had been killed along with Alexander rather than watch what Darius was turning the institute into. He laid his head back on the pillow and wept as he fell asleep.

Chapter 27

Michele kissed Ryan lightly on the forehead. "Don't blame yourself, honey," she said. Ryan looked into her face. She smiled slightly and said "It's going to be okay. We'll get through this." He looked over and saw Jackson. He was crying softly and was sitting in a wheelchair!

"Nooo!" Ryan screamed as he sat up. He was dripping with sweat and scared out of his mind. After a few seconds, he realized he was on his mom and dad's couch. It was a dream. Just a dream. He was shaking uncontrollably, though. Suddenly, the light came on. "Ryan, are you okay?" It was his mom. She came over and sat down next to him.

"Yea, I'm fine Mom. I just had a bad dream."

"You're absolutely drenched, Ryan. Are you sure you're okay?"

"I'm sure. I'm just going to go splash some water on my face. Sorry about the couch." The couch was wet with his sweat. Hopefully, it will be able to be cleaned.

"Don't worry about the couch," his mom said. "I'm sure this has all been very stressful for you, dear. Is there anything I can do?"

"No. It's okay. I'm sure this has been pretty stressful for you, too," Ryan said without looking at her.

"To be honest, Ryan, I still don't know what to think. I believe you. I do. But it just seems so impossible," she said as she stood up.

"I know, Mom. It seems impossible to me, too. I have no idea why this is happening. All I know is that I'm telling you the truth and I have to do whatever I can to get back to my family."

"I know, dear. I'll try to be strong. But I can't promise I'll be happy about what's going on," she said. Ryan smiled and looked at her. She had tears in her eyes, but she smiled weakly and went back upstairs.

He glanced at his watch. It was 4:00am on Tuesday, September 14th, 1982. There was nothing he could do to change that. At least not right now. There was no way he was going to be able to go back to sleep. So he went into the kitchen and reached for the light switch, but stopped. A dark figure ran by the bay window. Ryan crouched down and inched his way to the back door. He looked out but didn't see anything. The gate to the backyard was open and was still swinging slightly. He ran back into the living room and got the 9mm out of the backpack. He checked the magazine and crept out the back door. He realized he was only wearing Levi's and a T-shirt. He cursed himself for not putting shoes on. His arm was stiff and was burning where he'd been grazed. He crept down the driveway and crouched behind his mom's station wagon. He looked down the street and saw the same black SUV but couldn't tell if anyone was inside. Suddenly, the dome light went on inside the truck. He couldn't see any faces but could tell there were two people in the front seat. The driver was looking through binoculars in his direction. He put the binoculars down and put his finger and thumb up in the shape of a gun, pointed at Ryan and flicked his hand up like he was firing. The dome light went off and the SUV turned around and drove off. Ryan's heart was racing. He was holding a Glock 9mm but felt absolutely helpless. He walked back up the driveway and went inside.

Chapter 28

It was only 4:30 am, but Ryan knew he needed to talk to Sean. He called Sean's house. "Hello?" a sleepy voice mumbled. "Hello, Mrs. Jensen? This is Ryan. I'm so sorry for calling so early, but could I speak to Sean, please?" he asked as politely as possible. "Just a minute, Ryan," she said with obvious annoyance. A few minutes later, a voice came on the line. "Dude, you know what time it is?" Sean asked sleepily. "Yea, I know. Sorry. But I just had a visitor in our backyard. It was them. I think we need to get going. Now!" he said. "Pack a bag for at least 2 or 3 days. I hope we won't be gone that long but bring whatever you're going to need."

Ryan hung up the phone and went downstairs to pack. In his room, he stopped to look around. He hadn't really had the chance yet. It had been over 30 years since he'd lived in this room. There were a lot of memories here. It sounds corny now, but he always felt safe in this room and in this house. His parents had bought this house just before he was born. Therefore, he never knew any other home or neighborhood. This was his neighborhood and his family. There's no way in Hell he was going to let those assholes ruin his life or the lives of his family, past, present, and future. He was ready to do whatever it took to get out of this mess and get back to where (and when) he belonged.

Ryan packed enough clothes for a couple of days. The problem of evading the other team had been in the back of his mind. Now, he needed to start to think in earnest about how to get to Southern California without them finding out. Then a thought hit him that made his heart skip a beat, and the hairs on his neck stand up. His family and Sean's family knew where they were going. The other team knew that or at least they would suspect it. If they got on that plane without the other team knowing, they would simply come back and find out from one of his or Sean's family members. His mom, dad, and sisters were tough, but those assholes could easily convince them to reveal where Ryan and Sean had gone. The thought of his mom duct taped to a chair while they beat his dad or raped one of his sisters turned his stomach. There was no way he was going to let that happen. He and Sean would have to try and lose them in California. They HAD to let the other team follow them! Ryan couldn't believe he hadn't thought of this before. Just then, he heard Sean upstairs, "Dude, you down there?" he said. "Yea, come on down," Ryan said as he zipped up his suitcase.

When Sean came down to Ryan's room, he told him about his thoughts regarding their families.

"Damn, I hadn't thought of that either," he said. "I agree. So, we'll let them follow us onto the plane? What's going to keep them from grabbing us once we land?" he asked.

"I thought about that," Ryan said, "but I don't think they will. They need to know where the second clue is and they want us to get it for them. I figure we'll try and lose them between the airport and whatever hotel we decide to stay at. If that doesn't work, we'll try losing them before we get to Disneyland." He wasn't very confident in his plan. It wasn't really much of a plan. Just an idea. But for now, they had to focus on getting to California and figuring out how they could get into the Matterhorn.

It was now about 6:00am. Ryan's dad had been awake for a while. He was always an early riser. The two boys went upstairs, and he was reading the paper, as usual.

"You guys about ready?" he asked. He was very calm, which made Ryan nervous.

"I guess so," he said as he looked at Sean. He shrugged his shoulders as if to say, 'that was easy.'

"Dad, you're being awfully calm about what's going on here," Ryan said, questioning.

"Well, Ryan, last night I started thinking about what you told us. You know how you got here. The whole time travel thing. Well, even with the whole Grace Kelly proof and all, I can't say I completely believe you. But," he held up his hands to stop his son from butting in, "I also realize that something is going on and even though I don't know exactly what it is, I do know that there's not much I can say to stop you. So, if I can't stop you, I might as well help you as much as I can. If I had my way, I'd be going with you. But you've made it clear that that isn't going to happen. So, if you're ready. I'm ready. What can I do to help? You guys still set on going to the airport on your motorcycles?" He gave me one of his little crooked smiles and got up.

"Dad, sit back down for a minute," Ryan said as he sat down next to his dad. He looked out toward the foyer and made sure his mom wasn't within earshot. "Dad, last night I saw someone in our backyard," he kept his voice down, "and when I went outside to check it out, I saw him get into a black SUV down the street. Right across from Stanton's house. There were two of them in the truck. They didn't come in the house but the bottom line is that they know where I live. And I would guess they know where Sean lives. The undeniable truth is that you guys aren't safe if we try to lose these guys. They'll just come back here and demand you tell them." Ryan left out his fears of beatings and gang rape. "So, we figure the safest thing for everyone involved is to let them follow us to California and deal with it down there. We know they won't try to hurt us, at least not now. They need us to get the clues. But Sean and I agree that your safety and the safety of his family is a top priority. So, we're not going to go on our bikes. But we'll take a ride to the airport if you're willing."

Ryan's dad was silent for a moment and just stared at his son. It was obvious that he hadn't thought about this whole thing spilling back onto all the others involved.

"If what you're saying is true, we're in more danger than you are until this whole thing is resolved," his dad said thoughtfully.

"Not necessarily," Ryan said. "As long as we lead them along, they have no reason to threaten you. And, just to make sure, we won't involve you in any way from here on out, if at all possible."

"No. That's where I draw the line," his dad said and stood up.

"You will keep me posted on everything you're doing. I can protect the family but I'm not going to let my son go through this alone. And, I think you should tell everyone about the possible danger. It will be important for all of us to know and to be aware."

"Alright, Dad. But keep your eyes open." Ryan knew in his heart that, despite his father's adamant intentions, Ryan's and Sean's family's involvement in this whole mess had come to an end. No matter what happened from here on out, they were on their own. Ryan was not going to put his family or Sean's family in any more danger.

"Fine. So, are you guys ready to go?" Ryan's dad asked.

"Yea, but I was hoping to get everyone together before we leave. At least Jessica and John. I'm going to give them a call." Ryan called Jessica, and she was getting her kids ready for school. But John was still home and she said he would be right over.

John came in about ten minutes later. And Jessica was with him. She said she had dropped her kids off at a friend's house. "What's going on, Ryan?" she asked. "I didn't think you were leaving until later."

"I know. That was the plan, but we've moved it up a little. Last night, I saw a couple of the other team members down the street watching the house. They obviously know, or think, we're going to be going somewhere. So Sean and I have decided to let them follow us," Ryan said, knowing what response he would get.

"What!!??" his mom said emphatically. "You can't just let them get on a plane with you and follow you to Disneyland! They'd kill you to get that second clue!"

"That's the point. I don't think so, Mom. This thing isn't over yet. They need us. They haven't got a brain between the four of them and they need us to lead them to the clues. However, I agree that they will do whatever they can to get the clues. So, if we leave and they don't know where we've gone, I'll give you three guesses where they'll come next," Ryan paused for effect. His mom opened her mouth to speak, but then he saw the realization in her eyes. "Oh my," she said. "They'd come here."

"Holy shit," John said under his breath. "Ryan's right. We all know where they're going. It wouldn't take much to get it out of us. We're not exactly Israeli commandos trained to withstand torture," he said.

"So, you see," Sean said, "we have to let them follow us down there. Ryan and I are going to do whatever we can to lose them once we're there. But we have no choice. They need to know where we're going."

Just then, Sean's mom and dad showed up. They let them in on what they had been discussing and they reluctantly agreed.

Ryan and Sean went outside and loaded up the suitcases in the wagon. Ryan looked down the street. He didn't see the SUV but he knew it had to be close. His mom and Sean's mom kissed them goodbye and started crying again. That much was expected. As they pulled away, Ryan looked back at his mom and sisters standing in the driveway. As much as he loved them, he hoped that the next time he saw them would be 34 years from now.

Chapter 29

As they drove down the street, Ryan kept an eye out for their 'friends.' They had to be close. "Dad, keep an eye out for a black SUV. I think it's a suburban."

They stopped at an ATM to get some cash. Before Ryan could put his card in, though, Sean reminded him of his substantial withdrawal from yesterday. "Holy crap," Ryan said. "I totally forgot it. It's in my bedroom on the shelf."

"You forgot 10,000 dollars!" Sean said and almost started laughing. "Dude, how could you possibly forget 10,000 dollars?"

"I don't know. I guess I just didn't think about it. Oh well. I'd love to see my mom's face when she finds it dusting my shelf." Despite her insistence to the contrary, Ryan's mom always dusted his room. Something teenage boys are usually remiss in accomplishing.

Rather than go back, they went to several ATMs since they could only take out $300 each at a time. They figured they could pay for the tickets with their 'credit cards.' They'd worked everywhere else. As they were leaving the final ATM, Sean looked behind them, and about 3 cars back was the black suburban. He couldn't tell how many people were in it. "There they are," Sean said. "About 3 cars back." Ryan turned around to see them. "Well, at least we know they're following us. That's good, I guess," he didn't sound overconfident.

"It is good. Once we get to the airport, try to get a look at their faces. We need to know what these guys look like," Sean said.

"Don't lose 'em, Dirk," Jerry said.

"Don't worry, their old man drives like my Grandma," Dirk said. Willy was in the backseat cleaning his .45.

"You're wastin' your time, Willy. If they're goin' to the airport like we think they are, you're not going to be able to take that thing with ya on the plane. Just put it in your suitcase," Jose said. He was sitting next to Willy in the backseat.

"So, where do you think these little pricks are goin', Jerry?" Dirk asked as he drove.

"Don't know. All I know is we're going to follow them to the next clue. As long as we stay on their trail, it should be easy to win this thing. Once we have our hands on that orb, we waste the punks and get back to where we belong and start spending our money," Jerry smiled as he thought how easy this had been so far. He also was smiling because he had contacted some friends in Orange County that would set him up with more weapons and transportation. He didn't have to tell them anything about the contest so technically, he was still within the rules.

As they neared the airport, Jerry said, "Jose, I want you to follow those two and find out what flight they're getting on and where it's going. We'll park the car and follow you in. Buy four tickets for the same flight. See if you can get us in the back of the plane so we can watch them during the flight."

They followed a few car lengths behind the station wagon as it pulled up to the terminal. They watched as both boys got out with their suitcases and hugged their dad."Oh, how sweet," Willy said through gritted teeth. "I'm going to enjoy spillin' their guts," he said.

"Just don't do anything til I say so, you freak," Jerry said as Jose got out to follow them in.

"See you in a couple of days, Dad," Ryan said as he gave him a hug. "We'll give you a call when we land."

"Be careful, Ryan. You know these guys are serious. They won't hesitate to kill you once they don't need you anymore," he said as his voice quivered.

"We will be careful, Dad. But we have to do whatever is necessary to get this clue." Ryan gave him a pat on the shoulder and they turned to enter the airport. He looked back at him from the door. His dad waved and wiped a tear from his eye. Ryan gave him a small smile and turned and went inside. As they walked toward the Delta counter, he was thinking how nice it had been to spend some time with his dad again. A few months ago, he had attended his funeral. The man he had just left behind was vibrant and alert. It had been quite a while since he had seen him like that. If there had been anything good that had come from this, it was the blessing he had been given to spend time with his dad again. For that, he was grateful.

They got to the Delta counter. They figured Delta would be the best option. The Salt Lake City airport was a Delta hub, even in 1982. There was a good chance that they had a flight to Southern California. As they stood in line, Ryan turned to Sean, "So, do you see anybody suspicious checking us out?"

"I've been looking but haven't seen anyone yet," Sean said. Ryan casually looked around as they waited for their turn. Just then, he noticed a guy standing against the wall behind them. He didn't look familiar, but then why would he? Ryan nudged Sean,

"Check the guy out at six o'clock." Sean turned slowly and looked in his direction. "Oh yea, I think that's a very bad guy. And he's coming in our direction." Ryan turned, and the guy got in the back of the line about 10 people behind them.

"I think we can assume we are officially being followed," Ryan said. "Let's just buy the tickets and get going." They got to the counter and found out that the first plane leaving for Orange County was leaving in about an hour. Sean asked the attendant if the plane was full. She said that there were plenty of seats available. He asked if they could be seated as far forward as possible. She said she didn't have anything near the front unless they wanted to buy first-class tickets. There were three first-class seats left. They figured money wasn't exactly in short supply so they bought the first class tickets and checked their bags. As they had hoped, their credit cards worked fine. As they walked away from the counter toward the gate, Ryan looked back and the guy was staring at them. "Not exactly hiding his interest in us, is he?" Ryan asked Sean.

"No. Not really. I think we can assume that they'll be on the same plane." Sean said as they got in line for the security check.

They made their way to the gate and had about 45 minutes before they boarded.

"So what's the plan?" Sean asked.

"Well, the first thing we'll need to do once we land is rent a car. I figure we should get something small and fast, if possible. Then I guess we go find a hotel and decide our next move from there." For the first time, Ryan realized that he hadn't really thought this out completely. That was bad. They should have a definite plan, but he didn't know where to start.

"I don't think we'll have much of a chance of losing them between the airport and the hotel. With four of them, they'll easily be able to watch us," Ryan said as he kept an eye out for them to arrive at the gate.

"That's if they all come," Sean said. "What if one or more of them stays behind in case they do lose us? Then they'll go back and beat it out of our families."

"You're right. We'll let them follow us to Disneyland. Once we get the clue, that's when we'll need to start worrying about losing 'em," Ryan said.

"Hey, Sean, what do you think our families are doing back home?" As soon as he'd said it, Ryan realized it was a stupid question.

"I guess nothing since right now, they don't even exist, right? Well, at least our kids don't exist." He looked at Sean. Sean looked as sad as Ryan felt.

"All I can think about is getting back to them," Sean said sadly. "It's like the old saying, you don't realize what you've got until it's gone."

"It's not gone," Ryan said with new resolve, "we're going to win this thing and get back to them. We just have to stick together and figure this out." A voice came over the intercom and called for their flight to begin boarding. They made their way to the line and walked down the breezeway to the plane.

As soon as they were seated, Ryan turned to Sean. "When we see that guy come on, don't look right at him. Try to see where he sits and who sits down next to him. I'd like to know if all four of them get on." They were seated in the second row of first class. There were only five rows in first class and most of them were already occupied so they knew they'd be able to see everyone that got on board. They watched as people passed them on their way to the coach. After about twenty people had passed, the same guy they had seen in the terminal passed by their row. Ryan didn't look up but could feel him staring at him as he passed by. Directly behind him were three other guys that fit the general description. Both Sean and Ryan looked at them as they passed. Only one of them looked down at the two boys. He had a crazy look in his eyes. He smiled as he walked by and whispered something to the guy in front of him. The guy in front looked back and stared down at Ryan. Ryan looked away after he burned his image in his memory.

"I think they're all here."

"That's good," Sean said. "At least we know our families are safe for the time being. Did you get a good look at them?" Ryan was sitting in the aisle seat so he had a much better view of them as they passed.

"Yea. At least two of them. The guy we saw in the airport and another guy that reminds me of Charles Manson. He's got a really crazy look. I didn't see the other two very well but they're all sitting together." Ryan had leaned out and looked back. They were about 10 rows back in coach. Two were sitting on one side, and the other two were sitting on the other side, directly across from each other. "When we land, we'll just act natural, get our bags, and get our car. Then, we'll drive towards Disneyland and find a hotel close by. There are a bunch of hotels right around the park. Most schools around the country have started so I don't think the park will be very busy with tourists." They continued to talk about their plan, as it were. They decided they'd go right over to the park and figure out how hard it was going to be to get into the Matterhorn and find the clue. All Ryan's Disneyland experience was from the 21st century. But he figured everything around the Matterhorn was pretty much the same. The only idea they could come up with is to try and get inside and hide until the park closes. At this time of year, Ryan thought the park closed at 8:00 pm. At least it does in September of 2016.

Ryan started to reminisce about his trips to Disneyland over the last several years. Their favorite part of the park was actually the California Adventure side. In 1982, that portion of the park wasn't even there. He always loved going to Disneyland. As soon as he walked into the park, he felt like an 8-year-old kid. He and Michele would run around like kids and try to keep up with their two boys. Now, he was heading to the same park in an attempt to win this crazy contest and get back to his family. "If we ever get out of this," he thought, "we'll go to Hawaii for our next vacation."

They landed a little ahead of schedule. Of course, the first-class passengers were the first to leave the plane. As they headed out toward the baggage claim, Ryan could feel the stares from behind them. He looked back a couple of times. All four of them were about 30 yards behind them. "Why don't you go get our bags. I'm going to go get us a car. Meet me at the rental car counter," Sean said to Ryan as he headed for the car rental section. He figured there still wasn't any danger. At least until they found the clue, that is.

"So, did you get us a Ferrari?" Ryan asked as he came up to the counter, lugging their bags. "No, the only cars they have are pretty crappy. But it will get us where we're going." As they left the airport in their Ford Escort, neither of them could see the other team.

"Did you see those guys at the baggage claim?" Sean asked Ryan.

"Oh yea, they were there. Staring at me the whole time."

"Well where are they now," Sean wondered out loud.

"I don't know," Ryan said, "but I expect we'll see them soon enough. Maybe they had somebody meet them here. Probably some low life that's setting them up with Uzis and rocket launchers."

Ryan knew the fastest way to Disneyland. As usual, the first thing you see as you approach Disneyland is the Matterhorn. On their recent trips to Disneyland, they'd always try to be the first to see it. Either Michele or Ryan would see it first, but they'd always keep their mouths shut and let the boys scream out when they saw it. This always led to a shouting match about who actually saw it first. The fights in the backseat usually led to either Michele or Ryan yelling for it to stop. Right now, Ryan ached to hear his two boys screaming at each other.

They circled the park a couple of times looking for a hotel. There were a bunch of them right across the street from the entrance. They chose the best-looking one and pulled in. Just as they pulled in, Ryan looked in the rearview mirror and saw a Cadillac behind them slow way down and then speed up once they pulled up to the lobby. "I think our friends just saw us pull in here," Ryan said to Sean as he turned around to look.

"Where?"

"I saw a Caddy slow down and then speed up once we pulled in. I couldn't tell how many were in the car, but I noticed bodies in the front and back."

They checked in and told the front desk they were expecting several members of their group later so they needed four rooms. Ryan figured since money was no object, they shouldn't make it easy for the guys following them. Two guys checking into a room in 2016 would have raised eyebrows. In 1982, the girl that checked them in didn't even bat an eyelash. A sign of the times, Ryan thought. Just for fun, Ryan hooked arms with Sean as they left the front desk and said, "You ready for the night of your life, big boy?" Sean caught on quick and said, "Be gentle, sweety. You know how tender I am." Ryan looked back as they walked out and the girl's mouth was still hanging open. They laughed all the way to the room. It felt good to laugh. Somehow Ryan didn't think they'd be laughing much from that point on.

Chapter 30

After they settled in, they each sat down on their respective beds facing each other. "You ready for this?" Ryan asked.

"I'd be lying if I said I wasn't worried, Ryan. I still don't know how we're going to pull this off. But I'm as ready as I'll ever be, I guess," Sean said with the same trepidation that Ryan was feeling.

"Alright, let's go. Grab the backpack but leave the gun for now. In 2016, they checked bags. I'm assuming they won't do that now, but we can't be sure. If we think we'll need it, we can come back." They walked out and headed across the street.

As they neared the ticket booth, Ryan couldn't believe how different the park was. He looked over where California Adventure is (in 2016) and it was just a big field and some parking areas. They walked up to the ticket booth and got in line. It was mid-afternoon and there was still a line to get in. As they waited, Sean noticed a sign in the window of the ticket booth next to the one they were waiting in.

"Wait here," he said to Ryan as he walked up to the other window. As he read the sign, his mind was reeling with the possibilities. The sign was a job posting. It read:

Immediate Job Openings:

Park Maintenance Workers

Cleaning Crew

Administration Positions

No experience is necessary. Will train. Part-time and full-time.

Apply at Administration Office

It was perfect. If they could actually get a job here, they'd have a much better chance of accessing the Matterhorn. Sean walked back to Ryan and told him what he'd found. They left the line and walked toward the administration building. Neither of them had any idea if they could get a position. They didn't have a Southern California address. They didn't have any documentation except for their driver's licenses. Utah driver's licenses, for that matter. But they agreed that they should give it a shot.

When they got to the administration building, they walked to the counter, where there was one girl sitting at the desk. When she saw them approach, she put on her Mickey ears and a fake smile and said, "How can I make your day a happy one?!" Sean and Ryan looked at each other. "Who do we need to talk to about the maintenance positions?" Sean asked.

"Oooh, I don't think I know the answer to that question. Would you like a map?" Again, Sean and Ryan looked at each other. Obviously, she wasn't the sharpest tool in the shed. She handed them a map and a couple of lanyards.

"No, we don't need a map. We'd like to apply for the maintenance positions that are listed on the sign at the ticket booth," Ryan repeated a little slower but with little hope of a positive response.

"Well, I'm really not sure. My boss is at lunch," she said with her fake smile plastered on. Just then, a lady walked in the front door and walked behind the counter.

"May I help you," she asked. Her name tag read Barbara.

"Yes," Ryan said trying to hide his exasperation. "We'd like to apply for the maintenance positions that are posted."

"Okay. Well, I think we may have filled those positions, but if you could wait for a few minutes, I'll check."

Ryan sat down on a puffy Donald Duck chair and Sean sat down on a puffy Goofy chair. Ryan looked at Sean. He shook his head as if to say 'What the hell are we doing'? Sean got up and walked over to Ryan.

"Dude, if even one of us can get this position, we're in. Just give it a chance."

"Well, I have good news and bad news," Barbara said as she returned. "We do have maintenance worker positions still available but they are only part-time."

"Well, we were hoping for full-time," Ryan said, feigning disappointment. He couldn't care less. "But we're still interested in part-time work."

"Okay, please fill out these applications and I'll see if the maintenance supervisor can see you." She handed them two clipboards.

"Um, one question," Sean asked, "we just moved here and haven't found an apartment yet. We're staying at a local hotel. Will that be a problem?"

"I don't think so. Just list the address of the hotel, and then you can update the application once you find an apartment." Whew, they both thought. That was lucky. In 2016, they'd probably want a complete background check and a pint of blood. They filled out the applications and listed their hotel as their address. They gave the clipboards back to Barbara. She said she couldn't reach the maintenance supervisor, so they'd need to wait.

They sat back down. Ryan leaned over to Sean. "Look, even if we get these jobs, we're going to have to go through training, orientation, and who knows what else. We could be here for weeks!"

"Relax. It's maintenance. I don't think there will be any intensive week-long training. Probably just on-the-job training," Sean said, although he didn't really know.

Maybe Ryan was right. But it was still the best chance they had.

About 20 minutes later, an old black guy came in and approached the two boys. He was about 6'5" and looked a lot like an aged Denzel Washington. "Hello, boys. My name's Clifford. I'm the maintenance supervisor. I understand you want to work for me?"

"That's right. We're both pretty good with our hands and we learn quickly," Ryan said as he shook Clifford's hand. A hand that completely enveloped Ryan's.

He stood looking at them for a few seconds as if he was sizing them up. "Well, it's only part-time, but I can probably give you a few weeks of near full-time. But we're coming up on our slow season, so it will go back to part-time pretty soon. Will that be okay?"

"Sounds great," Sean said and also shook Clifford's meat hook of a hand.

"Follow me. We'll get you set up in payroll and get you a maintenance uniform and name tags."

Sean nudged Ryan and gave him a thumbs-up. They followed Clifford to payroll and went through the whole W-4 process. Then they moved to what Clifford called the maintenance shack. As they walked down Main Street, Ryan got the same feeling that he got when he came here with his family. It truly was a happy place. Kids were all smiles and parents were frustrated. Just like it should be. They went through the castle into Fantasyland. These were some of Ryan's favorite rides when he was a kid. Peter Pan, Mr. Toad's Wild Ride, Dumbo, the Carousel, Snow White. It was amazingly crowded for September, Ryan thought. They headed toward Frontier Land where Big Thunder Railroad was. Before they got there, though, they headed back into the "Employees Only" area. The maintenance shack was basically a big garage with all kinds of tools, machines, manuals, and spare parts. They went into Clifford's office. Clifford Haskill was stenciled on the door.

"Go find yourself a uniform that fits in that closet. Then come back here and we'll get you started," Clifford said as he went to the other side of the garage to talk to a couple of guys playing hacky-sack.

"Dude, we're in," Sean said. "We'll do whatever Clifford wants and then when it gets close to closing time, we'll make our way toward the Matterhorn and sneak in. We wait for a couple of hours until everyone's gone and then go check out the monsters. It's perfect."

"I don't know, man," Ryan said. "It can't be this easy. What about night security? What if we all have to sign out and get escorted out or something? Maybe we should wait and do it tomorrow?" Sean didn't blame Ryan for being nervous. He felt the same way but didn't want to wait.

"I say we go in tonight. But let's play it by ear and see what happens." They put their uniforms on which were essentially a set of coveralls. Clifford came back in. "You guys find everything you need?" he asked.

"I think so. Except for name tags."

"Don't worry about it. I'll get you some later. For now, I need both of you to review this book." He slammed down a huge, tattered three-ring binder. "It's every ride in the park. You don't need to know everything about every ride but you need to know where everything is. I know this isn't too exciting, but it's what every maintenance worker has to do on their first day. Go through each section: Fantasyland, Tomorrowland, and so on. Make sure you know where everything is and how to get there from anywhere in the park. I'll be back in a couple of hours, and we'll tour the separate areas. Take these. You'll need them later. Just set the channel to 6." He handed them two radios and walked out of the garage and out of sight.

Ryan looked at the book. It had a bunch of pages sticking out of it and it didn't look like it was in very good shape. It might fall apart when they opened it. Ryan carefully pulled the book open. It was separated into sections of the park. Ryan immediately turned to Fantasyland where the Matterhorn was located. He found the section on the Matterhorn. It was like a gold mine of information. There were maps, drawings, descriptions, exits, entrances, everything. "This is incredible," he exclaimed. They started to read the description of the Matterhorn.

Chapter 31

The ride opened in 1959. It was conceived by Walt Disney himself while he was in Switzerland making his film "Third Man on the Mountain." It was based on the actual Matterhorn mountain in the Swiss Alps. The attraction opened on June 14, 1959, as one of three new major attractions for Tomorrowland that year. It was the first tubular steel roller coaster in the world. It consisted of a wood and steel infrastructure surrounded by manmade rock. Trees could be seen on its sides; by making the trees at higher altitudes smaller, the designers used forced perspective to augment the mountain's height. Waterfalls cascaded down its sides and frequently misted riders. Inside was a large, open space through which the bobsleds traveled. In the early 1970s, the ride was officially made a part of Fantasyland, but this was merely a prelude to far more significant changes. In 1978, the Matterhorn received a major refurbishment. The designer's biggest task was to break up the interior space into a number of small, icy caves and tunnels with far more convincing theming. They also had actual mountain climbers that scaled the mountain. Another major addition was the Abominable Snowman, a yeti by the name of Harold. Harold exists as three similar Audio-Animatronic figures that roar at the bobsledders; the first is visible from both tracks, while the other two are visible only from their respective tracks. Each track also features a pair of red eyes that glow in the dark shortly after the lift hill while Harold's roar is heard.

"So, there're three monsters we have to check," Sean said to Ryan, who was still reading. The description of the ride went on. One section caught Ryan's eye.

There was a basketball half-court inside the structure above the coaster near the top. This court was really just a break room with a wooden floor where the mountain climbers could play basketball in between climbing sessions. It was not accessible to anyone else, as internal access to the mountain was locked for safety reasons. There is another cast member break room inside the mountain at the base.

"So, there're two break rooms. One at the top that doubles as a basketball court and another one near the bottom," Ryan said as the wheels inside his head started to roll.

"Yea, and did you notice that it states that access to the interior is locked?" Sean pointed out.

"Well, with these coveralls and name tags, that might not be a problem," Ryan reminded him.

Just then Clifford came back to his office. "Let's go, fellas. I know you haven't had a chance to read everything but you can get back to that later. It looks like our little friend, Mr. Toad, has taken a tumble. The ride's shut down and it's up to us to figure out why." They followed Clifford out of the office and headed toward Fantasyland.

When they reached Mr. Toad's Wild Ride, they walked past the "cars" that were lined up outside and into the dark interior. Clifford had a flashlight, but he only needed to use it for a few seconds. Once they were deeper inside, there was enough light from the attraction's lighting that they could easily navigate their way. About 30 feet along the track, Clifford turned sharply and headed for the wall. Amazingly, he pushed softly on the wall and a door swung in. It was cleverly camouflaged. They would never have known it was there. Inside the door was what looked like a break/tool room. There were piles of parts. Pieces of track, replacement lights, parts for the cars, etc. There was a small table in the corner with six chairs around it. Obviously, a place for the workers to take a break. There was a soda and snack machine with its door slightly open. Must be free drinks for the crew. There were also two large tool chests lined up against the wall.

Clifford went to one of the tool chests and grabbed a rather large sledgehammer. "Follow me," he said. They went back out to the main area and walked deeper into the ride. "Most of the time, one of the cars gets stuck and shuts the whole ride down. All we need to do is find out which one and give it a good smack," Clifford said as they hurried to stay up with him. For an old guy, he moved pretty quick.

They spent the next half hour checking each car until they found one that had indeed slid off the track. Its rear wheels were on the track but one of the front wheels had slid off. Ryan suddenly didn't feel very good about the overall safety of these rides. Mr. Toad's Wild Ride was a slow-moving ride that couldn't really hurt anyone. But if this was the way that they fixed rides like Space Mountain and the Matterhorn, he wasn't about to experience those thrills again any time soon.

Clifford had Sean and Ryan lift up on the front of the car and he banged the wheel back in place. "Good as new," Clifford said with satisfaction. They continued to check the rest of the cars but didn't find any more out of whack. They followed Clifford back out of the ride and waited until the girl running the ride gave them the thumbs up that everything was working again.

"Easy as that," Clifford said with a smile. "As long as we're here, we might as well start your tour." They spent the next two hours walking the park and getting familiar with all the different areas. Ryan already knew where all the rides were but he was amazed at how many different 'work areas' were scattered around, cleverly hidden from the public's view. If he hadn't been in the predicament that they were in, it actually would have been a really fun part-time job. They ended up back at Clifford's office, and it was getting dark. "Well, it's just about time to close up shop," Clifford said as he sat down at his desk with a tired groan. "How did you like your first day?"

"It was great," Sean said with a little too much enthusiasm. "I mean, it's hard work but we learned a lot about the park and how things operate."

"I never knew there were so many people that worked here," Ryan said. "You don't really notice it when you're here for fun."

"Well, that's how it's supposed to be," Clifford said as he lit a cigar. Funny, Ryan thought. In 2016, there's no way he would be allowed to smoke in his office.

"So, when is our shift over?" Ryan asked. "Not that I'm a clock watcher. Just curious."

"The maintenance crew usually leaves about a half hour after closing time. I walk the perimeter of the park with the security folks to make sure all the guests have left. Then they close up after the crew is gone," Clifford explained. "I'll need both of you to be here at 8am sharp tomorrow. The park opens at 10 and we have to make sure everything is running smoothly before the guests are allowed in. Any problem with that?"

"Not at all," Sean said. "We're actually staying in a hotel right across the street while we look for an apartment." Ryan glanced at Sean somewhat disapprovingly, but Clifford surprised him.

"Great. So I know where to find you if you're late," he smiled and blew a big smoke ring into the air.

"It's 9 o'clock now. The park closed at 8 so most of the guests should be gone. Why don't you boys walk the perimeter with me tonight?" Clifford asked. Ryan's mind was racing. If they walked with him, he was sure they'd end up at the front gate and would have to leave. But if they refused, it might raise suspicions. Ryan figured they could walk with him, and he'd figure something out.

"Sure. Sounds great," Ryan looked at Sean with a furrowed brow and slightly shrugged his shoulders. He nodded. Ryan could tell his mind was reeling as well.

Chapter 32

They quickly took their coveralls off and grabbed their backpack. Ryan grabbed the two radios and stuffed them in the backpack. As they followed Clifford out of his office, it was completely dark and Ryan and Sean fell back so Clifford couldn't hear them.

"Now, what are we going to do?" Sean whispered. "He's going to end this little perimeter walk at the front gate and we're screwed."

"I think I have a plan. But I don't know if it will work. It depends on how tight the security is. Here, hold this," Ryan whispered back and handed Sean his wallet. They caught up to Clifford and two security guards joined them. They were walking toward Splash Mountain at one end of the park. Seemed like a good place to start. As they passed by Pirates of the Caribbean, Ryan figured now was as good a time as any. "Oh shit," he said as he padded his shorts, pretending to look for something. "Clifford. Sorry, but we're going to have to walk with you tomorrow night. I left my wallet back at the maintenance shack." In his mind, it sounded a lot more convincing than it did when he actually said it. He was completely convinced that they would be walking back to the maintenance building with one of the security guards. But again, Clifford surprised him. "Well, I assume you know the way out?"

"Yea, and again, sorry. We'll be here bright and early at 8am sharp," Ryan said as he and Sean turned and began to walk back the way they had come.

"Don't doddle, gentlemen. One of these guys finds either one of you here after I leave and it's my ass," he said as he walked off with the two security guards.

"Well, that was easy," Sean said.

"Too easy. We'd better hurry and get out of sight," Ryan said as they broke into a run once Clifford was out of sight.

They rounded the corner from Frontierland and ran through Fantasyland. They hadn't yet seen any more security but they were sure there had to be more than two for the whole park. It was weird to see Disneyland at night. With the rides shut down, it was amazingly dark. The castle was softly lit, and there were a few streetlights but other than that, all the other lights were out. They could see where they were going but couldn't see much more than 20 or 30 feet in front of them. As they ran towards the Matterhorn, Ryan glanced down toward the entrance to Tomorrowland and thought he saw three people standing near the bathrooms. He stopped and looked again, but there was nobody there. Ryan stopped Sean. "Hey, did you see that?" he asked.

"See what?"

"I could have sworn I just saw three people down there about 100 yards by the bathrooms. I couldn't make out any faces but I know there was someone there."

"You think our friends hung around?"

"I don't know. I assume they were here today. But let's get inside the mountain before security sees us. If they do, we'll be out of a job and probably be arrested. We'll deal with whoever that was later," Ryan said as they started running again toward the Matterhorn.

As they got close to the mountain, Ryan didn't know the best way to get in. So, they just went through the normal line area and crawled into the mountain where the bobsleds usually enter. Once inside, it was totally black. They couldn't see a thing.

"Well, we're inside. Now what?" Sean asked.

"I'm not sure. At least we're out of sight. The problem is we can't see anything. We should have brought a flashlight," he said as he held his hand out in front of his face.

He could see his hand but not much further. Ryan then realized that a flashlight wouldn't do them much good since it would probably be seen by security from outside the mountain. He knew from going on this ride about a million times that the track led up to the top and then started its descent. "I know we need to go up. The description from the manual said that there are three separate monsters. The first is visible from both tracks and the other two can only be seen from their respective tracks. If I remember right, there's one monster at the top of the tracks. Then the other two are located near the end of each track. But it's been a while. I can't be sure. This could be a long search," Ryan said as they headed up the track, hand over hand feeling their way along.

It was slow going. They found after a few feet that there was a small walkway next to the tracks that made it easier to move up. Near the top of the tracks, it got easier to see. Some of the light from the park and surrounding areas shone through the opening to the mountain at the top of the tracks. With that light, they could see the first monster between the tracks at the top. Sean put the backpack down and reached inside. He had put a small first aid kit in when they left Salt Lake and he thought he remembered some matches being inside. Two matchbooks. One was only half-full. He lit one of the matches and held it close to the base of the monster.

"See anything?" Ryan asked.

"Nothing that looks out of place."

The match burned down to his fingers. "Crap!" Sean threw the match down.

"This isn't giving us enough light. Is there anything in the backpack we can burn?" Sean dug around and pulled out the Disneyland map they'd gotten at the administration building.

"Just this," he said.

"Perfect. Tear off the front page and roll it tight." As Sean did that, Ryan stood up and walked toward the opening, where the tracks began to lead down. He could see Tomorrowland but couldn't see down to the base of the mountain because of the angle.

He walked back to Sean. He had lit the paper and was looking around the monster. "I don't think there's anything here," he said.

"Alright, let's move down these tracks toward the end. I think the other monster on this track is near the bottom."

They started going down when something ricocheted off the wall next to Ryan's head. They both instinctively fell to the ground and hurried back inside.

"What the hell was that?" Sean said.

"Pretty sure it was a bullet. But I didn't hear the shot."

"Where did it come from?"

"I don't know. But I'm not sticking around to find out. Let's move to the other track and go down the other side. Stay away from the openings," Ryan said as they jumped the track and moved to the other side.

What Ryan couldn't figure out was why they were shooting at them now. It would make a lot more sense to wait until they had the clue and then take them out. These guys were obviously not the smartest criminals in 2016 or 1982.

As they felt their way along the track, Ryan lost his footing and fell into the wall. It moved! "Sean, wait. Come here," he said as he pushed on the wall and a door opened. They walked inside and closed the door behind them. They couldn't see much, but there was a dim light glowing on the other side of the room. They moved toward it. They could tell they were walking on a wooden floor since it creaked with about every step. From what they could see, the room was about 30' x 30' and had high ceilings. They reached the light. It was an exit sign. Ryan felt around on the wall and felt a switch. "Here goes nothing," he said and flipped the switch.

Chapter 33

"You idiot," Jerry whispered loudly at Willy. "What the hell are you trying to do?"

"Hey, sorry, but I saw one of them come out. I figured they had the clue," Willy said as Jerry grabbed the gun away and put it in the waist of his own pants. With the silencer, it didn't fit very well.

"You figured! You're a damn idiot, Willy. What if they did have the clue? You gonna climb up there and take it out of his dead hands? Don't figure from now on. You're too stupid to think. Just do what I say and shut up!" Jerry turned to Dirk. "We've got to get off this path. Security could be coming by anytime. Dirk, you and Willy go to the other side and find a way in. Jose and I will take this side. And," he looked at Willy, "no shooting until I say so. Got it?!" Willy scowled but nodded his head. Dirk and Willy hopped on the fence surrounding the mountain and climbed up to the track. Jerry and Jose started to move around to the other side. As they neared the front of the mountain, a security guard rounded the corner in front of them. "Hey, hold it right there. The park is closed. What're you doing in here?" The kid couldn't have been more than 18 or 19. Cocky and indestructible.

"Hey, sorry, man," Jerry said. He'd already come up with an excuse if security stopped them. "I think I left my keys here and I've been looking for 'em. We're stuck unless I find those keys, and my wife is not too happy about it." Jerry put on his best tourist smile as Jose moved slowly around the security guard who was moving up to Jerry. As soon as Jose was behind the guard, he quickly pulled out his knife and stuck it deep into the security guard's back. The teenager's eyes opened wide. He tried to scream. Nothing came out but a small trickle of blood at the corner of his mouth as his lungs filled up. Jose had done this to a number of men, and even one woman, so he knew just where to place the knife that would do the most damage. Jose grabbed him and the two of them tossed his body over the small wrought-iron fence that separated the path from the ride. Jose pulled his knife out and wiped it clean on the guard's shirt. "Stupid kid," Jose said with a slight grin.

"Let's get to the other side before more security shows up," Jerry said as they both walked on as if nothing had happened.

Dirk and Willy had started to walk up the track starting from the end of the ride. Dirk turned to his brother. "Willy, you go around front and walk up the track from the start. I'll keep going up this way. There's no way they can get through this side without one of us seeing them." Willy went back down and followed the track to the starting point. "And Willy," Dirk whispered loudly, "remember what Jerry said. No damage to either one of these kids until we get the clue. Don't screw this up." Willy turned away and said under his breath, "Screw that. Whoever I find is as good as dead," and smiled as he walked to the front of the mountain. Dirk kept walking up the opposite way.

Jerry and Jose also split up. Jose went through the opening at the start and Jerry started walking the track from the end.

There was no way out but through at least one of them.

Chapter 34

A basketball court! It was a damn basketball court. Not much of one. Just one hoop and what looked like about half a court. Ryan's first thought was to turn the light back off but he quickly noticed that there were no openings or windows and only two doors. One they had come through and the other was next to the light switch where they were standing. They started looking around for anything they could use. Both Ryan and Sean had realized they had come very ill-prepared. In one corner was a large red tool chest. Sean opened the drawers. Lots of tools but nothing very useful. In the bottom chest, however, there were three heavy-duty flashlights. They each grabbed one.

"Dude, if we go back out there, they could be just waiting for us," Sean said.

"Yea, but if we don't, they'll eventually find this place and we'll be sitting ducks. I wish we would have brought the gun," Ryan said as he tried to think of what their options were.

"We don't have a choice. We gotta go. Let's go back out the way we came. At least we know where we were." Sean turned off the light. They both checked their flashlights and moved back across the court.

"Wait a minute," Sean said. "What else was in the tool chest? Anything we can use as a weapon? It's not a gun, but it's something." They went back to the tool chest, and each grabbed the biggest crescent wrenches they could find and went back across the court and slowly opened the door to the track.

They listened for a few minutes. No sound. They kept walking slowly along the track. This side of the ride looked out onto Fantasyland. Ryan looked out over the edge and could just make out the Teapot ride below. They kept their flashlights off as there was enough light to navigate. The track started to go down steeply. The footing was uneven and difficult but they found the walkway again next to the track and were able to get down the first hill okay. They went around a bend in the track. Sean heard him before Ryan did. "Shit," he whispered. He pointed down the track. About 20 feet away, a dark figure was coming up the track toward them. Before they could turn and run, a bright light hit them right in the eyes.

"Don't move, gentlemen, or I'll put a 9mm slug right between those baby blues," Jerry said as he walked toward them. Sean and Ryan instinctively put their hands up. The wrench Sean had taken from the tool chest was in his back pocket. Not much use with his hands in the air.

"Well, at last, we meet," Jerry said. It seemed odd, but he was very polite. "I guess I should thank you boys for making this so easy for us. My name's Jerry, by the way. Of course, I know your names already. Obviously, neither of you has ever been in the Marines. See, in the Marines, they teach you how to track and not be tracked. I could have tracked you both with my eyes closed." He was in front of them now. Even with the light, neither of them could see his face very well. He looked like he was about 25 at least in this time frame.

"Sorry to disappoint, Jerr, but we haven't found the second clue yet. So maybe you and your buddies should just go back to your hotel room, and we'll deliver it later tonight with a big bow tied to it," Ryan said with too much sarcasm. The blow came from nowhere and was lightning quick. Ryan fell to his knees. "I give the orders around here, got it you little smartass?!" Jerry screamed. As he turned to kick Ryan, Sean grabbed the crescent wrench out of his back pocket and swung it as hard as he could toward Jerry's head. He couldn't see exactly where he was swinging. Most of the wrench missed but his fist holding the wrench caught Jerry in the side of his neck. The wrench flew from Sean's hand and hit the side of the wall. Jerry fell to his knees. Sean brought his knee up quick and caught him full in the face. His head swung wildly back, and he rolled down the walkway the way he had come. He landed with a thud at the bottom of the hill they were on and lay still.

"Ryan, you okay?" Sean said as he helped him up.

"Yea, what the hell happened?"

"You got your ass kicked, man! But I got him with my wrench. He's down there." Sean pointed down the hill to where Jerry had landed. They walked slowly down toward him. Sean felt his pulse. He was still alive but was out cold. Ryan felt around his waist and found the gun. He pulled it out and for an instant, actually considered finishing him off. He looked at Sean. They both knew Ryan couldn't kill a man in cold blood. He put the gun in the backpack. Sean then put the backpack down and started rummaging through it. "What are you looking for," Ryan asked. "Remember that ditz at the administration building? She gave us those two lanyards. Let's at least tie his hands." They tied his hands behind his back and took off down the track. Both of them knew they'd better get this clue and get the hell out of there. Jerry was going to be pissed when he came to. And he'd have one hell of a headache.

They made their way quickly down the track and came upon the second monster. They both got their flashlights out and started searching around the creature. Nothing at first seemed out of place or out of the ordinary. They had been restricting their search to the base of the monster. Ryan started to look up and down the body. When he got to the head, he had to crane his neck around the creature to see behind. That's when he saw it. A small black box was attached to the back of the creature's head. At first, it looked like it belonged there. Maybe a power pack or hydraulic actuator. Ryan pulled on it and it came off rather easily. "Here, I've got something," he said. He set it on the ground and Sean shined his light on it. It was a metal box, maybe 6 inches square and about 4 inches high. He carefully opened the lid and looked inside. There were two pieces of paper inside. Ryan pulled both out and looked at them. They both looked like they were the same. Another code. Multiple sets of numbers.

"Lay them flat, and I'll take some pictures," Ryan said to Sean as he was already pulling out the camera. They took several shots and put the papers back. Ryan didn't know how the box had been attached to the monster's head, so he just tossed it back behind.

Suddenly they heard some commotion coming from the track above. They put the photos and the gun back in the backpack and stood to leave. Just then, a bullet ricocheted off the wall and into the monster behind them. "Go!" Ryan yelled. They took off down the track. Several more bullets hit the wall behind them as they ran. They jumped off the track near the bottom and ran through some bushes that lined the wrought-iron fence next to the path. They jumped over the fence and ran toward Fantasyland. It was pretty dark here and Ryan had dropped his flashlight when they left the track. As they ran, Ryan could hear Sean behind him. He ran toward the carousel and veered off toward Mr. Toad's Wild Ride. He ran past the cars and into the ride, just as they had done earlier with Clifford. Once he got inside, he turned around, and Sean was gone.

He looked out but didn't see him. "Sean!" he whispered as loud as he dared. "Sean!" Nothing. Just then, someone came into view and looked right at him. He raised his gun and fired. It hit the wall 3 inches from Ryan's face. Ryan turned and ran into the ride. He went for the door to the break room. He was sure someone was following pretty close behind, but he didn't have any choice. He slammed into the wall. The door opened, and he stepped quickly inside. The room was bathed in a soft grey glow coming from a light under the cabinet. Ryan looked around for any type of weapon. The only thing he saw was a short piece of metal, about 2 ½ feet long. It looked like a piece of track. It had been cut with a torch on both ends. He picked it up and crouched behind the tool chest closest to the door.

For a minute, he thought he'd lost his pursuer. But then the door slowly started to open. Ryan saw a flashlight followed closely by a gun come into view. The gun had a silencer like the one that they took off Jerry. From Ryan's vantage point, he was at a 90-degree angle to the door, so he couldn't see who it was or if he was alone. He followed the light from the flashlight as it shone around the room. It settled on a light switch that was just inside the door. Ryan knew that if that light went on, he was a dead man. Most of the guy's arm was inside now and his hand was reaching for the light. It was now or never. Ryan jumped out from behind the tool chest and swung the piece of track down hard on the guy's arm. He could actually hear the arm break. It snapped into an impossible angle and his limp hand dropped the gun and he let out a wail, unlike anything Ryan had ever heard. He took one more step toward him and swung the pipe again. This time at his head. But the guy ducked and the piece of track hit the wall and fell out of Ryan's hands. With his good arm, he reached for his gun. Ryan threw his body into him with as much force as he could generate from the short distance between them. They both hit the wall and fell to the ground. His pursuer landed on top of Ryan and pinned him with his good arm. "You broke my arm, you little shit!" he yelled. His face was contorted with pain. Ryan looked over, and he was cradling his broken arm near his body, so he reached up and grabbed his arm and squeezed right where it was broken. Ryan could actually feel the two broken bones. He screamed, and Ryan thrust his body up and threw him off. He landed on the pile of cut-up tracks. His head landed hard, and he didn't move. Ryan scooted away from him and waited for him to get up. He stayed where he was.

Ryan looked around frantically for some way to tie him up. The only thing he saw was a pile of zip ties lying on top of the tool chest. He grabbed several and put one around each wrist and tied his wrists together. Then, he pulled one of his legs up and put one zip tie around his ankle. Then, he looped several together until they reached his wrists. He was hogtied, for lack of a better term. Satisfied, Ryan grabbed his gun and went back out to Mr. Toad's Wild Ride track.

He stood there for a moment and listened but didn't hear anything. So he slowly walked out to the front of the ride. 'He most likely wasn't alone when he chased after me,' Ryan thought. He crouched behind the nearest buggy. Where the hell was Sean? He walked slowly out toward the carousel. He looked toward the Matterhorn but couldn't see anyone. It was totally deserted. "Sean!" he whispered loudly. "Ryan!" He barely heard coming from the left toward Frontierland. He ran in that direction. A bullet whizzed by his ear and he hit the ground and rolled behind the Dumbo ride. As he looked toward Frontierland, he saw Sean being pushed along by someone. They were at least 200 yards in front of Ryan. He veered around the Dumbo ride and came out close to where they had entered earlier into the maintenance area. He stayed close to the rail that ran along the path from Fantasyland to Frontierland. He couldn't see Sean or whoever was with him anymore.

Ryan started to run toward Pirates of the Caribbean when he heard "Get in there, you little shit!" from down toward Big Thunder Railroad. Ryan went through the exit to Big Thunder, where he could look down into the ride. Sean was on his knees on the path where people wait in line for the railroad ride and the guy that had been pushing him along was pointing a sawed-off shotgun at his head!

Chapter 35

Ryan quietly maneuvered his way down to where he was about 20 feet away from them. He could clearly see both of them from the illumination of a mock street lamp that lined the path. Sean was on his knees. The guy pointing the gun at him was rummaging through the backpack. He took out the gun and put it in his jacket pocket. Then, he pulled out the photos and a sickening grin came across his face. He looked at Sean and said "Well, well. Isn't this nice? Looks like we don't really need you anymore." He stood up and pointed the shotgun at Sean's head. The evil, sickening smile once again appeared on his face, and he said, "Too bad for you!" and put his finger on the trigger. Ryan had 12 rounds in the gun he had taken off the guy in the break room of Mr. Toad's Wild Ride. When he was through firing, the gun jammed open. All twelve rounds had been spent. Ryan hadn't taken a breath while he fired. He gasped for air as he stared at the scene in front of him. Sean's eyes were still closed tight. When he opened them, he saw Willy (he had found out his name by then) dead in a heap in front of him. Ryan rose slowly from where he had shot Willy and walked toward Sean.

As he approached Sean, that little voice inside his head was telling him that his life had just changed irreversibly. He had just killed a man. Dirtbag or not, he had taken a life and he was shaking uncontrollably from the adrenaline coursing through his veins. As Ryan reached Sean, he looked over at the man he had just killed. The man looked back at him with cold, dead eyes, opened wide. The sickening smile had been replaced with a look of sheer disbelief. Ryan stared at his eyes, half-expecting them to blink or give some indication of life. There was none. He was dead, and Ryan had killed him.

Sean got up slowly on unsteady legs. He put his hands on his knees and immediately threw up on the path. Ryan walked over to him and put his hand on his back.

"We need to get moving," he said quietly and started walking back up the path toward the entrance to the ride. Sean wasn't far behind once he'd put everything back in the pack. Once they got to the top of the path, they looked in all directions but didn't see anything. They then started running toward the front of the park, faster than either of them had run in a long, long time. Neither of them said a word the entire way.

Chapter 36

July 2163

Maxwell sat waiting outside Darius' office. He wasn't sure how Darius would take the news of Willy's death or that of the security guard. Maxwell had witnessed it all. He was bound by his handler's 'code' to not interfere in the competition's proceedings as they occurred. He was only allowed to aid his team with vague clues and implications. He had witnessed the action in the Matterhorn but had lost the team briefly until he caught up with them at the Big Thunder Railroad ride in time to see Willy point the gun at Sean's head and then see Ryan empty his gun into Willy. It was obvious that Ryan had fired in order to save Sean's life but he was not sure of the eventual effects to the competition, if anything happens at all.

"Mr. Ramsey will see you now," Darius' secretary said as she held the buzzer for the door. Darius had recently installed a holographic door as the entrance to his office. As his secretary held the buzzer, the door slowly disappeared as Maxwell entered. Once she let go of the buzzer, the door re-materialized and looked like a regular door. Only the best for the leader of the Life Force Institute, Maxwell thought with disdain as he crossed Darius' office. As usual, he hugged the wall in order to not walk directly beneath the huge ship that hung from the ceiling.

"Maxwell, it's good to see you my friend," Darius rose from behind his desk. "I hope you have good news to report."

Maxwell sat down and cleared his throat. "Unfortunately, the news is not good, sir. There have been two deaths and one serious injury." Maxwell paused to gauge Darius' response, but

Darius just sat back down with little outward emotion and calmly asked, "Who and how?"

"Um, one of Tyler's team members. A Willy Bendar was killed by Ryan White. There was a violent confrontation at a theme park in Southern California. All indications are that Mr. Bendar was preparing to execute Sean Jensen and Mr. White intervened and shot Mr. Bendar in an attempt to save his friend's life. The other fatality was a 19-year-old security guard who was stabbed to death. At this time, we are uncertain of who committed the act. Jose Alvarez suffered a fracture to his left arm in a confrontation with Mr. White. The research team is now conducting background checks on the security guard in an attempt to ascertain any historical implications. So far, none have been uncovered." Maxwell sat very still ready for whatever reaction Darius would have.

"Excellent," Darius said quietly with a slight grin.

"Excellent?" Maxwell said with some incredulity. "Excuse me, sir, but I don't think that the murder of a young boy is excellent."

"Yes, yes, of course, the death of the security guard is regrettable." Darius stood up and walked around his massive desk. "Please keep me posted on the historian's progress."

"Yes, of course sir, but..." Maxwell began as Darius held up his hand to stop him.

"The fact that Ryan had the fortitude and bravery to save his friend's life by killing this Bendar fellow is very interesting and encouraging. You see, my friend," Darius sat on the front of his desk, a little too close for Maxwell's comfort, "when we set out on this adventure, we knew the risks. But it is vital that we push our contestants as far as possible in order to better understand their inner strengths...what drives them and makes them take chances. Even chances that might end up in someone losing their life."

Maxwell was stunned, although he kept his emotions well hidden. He had assumed that Darius would end the contest immediately, not due to Willy's death but certainly since the security guard had been killed. A sickening feeling was building deep in Maxwell's gut that something very wrong was going on and he had no way of stopping it.

"Please instruct Tyler to take one of our emergency personnel with him to fuse Mr. Alvarez's arm. We can't have one of our contestants in a 20th-century cast, now can we?" Darius said. "Bring Mr. Bendar's body back to the institute to be disposed of. We will have to let the 20th-century authorities deal with the security guard, of course. And when Tyler returns, have him report to me immediately. That will be all." Darius returned to his seat, sat down, and turned away from Maxwell.

As Maxwell stood up to leave, Darius turned around. "One last thing, old friend. Please don't think for a minute that this contest is over. It's just getting interesting." He laughed and turned back around.

Maxwell hurried as fast as he could out of the office to the nearest restroom and wretched violently into the toilet. As he stood up and looked at himself in the mirror, he had the unmistakable feeling that his life would soon be over. He had just passed his 70th birthday and for the first time in his life, he felt old. Very old and very tired. So, so tired. Holding onto the walls, he made it to one of the stalls, sat down, and wept openly.

He didn't know how long he had sat there, all alone, when a thought came to his mind that seemed to have been with him a long time but just now was coming to the surface. He had worked for Alexander and now Darius for his entire life. Much of that time had been spent trying to isolate physical and psychological data in order to bring to pass Darius' grand plan. He had gone along with the theory behind the plan since it had been originally laid out so honestly and with great passion by Alexander. As he sat in the bathroom stall alone with his thoughts, he began to go over the past 20 years or so since Darius had taken over the institute. Somehow, he had never allowed himself to seriously contemplate what was happening. Possibly out of fear. Or more probably, due to a deep seeded desire to carry on his friend Alexander's work.

What was it that Darius had hoped to accomplish? From a sociological standpoint, the data that Maxwell's team had compiled made sense. But what exactly did Darius intend to do with it? Maxwell realized that the eventual "endpoint" of their work had never been delineated. Darius simply spoke in generalities and with vague references to a better life for all. What had crept to the front of Maxwell's mind was the thought that all his work was somehow meaningless. What amazed Maxwell the most was that he had never stopped to truly contemplate this before now. Assume that somehow he was able to gather all the data necessary? How would Darius implement any significant change? It made no sense. Had Maxwell and his team been so blind that they carried on their work for years without ever seriously considering how the information would be used? The fact that Darius had so carefully compartmentalized everything now started to make sense. It was now becoming clear that most, if not all, of the institute's personnel, had been motivated solely by the 'grand dream' that Darius had spun for so many years. Darius' expertise in concealing his objectives with flamboyance and well-crafted speeches was becoming more and more evident as Maxwell considered recent events.

A new emotion began to build inside Maxwell. Not sadness, fear, or even guilt but pure anger. What was Darius' endgame?

Why did he not cancel the contest? He wiped his eyes and stood up. He didn't feel old anymore. He just felt pissed!

Chapter 37

"Jerry! Jerry, wake up." Dirk had found Jerry still unconscious on the tracks and was cutting the lanyards that held his wrists. "What the hell happened here?"

"Last thing I remember was smacking the taller one. The short little shit must have cold-cocked me with something. My head is still ringing," Jerry said as he held his head in his hands and struggled to get to his feet. "Did you see where they went?"

"No, I was on the other tracks. I think I saw Willy run back down the track and out the front. Maybe he saw one of them after they knocked you out. I have no idea where Jose is."

"All I know is, next time I see either one of those little pukes, I'm putting a bullet through their head. Clues or no clues, I'm done messing around," Jerry said as they stumbled down the track.

"And I suppose you're going to figure out the next clues yourself?" Dirk said somewhat sarcastically.

"Why not? They can't be that hard if those two idiots figured them out."

"All I'm saying is maybe we rough 'em up a little, but we might as well use them while we can," Dirk replied as they exited the Matterhorn. At this point, Dirk was the only one thinking clearly.

"Fine. Let's just find the others. I think we're going to have to use our backup plan."

They started walking toward the carousel when they saw Jose stumbling toward them. He was cradling his left arm.

"What the hell happened to you?" Jerry asked as they got closer.

"That lucky little bastard busted my arm. He also got my gun." Jose groaned as he explained the chase through Mr. Toad's Wild Ride and how he had to use the sharp end of a piece of track to get out of his restraints.

"Maybe these two are more than we thought," Dirk said.

"Bullshit!" Jerry said through gritted teeth. "They're just damn lucky, is all. At least we know they won't be driving anywhere real soon. Where the hell is Willy?" They all looked around and decided to split up when they saw someone walking toward them from the other side of the Matterhorn.

"Willy, that you?" Dirk whispered as loud as he could.

"I'm afraid not, Mr. Bendar," Tyler said as he approached the trio. "We have a few things to discuss. But we must leave the park immediately."

Jerry walked up to Tyler and literally lifted him off his feet. "You've been here the whole time while we got our asses kicked and didn't even help?!" He tossed Tyler like a rag doll, and he landed hard on his back.

"Please, Mr. Stillwell! I told you in the beginning that I cannot help you, only guide you and give you instructions. The completion of your tasks must be accomplished by you and your team without any outside assistance," Tyler said as he got up and dusted himself off. "I would remind you that harming me will only result in your immediate disqualification and prompt return to incarceration."

Tyler looked directly at Dirk. "I'm afraid I have bad news about your brother, Mr. Bendar. Apparently, he took one of the members of the other team hostage across the park and was about to execute him when his partner intervened and shot your brother. I'm sorry to tell you that he is dead."

Dirk didn't say anything right away. He just stared at Tyler as if he hadn't heard him clearly. "Willy's dead?" he said finally. Not with a great amount of emotion. Just bewilderment.

"That idiot!" Jerry said, somewhat under his breath.

"I'm afraid so. And the security guards were on their way toward where his body was located and will certainly be alerting the authorities. They will also, I'm sure, find the body of the security guard that Mr. Alvarez dispatched earlier. I'm sorry, but we must leave immediately."

"Wait," Jerry said. "Willy is dead? Are you sure?"

"Quite sure, Mr. Stillwell. We will take the appropriate measures to care for his body and personal effects, but we must leave now or we will most assuredly be detained which will greatly hinder your chances for success. We can also take care of Mr. Alvarez's arm. But not here. Now, please!" Tyler began to walk away from the three of them when Dirk grabbed Tyler from behind, cocked his gun, and put it up against his temple. "Just tell me one thing," he said in what could only be characterized as a low growl, "what the hell were you doing while my brother was getting blown away?" Dirk knew his brother was evil and an altogether loser, but he was still his brother. Dirk was no longer thinking clearly.

Tyler stood perfectly still. For the first time, he was truly frightened for his life. "I assure you, Mr. Bendar, there was absolutely nothing I could have done. I was nowhere near your brother and the other two when it happened. I am very sorry for your loss. I truly am."

"Let him go," Jerry said from behind. "We have no chance without this little piece of shit showing us the way. Let's get the hell out of here."

The four of them began running and hobbling in Jose's case, toward the exit of the park.

Chapter 38

"Whoso sheddeth man's blood, by man shall his blood be shed."
– Genesis 9:6

As Sean and Ryan ran through the exit, Ryan's mind was racing so fast, he felt as if his head was literally going to explode. He was struggling to remain in control but was not succeeding. He knew they couldn't stay at the hotel they were at, but he also knew they had to go back and get their suitcases. Sean had pulled ahead of him but stopped abruptly as they cleared the exit from the park.

"Holy shit, Ryan! What the hell are we going to do?"

"I don't know. Just keep running toward the hotel. They might be watching but I doubt it. We've got to get our stuff and get to a different location right now!" Ryan said breathlessly as they continued running. Their hotel was directly across Harbor Boulevard, which ran right next to the park. They got to the street. By now, all the buses had left and most of the people were gone. There were a few stragglers at the local restaurants and wandering outside. Sean looked back but didn't see anyone behind them. As the light turned green and they turned to go, Ryan looked back and thought he saw some movement but couldn't be sure. The lighting was such that it was difficult to see all the way back to the park exit.

They got back to the room that they had put their suitcases in and immediately threw all their stuff together and went back out toward the parking lot. They bypassed the main lobby and went out a side door at the bottom of the stairs. They didn't check out. They figured the hotel would charge whatever they needed to their cards. There were a lot of things running through Ryan's mind, but he knew he had to get somewhere safe before they could rationally go through it all. They ran around the corner to where they had left the rental car. As they approached, Ryan got a sinking feeling in his stomach.

The car was tilted at an odd angle, and when they got close, it was obvious why. Three of the tires had been slashed! Either those dirtbags planned ahead, or they were already here watching them. Both thought the same thing and instinctively crouched down and started looking around. Sean reached into the backpack and took out the 9mm. Ryan still had the gun he'd taken off the guy in Mr. Toad's Wild Ride but he didn't have any ammunition.

"Forget the car. Let's just get the hell out of here," Sean said as they both grabbed a suitcase and Ryan put the backpack on. They started to run toward the street when Sean grabbed Ryan's arm. "Not that way. I think I saw a way out through the back." In the back of the hotel, there was a large group of palm trees. Through the palm trees was the Santa Ana freeway. As they made their way through the grove of trees, they realized that there was a frontage road that ran along the freeway. They took off down the street.

"Well, where now? You've been here before, right?" Sean said as they stopped to catch their breath.

"Yea, in 2016. It all looks different," Ryan said as he put his hands on his knees, breathing hard. "If nothing has changed that much, there are a lot of hotels south of here. Let's just keep going."

They picked up their suitcases and walked briskly south toward what they hoped was a quiet hotel room where they could collect their thoughts.

Ryan was constantly looking back but never saw anyone following them. They made their way to Katella Avenue where the frontage road ended. They either had to go left or right.

"Well, which way now?" Sean asked. He dropped his suitcase and stared back the way they came. There was nobody for as far as he could see.

"We're only a couple blocks from the park, but we need to get off the street," Ryan said as he looked around for a hotel. There were several hotels that looked pretty run down but were relatively full judging from the number of cars in the various parking lots. "Let's just check into one of these and get out of sight."

They walked into the lobby of the closest hotel, The Castle Manor of Anaheim. The outside of the hotel was deceiving. It looked like a rundown motel where you could rent rooms by the hour. Inside, it was remarkably clean and well-furnished. Ryan sat down in one of the lobby chairs that couldn't be seen from the outside. He put his head in his hands.

"Hey, I'm the one that almost got shot," Sean's attempt at humor went unnoticed. "I'll get us a room," he said as he crossed the lobby to the front desk.

"Excuse me, do you have any rooms available?"

"One bed or two?" The lady working the front desk had to be over 100 years old, Sean thought.

"Two, please. And could we please have two rooms? We're expecting some friends later tonight," Sean said as he looked back at his friend. Ryan was sitting up but had a blank stare that was making Sean a little worried.

"How many nights?"

"Well, I'm not sure. I think we'll be here all week." Sean managed a smile.

Without looking up, the ancient clerk handed Sean a key. "Welcome to the Castle Manor. Your suites are 113 and 114.

There are two doors to your abode. One from the Queen's garden and one from the outside world. You may park your chariot in the designated stable. There are no beasts allowed in our castle. Please enjoy your stay."

After her rehearsed spiel, she slowly returned to her chair and her crossword puzzle.

"Let's go, dude," Sean motioned to Ryan, who stood slowly and picked up his suitcase. They walked to the "Queen's Garden," which was essentially a bunch of fake flowers and trees in the middle of the hotel. The rooms were arranged around the garden. There were probably 50 rooms with a second floor having the same number of rooms above.

Sean opened the door to "suite" 113. They both went inside and each sat down on a bed opposite each other. Ryan looked at Sean with tears in his eyes. "Sean, I killed him." Sean slowly began to realize that Ryan was probably in some sort of shock. Even though it had been Sean that had almost been killed, it was Ryan that was actually more traumatized since he killed Willy.

"You saved my life, Ryan. If you hadn't killed that psycho, he was going to kill me." Now Sean started to tear up when the realization finally sank in that, by all rights, he shouldn't be alive right now. "Holy shit! This is out of control," Sean said as he got up and headed to the bathroom. Before he got there, someone knocked on their outside door.

Chapter 39

July 2163

Maxwell sat quietly in his darkened office. His window gave him a perfect view of the helipad where Darius always met his pilot for his flight home. The helicopter's blades had been spinning for at least 10 minutes. That meant that Darius would soon be leaving. The institute had received approval from the government for the luxury of a helicopter due to their need for "environmental observations." As far as Maxwell knew, the only use of the helicopter had been to shuttle their precious leader to and from his house 50 miles away. A little before 10:00 pm, he watched as Darius exited the building and boarded the helicopter. Seconds later, it pulled away and flew out of sight.

The night staff at the institute was a skeleton crew. Mainly technicians in the travel division monitor events as well as campus security. Maxwell left his office and made his way toward Darius' wing. Ironically, with all the security set up in and around the travel section and outer buildings, there was actually very little security elsewhere. Darius once told him that if anyone was able to breach their firewalls and physical security around the institute, there wasn't much that could be done to stop them once inside. It had never occurred, so additional security had never been installed inside. Maxwell had often thought that maybe Darius just didn't want anyone spying on him in his office through surveillance cameras.

The hallway leading to Darius' office was dark. Only soft light from an occasional emergency light led the way. Maxwell approached Darius' secretary's desk. He had watched her open his door countless times. She simply pushed a small illuminated button on her desk. Previously the door had opened. More recently, the holographic door disappeared and allowed entrance. However, that button was not illuminated now. He pushed it anyway. Nothing happened. There had to be a way to turn it on. He felt around and under her desk. He couldn't find any switch or power source. It was then that he realized his stupidity. The door was holographic! There was no door. He came around from the desk and approached Darius' door. It looked like an ordinary door, even up close. Amazing technology, he thought to himself. He reached out his hand and slowly pushed it through the door. No resistance, just a small ripple in the field immediately around his hand. He pulled his hand back and walked slowly but deliberately into Darius' office.

Chapter 40

Maxwell stood still for a moment, half expecting an alarm or siren to start blaring. Nothing but silence. It was considerably darker inside Darius' office, so it took Maxwell's eyes a few moments to adjust. He looked up and saw the giant ship above his head. In its darkened state, the office seemed even larger than in daylight, if that was possible. Each step he took seemed to echo throughout the great room. He had always noticed them but now took a longer look at the huge monitors that encircled the room. Why so many, he thought? He slowly crossed to Darius' desk. He was certain nobody had ever been inside this office without Darius present. He had even stipulated that the cleaning crew be accompanied by his secretary at all times. Maxwell felt a slightly guilty sense of power as he sat down in Darius' $10,000 chair. Not especially comfortable, thought Maxwell with a slight grin. As his eyes had completely adjusted to the dark, he could now see things quite clearly. Much to his dismay, there were no drawers visible anywhere on the desk. Just lavish, very expensive hardwood. He was about to get up to explore the rest of the office when his knee grazed the desk. A drawer suddenly opened. It seemed to appear out of nowhere. There were no visible seams, at least in this light. He touched higher up and another drawer opened. He didn't dare turn on any overhead lights, but he couldn't see much without some additional illumination. He pulled out a small flashlight from his pocket. It wasn't much but it would have to do. He began going through each drawer one by one. He had no idea what he was looking for but figured he'd know it when he found it. Most of what was in the drawers was meaningless paperwork. Reports from various divisions, pointless data, and photographs from environmental observation flyovers (apparently, they had actually occurred). As Maxwell searched the bottom drawer on the left side of the desk, he came across a file folder marked "My Turn." He took it out and set it on top of the desk. As each page was turned, his stomach tightened and his anger grew. He went through the folder twice, committing as much as he could to memory. He hadn't thought to bring the duplication device from his office. As he considered returning to retrieve it, he saw a light bouncing off the walls of the hallway outside the office. He hadn't noticed until now but apparently, when he entered, the holographic door had not reappeared. Someone was coming down the hall. He hurriedly put the folder back where he found it. He cursed himself as he realized he hadn't returned all the papers to their original order. He looked around but there was no place to hide in the sparsely furnished office. He had no choice. He pushed the chair back into the desk and crouched behind it. It was a large chair, but if whoever was approaching came anywhere near the desk, he would be in plain sight.

Suddenly, the overhead lighting in the office came on. It was so bright that Maxwell had to close his eyes and then open them slowly to adjust. He felt as if his breathing was octaves louder than it actually was. He breathed shallowly and waited. He heard footsteps sound as someone crossed the room. He crouched lower until he was almost lying on the floor. He didn't dare look up. The footsteps continued, then suddenly stopped just short of the desk.

"Director's office clear. But get a technician up here to check that damn door. It appears it's malfunctioning again. The holographic image won't reanimate. For now, I'm going to alarm it. Stupid fake door..."

"Understood. Check section 17. We got a motion alert. Probably another rat or that flea-covered cat. If you find it, screw protocol and kill it!"

The footsteps retreated and the light went out. Maxwell stayed where he was until he was sure the guard was gone. He slowly rose from behind the chair and stared out across the office. He could see a small box with a green light affixed to the wall to the right of the door. There was no other way out of the office. He was trapped.

He hurried across to the door and closely inspected the alarm. It was essentially a scatter laser that covered the door from top to bottom. Anything that penetrated the door would interrupt the laser and trip the alarm. The box had a digital keypad and an iris scanner. Maxwell was certain that even with his high-security clearance, his iris was not included in the list of personnel authorized to clear the laser alarm. Plus, he didn't have the code. He started to list in his mind his options. It was a very short list. Essentially only one choice. Make a run for it! He figured the guard had to be close to section 17 by now which was at least 2-3 minutes away. If he ran, he could be back to his office in less than a minute. The only glitch was if the alarm would trip locally or if it was wired to trip the entire facility. Maxwell knew he had no choice. He waited a few more seconds, took a deep breath, and bolted through the opening.

Immediately a high pitch alarm sounded, nearly making Maxwell trip. But he continued running down the hallway. No other lights or sirens came on, indicating that the alarm had only tripped locally. As he turned the corner from the long hallway leading away from the office, he turned to see the lights in the lobby to Darius' office come on and he could hear voices as they crossed towards the office.

Maxwell slowed down and walked the rest of the way to his own office. He went in and sat down, breathing hard. His heart was racing not only from the run but also from the information he had obtained in the file. He cursed himself again for not arranging the file back to its original form. Darius was extremely detail oriented. He would likely know someone had been in the file. Maxwell pushed it out of his mind. There was nothing he could do about that now. Right now, he had only one thing he needed to do. He had to get to Sean and Ryan.

Chapter 41

Sean still had the 9mm in his waistband. He pulled it out and crouched down near the door. Ryan immediately jumped up and hugged the wall next to the door. Neither one said anything or even made a sound. Sean slowly checked the gun. There was already a round in the chamber. An old episode of Magnum PI suddenly jumped into Sean's mind. He pushed it aside and listened. For a minute, both of them thought they may have heard a knock on the door next to theirs when they heard a voice outside.

"Master White? Master Jensen?"

"It's Maxwell," Ryan whispered.

"How did he find us?" Sean asked.

"How the hell should I know?" Ryan slowly crept toward the door and looked out through the peephole. He could see Maxwell. From his fish-eye view, it looked like it was just him.

"Are you alone?" Sean asked, not too loudly.

"Yes. Please let me in. We have much to discuss and I feel quite exposed out here," Maxwell replied.

Ryan opened the door slowly and looked out. Maxwell was indeed alone. He opened the door the rest of the way and Maxwell came quickly inside.

"How did you know where we were?" Ryan asked as Maxwell sat down on one of the beds.

"It wasn't difficult. We know where you are at all times. You're both wearing tracking devices."

Ryan started to feel around his shirt and down his pants.

"Don't bother looking for it. It's not part of your clothing, it's on your skin," Maxwell said with some apprehension. "It's part of the contest protocols. It allows us to monitor your location for a variety of reasons. It can't be washed off. It eventually will wear off over several weeks. It's actually in place to protect you as well as for surveillance."

"I'm not surprised. But I'm too tired to be mad," Ryan said as he laid down on the other bed and put his arm over his eyes to shade the light.

"So I assume you're aware of what happened tonight?" Sean asked still holding the Glock.

"Unfortunately, yes, Master Jensen. I'm sure it was a horrific incident for you both." Maxwell looked quizzically at the gun Sean was holding. Sean looked at the gun and set it on the table, as if he hadn't even realized he was still holding it. He leaned against the wall and slid slowly down until he was sitting on the floor.

Nobody spoke for what seemed like hours but it was actually only a couple of minutes. It seemed as if the prospect of reviewing the details of the night's events would be physically and mentally overwhelming. Neither Ryan nor Sean wanted to relive it. Finally, Ryan spoke. His eyes were still closed as he lay on the bed.

"So, Max. Great contest you guys put together. Turned us into fugitives and me into a killer. Everything going as planned?"

"I assure you, Master White. I had no idea things would get this out of control. I've tried to have the contest called off. In fact, that's what I'm here to talk to you both about," Maxwell got up from the bed and sat down at the table.

"What, we just go back to 2016 like nothing ever happened? I killed a man, you son of a bitch! And I blame you for that!" Ryan still didn't get up off the bed but his eyes were open and staring straight at Maxwell. Maxwell didn't say anything but did hang his head. It was the first true sign of emotion they had seen out of the man. It seemed to stop Ryan in his tracks as he was ready to let go with another barrage of criticism. Sean looked up at Maxwell, then looked at Ryan. They couldn't be sure but it sounded like Maxwell was crying.

Maxwell wiped his eyes and took a deep breath. "It doesn't please me to let you men see me this way. I seem to have lost my cold exterior," he chuckled through sobs. "I understand your anger, Master White. And I do feel that I should bear some of the responsibility. But not all, as you will certainly understand in a minute. It's even worse than you know, gentlemen. First of all, another man was killed tonight. And not in self-defense but in cold blood. An innocent young security guard was killed by one of your opponents. It was quite brutal and horrifying."

"Why?" Sean asked.

"As far as we know, there was no good reason. We were able to capture it on video. He was questioning two of the other team members near the Matterhorn ride and, for no apparent reason, one of them stabbed the young man from behind. They then just tossed him over the railing as if he were a piece of refuse."

"And that wasn't enough to call this whole thing off?" Ryan asked.

"No, I'm afraid not. It would appear that things have spun quite out of control."

"You said that was the first thing we didn't know. What's the second?" Sean asked as he got back on his feet and sat down on the bed recently vacated by Maxwell.

Maxwell looked at them both as if sizing them up for what he had to say next.

'The second thing, Master Jensen, is quite a bit more disturbing and quite difficult to explain. But I will do my best," Maxwell got up from the table and paced a few times before starting. Ryan and Sean just looked at each other, puzzled.

"To begin, I need to explain a little bit more about the contest protocols. First, in order to keep tight surveillance on all our subjects, we tag them with a locating spray. That you already know about. But second, we have set up a very elaborate system of closed-loop digital recording systems. Video cameras, I believe they were often referred to as camcorders, would be the closest thing to what you understand. These "cameras" have been placed in every conceivable location throughout the contest geography. On the mountain and in the canyon for the first clue, at the golf course, in and around your homes, your school, in your vehicles, on the plane, in your first hotel room, many in the amusement park, and even several on the streets in and around the park. It's very likely that we will have you entering this hotel on video. The only thing I can say for sure is that there are none in this particular hotel room."

"Wait a minute," Ryan interrupted. "How could you possibly place that many cameras without being seen?"

"My employer, the ultimate architect of this contest, has endless resources, Master White. With the time travel device, it would be quite simple to place cameras without being seen."

"If these cameras were in our cars and in our houses, how is it we didn't see them? What, are they invisible?"

"Quite," Maxwell said matter of factly.

"Bullshit," Sean said somewhat under his breath.

"No, quite real, Master Jensen. We also possess technology that, while not completely, will quite effectively camouflage a person wearing it or a camera with it installed, in this case. We call it the Visual Concealment Device or VCD for short. I believe your government will have something close to it around 2025. It's quite incredible. It's not widely used in my time since there is really no need. Except for the military, that is. Even that application is becoming increasingly rare. I'm not intimately familiar with the physics of the devices but I do know they use light bending and holographic imaging to achieve the lower visibility."

"So how do you know there are no cameras in this hotel room?" Ryan asked as he looked around the room.

"With this." Maxwell took a small handheld object that looked like a small cell phone out of his pocket. "This tracks all video placement and can detect as well as make visible any camera that has been placed. Or any person utilizing the VCD. Of course we have another acronym for it. It is called the Holographic Detection Unit." He flipped a switch and a high-frequency sound emitted as he waved it across the room.

"If there were any cameras present, they would immediately lose their holographic concealment and become visible. It's quite useful."

"Okay, so we're being videotaped everywhere we go. I can't say I'm surprised," Ryan said.

"Well, not everywhere. Of course, we can't know every step you will take. But it's quite comprehensive. As I said before, much of this was put in place to protect you as well as surveil you. But I digress," Maxwell walked back over to the table and sat down.

"So who is this employer of yours?" Sean asked.

Maxwell looked somewhat forlornly at Sean. "Believe me, I'll get to that, Master Jensen." He took a deep breath and started again. "This contest you two are competing in was originally conceived by a man by the name of Alexander Ramsey. This was many years ago and, of course, when he first came up with the idea, it was only fantasy and very theoretical. You see, gentlemen, the world is a very different place in my time. The people have lost their drive, their desire for success. I won't bore you with the details at this point. But suffice it to say that Alexander wanted to change things. To bring back the human spirit that so many had lost. His goal was to re-engineer the human race. To bring back the greatness that this world once had to offer. It was a grand quest but sadly, he was cut down in his prime, and his ideals and dreams died with him," Maxwell paused for a moment as if recalling a fond memory.

"Which brings me to Darius. Darius Ramsey is my current employer and is Alexander's son. For many years, it was apparent that Darius was attempting to complete his father's mission. But for the past several years, I have seen a different side of Darius emerge. He had lost his father's ideals and I question whether he ever truly understood his father's true mission. Alexander's goal of improving the human race has now become a quest for power and control. You were right, Master White when you assumed a few days ago that we have done this before. We have. With quite moral and ethical intentions, but quite different results."

"Exactly what type of results are you looking for?" Sean appropriately asked.

"As I stated, Master Jensen, we have been trying to find those qualities and capabilities that the human race was sorely lacking. A monumental feat, I grant you, but nonetheless, that was our intention."

"So, we're basically guinea pigs in a giant experiment?" Ryan asked.

Maxwell smiled. "I suppose you are correct, in a way, Master White. But I need to explain further for you to completely understand."

Ryan rolled his eyes. "Go ahead."

"Ever since I started this work with Alexander many years ago, I have been intimately involved with these contests and gathering the data. It started out with people selected from our own time. You see, back then, there wasn't a time travel device. We could only work with subjects from our own "world," for lack of a better term. The results were most often inconclusive and did not glean any useful information. The problem was obvious. The people we were recruiting were already afflicted with the symptoms we were trying to correct. It was useless. Until Darius and his engineers perfected the time travel device and made it safe to utilize. Or at least we thought it was safe. There was one contest that ended quite tragically. All the subjects had been killed during the time travel process. For obvious reasons, we could not explain their deaths to their families. So, as far as they knew, their loved ones simply disappeared. It was quite horrible," Maxwell hung his head again but stayed in control.

"In fact," Maxwell continued, "the two of you didn't actually travel back in time." This got both Sean's and Ryan's attention.

"Excuse me?" Ryan asked. "What exactly do you mean by that?" Maxwell took a minute to explain how the consciousness transfer had been used in lieu of actual time travel. His explanation didn't go as smoothly as he had hoped and Maxwell realized it would have been better to wait until later to explain the whole consciousness transfer vs. time travel argument.

He continued. "Ok, more about that later. After the time travel "accident," the contests were halted. I thought permanently, but then recently, Darius suddenly wanted to restart the program. That's where you two gentlemen entered the picture. But after tonight's unfortunate events and Darius' refusal to stop this contest, I began to see the "big picture," as they used to say in your country. I began to realize that the data we were collecting was not relevant to Alexander's original plan, or any plan for that matter. Of course, we can learn about human ingenuity, bravery, loyalty, and other qualities. But, realistically, what would we do with the information? I must admit, gentlemen, that I am shocked at my inability to have seen this before now. Most of our models are built on theoretical factors. The process of putting actual subjects through specific tests does not necessarily improve those models."

"Max, you're losing me," Ryan sighed. "Here we are in 1982 but you say we didn't actually travel back in time. Only our minds did. Now you're going on about theoretical data and human engineering."

"Forgive me. Suffice it to say that I believed that there were other factors at play here and earlier this evening, I found the proof I needed."

"What factors?" Sean asked.

Maxwell took a moment to gather his thoughts. "I believe Darius is simply using you two and the others as part of some sort of...I'm not sure what...a game, perhaps?"

"A game??" Ryan asked in disbelief.

Maxwell looked at them both. "It would appear so. Earlier this evening, I waited until Darius had left and snuck into his office. I was about to leave when I came across a file that was labeled "My Turn." Inside, there were several photos of you two and the other team, along with pages and pages of transcripts from your journey thus far. I didn't consider this out of the ordinary until I came across a page that had several names listed. Under each name was a ten-digit code and under the code was a line that simply said "Winner: Team A, Team B." And one or the other had been circled. I wasn't familiar with all the names but I recognized a few of them. They are extremely wealthy acquaintances of Darius'. I counted nine in all. The next page had a title at the top that read 'Proposed Payouts.' Each winner was to receive six million dollars and 15 points. I have no idea what the points mean. I wasn't able to read anymore since a security guard came to check on the office." Maxwell then retold the story of his near capture and escape.

When he was through, all three sat quietly for a few moments. Finally, Sean broke the silence. "So, who are we, Team A or Team B?"

"I honestly don't know, Master Jensen. But seven out of the nine picked Team B." "Great. I can guess who Team A is," Ryan said. "So, what you're saying is that we're just a couple of gladiators fighting the lions waiting for a thumbs up or thumbs down vote at the end?"

"Quite a colorful and historically correct analogy. Actually, I'm not sure how this will end, Master White. But I am sure of one thing. I'm not going to sit this one out. I am here, gentlemen, to help you. I'm not just your guide any more."

Chapter 42

"Please hold still, Mr. Alvarez. This will only take a moment," Tyler pleaded as the technician moved the stabilizer over Jose's arm.

"It feels like he's breaking my other goddamn bone," Jose yelled through gritted teeth.

"The pain is only temporary. The bone is actually re-fusing. It's better than wearing a cast for six weeks," the technician said rather coldly. "Now, hold still."

Jose started to breathe more regularly and he was noticeably relaxing. "It's actually starting to feel a little better," he sighed.

Jerry, Dirk, Jose, and Tyler had exited the park only minutes after Ryan and Sean. But they hadn't been watching and had no idea where they went. The four of them ended up back at their hotel, which was right next door to the hotel where Ryan and Sean had stayed. Dirk motioned to Jerry to join him outside the room.

"So what do we do now?" Dirk asked as they stood in the hallway. "We don't have the clue and we have no idea where those little pricks went. I don't want to use our backup plan unless we have to. If the cops get involved, things could get complicated."

"Too late," Jerry said in a whisper. "I made the call earlier today. We've got all the leverage we need now."

"You son of a bitch! We agreed we'd decide together!" Dirk replied in as loud a voice as he dared.

"We don't have a choice at this point. I don't give a shit about some punk from 30 years ago. I just want to end this thing, get my money and get back to where we belong," Jerry turned and went back inside the hotel room.

Dirk stayed out in the hall a moment longer. He was still pissed about Willy but he also knew that Jerry wasn't thinking clearly anymore. The road they were now on wasn't just risky but stupid in his mind. It could backfire in a big way. But he also agreed that they didn't have much of a choice.

Chapter 43

Darius sat in his Jacuzzi, sipping a scotch and water (very little water). Something had been bothering him for some time now but he couldn't figure out what. The three girls he had "ordered" on the flight home were giggling and splashing each other in the enormous pool that sat next to the Jacuzzi. One of them got out and slipped in next to Darius.

"Come on, sweetie, why don't you come in the pool and play?" she asked as she slid her hand under the water onto Darius' leg.

Darius slowly moved his gaze to the strikingly beautiful, naked young girl. "Get out," he said flatly.

"What?"

"Get out! Take your whore friends and get the hell out of my house."

"But you paid for the whole night. Where are we supposed to go?"

"I don't really care. Get out before I throw your asses out!"

The other two girls had already gotten out of the pool and were hurriedly putting their clothes back on. The girl in the Jacuzzi stormed out and, without dressing, walked up to the nearest servant standing guard and demanded a ride home. He looked at Darius who waved his hand. The guard left with the girls leaving Darius alone.

Darius sat thinking about the call he had received just before he and the girls had come into the spa. It was from the night security team at the institute. He was automatically alerted when any security breach was monitored. The agent on the phone had assured Darius that it was another innocent false alarm from a rodent or small animal that had gotten in from the surrounding forest. Even though they couldn't rationally explain why the temporary laser field across his door had been breached. But something gnawed at Darius. For some reason, he didn't believe it was so innocent. The more he thought about it, however, the further it slipped away.

It wasn't just the security breach, Darius realized. The contest was going very well. Actually, with the recent events, things were going extremely well. Better than he could hope for. What was concerning him was how the contest would play out. He had chosen Sean and Ryan for a reason. They had saved Taz on that cold night so many decades before. The story was legendary. Although he was sure it had become embellished over the years, he had no reason to think it was anything but completely truthful. So, what was bothering him?

He began to think about the time travel paradox. A nasty little theorem that had never been completely proven and always seemed to succeed in giving him a headache. As he sat soaking in the hot mineral water, he thought back to how the paradox was originally described to him by his father, Alexander. Suppose a person travels to a time before he was born and does something that breaks a causal chain that led to his birth. For example, what if you killed your own mother before she first conceived? The apparent paradox is quite obvious. If you kill your mother then you would not be born, which in turn would bring it about that you did not travel into the past, thus you would not kill your mother, thus you would be born causing you to again travel into the past to kill your mother and on and on. It was one of the moral questions that prompted the complete moratorium on time travel. Many scientists believed in the paradox, as confusing as it was. However, there were a number of theoretical physicists that felt that there would not be any change in the eventual effect. The change in the past would simply result in a different "chain of events" or "reality branch" that would cause another reality to emerge. In essence, there would be an infinite number of parallel realities. This "branching effect" had been proven through short-term experimentation, at least to Darius' satisfaction, by the Institute engineers. Thus a fundamental problem existed. How could someone be sent back in time and guarantee that they would return to their own reality, whether they made a causal change or not? It was a mind-numbing conundrum and one that had taken nearly a decade to figure out. Finally, a combination of software and hardware had been developed that would accurately track a traveler's initial point of departure and ensure that they would return to that original point whether they had made any significant change in the past or not. Darius had always felt that just the transportation of a traveler back in time would be sufficient to alter the reality of that time. Thus the concept of an infinite number of alternate realities had somewhat of a calming effect on those that had a moral problem with the notion of time travel. For any change that occurred, a new reality existed for everyone who existed at the point where the change was made. That new reality might be better for them or it might be worse. But the fact remained that Darius' world would go on unaltered forever.

Of course, this proven fact had remained a carefully guarded secret. As far as the general scientific world knew, the paradox still existed with no generally accepted explanation or way around it. It was this secret, along with the necessary technology, that was being so coveted by Darius' "partners" in the contest. Even though Darius had been purposely vague about the prize they were all playing for, they all knew it would be something worth more than money or jewels or drugs. Even the rare ownership rights of real estate would not compare with the power that Darius had "dangled" in front of his cohorts.

"Excuse me, sir?" Darius bolted upright in the tub. He had actually fallen asleep, a very rare occurrence.

"What is it!?" he replied as he gathered his senses.

"It's quite late, sir. I thought you would prefer to retire to your suite," the servant gave a slight nod to the large holographic clock floating on top of the pool. It was 3:00am. Darius had been asleep for over four hours!

"Yes, quite. Thank you, Jeffrey." Darius pulled himself slowly out of the tub. The water seemed to have drained the energy out of his body. It was difficult to stand for a few moments. To say he was "pruned" would be an understatement.

"Are you alright, sir?" Jeffrey asked with genuine concern. However Darius behaved in other aspects of his life, he took very good care of his household servants. He had never known what it was like to not be waited on, hand and foot. But somewhere along the path of his quite sordid life, he had gained an understanding of how important these people were to his existence.

"Yes, I'll be fine. Please fetch my robe if you would be so kind, Jeffrey."

"Right away, sir."

As Darius stood naked with steam rising from his body, the nagging uneasy feeling was only getting stronger.

Chapter 44

"Wait a minute," Sean interrupted. "Ryan, I just thought of something." Ryan had never seen a more fearful look on Sean's face. "If nobody intervened to save that security guard tonight, that means everybody's fair game, right? What about our families? Those bastards could be sending someone over there right now! We've got to warn them!"

"But our families don't even know where we are," Ryan said.

"They don't know that!" Sean exclaimed.

Ryan looked at Maxwell. "I'm afraid Master Jensen is correct. There is no active protocol to protect anyone involved. In fact, we are forbidden from interfering even if an innocent bystander is threatened, much like tonight."

Ryan sat quietly for a moment, then finally spoke. "So, what do we tell them? That they have to leave? Check into a hotel? All of them?"

"I don't know," Sean said. "We should at least tell them what's going on."

"Uh, I'm not calling my mom and telling her I just shot someone, Sean. She'd freak out more than I am."

"Well, okay, not everything. Let's just let them know that things have taken a bit of a downturn and we need them to...what...?"

"Let's just tell them to stay together for the next few days. Nobody goes out alone," Ryan said as he stood and walked toward the phone.

"You're sure they don't know where we are, Max?" Ryan asked as he passed him.

"Not at all, Master White. The only thing I'm sure of is that there are no cameras in this room. I have no idea where the other team is located at the moment or if they are aware of your location. I would have to return to the institute to gather that type of data."

"Great," Sean mumbled as he lay back on the bed.

Ryan picked up the phone. "Good ol' 801-528-8599. That's been our number for as long as I can remember," he said as he dialed.

"Hi, Dad. Sean and I wanted to call to...," Ryan stopped talking and all color seemed to run out of his face. "What?! When...how?!"

Sean sat upright on the bed. "What is it?" he asked. Ryan seemed to ignore him. Both Maxwell and Sean could hear Ryan's father speaking on the other end of the phone but couldn't make out any words.

"Alright, we'll call you in an hour," Ryan said as he hung up the phone.

"What the hell is going on?" Sean asked.

"Mason's gone. He's been kidnapped."

Chapter 45

Dirk walked slowly back into the hotel room. The technician was finishing up with Josc's arm.

"So, what now, doc? Good as new, right?" Jose asked as he massaged his recently broken arm with his other hand.

"The bone has been fused, yes. But the internal structure will need some time to completely heal. You should not strain the arm more than is necessary for three to four weeks."

"No problem. I can shoot fine with my right," he said as he raised his 9mm and aimed toward the door. "That little punk'll never know what hit him. What'd you say his name was? Ryan?"

"Yea, Ryan," Jerry said as he walked toward the window and looked out.

"Master Stillwell, if I may be so bold," Tyler said tentatively, "what is your plan at this juncture?"

"Well, Tyler, my man," Jerry began, still looking out the window, "I'll tell you what my plan is. Since we don't have the next clue, I think I'm going to string your bony ass up on that wall until you tell us where we need to go. How's that for a plan?" He let the drapes fall and turned to look at their handler, quite shaken.

"W...Well, of course I will do whatever I can to assist, of course. The problem is that, as handlers, we are not permitted access to the clues as a security measure." Tyler was looking at the ground and shaking uncontrollably. "But...but I might be able to get some information back at the institute. I will explain the situation and can, in all likelihood, get a variance. Considering what has occurred." He still didn't look at Jerry but kept his gaze on the floor.

"Well, that sounds just peachy, Master Tyler," Jerry said with as much sarcasm as he could muster. He walked over to where Tyler was sitting. He reached down and grabbed Tyler by the hair and turned his face so he was staring right at the scared little man. "I'll tell you what. I'll give you exactly one hour to go get your variance and get back here with the next clue. And you can tell your boss or whoever is running this little circus that if we don't get the next clue, little Mason White has earned his last merit badge!" He let go of Tyler's hair and walked back toward the window.

"What the hell, Jerry?" Jose broke in. "We were supposed to all agree on that! Now we got the cops and probably the feds comin' after us. That's great. Just great!"

"Shut the hell up, you piece of shit! We just got our asses kicked by a couple of kids. Willy's dead and, if it wasn't for Dr. McCoy here with his little bone healer, you'd be out one arm. The time to end this is NOW! We don't have the next clue. We have no idea where they are. We needed leverage and I got it. So deal with it!"

Nobody dared to say anything. Finally, Dirk said quietly, "Tyler, go get as much information as you can and get back here." He walked closer to Tyler, so only he could hear him. "And, if you can't get the clue, I would advise you not to return."

Tyler stood up and silently left the hotel room.

Dirk continued, "So now that we have our "leverage," what do we do with it?"

Jerry didn't say anything for several seconds. He just stared out the window. Finally, he said, "I'll call Doug back in Utah and see where he's at. By now, he should have the kid and delivered the letter to his family. If I'm right, Ryan and what's his name will be looking for a way to contact us. They'll give us the clue and we'll be on our way. At that point, we waste 'em and get back to where we came from." At that point, he let the drapes fall again and turned toward the room, and smiled. "Any questions?"

"Just one," Dirk said. "There's still one more clue to find."

Jerry didn't say anything. Just grunted and stared out the window.

Chapter 46

"Kidnapped?!" Sean asked as Ryan sat down hard on the bed. "How? When?"

"A couple of hours ago, my mom went outside and found Mason's bike on the front porch. It had a note attached. It said, 'We've got your little Boy Scout. No cops or you'll never see him again. Tell Ryan the game's over. We'll call you'. That was it."

"My God," Maxwell exhaled loudly.

"My dad said to call back in an hour to see if they'd heard anything," Ryan said as a tear ran down his face. "Maybe we shouldn't have told our families about this whole thing."

"We needed their help, Ryan. And their support. What the hell do we do?" Sean asked as he sat down on the bed across from Ryan.

Ryan had his head in his hands. Without raising his head, he said, "We finish it. They obviously want the next clue. So, we give it to them. In exchange for Mason." He got up from the bed. "Where's the clue we got from the Matterhorn?"

"I think it's in the backpack. I forgot all about it," Sean said as he grabbed the backpack and started rummaging through it.

"Here, got it," he pulled out the envelope and opened it.

Inside was what appeared to be, another puzzle of sorts. However, there weren't any letters or numbers. Just a bunch of weird-looking characters.

"What the hell is this?" Sean asked as he handed it to Ryan. Ryan stared at the parchment in his hands.

"I could be wrong but it looks like Korean. One of the engineers in our firm is from Seoul. He's got writing like this all over his cubicle. I mean it could be Japanese but it looks like Korean. It's hard to tell the difference." They both looked at Maxwell.

"You said you were here to help us now, Max," Ryan began, "can you make anything out of this?" He handed the envelope to Maxwell who still looked in shock. He took it and looked closely at the characters.

그는 왕좌에 앉아있다

대중을 내려다보고

사슬을 끊은 남자

뇌에 총알

"I don't know how much help I can be in deciphering. As part of the contest protocols, handlers are not privy to the locations of the clues. However, I believe Master White is correct. While I am not fluent by any means, I am familiar with several Asian languages and it does appear to be Korean. Unfortunately, I have no idea what this particular passage says." He handed the clue back to Ryan.

"Okay, so we find someone who knows Korean. I'd call my friend but we're a couple decades early for that," Ryan said as he put the clue down on the bed.

Sean got up to pace. "Well, we're close to one of the biggest cities in America. There's got to be a Korean Consulate or embassy in L.A., right? We go there and get them to translate for us."

Ryan looked up. "That's not a bad idea. We need to do something first, though." He looked over at Maxwell.

"Max, I need you to find the other team's handler. Tell them we're ready to deal for Mason's release. We need some time, though to get this clue translated. I want a face-to-face meeting with them."

"Are you crazy, Ryan?!" Sean almost yelled. "I'm not sure if you're keeping up with current events, but you just killed one of them and broke the arm of another one. I don't think they're going to be the best company right now!"

"I would have to agree with Master Jensen, sir. That is not a good idea," Maxwell said, again showing more emotion than either Sean or Ryan had seen up to this point.

"I don't really give a shit at this point. They've got my brother and could kill him or any member of our families any time they want. We've got the clue. They need it. They're not going to kill us or anybody else until they get it." Ryan got up and grabbed the yellow pages from the desk next to the bed. Sean had never seen his friend so resolute about anything before.

"Fine, I guess. At this point it would appear we don't have a lot of options," Sean said, much less resolutely.

"Very well. I will pass on the message. Where do you want to meet?" Maxwell asked.

"I don't know yet. Just pass the message on so we can buy Mason some time. Make sure they understand that we have the clue and are ready to deal. But," Ryan held up a finger to Maxwell, "also make sure they understand that I will need irrefutable proof my brother is safe before they get the clue. I'll decide where we meet after we get this clue translated. I'm sure you can use your little futuristic GPS unit to find us."

"I understand," Maxwell said. "But before I go, I want you both to know that I meant what I said. I am no longer just your handler. I will see this through if it's the last thing I do." With that, Maxwell pulled a small ball about the size of a large grapefruit from his bag. He entered several numbers and placed his hand on top. "Good luck," he said and simply vanished.

"Whoa," Ryan and Sean said in unison.

Chapter 47

July 2163

Darius woke with a start. He had only been asleep for an hour or so since he left the hot tub. It took him a minute to gather his bearings. The outside security lights that illuminated his large estate cast an eerie glow across through the large bay windows that circled his master bedroom. He realized he was alone. Normally, he had a warm body next to him. Some lucky girl had been given the honor of spending the night. Of course, he never remembered their names and the faces all seemed to blur together after a while. He was glad he was alone. He fell back on his pillow and realized he was completely soaked. The room was a perfect 71 degrees, but he was sweating as if he was in his sauna downstairs. His mind was racing. He felt as though there was a huge weight compressing his body and his mind. He wanted to scream but he didn't know why. He reached over and pressed the intercom button next to his bed. After a few moments, a tired voice replied, "Yes sir, how may I be of service?"

"Jeffrey, please pull my car around. I want to go for a drive. And have Marta report to my dressing room with something comfortable."

"Very good, sir. I will be out front momentarily."

Darius always thought more clearly when he was moving. Whether in the helicopter or his car. Of course, he never drove. He felt it was beneath him. That was what chauffeurs were for, after all.

Marta appeared momentarily with several outfits, of which Darius chose what he thought looked like comfortable "driving clothes." He then made his way to the front of the estate where

Jeffrey was dutifully waiting with the Cadillac's door open. Darius had often marveled at the luxury car company's endurance. Through all the failed experimentation with hovercraft and other transportation devices, nothing rivaled the comfort and power of the Cadillac limousine. And with so few people having the wealth or authorization to purchase such a vehicle, he was amazed that they stayed in business. But they did and Darius owned one of the few Cadillacs in Montana. He got in, and Jeffrey asked where he would like to go. "Nowhere in particular, my friend. Just drive."

"Very good, sir." They pulled out and accelerated down the long drive, through the gate and on into the night.

Chapter 48

"They want what?!" Jerry asked.

"Um, yes, well, that was the message I received. The other team would like a meeting in person. I must say this is quite rare, indeed. In fact, I don't think it has ever happened before," Tyler stammered out his message for the second time.

"And where exactly is this 'meeting' supposed to take place?"

"The location has not yet been relayed to me. However, there were a couple other points of note that I was requested to pass on," Tyler physically cowered as Jerry turned and approached.

"And what would those be?" he asked as he stood just inches from Tyler.

Tyler gulped. "Well, they say that they do, in fact, have a clue and will share that with you, of course. But,"

"But what?" Jerry now stood over Tyler, and Tyler fell backward. Luckily a well-placed chair caught him from falling to the floor.

Tyler gulped again. "But, the message given to me," Tyler was trying to dodge any culpability, "was that they need some time to decipher the message, and they will only share it with you once they are given proof that the White boy has been released."

Jerry stepped back from Tyler, who had lost all color in his face. By now, he knew how unpredictable Jerry was and he was relieved that he had moved away.

"That's bullshit!" Dirk said from the other side of the room. The three members of the team were still in their hotel room across from Disneyland.

"No. That's fine," Jerry said as he sauntered back toward the window. "I think they know if we got the kid once, we can get him again. Or anyone else in their perfect little family. Besides, if we do this quick, we can keep the cops out of the picture." He turned back toward Tyler but didn't approach him. "Tell them we'll meet and we'll give them the proof they want. But deliver this 'point of note,'" he said, mocking Tyler's choice of words, "if they screw with us, the kid's as good as dead. And we won't stop there. If we don't get that clue, we'll move on to good ol' Mom and Dad next."

"I understand, sir. I will relay the message and will endeavor to find out the location of the meeting." With that, Tyler got up and slinked out of the room.

Once he was gone, Dirk went on the offensive. "The second we release that kid, we've lost all our leverage. What if we need these pricks to find the final location of the orb? Have you thought about that, genius?" Dirk regretted it as soon as he'd said it. Jerry spun toward Dirk and clocked him with a hard right to the face. Dirk went down hard on the floor. Jose just stood frozen, not daring to enter into the fray.

Dirk brought a hand up to his face and wiped away the blood that had gushed from his lip. "Listen to me, you little shit! I'm in charge here and I make the decisions. If you don't like it, you can leave and try to win this thing on your own. But I guarantee you'll just end up like your stupid ass brother." Jerry walked back toward the window. Jose was wondering what the hell he was looking at but wasn't about to ask.

Dirk slowly got up and sat down on one of the beds. "Fine, you're in charge. Whatever. So what kind of proof are we going to give them that his brother's safe?"

"We won't need to. He'll talk to Daddy back home and find out. But we need to be ready to move. As soon as we get that clue, we go and finish this." Jerry turned slowly to look at Dirk. He didn't regret hitting him, but he did realize that Dirk made a good point. "Once we have the orb, then we slit their throats. There's no way in hell that either of them will ever see their families again."

Chapter 49

The Korean Consulate was located in the heart of downtown Los Angeles. Ryan and Sean had rented a car and made the two-hour-long drive through traffic as soon as the rental company opened. They made sure to use a different rental car company than they had when they arrived a day earlier. As far as they knew, their first rental car was still sitting in the hotel parking lot with its tires slashed.

Ryan had called his father the night before as planned. He told him to sit tight, and he was going to get Mason back. Ryan stressed that no police should be involved yet. He had a plan and would keep his father up to date. He also spoke to his mom. Which didn't do much good. She didn't stop crying throughout the entire conversation. But Ryan was sure that he got his message of "stay calm" across to her. After he hung up, he was more sure than ever that he HAD to get Mason back unharmed. That was their first priority now.

They entered the consulate and approached the receptionist. She was a tiny Korean woman who couldn't have weighed 80 pounds. She greeted them with a smile and asked with a heavy accent if she could help them.

"Yes," Sean said. He had been elected as the spokesman. "We were wondering if there was anyone here who could help us translate a message? We think it's written in Korean and we need it translated to English?"

"Oh yes, I think I could help you with that," she said as she jumped up, seemingly excited to have something to do. Amazingly, her height didn't change much from when she was sitting, Ryan noticed with a small smile. She came to the edge of the receptionist desk and Sean held out the parchment for her to see.

"Oh, yes, this is Korean. Would you like me to read it for you?"

"Yes, but I'd like to write it down, if I could. Would you have a pen and piece of paper I could borrow?" The receptionist produced both instantly. Again, it seemed as if she was over-eager to help.

"This is kind of strange," she said.

"I know. It's for...a school project. Kind of a riddle," Sean lied convincingly. He looked at Ryan, who gave him a thumbs-up under the desk.

"The first line says, 'He is sitting on a throne.' The second line says 'Looking down on people'. "Or the group of people?" She looked quizzically at the two boys.

"Then it says, 'Man unhooked... or actually, unchained?'. She handed the paper back to Sean with somewhat of a concerned look on her face. "And the last line says, 'Bullet to the brain.' That's a very strange riddle. So do you know what this means?" she asked with her nose somewhat crinkled.

"Well, like I said, it's for a school project so we don't really know yet. But thanks a lot," Sean said as they turned to leave.

Ryan and Sean walked back to their car. They both sat staring at the translation but had no idea what it meant. Sean had written down the following:

He is sitting on the throne

Looking down on group of people

Man unchained

Bullet to the brain

Suddenly, Sean's eyes lit up. "It's Lincoln! This is about Abraham Lincoln!" he exclaimed with excitement. Ryan still didn't see it. "What? How do you know?"

"It all makes sense, Ryan. Sitting on a throne. The Lincoln Memorial. The Civil War. Men chained. Or unchained, more correctly. Slavery. Getting shot in the head? It all makes sense."

"Damn, I think you're right," Ryan agreed. "But it doesn't say anything about where to find the clue. I've been to the Lincoln Memorial. It's huge!"

"Well, I guess we'll have to rely on Max for help. He said he's on our side now." Sean said.

"Yea, but he said that handlers were not privy to the location of the clues," Ryan reminded his friend.

"Well, this is all we have. So let's go ask him," Sean said as Ryan started the car and they drove away.

Chapter 50

Ryan and Sean drove in silence until Ryan spoke up. "I think the only way we're going to get out of this is to change the players on the field."

"Okay and what exactly does that mean?" Sean asked.

"Well, think about it. Either we keep evading the other team, or we trap them," Ryan said and glanced over at Sean with raised eyebrows.

"What do you mean 'trap the other team'?" Sean asked.

"Well, after what Maxwell told us, this whole thing is just a show for whoever's watching, right?"

"Yea, so what?"

"So, we have to assume that there will be cameras, 'invisible cameras,'" holding up his fingers in quotations, "placed all over the memorial and probably all over the area outside, right?"

"I'm still not getting what..." Sean started to say.

"So, I've been thinking," Ryan interrupted, "what possible reason is there for these "game players" in the future for sending either team back to where they started from? I mean, once the game is over, why not just eliminate both teams? Other than their word, which I gather from Max is rather tenuous at best, what possible reason do they have?" Ryan looked at Sean.

Sean was suddenly very quiet and didn't look back at Ryan. He took out the note that he had written the clue and scribbled something on the opposite side and handed it to Ryan.

'What if they're listening and/or watching us right now?' Sean had written on the note. Ryan handed the note back to Sean.

"Well, if you ask me, I say we trust Maxwell and just finish this damn thing. Leave the conspiracies to the experts," Sean said.

"Yea, you're probably right. Let's head to a hotel and get ready to leave," Ryan looked at Sean, who returned the look this time. Both of them knew they needed to get ahold of Max and his 'bug sweeper' before they talked any further.

They drove through downtown Los Angeles and found a small motel that sat right off a freeway ramp. They knew that every hotel in L.A. couldn't possibly be bugged. So, this motel seemed as good as any to provide some level of security. They parked the car and as they were heading toward the lobby, they heard a voice from behind them.

"Master White? Master Jensen?" It was Maxwell.

"Damn, these trackers they put on us are accurate as hell," Ryan said as Maxwell came up to them, somewhat out of breath.

"Hey Max, were your ears burning?" Sean asked.

"What, my ears..." Max felt his ears with his fingers.

"Nevermind, I assume you found us thanks to our little trackers inside our head? Or wherever they are?" Ryan said.

"Yes, well that is what they are there for, after all," Maxwell said as they continued on toward the lobby.

Ryan rented a room and the three of them walked in silence down the hallway. It was actually a pretty nice motel despite the outward appearance. The halls were clean and the carpet looked fairly new. And it was pretty full. A bunch of kids whizzed by them with towels and floaters and headed for the pool. It caught Ryan a little off guard as he had just taken his kids swimming recently. It seemed like a lifetime ago. He quickly put it out of his mind and tried to concentrate on what was going on in this timeframe.

Once inside their room, Ryan wasted no time. "Okay, Max, do your thing with your little gizmo there. Let's see if we're alone." Max took out his transmitter and slowly swept it across the room from several angles.

"As far as I can tell, there are no cameras or listening devices here," Max said as he put the unit back in his bag.

"Okay, so did you get our message to the other team? About the meeting?" Ryan asked.

"Yes, I did as you instructed. I must say, they were not overly pleased with the idea. But they did agree to meet," Maxwell said with some hesitation. Before Ryan could respond, Maxwell continued. "But I feel I must warn you, once again, against this course of action, Master White. As you are aware, the other team is made up of very dangerous individuals. I shudder to think what they are capable of."

"I understand your concern, Max. But right now, it's our only option and it's the best chance we have to get Mason back unharmed. Let me ask you another question," Ryan asked, changing the subject. "If there are no cameras or listening devices present, say, in this hotel room, for instance, how does Darius, or whatever his name is, find out if any rules are broken?"

"It is up to the handlers to observe each team and report any infractions to Darius. At that point, he decides what punishment, if any, is to be imposed on that team."

Ryan made a mental note but didn't respond. "One other question. And please be honest, Max. Since you've been a part of these "quests," as you call them, how many teams have won and have been sent back to their original time or rewarded with money or freedom or whatever else had been promised to them?"

Maxwell stared at Ryan for a moment. He started to speak but then stopped and looked as though he was deep in thought. "Max?" Ryan prodded.

"Yes, I understand the question, Master White. I am just trying to ponder for a moment." Slowly, a look of what could only be called sad anger began to appear on Maxwell's face. He was slow in responding. "There have only been two successful contests in which we used participants from another time. In both those cases, there was a winning team and a losing team. I cannot say for sure what happened to the victorious team. At that point, my involvement had been suspended, and I was not privy to the eventual outcome. But, now that you mention it, I would have surely received some indication since I am also a member of the memory reprogramming committee. At least, I was in the second contest. But I was never involved with any post-contest memory adjustments. And protocol stipulates that all memories must be erased upon completion of the contest. I guess I just didn't think about it. You see, in the second contest, there was an unfortunate outcome near the end. One of the losing team members was killed. At that point, a moratorium was put in place on all-time travel-related contests. Obviously, that moratorium was lifted." Maxwell sighed and sat down softly on one of the chairs next to the bed.

"So, you're saying that, as far as you know, no team has ever been sent back to their original time or rewarded in any way?" Ryan asked.

"No, not that I can prove. Of course, there were reports of the teams being sent back but I was not directly involved."

Ryan was quiet for a moment. He paced slowly back and forth as he chose his next question carefully.

"Maxwell, you said last night that you were not simply our handler anymore but you would see this through. What exactly did you mean by that?" Ryan asked.

Maxwell slowly stood up and walked toward the window. "Master White? Master Jensen?" he started. "I have been working for the institute for as long as I can remember. I helped Darius' father, Alexander, start the business over 40 years ago. I know nothing else. The institute has provided for me and my family. I have seen times of struggle and times of great success. But recently, I looked at myself in the mirror and realized that I have been enabling a man who has lost all sight of his father's dream. Who has become so drunk with power that he will stop at nothing to propagate his kingdom? My son was killed in an automobile accident 15 years ago. My daughter lives with her own family many miles away. And 9 months ago, my wife of 46 years passed away after a long and painful illness." He turned to look at both boys with tears in his eyes. A show of emotion that neither Sean nor Ryan had seen to this point. "I am telling you these things because when I looked in that mirror, I knew my time on this earth was limited. I'm leaving the institute as soon as this is over. I don't want my legacy to be the unnecessary and meaningless deaths of two young men. I'm not sure how but I want to stop Darius, and I want to get both of you back to where you belong." Maxwell sat back down and wiped his tears away. Neither Sean nor Ryan spoke. What could they possibly say?

"I apologize for my emotional breakdown. I'm not usually one to wear them on my sleeve," Maxwell said after a moment or two.

Ryan had sat down during Maxwell's explanation. He slowly stood up and walked over toward where Maxwell was sitting, and sat down on the bed near him.

"If what you're saying is correct, Max, it would seem like we have an additional objective to finish this thing. We need to somehow stop Darius." Ryan said and looked at Sean.

"Why do WE need to stop Darius?" Sean asked and emphasized, "WE."

"Well, think about it. Let's say somehow we get to the orb first. What then?

Either we have our memories erased and our consciousnesses put back where they belong or Darius sends his "hit squad," and we're both eliminated? From what Maxwell has told us," Ryan glanced at Maxwell, "there is not a preponderance of evidence that we can trust Darius to keep his word. And whether or not Max leaves the institute, there's nothing to say that Darius won't grab us again or do this same thing to somebody else."

Both Sean and Maxwell were quiet. "I don't know about you but I don't feel like letting Darius keep screwing around with people's lives with his little time machine. Seems to me we need to put him out of business."

Ryan turned to Maxwell. "Max, I'm sorry about your wife and son. Neither of us knew you even had a family. To be honest, we didn't even know you were married," Ryan said trying not to sound too "fatherly."

"That's quite alright, Master White. None of that is really your concern. Right now, our only concern is getting Mason back and finishing this contest. Right?" he said, trying to cheer things up. Obviously, Ryan's speech about stopping Darius had made an impact but Maxwell wasn't ready to discuss it further. At least not now.

"Quite right, Max," Sean said, standing up. "Now the problem is how do we do that, exactly?"

"Well, as far as Mason is concerned, I have an idea about that," Ryan said. And they all huddled together around the table as Ryan described his plan.

Chapter 51

Thursday, September 15th, 1982

The biggest problem, Ryan had surmised, was keeping his family safe once Mason was returned. Unfortunately, he couldn't risk getting the police involved. There would be too many questions that simply did not have believable answers. He figured the only way his family would be safe would be to simply remove them from the equation. Both he and Sean had been given bank accounts with $125,000 in each. They had used very little so far. Only a few thousand dollars for their airfare and rental cars. Ryan wasn't sure if his father, or Sean's father, would go for it, but he wanted to send his entire family and Sean's entire family on a cruise. It was the only way to make sure they would be safe. Even if Jerry's henchmen followed them onto the ship, there wouldn't be much they could do. And Ryan doubted they would follow them on the cruise anyway. Ryan and Sean had spent the early morning hours calling the cruise lines in Florida to see when a cruise would be available. It turned out that there were various cruises leaving port weekly. They took note of the best options and returned to the task of getting Mason home safely.

As for the meeting place, Ryan wanted a place with a lot of people. He knew the other team would not hesitate to kill him the second they got the clue. The only thing leaning in their favor was that there was most likely one final clue that he would need to solve for them.

Through Maxwell and then Tyler, he relayed the message that the meeting would take place on Thursday morning at 10:00am in the main parking lot at Knott's Berry Farm. Ryan had been there once before with his family in the late 70s and remembered it was a very busy place. He also relayed the message that he would need proof that Mason had been returned unharmed. Even though he knew he would not believe anything they said and would call his father anyway. Ryan had talked to his father the night before and assured him they would be seeing Mason very soon. He hadn't yet broached the subject of the cruise.

Ryan and Sean arrived at the parking lot early. They suspected the other team might also arrive early, but as far as they could tell, they were not there yet. "I don't like this Ryan. This place is pretty empty," Sean said as they stood near the entrance but off to the side slightly hidden by one of the entry gates. They had sweet-talked one of the parking attendants to let them in early. It wasn't too hard. The attendant was a 19-year-old college student who was much more worried about the upcoming Chemistry test she was studying for. Plus, she took an instant liking to Sean, who turned the charm on 100%. After that display, Ryan's only response was, "I think I'm going to be sick!" Sean was always more of a lady's man back in the day.

"Hey, we're in, right?" was Sean's response.

"Don't worry. People will start showing up. Pretty soon, we'll have to look hard just to notice the other team in the sea of people," Ryan said as they stood waiting. It was 8:30am. Just an hour and a half before meeting time.

Over the next hour, Ryan was right. The parking lot was quickly filling up. The park didn't open until 10:00am so everyone was lined up at the ticket booth and entry gate. Ryan and Sean wandered over closer to the crowd. They were almost to the gate when Ryan felt something hard push against his back and a voice said, "Just keep walking." He didn't dare turn around. He was definitely planning on being in charge of this meeting, and, at this point, that didn't seem to be happening.

Ryan kept walking with Sean right next to him. Sean had turned around just enough to see Jose walk up behind Ryan but didn't have a chance to warn him.

"Where're we going?" Ryan asked quietly.

"Just keep walking and keep your mouth shut!" hissed Jose. He pushed the .45 harder into Ryan's back. Ryan jerked slightly with the pain from the muzzle of the gun. They walked past the crowd of people at the ticket booth. Jose was pressed tightly against Ryan's back in order to hide the gun. Ryan was amazed. Nobody even looked in their direction. It seemed to him that it would look quite odd for a grown man to be pressed up so tightly to a teenage boy. Even though Ryan was actually a little taller than Jose, it was obvious he was younger. Nobody was behind Sean so he just kept pace with Ryan. It didn't make much sense to run at this point.

They made their way through several rows of cars and the density of people was diminishing rapidly, much to Ryan's chagrin. He knew if they ended up alone with these guys, this meeting could go much differently than he had planned. He knew he needed to do something to stop this.

Suddenly Ryan stopped and put his hands up about shoulder height. "That's far enough. I want to talk to Jerry now!" The pain he felt then was deafening. In his youth, he had watched cartoons like every other kid and when someone was hit over the head, there was always a little circle of chirping birds that flitted around the person's head as he fell down. Ryan didn't see or hear any chirping birds. But he did go down. Hard. He fell to the asphalt and grabbed the back of his head. Everything was dark for a few seconds. His head throbbed so hard he felt like it was going to actually explode. Sean immediately tried to grab him but got a knee to his face for his efforts. He fell next to Ryan as his nose gushed blood and ran onto the parking lot. He grabbed his face and rolled away from Jose.

"GET UP NOW!" Jose barked. Ryan had honestly not heard him due to the brass quartet playing in his head. Jose kicked him hard in the ribs. Ryan's breath completely left him. He gasped for air and coughed spastically as his lungs searched for any type of relief. He still couldn't move to get up. He was bracing himself for another kick when he heard some commotion above him. He was able to suck in a small breath and then a larger one until he was breathing more regularly. He opened one eye and looked up. Jose was gone! He pulled himself to his knees and looked over at Sean who was still lying on the ground holding his face.

"Sean, you okay?" Ryan asked, barely above a whisper.

"Yea, I think. What the hell?" Sean replied as he slowly got up on his knees and tilted his head back.

"I guess our welcoming party wasn't ready to make any deals," Ryan said and actually eked out a small chuckle as he stood up.

"Where are they?" Sean asked with his head still tilted back.

"I think they're gon...oh shit."

Sean dropped his head and looked in the direction Ryan was looking. The guy from the Matterhorn was walking toward them at a rapid pace. The guy who had just kicked the crap out of them was following closely behind.

"What do we do?" Sean asked.

"Do as we're told. Right now, they're in charge," Ryan answered and pulled himself up as tall as he could muster. He held his side with his right hand. He just hoped there were no broken ribs. His head still hurt like hell, and he felt a small trickle of fluid run down his back. It was either blood or sweat. He couldn't tell. He gingerly felt the back of his head. When he pulled his fingers away, they were covered with blood. He felt nauseous and knew he probably had a concussion.

Jerry slowed down as he neared the boys. He desperately wanted to continue where Jose had left off, but he also knew he needed them to be at least somewhat coherent. He walked directly up to Ryan. Ryan took a half step back but maintained his position.

"My colleague has informed me that you wanted to talk to me. Let me introduce myself. My name is Jerry Stillwell. You've already met Mr. Alvarez. And our third musketeer is close by with a high-powered rifle aimed at your head. So please don't entertain the thought of running or trying anything stupid. There was a fourth member of our team, but you took care of him last night. I can't really blame you. You were saving the life of your pitiful little friend here. But just so you know. His name was Willy Bendar. He was a murderer and a rapist, so you probably did the world a favor. However, the man with his finger on the hair-trigger of that rifle is Willy's brother. So please behave," Jerry smirked as he took a half step back and threw a paper towel at Sean, who took it and pressed it against his nose.

Ryan had not even remotely thought there would be this much animosity. He knew it was risky to meet face to face. But this was way beyond 'out of control.' He had to think quickly, but nothing was coming to mind. He was surprised at how well-spoken Jerry was. For a low-life criminal, that is. He figured he would try to return the favor.

"Mr. Stillwell. It's good to finally meet you. My name is Ryan White, and this is my colleague, Sean Jensen. I apologize for my rude behavior. I was taken by surprise by Mr. Alvarez. I was simply trying to initiate our meeting," Ryan said with as much clarity as possible. The throbbing in his head had stopped but had been replaced with an annoying ringing in his ears and a terrible headache.

"I believe we each have something of interest to each other. But you have made it clear that you are in charge of these proceedings, so please tell me how you would like to move forward," Ryan was trying to sound businesslike and not be a smart ass but it was tough.

Jerry smiled and put his hand roughly on Ryan's shoulder. "Well, Ryan, I'll tell you something," he moved his hand to the back of Ryan's neck and squeezed. He moved his face closer to Ryan's. "The fact is that we don't really need both of you. We really just need you." Jerry pulled a 9mm from his waist and pointed it directly at Sean's stomach. Ryan didn't know what to do so he just took a chance. He whipped his arm up and knocked Jerry's hand away from his neck, and took a step back. "You pull that trigger, and you'll never see the next clue!" Ryan nearly yelled. Immediately, Jose brought his gun up and pointed it at Ryan but Jerry knocked his arm back down. "Not yet!!"

"Well, Mr. White, I'm impressed. I didn't think you had it in you. Don't worry. I'm not going to kill your friend or you. Not yet, that is. We don't even care about your little brother. Who, by the way, is home safe and sound with mommy and daddy. We just want the clue. Nobody has to get hurt. Well, hurt anymore, that is. So... Let's see it," Jerry held out his hand.

Ryan's heart was still racing from his sudden decision to break away from Jerry's grip. He looked at Sean, whose eyes were wide but in control.

"Okay, Mr. Stillwell. You'll get your clue. Of course, you won't mind if I make a quick phone call first? After all, I did say

I wanted proof that my brother is safe," Ryan made a gesture towards the ticket booth where there was a bank of payphones.

Jerry was quiet for a few seconds. "Very slowly. And please remember our friend on the other side of the scope."

Ryan had actually forgotten about the other team member with the rifle. It really didn't make much difference as he wasn't about to try anything anyway. Ryan and Sean moved slowly together toward the ticket booth. They were several hundred feet away. Ryan desperately wanted to talk to Sean, but Jerry and Jose were right behind them. As they neared the ticket booth, the crowd of people grew thicker. They actually had to excuse themselves several times to get through the throng to the other side where the phones were located. Ryan got to a phone and called his home phone number. His father picked up on the second ring.

"Hello?!" his father sounded a little out of breath.

"Dad, it's Ryan. Is Mason okay?"

"Ryan! What's going on? Are you okay? Yes, Mason was dropped off this morning down the block. He said he was being held by three men in a dark room. He didn't seem to know anything else. But he seems to be okay."

"Is he hurt at all, Dad?"

"No. Doesn't seem to be. Just a little scared but says he wasn't hurt. Where are you? What's going on, Ryan? Your mother and I are worried sick about you."

"Sean and I are fine, Dad. But we've still got some things to work out. Don't worry but stay by the phone. I need to talk to you more but not right now, okay?"

"Okay. But please call me and be careful, Ryan."

"I will. Talk to you later. Love you, bye." Ryan hung up the phone and turned back around. Jose was standing next to Sean with his hand inside his jacket. He pulled back the jacket enough to let Ryan see he was pointing his.45 at Sean's side. Ryan knew that Jose was probably not going to shoot Sean in front of all these people, but he wasn't going to take any chances.

It would be an understatement to say that Ryan's plan had not played out as he had hoped. The plan was to give the other team the clue and clear out before they had a chance to look at it. As it stood, Ryan was certain that Jerry would inspect the clue and quickly come to the realization that he had no hope of deciphering it. Then, they would be back where they started. Their family would be at greater risk, even if they agreed to go on the cruise as Ryan had planned. He was running out of options. What he didn't know was that Jerry was about to solve that problem for him.

Chapter 52

Darius slowly began to relax as he languished in the back seat of his Cadillac. He had told Jeffrey to simply drive and that was exactly what Jeffrey was doing. They were going nowhere in particular, and that was what Darius wanted.

As they drove, Darius was going over in his head why he had felt so disconnected and worried the past couple of days. He began to put his thoughts together. Right now, Darius had all the power he could dream of. It was a carefully guarded secret that he had perfected the time travel orb. The other 'players' knew very little about the institute's time travel abilities and had left that completely up to Darius. Darius had promised a reward worth more than all the gold in Ft. Knox to the winner of these damn contests. Of course, he had not elaborated as to the fact that the reward would be full access to his institute's time travel system. He had assumed all along that his contest would win and he would be able to keep his prize all to himself. Now, he wasn't so sure. Although his plan had so far exceeded his wildest dreams, what with Willy's murder and the other things that had transpired he was still worried what would happen if the other players voted down his contest. He would lose all the power he had worked so hard for. He had all but forgotten his father, Alexander, and his dreams of a better world. Darius was now completely self-absorbed and would never let someone else into his world. "How could he have been so stupid?" he thought to himself as he was now fully awake. That was the problem that he now had to deal with. Somehow the players must be eliminated and these contests would have to end. Starting with the one that was now in play.

Chapter 53

Thursday, September 15ᵗʰ, 1982

The four of them walked some distance away from the crowd toward a black Suburban parked illegally near the end of the parking lot.

"Okay, Mr. White. You've got your proof that your brother was returned safely. Now, my patience has run out. The clue please," Jerry said as he stuck out his hand.

Ryan reached into his pocket and retrieved the clue. He had no option at this point. He handed the clue to Jerry and turned to Sean. "Let's go, Sean," Ryan said.

"One minute, Mr. White," Jerry said as he opened the clue. Ryan didn't look directly at him. He was sure that Jerry would insist he solve it for him. He knew that these idiots would never take it upon themselves to figure anything out. He was right.

"As I suspected. More gibberish," Jerry said as he threw the clue back at Ryan's feet. "I'm sure you are aware, Mr. White, that our colleagues back in Utah still have access to your family and Mr. Jensen's family, as well. I would certainly hate to see any harm come to any member of your family as I'm sure you would as well. Therefore, I've decided to buy a small insurance policy." Jerry turned to Jose and nodded. Jose opened the door to the Suburban, turned and cold-cocked Sean in the face. As Sean fell back on the Suburban, Jose grabbed him and threw him in the backseat and slammed the door.

"What the hell?!" Ryan yelled as he lunged for the Suburban. Jose pulled out his .45 and pointed it at Ryan's head. Ryan stopped and reflexively put his hands up and stepped back.

"It's very simple, Mr. White. You go back to your hotel and do whatever you had originally planned on doing. The only difference is that Mr. Jensen will stay with us until we reach the next clue," Jerry said with a sick grin.

"And how do I know you won't just kill him between now and then," Ryan said, sincerely worried.

"I would be lying if I said I gave a rat's ass about your friend. Because I don't. But, unlike our friend you murdered last night, I don't kill just for the fun of it. And neither do my other two companions. Therefore, I will tell you that if you would be so kind as to get us to the next clue, I will return Mr. Jensen unharmed. Believe me or don't believe me. I really don't care. Call us at this number when you're ready," Jerry said as he tossed a piece of paper at Ryan's feet, opened the passenger side door, got in, and drove away.

Ryan stood alone in the parking lot amidst the dust from the tires of the Suburban. His head was swimming. He felt very alone and felt like crying, but no tears came. He just stood there, not knowing what to do. His best friend in the world and only companion through this nightmare was gone. He had no idea if he'd ever see him again. Suddenly, the tears did come. Ryan fell to his knees and openly wept. He fell to his butt and pulled his knees up close and buried his head between them. He didn't know how long he had been sitting there when a woman came up from behind. "Are you okay, son?" she asked. Ryan jerked his head up and slowly got to his feet. "Yea, I'm fine," he said as he wiped his face and looked around. He didn't know what to say. He must have looked like an idiot sitting in a parking lot crying. "I just got some bad news from home. That's all. I'll be fine," he said as he began to walk back toward the ticket gate. The woman continued on her way with a worried look on her face.

As he walked, Ryan began to put together what just happened and what he should do. He had to find Maxwell. He half expected him to materialize out of the bushes and come to his rescue. No such luck. He had gotten about halfway to the ticket booth and the bank of phones when he suddenly realized that Sean had the keys to the rental car. He stopped and hung his head. 'This day just couldn't get any worse,' he thought as he continued on.

He got to the ticket booth and asked where the nearest rental car agency was. Luckily there was one about a mile down the road. He rented a car and drove back to their hotel. He had almost called his dad from the phone booth at the park but decided he would wait until he got back to the hotel. He needed to gather his thoughts and decide what he was going to say. As he drove, he made the decision not to tell anyone about Sean. Not yet, anyway. There was no need to add any more worry to the mix. If Sean's parents were with his parents when he called, he would have to do some quick thinking.

When he arrived back at the hotel, Maxwell was sitting on the bed reading a People magazine.

"How did it go?" Maxwell asked.

"Where the hell were you?" Ryan asked, sounding more upset than he meant to.

"I stayed here, as you requested, Master White," Maxwell answered.

"Don't call me that anymore. My name's Ryan." Ryan had forgotten that he had told Maxwell to stay in the hotel. He was certain he and Sean could handle the meeting themselves.

"I'm sorry, Mas... Ryan. What has happened? Where is Master Jensen?" Maxwell asked as Ryan shut the door.

"Don't call him that either. His name is Sean. And he's gone. They took him," Ryan sat down heavily on the bed.

Maxwell sat straight up on the bed. "Took him?! Took him where?"

"How the hell should I know? They surprised us in the parking lot. Beat the crap out of us is more like it," Ryan said as he felt the lump on the back of his head. He pulled his fingers away and looked at them but there was no blood. Luckily, it had stopped bleeding. Ryan then described the meeting to Maxwell.

Chapter 54

"Jeremy, get your ass up here right now!" Darius slammed the phone down. Jeremy Carmichael had been a security guard at the institute for over ten years. He had heard Darius yell plenty of times but never directed solely at him. He hurriedly threw away the donut he had been eating and sprinted toward Darius' office. He didn't stop to announce himself via the secretary but went straight through the "door" and into his boss's office.

"You wanted to see me, sir?" Jeremy eked out his question as he crossed the large office to Darius' desk.

"Yes," Darius replied with an eerie calm. "I understand you were on duty last night when my office alarm went off?"

"Yes, sir. We received the silent alarm that your door had been breached. When we arrived, the door was open ...or not engaged... so we cleared the office but were unable to re-engage the hologram. So we lasered the door until maintenance could check it out today."

"And then what happened?" Darius was still calm but looking directly at the squat little security guard.

"Well," Jeremy stuttered, "we received a second alarm shortly after we left. We assumed that whatever small animal had breached the door had then exited and tripped the lasers."

"Uh-huh," Darius rose and walked slowly around his desk to stand directly in front of Jeremy. "Well, that must have been one hell of a smart rabbit!" Darius' calm veneer was officially gone.

"I'm not sure I understand, sir." Jeremy was literally shaking at this point.

"It would seem your "small animal," while looking for a place to crap, found it necessary to rummage through my files!" Darius grabbed the security guard by the collar and nearly threw him over the desk. Only Jeremy's sizeable waist stopped him from completely clearing the desk. The security guard looked down at the floor as he lay prone on the desk and saw an array of files spread out over the ground. He didn't dare move so he just stayed on the desk.

"Get your fat ass off my desk, you idiot!" Darius screamed as he returned to his side of the desk. Jeremy, as quickly as he could, scrambled back to a standing position in front of the desk.

"I'm very sorry, sir, I don't know..."

"Shut up," Darius barked. "Come over here." Jeremy quickly walked around the large desk and stood attentively. Darius pointed down at the array of files spread across the floor.

"Do you know what those are?" He asked in a slightly toned-down voice. Jeremy pretended to look but had no idea what he was looking at.

"No sir, I mean, yes sir. They are files." He somehow knew that wasn't the correct answer. Or at least not the completely correct answer. "Your brilliance amazes me, Jeremy." Darius was nearly back to his eerie calm. "But do you know what type of files they are?"

"Well, no, sir."

"They're MY private files!!" Darius bellowed in another maniacal twist of attitude. "And they have been rummaged through like a whore's panties!" Jeremy had no idea how to respond to that.

"So, either you went through my personal files or your small animal had very nimble paws!" Jeremy started to say something but wisely kept his mouth shut. Darius pushed Jeremy out of the way and sat down hard on his expensive chair.

"So, if you want to keep your job here, get your pathetic group of rent-a-cops together and find out who was in my office." Darius turned his chair away from the belittled security guard and bent down to start putting his "private files" back together.

Jeremy stood for a moment but realized his beating was over for the time being. He turned and quickly exited the office. As he walked through the holographic door, the secretary saw him wipe his face and walk slowly down the hall.

Darius sat back up and looked at the files on the floor. As is his practice, every morning he removes the contest files and reads and re-reads them. On this particular morning, two of the files had been out of place. One that was of no consequence. But the other one spelled out the details of the current contest. As his anger started to dissipate, Darius began to think of who could benefit from knowing what was actually going on? He immediately thought about Maxwell and Tyler since they were so intimately involved. But he couldn't come up with any reason why either of them would be going through his files. Of course, the most obvious explanation was some sort of corporate espionage. One of his "groups" could have sent someone in to gain more in-depth knowledge of the contest in order to gain some sort of tactical advantage? It didn't seem likely, however. Darius sat back and gazed up at the massive ship that hung above his office. Somewhere in the back of his mind, he wished he could just sail away and never be heard from again.

Chapter 55

"Hi Dad," Ryan said with a tired voice. "I'm so glad Mason is back. How's he doing?"

"He's fine, physically. He said the men that took him were actually pretty nice, for the most part. But I get the feeling he's just trying to be brave."

"Dad, have you called the police?" Ryan asked somewhat tentatively.

"I was about to, but John advised against it until we spoke with you and Sean. I agreed, but it seems like we need to do something. We're all pretty scared here, Ryan. For a lot of reasons." Ryan's dad had a bit of an edge to his voice. Not anger exactly, more frustration.

"I know you are. I'm sorry I got you involved." Ryan truly felt horrible about putting his family in danger and he was going to do whatever he could to minimize their risk.

"Ryan, we are involved and I would have it no other way. Not everyone completely believes how this all started but everybody here agrees with one thing. You, Sean and all of us here are in danger. We're taking precautions but I just don't know the best way to keep us all safe. By the way, Ryan, Sean's mom and dad really want to speak with him. Is he there?"

Ryan grimaced at the request he knew was coming. "Dad, Sean's not here right now but I'll have him call as soon as possible."

"Ryan, I," his dad started.

"Dad, wait. Things have gotten a little crazy here. These guys are serious, and Sean and I have a plan that I hope will at least keep you and the rest of the family out of harm's way. Can everyone there take some time off work, like a couple weeks?"

"I have no idea, Ryan. What's this plan of yours?"

Ryan then proceeded to lay out his plan for everyone to take a 10-day cruise. At first, his dad objected vehemently but once Ryan explained the logic, there was little objection left. If they had just checked into a hotel somewhere, the danger still remained. It was just a change of location. But the cruise would at least put some distance between them and whoever was watching them. And even if someone got on the ship with them, there wasn't much they could do if they all stayed together. Plus, communication with Jerry and his group would be a lot tougher, if not impossible. At least when they were at sea.

"Ok, Ryan. I'll run it by everyone. One thing, and this seems kind of silly when we're talking about our safety. But how are we supposed to pay for this? We have some savings but..."

"Dad, don't worry about that. Sean and I made a few calls. There are cruises that leave practically every day from Miami. There are 16 people in total. One of the travel places we called said it would run about $1500 per person. And with a group that size, you'll probably get a deal. Remember I forgot that $10,000 in my room? Plus, I'll wire you $25,000 today, and that should be enough to get you guys on a ship." Ryan's head was pounding. He had to keep his eyes shut as he talked.

"Ryan, this is one hell of a mess you're in." Ryan's Dad wasn't a prude by any means but he never swore. He always said it makes you sound ignorant.

"I know, Dad. It's not something we chose. It kind of chose us."

"Dad, listen. You need to do this as secretly as possible. I can't be sure, but you're probably being watched." Ryan felt very strange having to say his family was "being watched." It just didn't seem right.

"Well, as of last night we are all here. All 16 of us. Jessica came up with a cover story about a sleepover party for the kids. They seem to have bought it but Mason now knows pretty much everything, of course, and Brit seems very suspicious." Ryan could hear the commotion as his dad spoke. It must be a madhouse.

"That's good," Ryan agreed, "it will be best if everyone stays together. Maybe only you and John or Sean Sr. should go get the money from Wells Fargo. Once you've got all your tickets set up, pack what you can and just GO! You can buy what you need in Florida." Ryan felt so strange giving his dad directions. Right now, he was acting like a 44-year-old father as opposed to a 17-year-old teenager. He had nothing but respect for his father and would never talk down to him. But this was urgent and he had other important things to get to. Although the safety of his family was a priority.

"Sound like a plan?" Ryan asked.

"Ok, Ryan. I'll get the adults together and discuss it." His dad still sounded somewhat unsure but he had agreed.

"Ok, I'll give you a call in an hour. Love you, Dad." Ryan hung up the phone and gently laid back on the bed.

"It sounds as though you were successful in procuring your plan?" Maxwell asked from across the small hotel room.

"Yea, I hope so," Ryan sighed tiredly. "I feel bad, though. John, my dad, Sean Sr., and Debbie all have jobs. And the kids have school. I'm not sure how they're going to pull this off...."

Maxwell stayed silent and listened as Ryan quietly fell asleep. 'He must be absolutely exhausted,' Maxwell thought to himself. He decided to stay and keep watch since he was concerned that Ryan had suffered a concussion. His face showed the worry he was also feeling about Sean's current situation.

Chapter 56

It was Thursday, 5:00 pm and as he does every Thursday, Darius was scrambling to finalize his presentation for "the meeting." Every Thursday night, Darius hosts a meeting in his office to discuss the current contest. Major events, ups and downs, future plans and such. And this week would be the best update yet, Darius thought as he sat at his expensive desk in his expensive chair. Exactly at 7:00 pm, the monitors that surrounded his office would come to life and 9 of his closest 'friends' would be joining him. Darius considered them more as competitors rather than friends. He had no real friends. A fact that he wouldn't admit to himself but deep down, he was very aware.

This week's update will include the death of an innocent, the death of a competitor, violence, kidnapping, and family strife.

Maxwell had been quite correct in his assessment of the current situation at the Life Force Institute. Darius had indeed completely abandoned his father's quest. He no longer cared about bettering the world or reinvigorating the population. Those ideals and values had vacated Darius' psyche long ago. Maxwell and all the others had not noticed it since Darius had continued on and let the scientists research to their heart's content. Everyone thought they were doing such important work. When, in actuality, their data was useless and, beyond a white paper or research text, nothing would come of it.

Darius needed the Institute to fuel his greed and support his sociopathic ego. These contests meant everything to him. Once his contest was complete, nobody would be able to rival his creativity and technology.

For a brief moment, Darius felt a twinge of sadness for what would ultimately happen to Ryan and Sean. As far as his inner circle knew, he was risking his own existence by using the two men who saved those two young kids so many years ago. But Darius was confident that his engineers and scientists had adequately planned for any negative outcome. And although the memory erase procedure was highly effective, there had been cases where it was not complete. Therefore, as with past contests, there would be no real reason to leave anyone alive once the competition was over.

Chapter 57

"Here." Jerry barked as he threw a wet towel at Sean. Sean stared at the back of Jose's head as they drove. He was hunched in the backseat of the Suburban and tried to wipe as much dry blood off his face as he could. The dry paper towel had done very little but stop the bleeding. He was pretty sure his nose was broken and possibly a cracked rib or two. It hurt every time he breathed in. Through his mouth of course since his nose was completely blocked with blood and snot.

'Great plan, Ryan,' Sean thought. Although he knew it wasn't Ryan's fault. And it wasn't like he had come up with anything better. Sean had no idea where they were going. He wasn't as familiar with this area as Ryan was. He looked out the window as they drove. All he saw was strip mall after strip mall. They had only made one stop to pick up Dirk, the sniper. As he got in, he gave Sean a dirty look. Sean was sure he was going to get another punch to the face and even mentally prepared for it but luckily nothing had come. He knew he was in deep trouble. What Jerry had said back at the parking lot was true. They didn't need both of them. Sean was confident in Ryan's ability to plan but wasn't sure his friend would be able to save him. He knew they would be heading to Washington D.C. but wasn't exactly sure when or how. And what would happen when they got there? That was the thought that made Sean's heart sink.

"Shit!" Jose suddenly shouted. "I got a cop behind me with his lights on." Jerry slowly turned halfway around from the front seat to look. "Dirk, get that rifle on the floor and cover it up. And you, you little shit," he pointed at Sean, "sit up straight and keep your mouth shut."

Jose slowly pulled off the road into an empty parking lot. It was away from the street but there was still traffic going by. The cop pulled in behind the Suburban. Jerry had his 9mm with a silencer on the side of his seat out of view from the driver's window. Dirk kept his handgun under a sweater and pointed at Sean's ribcage. Both Sean and Dirk were in the 2nd-row seat, the 3rd row was empty and Jerry and Jose were upfront.

The police officer approached cautiously, looking in at Sean and Dirk as he passed. Jose rolled the window halfway down.

"Hello, officer, what's the problem?"

"Could I see your license and registration?" the officer asked.

"Sure thing," Jose replied. Jerry had the glove compartment open, rummaging through papers. Both he and Jose knew full well there was no registration, and they didn't have driver's licenses. This Suburban belonged to a friend of Jose's in Anaheim. 'It was probably stolen,' Jerry thought in the back of his mind.

Jerry leaned toward the cop. "It's the darndest thing, officer, this truck belongs to a friend of mine and I can't seem to find his registration here."

The cop spoke to Jose, "I need to see your driver's license, sir." Jose looked at Jerry.

"I'm sorry, officer, we just went to pick up our friend here," he motioned to Sean in the back, "he was in a bit of a scuffle. And I walked out without my license." The officer took a half step back and unclipped his gun. "Please step out of the vehicle, sir." Again, Jose looked at Jerry. Despite his training, the officer was focusing on Jose. Jerry reached down on his side, grabbed his 9mm and shot the officer point blank in the chest twice. The cop was literally blown back with the impact and landed on his back. Jose hit the gas and peeled out of the parking lot. Unfortunately, the police officer fell near the base of a palm tree that shielded him from the view of the highway. Since Jerry had his silencer installed, there was very little noise from the two gunshots.

As Jose reached the main road, he slowed down and entered traffic at a normal speed.

"Holy shit!!" Dirk yelled from the backseat. "What the hell's wrong with you?"

"Shut up! Just shut up, dammit!!" Jerry yelled from the front. For a man who is normally under control, Jerry was clearly losing it.

"Okay! Okay!! We have to get rid of this truck." Jerry screeched as he started to hyperventilate. Normally shooting a cop or anyone else wouldn't have elicited this type of reaction, but in this case, there was a lot riding on them staying out of jail. In fact, everything was riding on them staying out of jail.

"You shot a cop!! Are you nuts?" Dirk reiterated.

Jerry swung the gun around and pointed it right at Dirk. Dirk raised his gun and pointed it right at Jerry. "If you don't shut up, you're next!! Put your goddamn gun down right now or I will end you right here." Dirk could see the craziness in Jerry's eyes. He'd only seen that before in his brother's eyes. Dirk slowly lowered his gun.

Sean hadn't uttered a sound. He was in complete shock and hadn't hardly breathed since the shooting began. He slowly slid as far away from Dirk as humanly possible. He felt like he was watching a bad HBO movie, but he was actually part of it. Unbeknownst to Jerry and his team, Institute engineers had outfitted the Suburban with 3 cameras with varying angles. The entire incident had been recorded.

Chapter 58

Tyler was sprinting as fast as his little legs could go. He rounded a corner and barreled straight down the long hall that led to Darius' office. He didn't say a word to the secretary but ran straight past her. "Hey, you can't go in there!" she yelled as Tyler flew by.

Darius was still preparing for his 'presentation.' "Sir, sir!" Tyler shouted louder than he should have as he ran towards Darius.

"Stop!" Darius bellowed and held up his hand. "You know better than to just come barging into my office unannounced! What the hell is the meaning of this?"

Darius' secretary had followed Tyler in. "I'm sorry, sir, I tried to stop him." Darius looked at a very disheveled Tyler, looked at his secretary and waved her out. She immediately left.

"Well, Tyler, if you can compose yourself and stop sweating on my oak floor, what in the hell is your problem?" Darius had calmed down but Tyler was still breathing very hard.

"I'm sorry...for the intrusion, sir...but there has been a terrible accident," Tyler said between heavy breaths. At that moment, Maxwell entered the office. He had been watching Ryan sleep but, after a couple of hours, was confident that he was okay.

"What type of accident, Tyler?" Maxwell asked from behind his counterpart.

By now, Tyler's breathing had somewhat normalized, and Darius was sitting at his desk as if he was about to receive a boring quarterly report. "Yes, Tyler, what type of accident are you talking about?" Darius repeated.

"Well, as you both know, my team has taken Master Jensen captive. And just now, I received a video that shows another shooting!" As Tyler finished his sentence, Maxwell's heart sank, but he maintained his composure. "The team was on their way back to their hotel when they were pulled over by a police officer. Apparently, there was some confusion and Mr. Stillwell shot the officer twice in the chest." Tyler said with resounding defeat in his voice.

Darius slowly put his hands together and up to his mouth. Nobody spoke for several seconds. "Is he dead?" Darius finally spoke.

"No. He's in surgery. He was wearing a protective vest, but because of the close distance, both bullets went through the vest and into his chest." Tyler was now sitting in one of the chairs in front of the desk. Maxwell, although relieved it wasn't Sean, was openly distraught by the news.

"And where is your team and Master Jensen now?" Darius asked.

"They are in the process of obtaining alternate transportation and getting rid of the Suburban," Tyler explained.

Playing the politician, Darius replied, "Okay, gentlemen, we knew there was the possibility of violence and even injury or death. That is the inherent risk in this type of endeavor. We will maintain high hopes that the officer recovers from his injuries. Stay on top of this, Tyler, and keep me abreast of any developments." Darius slowly turned away from the two handlers but not before Maxwell noticed a slight grin as he turned.

Maxwell placed his hand on Tyler's shoulder. Tyler jumped at the touch. "Let's go, Tyler," Maxwell whispered to his friend. Tyler rose on shaky legs and they walked slowly out of the Director's office.

Chapter 59

Maxwell and Tyler walked slowly past Darius' secretary, and once out of earshot, Maxwell said, "Tyler can you come with me to my office for a moment?" Without looking up, Tyler nodded his head and followed the older man down the long hallway.

Once inside his office, Maxwell removed his 'bug finder' and performed a fairly exhaustive search along his walls and around the furniture. It had been a longstanding tradition to not install any cameras or listening devices in handler's offices. But Maxwell wasn't taking any chances.

"What are you doing?" Tyler asked.

"Just making sure," Maxwell replied.

"Making sure of what?" Tyler asked, somewhat confused.

"That we're not being listened to," Maxwell explained.

"We've never been bugged before. What's going on?" Tyler sat down in front of Maxwell's desk.

Maxwell closed his door and sat down next to Tyler. "Tyler, we've known each other for a long time. You've been here, what, 20 years now?"

"Close enough, 21 actually," Tyler replied.

"I've been here well over twice that long. You never had the opportunity of meeting Alexander. He was a great man with a great vision, as you know. Alexander and I started this institute before Darius was born. He and I shared a dream, Tyler."

"Yes, I know all that. Everyone does," Tyler said rather emphatically.

"I know you do," Maxwell continued, "but what you don't know is that Alexander's dream died a long time ago."

Tyler crinkled his forehead in confusion.

"Recently, I have become aware of some things. Very disturbing things about this institute and its mission." Tyler began a question, but Maxwell put up his hands. "Let me finish. Or rather, let me ask you a question. What do we do here, Tyler?" Maxwell asked.

Tyler thought for a moment. "We collect data on human behavior in an attempt to…" Tyler paused, "…change the world. Right?" Tyler looked at Maxwell.

"That's what I thought as well. But I recently came to a startling realization. What do we do with all that data?"

Tyler thought for a moment. "I'm not entirely sure. That's up to the science team and the environmental folks. We only handle the contest participants," he answered.

"Right, it's called compartmentalization," Maxwell stated with certainty. "Each division and team is given a specific set of directives and goals. They plug away at their research and give projections and theoretical analyses and it is all given to Darius to compile and make sense of. Right?"

"Right," Tyler's wheels were beginning to turn.

"So who's to say that any of the terabytes of data that we collect is worth anything at all?" Maxwell paused for effect. "Who's to say that what we do is making any difference at all?"

Maxwell stared at Tyler who seemed to be deep in thought. He opened his mouth but didn't say anything and shut it again. Tyler got up from his chair and paced around the room several times. "So, why are we all here? Why do we all have jobs and get paid our weekly units and…" he trailed off.

Maxwell interjected, "I'm not saying we don't do good work. We have some of the brightest engineering and science minds on the planet working here. We've perfected a time travel orb that could revolutionize the world. Have you ever wondered why we were sworn to secrecy regarding the orb?"

"That's easy. Because time travel was outlawed, and we'd all go to jail if anyone outside the institute found out we were using it," Tyler stated with some satisfaction.

"Possibly, possibly. That is probably the primary reason. But think about it. What is the most valuable asset this institute has? Its gold reserves? It's real estate holding? Maybe the engineering staff? Our patent library? No. The most valuable thing we possess is safe and reliable time travel. As far as I know, and correct me if I'm wrong, nobody else on the planet has the software and hardware capabilities we have with regard to the orb. Right?"

"Okay, let's say you're right," Tyler countered, "So who cares? We work away at our pointless jobs, get paid, and go home to our families every night. What's wrong with that?"

"Nothing. Not a thing. Except..." Maxwell paused, "what if that safe and reliable time travel technology fell into the wrong hands? And who's to say it isn't already in the wrong hands?"

Again, Tyler was at a loss for words. Maxwell continued, "Tyler, I'm going to tell you something now that, if made public, will most likely cost me my life." Tyler perked up. "Two nights ago, I broke into Darius' office and went through his files." Maxwell didn't take his eyes off his friend. Tyler's eyes widened. "When I told Darius about the young security guard's death, and he didn't even consider canceling the contest, I had to find out. I had to find out why." Now it was Maxwell's turn to stand up and pace the room as he spoke. "What I found was a file labeled 'My Turn.' It was a complete summary of the current contest with Ryan and Sean and your team. Also included was a list of 9 names. Some of them I recognized as Darius' inner circle. You know, his inner circle of knowledge that he claims assists with our data and our mission. Anyway, next to each name was a number, and either Team A or Team B was listed. I don't know which team is A or B but all, except I think two, had chosen Team B. Tyler, this contest is not a contest. It's a game! A sick, twisted game to see who wins and who loses. It doesn't matter who gets hurt or killed in the process. In fact, I think 'accidents' like the one today and the security guard and the young White boy being kidnapped and Mr. Bendar being killed only serve to increase the entertainment value. I was interrupted before I could get any more information but I'm betting that the time travel technology is the grand prize for the winner! This is only the third time travel contest we've run. You know how the others turned out. Imagine 6 more with similar results." Maxwell's mind was reeling. He just entrusted his life to this man. It had better be worth it.

Tyler sat still for what seemed like a long time, processing what he had just heard. So Maxwell continued, "Tyler, let me ask you another question. Master White asked me this question yesterday. To the best of your knowledge, have any of the so-called winners in the past been rewarded with what they were promised? Have they ever been returned to their time or, in local contests, returned to their families upon completion? I honestly couldn't say yes to Master White's question. I simply don't know. Again, compartmentalization. Another division handled that."

Tyler thought for a moment. "Well, I'm not sure I can answer that question, but I think I know someone who can? Do you know Tom Freeman over in data reduction?"

"Sure, I know Tom. But he doesn't handle post-contest results and rewards," Maxwell answered.

"No, but his wife does. Tom and I snuck out for a beer the other night, and he let it slip that his wife, Dorothy, is involved in the post-contest wrap-up, I think they call it," Tyler said.

"The problem is, Tyler, that what we've discussed here today really can't leave this room. If rumors start, the investigations and security department will certainly find out where they started. And you and I will conveniently disappear. They've done it before, as you well know," Maxwell reminded his friend.

"So what are we supposed to do, Maxwell? If what you are saying is the truth, what CAN we do? Realistically?" Tyler queried.

Maxwell sat down and pulled his chair in close to Tyler. Not for effect, just because he didn't want to say it too loud. "We stop him," Maxwell said in a whisper.

Chapter 60

Darius sat quietly at his desk, trying to pull everything together for his big presentation to the group. It was almost time and since he wanted to include this latest skirmish with the police officer, he was furiously adding the details. He was internally chastising himself for being so foolish lately. He didn't know why he was so worried. There would never be a contest quite like this one. He would certainly be hailed as the greatest of all time, and his coveted time travel technology would remain his and his alone. And he would be the envy of the entire group. Hell, he would be the envy of the entire world!

Deep within his soul, there was a slight glimmer of sadness that barely flickered now regarding how this contest would ultimately end. But his narcissistic and sociopathic tendencies had been growing out of control over the last several months. Any human decency or compassion was almost completely gone. One of the teams would certainly be declared the winner in order to satisfy the group. But behind closed doors at the institute, all participants would conveniently "disappear." Michele White and Cindy Jensen would never know what happened to their husbands. They went to bed one night and when they woke up, their husbands were dead. Investigations would ensue, but there would be no resolution. Their children would be fatherless with no explanation. Darius very easily categorized this as 'the cost of doing business.' He smiled as he patted himself on the back for his ingenuity and creativity.

Suddenly, a quiet alarm sounded, alerting him that it was time to begin. He remotely secured his office door and reached inside a panel on his desk, and pushed a button to bring the monitors to life. He slowly moved to the center of the room near the world globe, where he would be visible to his 'inner circle.'

The monitors above his head that circled the room began to glow and all nine settled on a blue screen with the Institute's logo. In one fluid motion, he raised his arms and with a small remote in one hand, switched all monitors to live shots of the participants.

"Good evening, my friends! Or good morning to a few of you! I trust you are all doing well. As you all know, I have initiated my crowning achievement. A contest like no other in our history. A battle of wits and strength, of cunning and cruelty, a battle of death and despair, and one in which I have risked my own life to execute. Ladies and gentlemen, I give you "The Battle Royale"!!

With that, a large holographic projection appeared behind Darius, showing the police officer being literally lifted off his feet as two gunshots rang out and blood covered the screen. Oohs and aahs could be heard from each monitor, followed by a round of applause. Darius soaked it in, swung back around, and exclaimed, "And that's just the beginning!"

Chapter 61

Ryan slowly opened his eyes and moaned from the pounding in his head. It had significantly lessened from when he was speaking with his father, but it still throbbed. He had no idea how long he had slept. He was alone in a hotel room, and it took a few minutes for his mind to recall everything that had occurred. Slowly his eyes adjusted and he could make out that it was dark outside. Only a small lamp glowed in the corner of the room. Ryan sat up and noticed a small bottle of aspirin on the nightstand next to a glass of water. He opened the bottle and swallowed 3 aspirins. He had no idea how many he should take. He was used to taking Advil or some other pain reliever for a headache. It had been years since he had taken simple old aspirin.

He was trying to sort things out in his mind when there was a light knock on the door. Ryan froze, unsure if he should answer it or not. "Master Whi...I mean Ryan, it's Maxwell. Are you there?" Ryan got up on wobbly legs and slowly walked to the door, and opened it. Standing there was indeed Maxwell but also another man he had never seen before. He was much younger than Maxwell and small in stature. They both came in quickly and shut the door.

"Ryan, I'd like you to meet Tyler," Maxwell pointed to the younger man. "Tyler is my counterpart in this contest. He is the handler for the other group."

"Nice to meet you, Master White," Tyler put out his hand, and Ryan tentatively shook it.

"I trust you were able to get some sleep," Maxwell continued. "You were thoroughly exhausted so I wanted to let you sleep for as long as possible." Maxwell moved past Ryan farther into the room, as did Tyler. Ryan had said nothing to this point.

Maxwell again pulled out his SDD (Surveillance Detection Device) and swept the room.

"You already did that, Max," Ryan said quietly.

"Believe me, Ryan, it would have been very easy for our technicians to enter this room, plant several cameras, and leave without any sound," Maxwell stated as he continued his sweep. "However," he put the SDD back in his pocket, "it would appear we are still alone." Ryan moved to one of the beds and sat down. Maxwell moved to the other bed and sat down directly opposite Ryan.

"Ryan, I brought Tyler with me because we have a shared concern. As I explained to you and Sean earlier, it has become apparent to both of us that our boss, Darius, is completely out of control and, well, very dangerous," Maxwell said as he looked at Tyler. Following Maxwell's gaze, Ryan also looked at Tyler, who so far had said very little beyond 'Nice to meet you.' Sensing the need to support his colleague, Tyler spoke up. "I completely agree, Master White. Sorry, Ryan," Maxwell had mentioned the name preference before they arrived. "As Maxwell has explained, neither he nor I realized what has been going on. For all his faults, Darius is brilliant and has quite effectively 'compartmentalized' his entire business so that no one person, besides him, knows everything that is happening," Tyler looked to Maxwell as if to gain approval of his using Maxwell's terminology. Maxwell nodded.

"He's quite right, Ryan. We have been able to determine that each department has been set up to execute its own specific duties and objectives with no real correlation to how they affect the rest of the Institute. Quite brilliant, indeed," Maxwell confirmed.

"Hold on, guys," Ryan rubbed his eyes and ran his hand through his quite disgustingly dirty hair. He even looked at his hand as he pulled it away. "You've kind of lost me. You're talking about departments and compartmentalization. Okay, so this Darius character is a dirtbag, great. How does that help me get Sean back and get us both back to where and when we belong?"

Maxwell was silent for a few seconds as he chose his next words carefully. "That is another reason I brought Tyler here with me. It is painfully obvious at this point that whether you and Sean win or lose, you will not be sent back to your families. In fact, you will most likely be executed," Maxwell slightly grimaced. His choice of words had sounded better in his head.

Ryan closed his eyes and slowly laid back on the bed. "You know? I should be really upset. But somewhere deep down, I think both Sean and I knew this was going to end badly, no matter what we did. Go on..."

Tyler stood and walked over, and sat down next to Ryan. Ryan opened one eye and looked at Tyler as he sat down. "I won't lie to you, Ryan. This is indeed a very difficult situation. But one thing you have in your favor is the man sitting across from you," Tyler motioned to Maxwell. "Your handler, or at this point, your friend, is every bit as smart as Darius. He has a plan that you need to hear."

"Oh shit!" Ryan sat up. "My dad. I was supposed to call him back in an hour to set up the cruise," Ryan reached for the phone and dialed.

"Hello?" It was Ryan's mom. Crap!

"Hi, Mom," Ryan said, trying to sound as normal as possible.

"Ryan, honey! Are you okay? We were expecting you to call hours ago."

"I know, Mom. Sorry. How's everyone doing?"

"We're not doing very well, Ryan. I am so scared I can't tell you!" Ryan's mom had started crying.

"I know, Mom. I'm really sorry, but can I talk to Dad for a minute?" Ryan's mom, sobbing, handed the phone over.

"Ryan, that was a long hour, son?" Ryan's dad sounded more aggravated.

"I'm really sorry, dad. I'll be honest with you. I haven't slept much since we got here, and I fell asleep. But I feel better now. What did you find out about everyone's schedule?" Ryan was hoping for the best.

"It took some convincing, but I think everyone will be able to take the time off. As for the kids, we decided to just pull them out of school and say something like a death in the family or something," Ryan's dad could never have known how inappropriate that comment was. But Ryan understood.

Ryan's dad continued, "So we started calling around and found a 10-day cruise leaving Florida in two days. We used the money you left behind as a deposit. We have our plane tickets and we're getting ready. We leave tomorrow night."

Ryan was impressed. "That's great, Dad! So I will send you the extra money by Wells Fargo tomorrow. Remember, you might be followed but don't worry about it. I doubt you'll be followed onto the ship. Communication might be tough. Normally, I would say text me when you get to a port, but unfortunately, that won't work."

"What does 'text me' mean..." his dad started.

"Nevermind, Dad. I will find a way to get in touch with you," Ryan managed a small grin. How did they ever survive without cell phones, he thought? "I love you guys. Trust me, this will all be over soon," Ryan said as convincingly as possible.

His dad continued to tell him the cruise line and cruise number, and they said their goodbyes. Luckily Sean's parents weren't there, so he didn't have to come up with another lie about why they couldn't talk to him.

Ryan hung up the phone, looked at Maxwell and Tyler, and said, "Okay, what's this plan you have?"

Chapter 62

Sean wasn't sure where they were. Since the shooting, everything had been essentially out of control. Jerry had threatened to shoot Dirk about a dozen times, and Jose seemed to be trying to stay out of it and just drive. "We need to get rid of this truck," Jose said as he weaved in and out of traffic.

"I'm aware of that," Jerry said, "just let me think."

"Jose, try to find a news station on the radio," Dirk said from the back. Jose turned on the radio and started scanning stations. Finally, what sounded like a news station came on. After a couple of commercials, "returning to our main story, a police officer was shot during a traffic stop in Anaheim today. We are waiting for confirmation on the officer's condition. At this time, the suspects are at large, and the latest information we have is that they could be driving a large SUV, either black or dark blue. Our reporter is on the scene now. Vivian, are you there? Can you tell us what the current situation is?"

"Yes, Vince, we just arrived here at the scene where the officer was found approximately 15 minutes ago by passersby. The information on the suspects is very sketchy, and we cannot confirm their vehicle description at this time. Officer Matthew Landis was rushed to Orange County Hospital in serious condition. We have been told that he was wearing his protective vest, and the EMTs we spoke with are very hopeful that most of the damage was curtailed by the vest and that his injuries are not life-threatening. We will stay with this story here and continue from the hospital. Back to you, Vince."

"Lucky bastard," Jerry mumbled. "But we still need to get rid of this thing. Jose, pull into the first gas station you see that is out of the way so we can find a damn phone."

After a few minutes, Jose pulled off the road and drove a short distance down a side street to a Phillips 66 station and parked along the side of the building. Dirk got out and made his way to the pay phone. Sean had to smile. A pay phone. How long had it been since he'd used a pay phone? He was still hunched down out of view holding the rag to his nose. He had stopped bleeding but it still hurt like crap. He could tell his face was swelling up. He glanced up at Jerry, who had lost a little of the crazy in his eyes but was still spinning his head around, keeping an eye out. Sean knew that he was in trouble, but he also knew that he was in no position to try to escape.

Dirk jumped back in. "Let's go. Bernard has another vehicle at this address." He handed a piece of paper to Jerry. Sean could tell Dirk was looking at him, but he didn't make eye contact.

About 15 minutes later, they pulled into what looked like a mechanic's shop parking lot. Jose pulled the truck around the back and shut the engine off. "Over there," Dirk pointed to the corner of the lot. Sean could make out a piece of crap station wagon that didn't look like it had been driven in a while. Dirk looked at Sean, "You move, you die." The three of them got out and walked toward the wagon. Dirk hung back and stared at Sean from a few feet away. Sean couldn't really hear what they were saying, but it was clear that Jerry wasn't thrilled with the vehicle exchange. Sean quietly put his hand down in the pocket of the door and rummaged around. At first, he didn't feel anything, but as he moved his hand toward the front, he ran into what felt like a small screwdriver. He quickly pulled it out and put it in his pocket. Suddenly, Sean's door swung open, and he nearly fell out as he was leaning on the door for support. "Let's go, shithead," Dirk said as he grabbed Sean by the shoulder and dragged him toward the station wagon. He opened the back door, which screeched like a banshee, "Get in." Sean climbed in and immediately started coughing as dust and dirt flew up from the seat. The other three jumped in, and remarkably the engine started right up. After loading all their stuff up in the back, they pulled out of the parking lot and headed out to where Sean had no idea.

Chapter 63

"Before we go any further, I need to tell you a few things. Especially fill you in on something that has just recently taken place," Maxwell said, still sitting across from Ryan.

Ryan sat up, "Is it, Sean?! Is he okay?"

"Yes, as far as we know, Sean is fine. A little beaten up but fine. No, it happened only a short time ago. As the other team, including Sean, was driving away, they were pulled over by a local police officer. We're still putting all the pieces together, but at one point, for some reason, Mr. Stillwell shot the policeman from inside their vehicle. The officer was standing at the driver's side window, and Mr. Stillwell shot him twice in the chest. Now, all indications are that the officer's protective vest saved his life. He's at the hospital now, and the last word we got was that he should make a full recovery." Ryan stood up and walked over to the small table, and sat back down. "Well, that's just great! Now they're shooting cops," Ryan said, somewhat exasperated. "So I assume they got away?"

"Yes, but we had surveillance cameras in the vehicle, and it would appear they made an exchange with another car a few miles away," Tyler chimed in. "At this point, all we have is their approximate location from their skin tags."

"So you see, Ryan, why Tyler and I are so concerned. This contest has spun completely out of control. And what makes matters worse is that Darius is thrilled."

"Thrilled!?!" Ryan nearly shouted. "Thrilled that a cop got shot and Sean and I got our asses kicked? Thrilled that I killed, what's his name? That an innocent security guard was killed? That my brother was kidnapped, and our families have been terrorized?! He's thrilled?"

"Yes, and that is why we are both here, Ryan," Maxwell said calmly, trying to bring the tension down a little. "Ryan, both Tyler and I want to end this thing and get you and Sean back home. We don't care about the contest anymore. In fact, we both want to prevent any further contests from happening."

"And just how the hell do you plan on doing that, Max? Aren't we constantly being tracked and surveilled? Aren't there multiple 'departments' back at this Life Force Company of yours watching our every move?"

"To a point, yes, but," Maxwell held up his hands, "most of the information they rely on comes directly from Tyler and me. It is true that the engineers at the institute can go in and check locations and cameras any time they want. But they very rarely do. The handlers are the primary source of information. Both Tyler and I turn in progress reports daily with events and updates. I do have a plan, at least the beginnings of a plan, but I think it is necessary to fill you in on some other things," Maxwell glanced at Tyler.

"Maxwell, no," Tyler said immediately.

"Tell me what?" Ryan asked. "Don't hold out on me now, Max."

"Ryan, what I am going to tell you is strictly forbidden. There are many reasons why but at this point, I think it's important for you to know everything," Maxwell said again, looking at Tyler. Tyler just sighed, "Okay, go ahead."

Maxwell rose from the bed and sat down at the table across from Ryan. "Ryan, I haven't told you much about our time. We come from the year 2163. Life is very different for the human race in our time. You witnessed the carnage of 9/11 in 2001. Sadly, that attack pales in comparison to what happens 25 years later. On September 11, 2026, a massive worldwide biological attack was launched from 20 locations across the globe. It was determined that a fundamentalist Islamic group was responsible, but it was never confirmed who. In 2163, the details are a little sketchy, but apparently, the virus that was unleashed spread more devastation than the terrorists probably planned. Or maybe not. Maybe they knew exactly what it would do. Anyway, the planet was decimated. When the anti-virals were finally developed and distributed, over 1 billion people had been killed."

"Holy shit," Ryan said under his breath.

"The loss of life was just the beginning. The world economy had crumbled and America was not spared. Within two years, the United Nations had been dissolved and replaced with what is called the New Global Union. This NGU essentially runs the entire planet. The United States Constitution was discarded, and the entire populace was placed under martial law and strict communism-like policies." Maxwell went on to further describe the aftermath and how life had changed since the attack. When he was finished, nobody said anything for what seemed like an eternity.

After a few minutes, Ryan spoke up. "So if you have this time travel device, why don't you go back and change things? Keep it from happening?"

"Well, that's just it. The time travel device, as you call it, is not available to everyone. In fact, it's not available to anyone but Darius. When time travel was shown to be theoretically possible, there were only a few laboratories that had the resources to try and perfect it. There were several horrible accidents and failed attempts. Finally, the NGU outlawed any experimentation with time travel and the penalties were severe. Although it didn't really matter since nobody had the resources or the motivation to continue the work. Nobody, that is, except for Darius. Someday, I will tell you the history of the Life Force Institute in more detail. For now, suffice it to say that we are the only corporation, at least that I know of, that continued the time travel perfection process and finally got it to work. And nobody knows about it but us. In fact, that is the next part of my story," Maxwell stood up to stretch his legs and continued, "Darius not only perfected time travel but also figured out a way around the paradox."

"Paradox?" Ryan asked.

"Yes, now this gets a little convoluted so just listen but don't try and figure it out just yet. It's hard to even explain adequately. Imagine that you go back in time to before you are born and kill your mother. Therefore, you will never be born and will not have the chance to go back and kill your mother. So it never happened. Or did it? Or think of another example. Say you go back in time and kill Hitler before the Holocaust. But one of the people he was going to kill turns out to be a much worse mass murderer and slaughters 20 million instead of 6 million. It was this time travel paradox and the obvious moral implications that so many feared. And, since resources were so scarce, proper research was never done."

"But you said Darius found a way around it?" Ryan asked.

"Yes, but I must admit that this is where my knowledge, shall we say, runs dry," Maxwell stated. "Tyler, I think you know a little more on this subject, correct?"

Tyler rose from the bed and joined the other two at the table. "Well, I can't say I completely understand the mathematics or the physics, but I do know sort of how it works," he started. "So, I dated a girl who worked in the theoretical division several years ago. She liked me a lot more than I liked her, so even though I am ashamed to say it, I 'used' that to my advantage to gain some insight," he glanced with a sly smile at Maxwell and Ryan, neither of which gave any response. "Anyway, as I understand it, the paradox actually doesn't exist. Well, it does exist, sort of. While it is true that changes can be made in the past that will affect the future, they don't affect every future," Tyler paused, seeing that Ryan had a very confused face.

"I told you this got quite convoluted," Maxwell interjected.

"What do you mean by 'every future'?" Ryan asked.

"The physicists in the theoretical time travel division postulated that changes made in the past didn't alter the current timeline but skewed it into another timeline entirely. For instance," Tyler said quickly to avoid more questions, "let's take Maxwell's example. If you were to go back in time before your birth and kill your mother, you would not immediately cease to exist. A new timeline would be formed from that point on that would not include you. Since you would never be born. But the timeline from whence you came would remain unchanged."

"I think I understand," Ryan said somewhat tentatively. "So every time anyone travels back in time and makes a significant change, a new timeline is formed from that point on?"

"Yes, but the change does not have to be significant. In fact, most physicists agree that ANY traveler that enters the space-time continuum will create a new timeline, whether a change is made or not. There are a multitude of implications; moral, spiritual, ethical, physical, and on and on. But the experiments and trials seemed to back up the theory," Tyler smiled sheepishly as if to say 'it wasn't my idea.'

"Okay, I think I understand, sort of," Ryan said. "But if there are essentially countless timelines created, how can you be sure to return to where or when you came from?"

Here, Maxwell spoke up. "That, Ryan, is the secret that Darius is keeping to himself."

"Quite right," Tyler agreed, "even Denise, my girlfriend, had no idea how that works. All she said was that it was a combination of algorithms and hardware and software that guaranteed a traveler would return to the exact timeline that he or she left from."

"And both Tyler and I agree that it is that technology that Darius is holding as the prize for these contests. Imagine, Ryan, you could go back in time, win a few lotteries and live out your life in that timeline like a king."

"Or, go back and commit all manner of evil and get away with it," Tyler said quietly.

All three were silent for several seconds after that.

"Guys, this is a weapon," Ryan said blankly. Again, complete silence.

After a few minutes, Maxwell broke the quiet. "Well then, that makes our plan even more important."

Chapter 64

Darius sat quietly at his desk. The presentation was over and as he expected, the group was astonished at the results he had displayed. Darius slowly sipped $1000 brandy as he patted himself on the back for his amazing creativity. As he congratulated himself, there was a nagging thought that kept creeping into his mind. How had his files been disturbed? Who was looking for information on this contest? He had completely dismissed the possibility that he had misfiled them. That was preposterous. He would never have replaced them in the wrong order.

He put his glass down and called security, "Bruce, could you please come to my office immediately?" Bruce Holstetter was the head of security and one of his most loyal employees. Bruce had been with the Institute since Darius was a young boy. Darius used to follow him around on his scheduled routes, and they had become quite close.

A few minutes later, Bruce entered the office and walked toward Darius at his desk. "Stop!" said Darius, louder than he had planned. Immediately Bruce froze in his tracks.

"Bruce, close your eyes," Darius commanded. Bruce closed his eyes. "Now, when I tell you to, open your eyes but remain where you are."

"Yes, sir," Bruce replied. Darius got out of his chair and crawled under his desk. "Okay, in 5 seconds, open your eyes and tell me what you see."

Bruce dutifully counted to five and opened his eyes. "I see the globe, the chairs in front of your desk, your chair, and your desk," Bruce was a little confused but played along.

Darius emerged from under his desk and sat back down. "Could you see me under my desk?" he asked.

"No, sir. I could not see anything beneath or behind your desk."

"As I suspected," Darius said. "Bruce, I have an assignment for you and you alone. Well, you'll need a technician but only one, and I want to speak with whoever you choose."

"Whatever you need, sir," Bruce completed the walk over to Darius' desk.

"I want you to install cameras outside my office from several angles and cameras in the hallway that are motion activated. I also want cameras installed here in my office but I want to have complete control of those. I will require a remote switch that I can turn on or off as I wish. Nobody is to have access to video from my office. Make sure they are hidden and nobody, including my assistant, knows about any of them. I want them installed by tomorrow at this time. Do you understand?" Darius was confident that Bruce did understand but needed to maintain the upper hand.

"Of course, sir. I will make the necessary arrangements. Will that be all?" Unlike Maxwell, Bruce was not scared of Darius or intimidated but was very professional in dealing with him.

"That's all, Bruce. Thank you." Darius picked up his brandy and turned away from Bruce. The head of security briefly hesitated. He wanted to ask why, but he knew it wasn't any of his business. He turned and walked out of the office.

Chapter 65

Maxwell, Tyler and Ryan sat silently for several minutes, each contemplating the situation. Ryan broke the silence. "Ok, I agree that stopping Darius is imperative, but it is more important to me to get Sean back safely and end this contest." Maxwell and Tyler nodded in agreement. "Maxwell, a few days ago, when this whole thing started, you described the technology that your engineers use to conceal the cameras?"

Tyler spoke up. "Oh, you mean White Out?"

"White Out?" Maxwell asked somewhat incredulously.

"Yea, we've always called it White Out because it basically erases anything that it is attached to," Tyler said with a slight grin. "Actually, we used to mess around with it during breaks before security took it away. They said we were abusing the company's property. It doesn't hurt or anything like that. And it's not foolproof but it does work pretty well," Tyler said.

Ryan was intrigued. "How does it work exactly?"

Maxwell spoke up. "Its actual name is Visual Concealment Device or VCD. When attached to a physical structure within its size range, it automatically scans the structure, envelops it with some sort of, uh, invisible screen, and uses light-bending technology to essentially make the structure disappear. For all intents and purposes."

"But you said it wasn't foolproof," Ryan said to Tyler.

"No, if you move too quickly, like try to run or jump, the screen has a hard time keeping up and part of the structure, as Maxwell calls it, becomes visible again until the device catches up," Tyler said, quite proud of his knowledge. "That was what was fun when we messed around with it. We'd try to see how fast the screen would catch up if we jumped or ran."

"Well, what is IT exactly? I mean, this White Out or VCD?" Ryan asked.

"It's a small box, about 3" by 3." It has to be small to fit on all the cameras that are placed," Maxwell said as he estimated the size with his hands. "And Tyler is exactly right. It works exceedingly well if the structure is static. But movement does cause a lag in the concealment. Why are you interested in the VCD, Ryan?"

"Well, we need to somehow gain the upper hand when we once again meet up with Tyler's team. And it might come in handy. Is there any way you can get a couple we can 'mess around with'?" Ryan asked, mimicking Tyler's terminology.

"Well, they're not as available as they used to be, but I'm sure I can get my hands on a couple," Tyler offered. "We'll need to be careful since they are logged in and out. But I know the girl that tracks the equipment. I think I can sweet talk her into forgetting to sign the logs."

"Max, you mentioned their size range. What is their size range?" Ryan asked.

"Probably two adults standing close together. They'd have to be touching. We tried it on a horse once. It covered most of it, but we could never get the head to disappear," Maxwell said with a slight grin.

Ryan reached into his pocket and pulled out the piece of paper that Jerry had tossed at his feet when they threw Sean into the Suburban. "Well, the last thing Jerry said was that I should do whatever I was planning on doing and they would keep Sean until they got to the next clue." Ryan stared at the phone number trying unsuccessfully to formulate a plan. His last attempt had resulted in getting Sean kidnapped. Right now, he wasn't exuding a massive amount of confidence in his planning abilities.

"Ryan, do you remember when I said that handlers are not privy to the location of the clues?" Maxwell asked.

"Yea, you said it was protocol or something like that," Ryan answered.

Maxwell looked at Tyler. "Well, it is also a protocol that handlers are given access to the location of the final orb." Tyler looked at the ground. He had to remind himself that everything was out in the open now, and all the rules had changed. Maxwell continued, "And I can tell you that you and Sean are correct. The final orb is located near the Lincoln Memorial. Please understand, Ryan. Tyler and I are here to help but with the understanding that once this contest is finished, you and Sean will assist us in defeating Darius before you return to your time."

"That, my dear Max, I definitely understand and agree wholeheartedly," Ryan stood and extended his hand.

As Maxwell stood to shake Ryan's hand, he added, "Also, Ryan, that location will be full of cameras. And since it is the final act of this disgusting saga, I'm sure there will be plenty of eyes watching. Tyler and I will need to remain essentially out of sight so as to not reveal our assistance. If you are planning on using the VCD, you will need to be careful as to how it is used and where."

Ryan dropped his hand and sat back down before shaking Maxwell's hand. "Crap, I didn't think about that. If we use the VCD, Darius and his security team will instantly know you helped us."

Tyler perked up, "Not necessarily."

Ryan and Maxwell both looked at Tyler. "You know Rudy in Field Tech?" he asked Maxwell.

"I know who he is. But I don't know him well," Maxwell replied.

"About 6 months ago, during the Prague mission, Rudy totally screwed up on a surveillance installation. It could have screwed up a lot of data acquisition. I covered for him and made it look like a mechanical error. He owes me for that. I might be able to convince him to give me a layout of cameras around the Lincoln Memorial. If we know where the cameras are, we can try and stay out of sight if and when we use the VCD," Tyler smiled.

Maxwell and Ryan looked at each other. After a few seconds, Maxwell spoke up. "I hate to involve anyone else in this plan, but it might work if Rudy does it. But what exactly are you going to tell Rudy you need this information for?"

"I won't tell him anything," Tyler stated matter-of-factly, "Rudy's a wimp. If I say I need it for the mission and it needs to stay between him and me, he won't say anything."

Maxwell turned and sat down at the table and exhaled loudly, "Well, it might be our only shot. Tyler, why don't you go back and get a VCD unit. Try to find one that is fully charged and in good working order. Talk to Rudy and see if you can get the camera layout. Ryan and I will stay here and try to put together some sort of plan. But if Rudy starts asking a lot of questions or seems to be overly suspicious, let it go and tell him you were just kidding or something to that effect."

Tyler looked a little worried but said okay, walked over to his bag, pulled out his orb, punched in a couple numbers, and disappeared.

"Holy shit, I don't think I'll ever get used to that," Ryan said as Tyler vanished.

He got up off the bed and walked over to the table and sat down. Maxwell reached over to his own bag and pulled out a folder. He opened it and took out a notebook with several loose papers inside. "On the positive side, we have a significant amount of documentation on the memorial itself and the location of the orb," Maxwell said as he spread out the papers on the table.

Ryan smiled. "Let's get to work. But first, we should probably make a call."

Chapter 66

"We need to get back to the hotel," Jerry said as Jose drove the station wagon through the Anaheim traffic. "Our friend might be calling. Without cell phones, the only number I could give him was our hotel room."

The rest of the drive to the hotel proceeded in silence. At one point, Sean glanced over at Dirk. His head was back, and he was asleep. They just shot a cop and this guy was taking a nap! A bump in the road jolted him awake. He immediately shoved his gun into Sean's ribs. "Feeling lucky, asshole?" Dirk asked, but Sean didn't look at him or say anything.

Jose pulled into their hotel and parked in the covered parking lot out of sight. "Get out," Dirk said. "My side."

After Dirk got out, Sean slowly slid across the seat and got out on wobbly legs. Even if the chance presented itself, he was in no shape to try and escape. Dirk roughly grabbed him by the back of his neck and started walking toward the parking elevator. Jose and Jerry grabbed some bags from the back and followed the other two. When they reached their hotel room, Dirk directed Sean toward the bathroom and shoved him into the bathtub. Luckily Sean had regained some of his coordination and sat down in the tub instead of falling head first. "You so much as make a sound, and I'll come back and finish you now. Remember, we don't really need you," Dirk said as he slammed the bathroom door.

After Dirk left, Sean let himself relax a little. He felt like crying but knew that wouldn't do much good. He looked around the bathroom. There was a small window but they were on the third floor, so that was no good. There was a phone on the wall, but who was he going to call? Sean felt very dejected and had no idea what his next move should be. Or if he even had a next move. He realized he was totally dependent on Ryan to save him. He loved his friend and had confidence in him, but he was sincerely worried that this might be the end for him. A couple of tears spilled out as he laid his head back and closed his eyes.

When Dirk came out of the bathroom, he saw that Jerry was lying on one bed and Jose on the other. 'Great,' he thought and sat down at the table. "So, what now?"

"Shut the hell up," Jerry said without opening his eyes. "We wait for the call."

Chapter 67

Ryan pulled out the scrap of paper Jerry had thrown at his feet and stared at it. "Huh, it's funny. It feels like I'm calling the shots but have zero control. They have complete leverage since they have Sean."

"Perhaps we should formulate at least a partial plan before calling them?" Maxwell asked.

Ryan thought for a minute. "Max, can I ask you a question? That little ball or orb or whatever of yours, can it transport two people? Like you and me, together?"

"Unfortunately, not the way it is currently calibrated. At the moment, it is only operable for one. And that one has to be me," Maxwell paused, "however, I can get it recalibrated at the Institute for two. It wouldn't be too difficult, but I would need to be careful as the technicians have access to all the calibration data. But," he thought for a moment, "re-calibration is a very regular and necessary maintenance function. And I can do it myself. So, the short answer to your question is yes. Why do you ask?"

"Well, I just figured it would be nice to arrive early at the Lincoln Memorial to get a lay of the land, so to speak?" Ryan gave Maxwell a small smile.

"That could work. The logistics of placing cameras on airplanes and in airports is complicated, so unless there is a defined need, the contest organizers rarely run surveillance during transport. They are usually much more interested in what happens when the subjects arrive at their destination. It's quite possible that whether you travel by air or by orb, nobody will be the wiser," Maxwell sat down and looked across the table at Ryan and gave him a small smile.

"Okay, so we tell the other team they need to make their way to D.C. We arrive early and set things up. I don't think they will relinquish Sean until they have their hands on the orb. So, I was thinking we give them an orb," Ryan said.

"I'm not sure that's the best course of action. If you just give them the orb, there's no telling what could happen. It might be very difficult to get it back," Maxwell stated.

"I didn't say; give them "the" orb, I said; give them "an" orb," Ryan said with finger quotes to emphasize "the" and "an."

Ryan got up from the table and sat down next to Maxwell. "I've seen your orb, Max. It's about the size of a bowling ball, right?"

"I suppose," Maxwell said as his mind began to track where Ryan was going.

"So, I have to assume the other team has had very little exposure to Tyler's orb, if any at all. So they don't know what it looks like. So, we get a bowling ball, new with no holes drilled, and put a couple of markings on it and maybe a fake keypad or something and make it look like an orb. We get these jokers to take it, let Sean go, and we use the real orb to get the hell out of Dodge, as they used to say," Ryan said.

Maxwell looked confused but mostly at the reference to Dodge. "I think I see where you're going, and I can do you one better. The Institute training department has several inoperative orbs just lying around for new technician training. Needless to say, we don't get many new personnel for obvious reasons, so they're just sitting in a closet. When I go back to recalibrate my orb, I can grab one and bring it with me," Maxwell gave Ryan a bigger smile this time.

"Alright, now we're talking. Ok, I'm going to call Jerry and tell him to make plans to get to D.C. Then you and I are going to pore over these documents on the memorial and figure out a way to get this done," Ryan said and walked over to the phone. He picked up the receiver, gave a big exhale, and dialed the number.

340

Chapter 68

Bill White and Sean Sr. herded their families along the walkway leading to the cruise ship. They had managed to get the money Ryan wired them and flew both their respective families to Florida. Neither Bill nor Sean Sr. had noticed anyone following them, but they were more concerned about keeping their families all together and weren't watching all the time.

"Ok, everyone, up the gangplank," Sean Sr. bellowed to the group. He led the way, and Ryan's dad was the last one behind everyone else.

Once on board, Bill White looked exhaustedly at his wife. "I understand Ryan's intention, but I still can't believe we're all on board a cruise ship headed to the Caribbean," he gave a half smile to Liz.

"Frankly, I don't understand Ryan's intention. I don't understand any of this. Last week everything was fine and normal, and this week it's all gone to shit," Ryan's mom grabbed her bag and followed the crowd. Bill raised his eyebrows. He had very rarely heard his wife swear but could easily understand her frustration.

Sean Sr. had finished directing his family and approached Bill. "Is your wife as pissed off as mine?" he asked.

"Worse, mine just said, 'Everything's gone to shit.' I don't think I've heard her say that more than 2 or 3 times in our married lifetime."

"Well, I figure we should cut them some slack. This is all very messed up. From all that we've seen and experienced, I know this is real. But every now and then, I get this nagging feeling that I will wake up any minute and this will all be a bad dream," Sean Sr. said as he grabbed the last of the bags and piled them on the luggage cart.

Bill White took a long look around. He didn't see anyone that seemed out of place. A couple of guys standing around, but they all seemed to either be with someone or looking for someone. In any case, nothing seemed out of the ordinary.

"I guess Ryan was right. At least we're safe for the time being. I just hope he knows what he's doing," Bill mumbled to himself as he walked toward the staterooms.

Chapter 69

Ryan suddenly hung up the phone before the call connected.

"What's the matter?" Maxwell asked.

"Something's been nagging at me, and I think I know what it is," Ryan said as he turned back toward Maxwell. "It's true that Jerry is a psychopath, but he's a smart psychopath. That's the problem. He always seems to be one step ahead of us. Sean is hurt, right? Not badly but I'm sure his face is swollen from the broken nose, and I'm sure he looks like crap. Dragging him to the airport and onto a plane to fly across the country will be problematic for them. I can easily see Jerry leaving him here with one of his buddies or worse, just killing him and forcing my hand at the exchange." Ryan sat down hard on the bed.

"A distinct possibility," Maxwell said as he sat down across from Ryan. "Do you have a better plan to get Sean back?"

"Maybe." Ryan laid back on the bed and stared at the ceiling for several seconds. He closed his eyes. "I'm not only going to tell them where the orb is," he sat back up and opened his eyes, "I'm going to take them to it."

"Master Whi...I mean Ryan, they would then have both of you," Maxwell stated matter of factly.

"You're right, but they essentially have us both right now anyway. At least they have complete control of the situation. The only way I can get Sean back alive is if I'm with him and can somehow regain some leverage. Or at least decrease their leverage." Ryan stood up and walked over to the table, glancing at some of the pictures of the Lincoln Memorial.

Maxwell got up and walked to the table and sat back down. He looked at Ryan. "Logic would dictate to stay as far away from your enemy as possible. But I must agree with your assessment. Do you think Mr. Stillwell will agree to the terms?"

"I guess there's only one way to find out," Ryan said as he turned and walked toward the phone.

Chapter 70

Bruce walked briskly into Darius' office. "You wanted to see me, sir?" he asked as he stood at attention at the foot of Darius' desk.

"Yes, I wanted to check on the progress of my office surveillance?" Darius asked as he poured himself a brandy, not offering anything to his security guard.

"I just finished my report for your review, sir," Bruce leaned forward and handed a folder to Darius and quickly stepped back.

Darius picked up the folder and started to leaf through the pages. "I really don't feel like reading a report right now." Darius tossed the folder back onto his desk. "Just tell me what you have installed."

Bruce described in detail what had been installed. Several cameras had been placed inside the office to capture every conceivable angle. Additional cameras had been placed in the hallway leading into Darius' office and down the hallway leading away. The regular security sweeps of the area had been doubled, and a guard would be in that particular wing of the building 24/7. Short of having a guard sit in Darius's expensive chair all night, there wasn't much more they could do. Of course, Bruce kept that last thought to himself but allowed himself a small grin when Darius wasn't looking.

"Fine, fine," Darius said quietly. "And how many people are aware of the surveillance?" he asked.

"Myself, of course. And the installation required two technicians. Their names are listed in the report. I chose them carefully and fully explained the need to keep the project confidential."

"And the increased security sweeps? How did you explain that to your department?" Darius asked as though he was trying to catch Bruce off-guard.

Bruce quietly cleared his throat. "I took it upon myself to increase security sweeps in two other wings so as to not alert any of the staff to your request."

"Good work Bruce!" Darius stood and Bruce jumped slightly at the sudden change of emotion.

"Thank you, sir. Will there be anything further?" Bruce had actually started to sweat in the 70-degree office.

"Just one thing, Bruce. I want all the feeds from my office surveillance sent directly to my personal monitor. Nobody is to have access to these video feeds at any time. Is that understood?" Darius came out from behind his massive desk and stood in front of Bruce, awkwardly close.

"Of course, sir. It will be done." Bruce took a half step back, turned and walked quickly out of the office.

Darius walked slowly to the brandy and refilled his glass. 'Let them try and spy on me now,' he thought as he took a gulp of liquor and stared up at the sailboat hanging from his ceiling.

Chapter 71

Jerry Stillwell tried to kill a police officer a few hours ago, yet he was sleeping like a baby when the phone rang. Dirk started to get up but quickly sat back down. He knew better than to test Jerry, especially today.

Jerry let the phone ring 4 times before he picked up. "Yea," was all he said.

"Mr. Stillwell, this is Ryan White. Before we go any further, I want to talk to Sean," Ryan demanded.

Jerry nodded to Dirk, "Go get the shithead from the tub."

Dirk threw the bathroom door open. "Get out here. Your boyfriend wants to talk."

Sean stepped out of the tub and past Dirk. He fully expected a slap on the head or a fist in the gut, but neither came. He walked slowly toward Jerry. When he got a couple feet away, Jerry tossed him the phone.

"Hey, Ryan," Sean said as boldly as he could muster.

"Sean, how bad?" Ryan asked.

"I'm alright. A busted nose is probably an improvement. He smiled but quickly stopped as it reopened the cut on his lip. I'll survive."

"Hang tight, pal. I have a plan." Ryan said, and Sean handed the phone back to Jerry.

"Okay, your friend's fine. Now where is my orb?"

"Well, Mr. Stillwell, I don't have your orb. But I know where it is and I would like to make you an offer," Ryan paused, but Jerry said nothing.

"Right now, I will concede that you have all the leverage. That's fine, and I accept that. So, in order to keep my friend and myself from further injury, I will offer to not only decipher the final clue but I will personally take you to the orb. I know where it is, but Sean and I will accompany you to it. At that point, we will tell you specifically where it is, no tricks, and you will let us go. I'll even pay for the plane tickets," Ryan threw in for good measure.

"You think I'm a fucking idiot?" Jerry seethed through the phone. "You two get lost in a crowd somewhere and we're left with nothing?"

Ryan had to think quickly. "Mr. Stillwell, you remember the parking lot as well as I do. I still have the lump on the back of my head. We are no match for you physically, you have the guns, and there are three of you. So you will now have two hostages instead of one. I'm willing to hand over the orb and take our chances with whoever is running this circus. All we want is to get out and stay alive. I promise we will not run. I know as well as you do that you can find our families back home. You've already shown us that." Ryan held his breath.

"Your promises don't mean shit to me," Jerry said but paused. "Okay, shithead, we'll play it your way. But understand one thing. Once I have that orb in my hands, all bets are off. I have two gentlemen here that want nothing else but to watch you die slowly. You tell our little butler, Tyler, the plan, and we'll be ready in the morning." Jerry hung up.

"Looks like you're gonna have some company," Jerry said to Sean who was still standing at the foot of one of the beds. Jerry picked up a towel and threw it at Sean. Sean didn't see it coming, and it fell to the ground. He bent down to pick it up and Dirk kicked him into one of the chairs. Sean fell headfirst into the chair but luckily got his hands up and deflected much of the blow.

"Knock it off," Jerry yelled. "You'll get your chance, but he has to be pretty for his boy tomorrow. Clean him up as best you can. He can sleep in the tub."

"Screw that! I'm not his mama," Dirk said as he picked up the towel and threw it back at Sean. "Clean yourself up and stay quiet in there. I'm going to get some sleep." Dirk laid back on the bed, much to Jose's chagrin. 'I guess I'm sleeping on the floor tonight.' Jose thought.

Sean picked up the towel, this time bending at the knees, and walked slowly back to the bathroom and shut the door. Jose had recently vacated the bathroom, and the smell was nauseating. 'Great,' Sean thought as he stared at his reflection in the mirror. He switched on the fan, but of course, it was broken. He felt like crying, but he simply didn't have the energy. His face was swollen and bruised from his broken nose. His lip was cut, and dried blood and dirt completed the ensemble. It literally felt like it was years since he was with his wife and children back home in his old bed and in his old body. Now he was beaten up in a 17-year-old body in 1982 and sleeping in a tub as a hostage. 'WTF?' he thought, 'WTF?'

Chapter 72

Ryan hung up the phone. "Well, I guess that went about like what I thought it would," Ryan said as he sat down on the bed.

"So he agreed to your terms?" Maxwell asked, still sitting at the table.

"I don't know if I would call it "agreed," but he said to tell Tyler the plan, and they would be ready tomorrow," Ryan stood and walked over to the table and sat down.

Just then, Tyler suddenly appeared in the corner of the room.

"Geez, Tyler, give me some warning," Ryan said with a start.

"I apologize, Master White," Tyler said, forgetting the preferred name change. "I wanted to get back as quickly as possible. I was able to procure a VCD. In fact, I brought two just in case," Tyler said as he produced two small boxes about the size of a pack of cigarettes.

Ryan went over and picked one of them up. There were two small loops on the back. "This is it?" Ryan asked. "This little thing is supposed to hide a complete person?"

"More than that," Tyler said. This model has an expanded range and better tracking technology. Whoever is wearing this device and whatever that person is touching will be completely camouflaged. Here, I'll show you." Tyler said as he hooked one of the units up to his belt and flipped a small switch on the top of the unit. He simply disappeared!

"What the hell?" Ryan said, completely shocked.

"Quite amazing, isn't it?" Maxwell said as he stood up, walked toward where Tyler had been standing, and put his hand on top of Tyler's head. But it looked like he was just patting the air.

"Watch carefully as I jump," Tyler said and jumped up. There was a slight disturbance in the air, kind of like blurred vision, but quickly settled. "Did you see the top of my head?" Tyler asked.

"No, I didn't see anything. Just a little flutter," Ryan said.

"That's the improved tracking technology. You can't run with it. But you can walk and it just shows a slight disturbance in the ambient air around the subject," Tyler said and switched off the device. He immediately reappeared.

"How long does the charge last?" Ryan asked as he picked up one of the units to inspect it more closely.

"Only about 10 minutes, I'm afraid," Tyler said as he looked at the side of the unit. "These lights on the side represent the charge remaining. They will go from green, as they are now, to blue, and then to yellow, and then to red. Once they turn red, there is only about 1 minute of charge left. After that minute, you are visible."

"The nice thing is," Maxwell interjected, "is that there is no degradation during the charge fall-off. The unit will work perfectly up until it loses its charge. But it won't flicker or start to fade as it's being used. Like they used to do."

"Can they be recharged?" Ryan asked.

"Not in 1982, I'm sorry to say," Tyler replied. "So we should probably try to keep them off as much as possible until you really need them." Ryan handed the unit back to Tyler.

"How did your conversation with Rudy go?" Maxwell asked.

"Like taking candy from a baby," Tyler said quite proudly. "All I had to do was mention Prague, and he was willing to do anything. I made up an excuse about needing the layout for a summary report. He ate it up. Here is the surveillance layout." Tyler handed a folder to Maxwell. "It's quite extensive, unfortunately."

"That's okay," Maxwell said. "We just need to know where they are located."

"We're just getting started on the layout of the memorial in relation to the orb. Wanna join us?" Maxwell asked Tyler.

"Sure," Tyler went to sit down.

"Wait a sec," Ryan intervened. We need to first figure out tomorrow and get Tyler over to their hotel to brief them.

The color seemed to fade from Tyler's face.

"Sorry, Tyler," Ryan said, "we need you to face them one more time."

"Alright," Tyler sighed, "but I hate my guys."

"Understood," Ryan said. With that, Ryan and Maxwell laid out the plan for the trip to D.C.

Chapter 73

Maxwell and Ryan spent most of the night going over their plan. They had sent Tyler on his way to the other team's hotel room with instructions for the morning. They finally concluded that the biggest hurdle they faced was the surveillance at the memorial. If Darius was alerted that Maxwell was helping Ryan and Sean or if they saw them using the VCD or any other Institute hardware, they would be immediately disqualified.

"There are cameras everywhere!" Ryan threw up his hands and pushed back from the table. "How many did we count? 35?"

"37, actually," Maxwell corrected him. "It is a daunting number, I grant you."

Ryan paced the room as he considered the options, finally sitting back down. "Okay, so if we can't avoid them, is there any possible way of shutting them down? Even a few?"

"Unfortunately not. They are all powered by the same element," Maxwell replied.

"Element? What the hell is an element?" Ryan asked.

"The closest thing I can compare it to in your time would be a network or maybe a server. Only much more complex and significantly more powerful. Computer systems changed significantly prior to The Incident around 2025. Not too long from your time, actually," Maxwell explained. "The Life Force Institute was one of only a handful of corporations that continued development after the attacks. Actually, it wasn't even the Life Force Institute at that time. Alexander's father and uncle were computer programmers and had authored many of the papers on the new organic computing system. I'm not an expert on the history of the 'living computer,' as it was called in the beginning. Suffice it to say, the new computer platform technology increased speeds by 100-fold. Supercomputers from your time would be slow compared to what these gentlemen came up with. In any event, one element back at the Institute has the capacity to run all the cameras currently placed throughout the world. Hundreds or even thousands at any one time."

Ryan was quiet for a minute. His engineering mind was turning. "Well, we don't need to turn them ALL off. Is there any way to shut them down individually in the field? Just a few of them?"

Maxwell shook his head and began to speak, then stopped. He looked at Ryan and said, "Actually, yes. The cameras that are regularly used for this type of field work are high quality, but they do malfunction from time to time. In fact, my Holographic Detection Unit," Maxwell pulled his 'bug sweeper' out of his pocket, "will quite effectively damage a camera if placed in close proximity to it for over 10 seconds. I can't believe I forgot about that. It is an integral part of the training for handlers. But the HDU has to be close, at least within a foot from the camera."

"Well, most of these cameras are within arm's reach," Ryan said as he pulled the surveillance schematic closer. "All we need to do is clear a path here, here, and through here," Ryan pointed to the layout. "Didn't you say that it was rare for the technicians to be watching in real-time as the contest played out?" Ryan asked.

"Normally, yes. Darius always relies on Tyler and me to fill him in on the progress and any noteworthy developments," Maxwell said. "But that will hardly solve the problem. Everything is being recorded. So we will be seen damaging the cameras."

Ryan looked at Maxwell. "Unless we're invisible," he said with a slight grin, holding up the VCD.

Chapter 74

The plan was to meet at the other team's hotel room prior to leaving for the airport. Ryan and Maxwell had debated the meeting location for some time. There were advantages and disadvantages whether they met at the airport or at their hotel. They had concluded that Ryan and Sean were important enough to Jerry that he wouldn't 'damage' them before they got the orb in their hands. After that, they both agreed that the game would definitely change.

During the planning stage, Ryan and Maxwell figured that going to the Memorial early would be counter-productive due to the complex surveillance system that had already been put in place. Their plan for dismantling the cameras would have to be done in real-time when they all arrived in Washington.

Maxwell had agreed to travel to Washington via his orb and meet them there. Ryan arrived at the hotel alone and took the elevator to the 5th floor. As he walked down the hallway, his heart felt like it would beat right out of his chest. He couldn't remember a time in his life when he was more nervous. Nervous and scared, he realized.

He arrived at the door and could hear the conversation on the other side. He knocked.

Jose opened the door but didn't say anything. Ryan slowly walked past him and into the room. Jerry was standing next to the table, and Tyler was standing next to him, looking very anxious. Dirk was sitting on the bed to Ryan's right. He was holding what looked to be a .45 with a silencer on his lap. Sean was standing on the other side of the table. Ryan walked toward Sean and stopped when he reached the table.

"Well Master White," Jerry said, emphasizing 'Master,' "you wanna tell us where the hell we're going? My patience is running a little thin." Even though Tyler knew where they were headed, Ryan and Maxwell had told him to wait and let Ryan explain the travel plans.

"Yes, of course," Ryan said as he set down his suitcase. "The final clue has pointed us to Washington D.C., more specifically, the Lincoln Memorial."

Jerry showed no outward expression that Ryan could detect. Dirk was the first to speak. "Well, isn't that convenient? We can pack the guns but can't carry them with us!"

He stood up and walked toward Ryan. But before he could continue, Ryan interjected with his hands up, "Look, that's where the clue says we need to go. If you want to drive, fine. But that's nearly 3000 miles. At least 48 hours driving or a 5-hour plane ride, your choice."

"No, that's fine. But get this through your head." Jerry grabbed Tyler's hand, pushed it onto the table, reached down to his side and pulled his knife out, and plunged it through Tyler's hand into the table below. Tyler let out a blood-curdling scream and fell to his knees, his hand pinned to the table. "I don't need a gun to kill you where you stand!!"

"What the hell?!?" Ryan shouted and began to lunge toward Tyler. Dirk stepped up and put his gun to Ryan's temple, and cocked the hammer. Ryan reflexively put his hands up and stopped in his tracks. "Okay, okay! Just stop! We understand you can kill us any time you want!" Tyler was moaning on the ground with tears running down his face. Jerry roughly pulled his knife out, and Tyler fell to the ground clutching his hand to his chest. Blood was running down his arm and dripping off his elbow. Jose picked up a small towel from the nightstand and threw it at Tyler. "Walk it off, big guy," he said.

Jerry walked over to the bed, pulled up part of the sheet and wiped the blood off his knife and put it back in its sheath. "Just so we understand each other," he said with a smile. "Have your Dr. McCoy from the future come down with his magic toys and fix that," he said as he stepped over Tyler and went into the bathroom.

Ryan looked at Sean. Neither one could speak. Dirk lowered his gun and sat back down on the bed. Ryan slowly walked around the table and knelt down next to Tyler, who was trying to wrap his hand in the towel. "Keep pressure on it," Ryan said and tried to help the smaller man tie the towel off. "I'm sorry, Tyler. Do you think you can get up to a chair?" Ryan helped Tyler to his knees and then fell into one of the chairs. He was sweating profusely and still moaning. Nobody spoke until Jerry returned from the bathroom. He looked at Dirk and Jose. "Well, get your shit packed up. Let's go!"

The ride to the airport was uneventful, and nobody said a word. Tyler had gone back to the Institute to get his hand looked at. Ryan desperately wanted to talk to Maxwell and tell him what had happened. He probably already knew by this point, however.

Earlier in the contest, Ryan would have expected there to be repercussions for injuring a handler. But he was sure Darius would be thrilled with the violent outburst. Sick son of a bitch.

When they arrived at the airport, Ryan used his credit card to purchase 5 tickets to D.C. The flight didn't leave for a couple of hours, so Jerry volunteered Ryan to buy them all breakfast. As they ate, Ryan leaned over to Sean, "Dude, with all that happened, I haven't even asked if you're alright?"

"I've been better. But yea I'm okay. The swelling has gone down a little, but I still look like I went 10 rounds with Tyson," Sean eked out a smile as he gingerly took a bite of toast.

"Good. Look, I need to talk to you before we get to D.C. Hopefully we'll have some time during the flight," Ryan said.

"I take it you have some sort of crazy plan?" Sean whispered.

"You could say that," Ryan said and gulped his orange juice.

Chapter 75

Maxwell sat quietly in his completely darkened office. The only illumination was from a small garden light outside his window. It cast an almost eerie glow onto his office wall. Every few minutes, a shadow would streak across the illuminated wood paneling as a rabbit or fox ran by. He had long since gotten used to the effect. The outside animal world continued on as if nothing had ever happened. Only humans knew how to destroy their own lives.

The ice in his drink had long since melted. He hadn't moved for what seemed like hours. He had been going over in his mind the plan that would ensue at the memorial. It should work. It had to work. But for the last hour or so he had been contemplating another problem. He and Ryan had spent hours discussing their plan, but they had never discussed what would happen after. Suppose Ryan and Sean are successful in retrieving the orb? Protocol states that they would be transported to the Institute with an orb where they would undergo memory reprogramming and have their consciousnesses transferred back into their older bodies. But now Maxwell knew that Darius most likely had no intention of performing that step. They would simply be eliminated. Maxwell had no idea what would happen to their physical bodies in 2016. Most likely, technicians would be dispatched to retrieve the bodies and dispose of them. Or just leave them lifeless for their families to find. Maxwell shuddered at the thought of that occurring.

In addition, both Ryan and Sean had expressed their intent to stop Darius from doing this to anyone else. Although Maxwell shared that desire, he couldn't help but think about what would happen to all the people who worked at the

Institute. They would, for all intents and purposes, be out of a job. He tried not to think about that. Darius had to be stopped. Time travel had become too dangerous to continue. People were dying. Maxwell thought of the innocent teenage security guard at Disneyland. He lost his life as a direct result of this damn contest, or whatever it had turned into. Tyler got a knife pierced through his hand. Maxwell had visited Tyler earlier in the infirmary. His physical wound was healed but his emotional scars remained. He was still quite shaken.

Maxwell sat in the dark, closed his eyes while sipping his watered-down drink, as he began to put together at least the beginning of a plan as to how to bring Darius to his knees. He would definitely not be able to do it on his own.

But for now, he had to get moving. He had quite a bit to do at the Lincoln Memorial before Ryan and Sean showed up with the other team.

Chapter 76

After a long wait, the plane was finally ready for boarding. Ryan had thought ahead and purchased 3 first-class tickets and 2 main cabin tickets. He was expecting Jerry to try and separate him and Sean. Ryan was hoping Jerry would opt for the more comfortable seat for the long flight. He figured there wasn't much they could do. They were all on the same flight. Luckily, Jerry had accepted the first class along with Jose and Dirk. Ryan and Sean had found their seats farther back in the plane.

As soon as they were airborne, Ryan went into full "briefing mode," describing in as much detail as possible the plan that he and Maxwell had come up with. Sean had a lot of questions, but after a couple of hours, they both felt comfortable with what they had to do. Ryan thought they might have some time to reminisce about their experience so far, but both young men fell asleep for the remainder of the flight.

After a little over 5 ½ hours, the plane finally reached Washington Dulles International Airport. Being in first class, Jerry's group exited the plane first. Ryan and Sean had no doubt they would be waiting patiently when they finally got off, and they were correct. Ryan walked up to Jerry but didn't stop. He just said, "I'll get a car," and kept walking. This irritated Jerry but he had no choice but to follow. Sean and the other three went to the baggage claim while Ryan rented a vehicle. The girl at the Hertz desk was horrendously slow, so Sean showed up before Ryan had finished with the contract.

"Hey, you about ready?" Sean asked. Ryan turned and saw Jerry, Dirk, and Jose standing about 20 feet away, looking very upset. What else is new?

"What's with them? They look pissed," Ryan asked Sean.

"Who knows? They're always like that," Sean replied as Ryan grabbed the keys and his suitcase and walked toward the rental car lot.

"Keys!" Jerry said as Ryan walked by. "You're not driving us to the nearest police station."

Ryan figured it would be pointless to argue. He'd probably get a knife through the hand. He handed the keys to Jerry, who gave them to Jose.

"Let's go, dipshit," Jerry said and gave Ryan a little push.

Ryan had rented a Suburban to fit everyone and their luggage. Ryan was sure there were several weapons of various calibers stuffed in their bags.

As they arrived at their vehicle, Ryan said, "Look, it's late. The memorial will be closing soon. We're going to need to get a hotel for the night and go in tomorrow."

"Bullshit, we go now!" Jerry said.

"Mr. Stillwell, security at a national monument is a little tighter than Disneyland. You won't be able to just stab a guard and keep going," Ryan said with more bravado than he had planned.

Whack!! Ryan doubled over and grabbed the back of his head. Dirk had cold-cocked him from behind with the butt of a rather large knife. "Alright, alright!" Ryan said as he stood back up. "Look, I understand you want to get this thing over with. So do we. But we go there now and we will be in police custody for who knows how long. That's simply a fact. We have to go when the memorial is open," Ryan took his hand away from his head. Luckily there was no blood, just a nice little bump.

"Okay, Mr. White, you make a valid point," Jerry said in a much calmer tone. "But, like it or not, we all stay in the same room."

"Yea, whatever," Ryan said, and they all piled into the Suburban.

There were countless options for hotels in D.C. They chose the first one that looked half decent, a Hilton that was relatively close to the National Mall.

Ryan spent some time at the front desk and came back to the group. "They don't have any rooms that will sleep 5, so I got two adjoining rooms on the 12th floor. We can leave the connecting door open. Okay with you?" he asked.

"Fine," Jerry said and walked toward the elevators. He was being strangely calm, and that made Ryan and Sean a little nervous.

Ryan desperately wanted to talk to Maxwell and get an update on the memorial. But there was no way to break away, even for a minute. He was sure Maxwell had found them and was probably in a room on their floor. He just hoped he had overheard them talking or watched them and knew the connecting door would be open. The last thing they needed was for Maxwell to materialize with Jerry standing right there.

They reached their room and went inside. The first thing Ryan did was open the connecting door between the rooms and throw his and Sean's bags on the two beds in that room. Jerry walked past Ryan toward the door to the hallway from Sean and Ryan's room. He locked the bolt lock and slid the chain lock across. He turned back toward Ryan and Sean. "It's very simple, boys. This door opens, and one of you dies." With that, he walked back into the other room and lay down on one of the beds. Sean and Ryan looked at each other and shrugged.

Jose spoke up from the other room, "So what's for dinner? I'm starving."

"Nobody leaves," Jerry said with his eyes still closed. "Order some pizza. Get a lot. Mr. White is paying for it."

Jose started thumbing through the yellow pages. "Just call the front desk. They'll get it for you," Dirk said as he threw his bags on one of the other two beds. Jose called the front desk, got transferred to the concierge, and ordered enough pizza for 20 people.

After about an hour, there was a knock on the main room door. Jerry, Dirk, and Jose had all fallen asleep, or so it seemed. Ryan answered the door. There was a cart with about 10 pizzas on it and the delivery man said, "That'll be $175, please." Ryan looked up at Maxwell in a very tight-fitting Domino's uniform and a stupid little hat. He winked and Ryan immediately turned around to see if anyone was looking. They hadn't moved. "Here you go," Ryan said as he handed Maxwell two hundreds. "Thank you, sir," he said and walked back down the hall. As he walked, he turned around, gave Ryan the okay sign, and turned back around out of sight. Ryan couldn't help but break a little smile. He rolled the cart into the room and closed the door.

The rest of the night was uneventful, thankfully. After they ate, Ryan laid down just to rest his eyes for a minute. He woke up and saw his alarm clock said 5:30am! He had slept the entire night. "I took your shoes off around midnight," Sean said as he slowly sat up. Ryan peeked around the corner of the door to see several guns laid out on the table, all fully loaded. He leaned, back. 'Well, here we go,' he thought.

Chapter 77

The Lincoln Memorial is a U.S. national memorial built to honor the 16th president of the United States, Abraham Lincoln. It is on the western end of the National Mall in Washington, D.C., across from the Washington Monument, and is in the form of a neoclassical temple. The memorial's architect was Henry Bacon. The designer of the memorial interior's large central statue of Abraham Lincoln was Daniel Chester French; the Lincoln statue was carved by the Piccirilli brothers. The painter of the interior murals was Jules Guerin, and the epitaph above the statue was written by Royal Cortissoz. Dedicated in May 1922, it is one of several memorials built to honor an American president.

What many people don't know is that as they climb the steps toward the massive sculpture of the former President and enter the main room, directly beneath their feet lies a cavernous three-story, 43,800-square-foot basement with architecture that resembles a World War II bunker. This section of the memorial was named the Undercroft.

This basement houses dozens of concrete columns used to support the surface structure. During the construction of the memorial from 1914 until its dedication in 1922, workers even drew cartoons on some of the columns, which can still be seen.

Some limited flashlight tours were offered of the Undercroft during the '80s but were not being conducted at the present time. This was most likely the reason that the technicians had chosen this location to hide the orb.

Ryan already knew where the orb was located. Actually, he knew where both orbs were located, the real orb which he and Sean would be using, and the fake orb that Maxwell had procured from the Institute. And, if Maxwell had done his job, the pathway to the fake orb would be free of all working cameras.

Ryan, Sean, and the other team arrived at the memorial parking lot shortly before it opened at 10:00am. As they approached the monument on foot, Ryan spoke up. "Okay, we need to go up to the statue of Lincoln to retrieve the final clue. The clue from Disneyland stated that both the final clue and the orb were at the same location," Ryan lied. Even though Ryan knew full well where the orb was located, he needed to feign ignorance to keep Jerry from becoming suspicious.

All five climbed the 58 steps to the main level where the Lincoln statue sits. Maxwell was to place a small box behind the statue on the former President's left side. As they approached the statue, they noticed a small chain strung between short stanchions that extended all the way around the statue. Not a formidable barrier, but certainly put there for a reason. Ryan approached from the right side, outside the barrier, and looked behind the statue. Nothing, as expected. Sean was walking with Ryan, but the other three stood off at a distance. Ryan and Sean walked around the left side and looked behind. At first, they didn't see anything but Sean walked a little closer to the wall and nudged Ryan. "There it is," he said and nodded in that direction. There were several guards milling about, but only one was close by. "I'm going to distract this guy," Ryan said and nodded toward the guard. "When I do, step over and grab it." Ryan walked over toward the guard and stood on his far side, so he was looking away from the statue.

"Excuse me, sir, do you know when this exhibit closes?" Ryan asked. As soon as the guard turned to talk to Ryan, Sean stepped over the chain and grabbed the box. Sean didn't know why, but his heart was beating a mile a minute. 'And this was the easy part,' he thought.

Ryan walked over to meet up with Sean as he opened the box. Jerry quickly joined them. The clue read:

Your prize lies beneath your feet

Once inside, 50 steps forward, 25 steps left, 25 steps left

"What the hell," Jerry asked, "beneath our feet?"

"Yep, that's what it says," Ryan said as he looked around.

"What are you looking for?" Sean asked.

"Someone who knows what is beneath our feet?" Ryan answered as he started walking toward a young girl with a Parks uniform on.

"Hi," Ryan said enthusiastically.

"Hello, how may I help you?" the young Park Ranger asked. Her name tag read Sally.

"Sally, my friend back in Arkansas told me there is a basement under this here monument. Is that true?" Ryan asked with a horrible Southern accent.

"Your friend is right. There is a very large area right underneath us where all the columns were poured to support this amazing memorial. It's called the Undercroft," she said, very eager to help.

"Well, I'll be," Ryan replied. "Is there any way to get a tour from y'all? My friend says there are all kinds of cool things to see down there." Ryan was having a hard time maintaining the accent. He wasn't even sure why he came up with it.

"Ooh, I'm sorry," Sally said. "They just discontinued the tours two weeks ago. They'll be starting them up again at the first of the year. I'm so sorry you missed it," she said.

"Oh, dag nab it," Ryan said. "Well, thanks for the info. I'll have to try and talk my folks into bringing us back next year."

"You're welcome," Sally said with a smile. "Have a wonderful rest of your day."

Ryan walked back to Sean and the others. Of course, he already knew practically everything there was to know about the Undercroft. But Jerry didn't know that and that was what Ryan wanted him to keep thinking.

"Okay, there is a basement underneath here. It's actually more like a cavern," Ryan embellished the Ranger's explanation. "They usually give tours, but they discontinued them two weeks ago. She did say the entrance was around the corner between the main level and the ground level on the North side of the building."

As they headed down the stairs toward the ground level, Ryan was focusing on the plan he and Maxwell had come up with regarding how to get into the Undercroft. They knew ahead of time that the tours had been discontinued and the door would be locked. He was hoping he could get Sally to give them a peek, and they could block it open. That was plan A, which didn't work. Plan B was to pick the lock, and Maxwell had some inside information that Ryan hoped would come to fruition in a few moments.

They headed around the North side of the building and Sally was indeed correct. There was a gated sidewalk that led down a slight embankment and ended at the door to the Undercroft. Ryan figured he'd take a shot. "Okay, you guys are the criminals. How do we get in?" he asked, hoping he didn't get a smack on his head. Nobody said anything but, as Ryan hoped, Jose was grinning.

"You're right, Master Ryan," Jerry said sarcastically, "we're not only criminals, we're damn good criminals, and Jose here is the best lock picker around." Ryan noticed that Jose was already digging in his pack for his pick set. "Okay, but it's going to be kind of tough with all these people walking around," Sean mentioned. "How long to get through that door, Jose?" Jerry asked. "Thirty seconds, maybe faster," Jose said as he found his pick set and looked through it. "Alright, so we have to somehow get down there and stand at the door for 30 seconds without being noticed," Ryan said, now somewhat unsure of their plan's viability. They all stood looking at each other, hoping for a brilliant plan to appear. Ryan couldn't believe he and Maxwell hadn't thought about how busy it would be.

Just then, Sean noticed a couple of kids throwing a frisbee at each other on a stretch of grass about 30 feet away. "Ryan, give me 50 bucks," Sean said. "Why?" Ryan asked. "Just give me 50 bucks and wait here." Ryan handed Sean the money. Sean went over to the kids, and within a couple of seconds, the kids were jumping up and down, and Sean was coming back with the frisbee. "Nice, Sean, but I don't really feel like playing right now," Ryan said as Sean got closer. "Yea, me neither, but how close to the door do you think you can get?" Sean asked as Ryan started to put it together. Ryan had been the neighborhood frisbee golf champion back in the day. It had been a while, but he was sure he could get close. "Okay, Jose, I'm going to throw this to you but don't catch it. Let it go by you. As soon as it does, hop this gate and head down to that door. You probably won't have 30 seconds, more like 10-15, so you better be as good as they say. Unlock the door, pick up the frisbee, and head back up here. We'll wait until the crowd thins and then go in," Ryan backed up about 10 feet and threw the frisbee right at Jose. He barely ducked in time, and the frisbee sailed down the hill. Jose jumped over the gate and ran down the hill. Ryan wasn't perfect. The frisbee landed about 5 feet short of the door. Jose ran past it and started working on the lock. At first, nobody seemed the wiser. But suddenly, a Park Ranger leaned over the banister from above. "Hey, that area is off limits!" he yelled. "Sorry, we lost our frisbee," Ryan pointed down the hill. From the ranger's vantage point, he couldn't see Jose or the frisbee. He left the banister and started walking towards the stairs leading down. Just then, Jose came jogging up the sidewalk holding the frisbee. "Sorry, sir," Jose said politely, "we'll be more careful." The ranger looked back at them, raised his hand, and walked back toward his post outside the memorial. Jose stepped back over the gate. "All done," was all he said and tossed the frisbee to Sean.

"Pretty good idea, dude," Ryan said to Sean. "Yea, unless someone goes down there between now and when we go in," Sean replied. "I know. I just wish I could talk to Maxwell and make sure everything is set up inside," Ryan said as he looked around. He was sure Maxwell was around here somewhere.

"Who the hell are you looking for," Jerry seemingly appeared out of nowhere.

"Nobody, just trying to figure out the best time to go in," Ryan said. "I think we should go back up top and see if we can figure out the guard's movements. You know, who's where, when, that sort of thing."

"That's fine criminal thinking," Dirk said from behind Jerry.

"Yea, well, ya gotta do what ya gotta do," Ryan said as he headed back up the stairs. They spent the next couple of hours watching the guards' movements, trying to be as inconspicuous as possible.

Ryan and Sean had found a bench inside the memorial out of the sun. The others were on the far side of the monument. "Hello gentlemen," Maxwell said as he rounded the bench from behind. "Max, where have you been?" Ryan asked as he nervously looked in Jerry's direction. Luckily he was engrossed in watching a soccer mom bend over to pick up her baby.

"I've been here all day, watching you," Maxwell said, staying a few feet away in case one of the others looked their way. "Nice job with the frisbee. I could have left the door open, but as we agreed, that would have been a little obvious," he said as he pretended to read a flyer about Lincoln's childhood.

"Is everything set up inside?" Ryan asked in a soft voice.

"Yes, you should be clear to the room with the orb. The fake orb, that is. You remember the navigation?" Maxwell turned away from Ryan. "Yea, I remember how to get there. The rest isn't so cut and dry."

"You could say that again," Sean mumbled from the other side of the bench.

"It's all about timing, gentlemen. All about timing," Maxwell slowly walked away and out of sight.

"Well, I guess now is as good a time as any," Ryan said and got up from the bench. Sean followed him over to the others. As they got closer, Jerry signaled to Ryan and Sean to meet outside. Once near the top of the stairs, Jerry approached Ryan.

"Look, we need to go now. The crowds are thinning out, and if we hurry, there's only one security guard who is covering this side of the top level. He should start a rotation in about 10 minutes. We'll be able to see when he moves from the ground level on the North side," Jerry didn't wait for Ryan and Sean to agree, he just started moving down the stairs, with Dirk and Jose close behind. Sean and Ryan followed.

Once on the North side, still trying to be unsuspicious, they waited until they saw the guard move out of sight. There were only a couple people around, but they were not paying the 5 men any attention. Jerry jumped over the gate and briskly began walking down the sidewalk. The other four followed quickly behind. It probably took 8-10 seconds to walk to the door, open it, slip inside and shut the door. They were inside the Undercroft.

Chapter 78

It was surprisingly well-lit inside. There was no natural light, but there were plenty of lights mounted on what looked like every other pillar. The space was massive. Huge cement pillars were used to support the incredible weight of the building above. The floor was mostly dirt but with some areas covered with wood flooring. Jose pulled out a flashlight and shone it toward the ceiling of the cavernous opening. There were actually stalactites hanging down from the rafters which only added to the rustic environment they were in.

"Okay, 50 steps forward," Ryan said as he began walking. He knew exactly where he was going but needed to stick to the clue they found. Ryan assumed Jerry would break out into the lead, but surprisingly, he stayed behind and followed. "48, 49, 50," Ryan stopped and turned left. "Okay, 25 steps left," Ryan said as they turned and began walking down a fairly steep grade, maybe 20 degrees. When they had walked 25 steps, Ryan turned left and was looking down a hallway of sorts, narrower than the passageway they had entered into. From what Ryan could make out, it looked like it dead-ended up ahead. "Alright, 25 more to go," he said and started counting the steps. As they had discussed the night before, Sean gradually caught up to Sean and stayed relatively close.

"23, 24, 25," Ryan stopped. They were standing in a space about 25' x 25'. There were a number of broken crates and what looked like broken chairs and tables strewn about. The area wasn't very well-lit. There were two lights near the entrance to the room and two on each wall. But only one of those lights was illuminated.

Dirk stepped up, drew his gun, and pointed it inches from Ryan's face. "No more fucking around! Get us our orb," Dirk stared at Ryan with a very serious look on his face.

"Look," Ryan said with his hands up, "I want out of this thing as much as anyone, but I don't know where the orb is. You know everything I do," Ryan lied. "But we know it's here, so let's just relax and start looking." Dirk didn't move, just kept the gun pointed at Ryan's forehead. Jerry spoke up, "Jose, stand over there near the entrance. If either of these two shitheads try to bolt, kill them." Jose pulled his gun from his pack and stood near where they had entered. "Let's start looking," Jerry said. Dirk slowly lowered his weapon and stuck it back in his waist.

"Okay," Ryan finally exhaled, "we know it's here but we don't have all day. We'll start in this corner and work clockwise toward you," Ryan said as Jerry walked across to the other side of the room. Ryan and Sean moved to the far corner and started moving crates and tipping over tables. "So, where is it?" Sean whispered. "About 20 feet to your right if Maxwell stuck to the plan. Remember what we do when we find it," Ryan said as he slowly moved right through the debris.

Ryan actually kicked it before he saw it. Unfortunately, it made an unmistakable metallic sound that turned everyone's heads. Ryan reached down and picked it up. It was remarkably light, made out of something even lighter than aluminum, he guessed. Jerry quickly came over and literally snatched it out of Ryan's hands. Jerry stared at it as if he was looking at a rare jewel. Dirk and Jose joined him, and all three were grinning from ear to ear. "Well, Mr. White, you delivered, but the sad fact is we just don't need you anymore," Jerry said as he pulled out his gun and pointed it. They were gone! "What the fu...?" Jerry said as he ran forward and kicked over a crate, and threw a couple chairs around. "Where the hell did they go?" Jerry stepped back and fired three shots into the wall where Ryan and Sean had been standing.

Suddenly the entire space erupted into multiple lasers dancing through the air.

"Freeze!! Drop your weapons," a voice boomed out from near the entrance. Dirk reflexively pulled his gun out from his waist and fired. No less than 7 rounds immediately ripped through his body, center mass. He dropped, and an ocean of blood poured from his body. Jerry raised his right hand above his head and tossed his gun to the side. Jose was already on the ground face down with a policeman's knee on his back. Jerry was still holding the orb in his left hand. "Put the device down very slowly," the team leader commanded. Jerry looked at the orb. His ticket home. He slowly lowered the orb to the ground and stood back up. "Now back away and get on your knees." Jerry was a psychopath, but he wasn't stupid. He did as he was told.

Ryan and Sean just stood very still. Obviously, from Jerry's reaction, the Visual Concealment Device worked as advertised. But Ryan knew they were fighting the clock before the power ran out. Ryan and Sean hadn't moved much when they turned the unit on. One of Jerry's shots missed Sean's head by centimeters.

There was a lot of commotion and a lot more light now in the enclosed area they were in. They had to somehow get out without being noticed. They were essentially hugging each other in order to stay hidden. They began slowly walking in unison around the edge of the room. But there was a lot of debris in their way. At some point, they were going to have to walk directly through the throng of police and forensic personnel who were streaming into the Undercroft. Ryan glanced down at the VCD. The light was yellow. Once it hit red, they would have one minute left before they were visible. And they had a long way to go.

Chapter 79

"What do you mean, malfunctioned?!?" Darius screamed at the technician. "How can six cameras all malfunction at once?" Darius slammed his hand down on the technician's desk.

"Sir, it was an error in the element. Those six cameras were allocated on one data acquisition string that inadvertently lost power. We're looking into it now," the terrified technician replied.

"I want a complete investigation! We just lost the video of my finale! Someone will pay for this! I want Maxwell and Tyler located immediately and brought back to my office for a debriefing," Darius swept his arm across the technician's desk, sending papers and a computer screen crashing to the ground. He stormed off and left a scared but also confused technician trembling. 'His finale,' the technician thought to himself? 'What the hell does that mean?'

Darius made his way back to his office, fuming at the loss of surveillance. Never before had so many cameras failed at once. This was obviously sabotage but he could not figure out who or why? He sat down hard in his expensive chair and pulled out his file, and set it on his desk. He stared at it in disbelief. His masterpiece. His grand plan. All ruined with no video of the final scene. He put the file away and poured himself a large glass of brandy. First things first, he needed to speak with Maxwell and Tyler. Then, there was only one thing left to do. Eliminate Ryan White and Sean Jensen.

Chapter 80

Sean and Ryan continued walking slowly around the perimeter of the room, being careful not to kick anything and give away their position. More than one policeman nearly walked right into them. It was only luck that they didn't all spill to the ground. That would have been very difficult to explain.

They continued moving, hugging the wall and taking baby steps, until they were out of the main room and heading back up the incline. It was very strange to have people look directly at them and not even know they were there. This little toy Tyler had gotten them was indeed worth its weight in gold.

When they reached the top of the incline, Ryan whispered to Sean, "Move over to our left and get behind that pillar. I'm going to get the other VCD and turn it on. This one is about out of...." Suddenly a small beep emanated from the unit. Sean looked down, and the VCD was shut off. Ryan quickly retrieved the other unit and turned it on. Just in time, too, as an officer walked past them on their side of the pillar with a flashlight, apparently clearing the remainder of the Undercroft. Sean and Ryan just froze and could barely breathe. The policeman was no more than 6 inches from Ryan's left arm. One wrong move, and they were in trouble. The policeman walked about 10 feet and turned and shone his flashlight directly at Ryan and Sean. He just stared and tilted his head as if he was confused at what he saw or thought he saw. He slowly started to approach where they were standing, still with a quizzical look on his face. He reached out his hand and waved it back and forth, literally inches from Ryan's nose.

"Fitzgerald, if that area's clear, get back out here. Sarge wants us all down in the main room," a voice said and the officer swung his arms out in front of him again but then turned and headed back toward the main passageway.

"Holy shit," Sean whispered.

"Yea," was all Ryan could muster.

Once they were safely out of earshot, Sean asked, "So where is the real orb?"

Ryan looked back to the top of the incline. "From the map, we measured about 4 columns past the top of the hill, then 10 feet to the right, and another 10 feet to the right. This is the second column so we need to head straight for another two columns."

It didn't sound like there were any police down in this area, but Ryan left the VCD on, and the two stuck together just in case. They made their way around the 4th column and walked ten feet, turned right, and walked another 10 feet. They were simply standing in the middle of another passageway. No rooms or enclosures.

"Okay," Sean said, "now what?"

"I don't know, did we..."

"Afternoon, gentlemen," Maxwell appeared around a corner, holding two orbs.

"Holy crap!" Sean practically yelled as both of them jumped in shock.

"Well, that was fun," Ryan said as he walked toward Maxwell. "Do we have you to thank for the swat team?"

The intervention of the police had never been part of the plan. Ryan and Sean were to just activate the VCD and simply walk away. Looking back now, that would have been quite difficult. Jerry probably would have emptied every gun in his arsenal, shooting the room to pieces.

"I thought it would be helpful," Maxwell said.

"How did you get them to come down here?" Sean asked.

"I told them I saw three men entering the Undercroft with what looked like an explosive device," Maxwell said with a small smile. "Once I said 'explosive,' they reacted quite quickly."

"I assume you are holding our way out of this place?" Sean asked and pointed to the orbs Maxwell was carrying.

"Quite right," Maxwell said and handed one of the orbs to Sean.

Sean felt its weight and handed it to Ryan. "Feels kind of like a small medicine ball," he said.

Ryan took the orb and turned it over like he knew what he was doing. He didn't.

"So, Max, you're telling me that this little ball is going to send Sean and me back to our beds in 2016 as if nothing has happened? Back to our families and chubby bellies and bald heads?"

"Hey, I'm not bald in any time frame," Sean joked.

"Yes, if that's what you wish," Maxwell said and suddenly donned a more serious look.

"And what is that supposed to mean?" Ryan asked. "Of course, that was the whole point of this whole nightmare we've just gone through."

Maxwell turned and began walking. "We need to get a little further away. I expect the SWAT team will do a more thorough search of the Undercroft."

Sean and Ryan briefly looked at each other and followed Maxwell down the corridor. They walked for about 100 feet, turned into a small alcove and stopped. Maxwell turned around and took a deep breath, more like a sigh.

"Gentlemen, as you well know, I did not plan this…nightmare…as you call it. Nor did I have any knowledge of what was actually going on. As I explained earlier, I have found out that Darius is not only carrying out some sort of warped version of a gladiator fight, but I fear that he has become dangerously psychotic. By now, I expect he has become completely unhinged after finding out that the final showdown that you two were just part of was completely missed by all the cameras and listening devices. I'm sure he is screaming at his security forces to locate Tyler and me to find out what happened."

"Yea, but…" Ryan started.

"No, let me finish, Ryan," Maxwell took another deep breath.

"This whole quest or contest, or whatever the hell it started out as, was actually Darius' master theater. I've thought a lot about what I saw in his office when I broke in a few days ago. These "contests" have not had anything to do with bettering humanity or reinvigorating the population. They are simply, I don't know, plays, for lack of a better term. Plays where the actors are real people fighting for their lives. There is no script, no production, other than what happens in real-time. His little circle of friends has been doing this for some time, I suspect. When it's over, they get together and drink their expensive brandy and laugh and grade everyone on their performance. Then, as far as I can tell, the participants are summarily executed. The last several days have been Darius' production. Or as he called it in his note, 'My Turn.'"

Ryan suddenly remembered the conversations he had with Maxwell. And how he had committed to helping stop the madman.

"So, what are you saying, Max? We're screwed?" Sean asked quietly.

"No, Sean. We're not screwed. Darius is," Ryan said and nodded to Maxwell, who replied simply with a slight smile and a nod of his own.

Chapter 81

Tyler sat in what seemed like a very large chair in front of Darius' desk. He'd never felt so small and vulnerable. He was shaking uncontrollably but was hiding it well. He had been sitting there for what seemed like hours but had only been brought in by security about 20 minutes earlier.

Darius sat across from Tyler in his expensive chair behind his expensive desk. He hadn't said a word for the entire time since Tyler had been brought in. Just stared at the smaller man and occasionally took a drink from his glass. Tyler didn't dare say anything and risk an explosion of violence from his boss.

Darius sat up, reached slowly into his drawer, and pulled out a coaster. He put his glass down softly on the desk. Without looking at Tyler, he said, "Where's Maxwell?"

"I don't kn..."

"SHUT UP!" Darius screamed and slammed his hand down on the desk.

Tyler jumped but quickly shut his mouth.

"I'll ask one more time," Darius said almost too quietly. He reached into the same drawer where he retrieved the coaster, pulled out a stun gun and placed it on the desk next to his glass. The stun guns of this century were quite different from those of the early 21st century. One shot, and you were out for hours. Extremely painful and debilitating for days. If you were shot at close range, it could be lethal.

Darius looked directly at Tyler, picked up the stun gun, and said slowly, "Where's Maxwell?"

Tyler was frozen. He had no idea where Maxwell was. He didn't know what to do. He could only think of one thing to say. "I will find him, sir."

Darius put the gun down and said, "You have one hour." He turned in his chair as Tyler got up and quickly exited Darius' office. Once outside and past the secretary, the little man broke into tears as he ran towards his office.

Chapter 82

"Okay, Max, you've sufficiently freaked us out. Do you have a plan in mind?" Ryan asked.

"I have what you might call a skeleton of a plan. But we can't discuss it here. We need to get back to my office."

"Your office in the future?" Sean blurted out before he realized it was a stupid question.

"Quite right, Sean. My office in the future. 181 years in the future to be exact."

Maxwell proceeded to show Ryan and Sean how to hold the orb and punch in the code.

"Wait a second," Ryan interrupted. "So does this hurt, or do we just disappear and fly through the air?"

"Actually, the experience is quite calming. You might feel a little lightheaded the first few times. Let me ask you a question," Maxwell had a little glint in his eye, "when was the last time either of you had anything to drink?"

Ryan and Sean looked at each other. "I guess a few hours ago. Why?" Sean said.

"Well, the engineers sometimes call this the yellow pipeline. You will feel an almost unbearable need to urinate. You might want to take care of that now." Maxwell said with a slight smile.

Ryan and Sean carefully put the orb on the ground and turned to the nearest wall. Once finished, they picked up the orb and punched in the code.

Maxwell stood across from them and punched in his own code. "I will go first. The code you input is the coordinates for my office. I have no idea what we will find. It could be empty or full of security personnel. Once I'm gone, count to sixty and then press the blinking green light twice. Good luck, gentlemen. This nightmare is not over yet."

With that, he pushed his button twice and simply disappeared, not like in Star Trek, where the people phase out. He was simply gone.

"Holy shit," Ryan and Sean said together. Sean began counting...

-58, -59, -60.

"Here we go," Ryan said. His finger was shaking so bad he could hardly control it. Sean grabbed Ryan's finger and guided it to the button. They both pushed it twice.

Chapter 83

Maxwell stood quietly, just outside his office, listening intently but heard nothing. It was about 6:30 pm and many of the employees had already left for the day. The lights were off in the hallway, so he turned on a small lamp just inside his office door. Suddenly, Sean and Ryan appeared inside his office. Maxwell quickly entered and shut his door.

"Congratulations, gentlemen. You are officially time travelers," Maxwell said as he moved across his office and "turned off" his window. Where his window used to be was now just a blank wall. 'Cool,' Ryan thought to himself and shook his head. They were definitely in the future.

"Well, that was an interesting experience," Sean said and sat down. "You're right about being a little lightheaded."

"And you were right about needing to pee," Ryan said. "Thanks for warning us. If I hadn't gone before, I'm sure I'd be looking for some towels to clean up."

"Yes, well, nobody has ever been able to explain that one. There are many theories, but we hardly have time to discuss the urination symptoms of time travel," Maxwell said and sat down at this desk. Ryan also sat down and handed the orb back to Maxwell.

"So Max, you say we are now officially time travelers. But weren't we officially time travelers when we appeared in 1982 a couple weeks ago?" Ryan asked.

"Not exactly," Maxwell said. "In addition to actual time travel, this institute has perfected something called Consciousness Transfer. Basically, your consciousness, your memory, experiences, and relationships, are all transferred to a younger version of yourself. Your bodies never left your bed in 2016 when the transfer was initiated," Maxwell paused to see Sean and Ryan's reaction. Both boys remained silent.

"Therefore," Maxwell continued, "what you just went through was the first time you have actually traveled through time."

Sean looked at Ryan. "Suddenly, I'm very tired," Ryan said and put his head back on the chair.

"So Max, when the time comes," Sean asked, "how are we supposed to get back to our 'beds' in 2016?"

"It's quite a simple process. Much easier than transferring the first time, actually. When your consciousness was transferred the first time, it required a technician to be on-site at your home. But the reversal can all be done from here. Once we initiate the transfer here, you will simply disappear, and your consciousness will return to your body in your time. Your current bodies," he pointed to both of them, "will be automatically transferred back to 1982. Normally, the policy is to erase your memories of the entire experience. But sadly, as I explained, I don't think we have ever actually reversed anyone's consciousness. So, I'm not sure how the memory erasure will go in your time or in 1982. It's possible you will remember everything," Maxwell said quite bluntly.

"How did some 'technician' creep into my bedroom and do whatever he had to do? I'm a very light sleeper. No way I would have slept through that." Sean asked.

"You were drugged," Maxwell said very matter-of-factly. "Don't worry. They use a completely safe vaporized spray that only lasts several minutes. I can assure you that neither you nor your wife were harmed in any way." Maxwell explained.

Sean was pissed but didn't want to hear any more about his wife being drugged.

Ryan lifted his head. "So what happens to the 'bodies' of the people who had their consciousness transferred?"

"Oh boy," Sean whispered.

"You are right, Sean. No cerebral activity. Essentially they would be considered brain-dead if found before their consciousness was transferred back. And the bodies you are in now are automatically sent back to the time you came from," Maxwell said. "It's quite horrible, I agree. But that is not the intent of the consciousness transfer. It is actually a much safer and more efficient method than utilizing the orb. The engineers have worked long and hard to minimize the effect of the orb. But prolonged use can, in theory, cause some damage. Mostly in the spinal area, I am told."

Maxwell stood up. "But we're getting ahead of ourselves. I don't think that will be a problem. The main problem is that, given Darius' history, you both are in serious danger. You could opt to return to 2016 right now but I would not be surprised if Darius immediately sent security to your time and have you executed. Whether your memories are erased or not."

"So, what do we do?" Ryan asked.

Maxwell was quiet for a moment and stared at his desk. Finally, he spoke, "We need to stop Darius and end time travel for good." Maxwell continued to stare at his desk.

Sean looked at Ryan. "Ok, and how do we do that?" Sean asked. "You said you had a skeleton plan, but I think we might need a more concrete plan at this point, don't you think?"

Maxwell looked up from his desk. For the first time, Ryan noticed how old Maxwell looked. Not wrinkly old but tired old.

He remembered that is how his father looked the last few months of his life.

"You are correct, Sean, but first things first," Maxwell sat down at his desk and fumbled through his top drawer. "Do you gentlemen remember when I told you we put trackers on your bodies so we could follow you as you progressed?" Maxwell asked. Both Ryan and Sean nodded. "Well, do you also remember I told you that there was no way to remove the trackers but that they would just wear off eventually?" Maxwell continued. Again, both nodded.

"I was truthful in that the trackers can't be removed, per se. But they can be blocked. Unfortunately, the procedure is not pleasant," Maxwell paused to gauge reaction, but neither boy seemed too concerned.

"So why do we all of a sudden need to block them?" Ryan asked.

"Fair question," Maxwell replied. "Protocol during the course of this contest, or whatever it was, is to limit the tracker data to the handlers. Myself for you two and Tyler for the other four. However, at this moment, I am betting that Darius has instructed his security team to alter the data tracking and open it to both himself and security. The advantage we have is that I happen to know that the process for altering those particular data streams, in this case, will take hours to complete. But it WILL happen and we must not let you two be discovered."

"You said the blocking process wasn't pleasant?" Sean asked somewhat apprehensively, remembering Maxwell's explanation from a minute ago.

"We don't have to cut your arm off if that's what you're afraid of. Just some mild burning for several minutes. You both need to take off your shirts," Maxwell said.

Ryan and Sean looked at each other and shrugged while they both removed their shirts.

"Now, turn around and arch your back," Maxwell instructed. Ryan and Sean complied.

"Now, this will burn, but it will subside rather quickly. And remember, security is walking the halls outside that door. So keep your voices down," Maxwell said as he donned a rubber glove and dipped his fingers into a small jar he had taken from his desk. He applied a small amount to both Ryan's and Sean's back just below their neck and gently rubbed it in.

"I don't feel anyth...," Sean started, then fell to his knees, and Ryan did the same. "Holy shit! Get it off!" Ryan said much too loudly.

"Keep your voices down!" Maxwell scolded. Both boys writhed in pain as they gritted their teeth, and tears came to their eyes. "It's not subsiding, Max!" Sean moaned.

"Give it a minute," Maxwell said, although he had never actually experienced this particular application before. However, one of the custodial staff was paid 100 credits to try it out. That guy ran around screaming for about two minutes before settling down.

Ryan and Sean began to slow their breathing and although still gritting their teeth, they both seemed to be improving. "Okay, it's not burning so bad," Ryan said, "but if I don't have a gaping hole in my back, I will be very surprised." They both stood up and took turns looking at each other's back. Amazingly, there was no mark. Nothing. Not even red or bruised. "What the hell?" Sean said. "You're saying that the trackers are gone?"

"Not gone, just blocked," Maxwell replied. Both Ryan and Sean put their shirts back on. There was still a dull pain but not bad. "So now what?" Ryan asked as he sat down.

Maxwell slowly opened his door and peeked out into the hallway. Luckily empty. "You two stay here. Do NOT, under ANY circumstance, leave this office. Remember, you are both expendable now. In fact, I would say you are both marked now. I can't be certain what Darius has planned but I know you two are in extreme danger. Tyler and I have to report to Darius to be de-briefed. When I can, I will return and we will proceed with forming Sean's "concrete" plan. I know this is a small office and only one couch but I think it would do both of you some good to try and get some rest. I'm going to lock my door. That won't keep security out but it will slow them down. Stay close to each other and use this VCD if someone tries to get in," Maxwell said and handed Ryan a freshly charged VCD. And without another word opened the door, walked out, and shut it behind him.

Chapter 84

Maxwell tapped his ear twice and said, "Tyler, where are you?" All senior administration, security, and handlers had been fitted with an internal communication device. Normally, you would just need to tap your ear once, and you were broadcast across the network. But it is possible to program two or more taps to reach a particular person and have a private conversation. The system wasn't used very much. Plus, it only worked inside the boundary of the Institute. The age-old technology of the intercom seemed to be more popular. But Maxwell, of course, couldn't risk that.

"Maxwell?" an out-of-breath Tyler replied.

"Yes, where are you, Tyler?" Maxwell replied.

"I'm in my office. Holy shit, Maxwell, we're in big trouble," Tyler exclaimed.

"Calm down and stay there. I'm on my way." Maxwell took a couple of turns and half walked, half jogged, towards Tyler's office. Once there, he knocked quietly, "It's me," he said.

Tyler opened the door, barely wide enough for Maxwell to shimmy through. "Darius has lost it. He threatened to kill me. He says I have one hour to find you and that was 30," Tyler looked at his watch, "no 35 minutes ago. He knows. I don't know how but he knows. I'm sure of it," Tyler was pacing back and forth as he rambled.

"Tyler, Tyler, calm down. Sit down for a minute," Maxwell pulled a chair out from the desk. Tyler sat down and put his head on the desk. He was either moaning or crying. Maxwell couldn't tell.

"Tyler, calm down," Maxwell said and slowly rubbed the little man's shoulder. "Tell me exactly what Darius said to you."

Tyler sat up, "he didn't say a damn thing for like half an hour. Just sat and stared at me. Then he asked where you were. I said I didn't know, but he freaked out. He pulled out a stun gun, pointed it at my head, and asked again where you were," Tyler explained, breathing fast again.

"That's it?" Maxwell asked.

"No, I didn't know what to say, so I just said I would find you, and he said I have one hour!" Tyler looked at his watch again.

"Okay, so he doesn't know. He just thinks he knows we had something to do with it." Maxwell walked back to Tyler's door and peeked out. Nobody could be seen or heard.

"I don't know, Maxwell, you should have seen his eyes. I've never seen him that mad before. He wasn't grilling his security team. He was grilling me!!" Tyler put his head back down on the desk.

"Ok, this is what we're going to do. We're going to go back to Darius' office..."

"No fucking way am I going back there," Tyler nearly shouted. Maxwell had never heard Tyler swear before. It was kind of refreshing.

"Tyler, we have to. We're going to go back to Darius' office and tell him we have no idea what happened. Yes, he'll freak out but he has no proof. We will tell him that we will stay all night with the engineering team going through the data strings and figure out what happened," Maxwell said but not very convincingly.

Tyler started to speak but Maxwell cut him off. "Tyler if we don't meet with Darius, he will have us hunted down and probably killed," Maxwell said, this time more convincingly.

"Clean yourself up. We need to go back to my office before we meet with Darius," Maxwell said and tossed Tyler a towel from his bathroom.

When Tyler was ready, they quickly walked back to Maxwell's office. When they got inside, Tyler headed for the bathroom to continue 'freshening up.'

As Tyler was wiping his nose and splashing some water on his face, Ryan got Maxwell in a corner alone. "Max, no matter how this turns out, I don't want my family or Sean's to remember what happened. With all we now know about Darius, I suspect he's not going to follow through and erase our family's memories as promised," Ryan said as Maxwell nodded. "You are probably right, Ryan," Maxwell replied, "The process is not difficult. But it will require a technician to visit each family member. And right now, correct me if I'm wrong, they are all on a cruise ship somewhere in the Caribbean?"

"Yea," Ryan said quietly, "but can it be done on the ship?"

Maxwell thought for a moment. "Not while they are at sea. Our technology is good but not that good. However, if they are docked, it wouldn't be a problem. We would just need to know where they are on the ship and, more importantly, where the ship is at any given time."

"Oh, right," Ryan said, "that does seem to pose a small problem. Seeing as they are in 1982 and we're in 2163. Any ideas on that one?"

Maxwell called Tyler over when as he was finished.

"Tyler, we have a small logistical problem that Ryan just brought to my attention. With all that has happened and all that is about to happen, we need to erase Sean's and Ryan's family's memories. But they are on a cruise ship somewhere in the Caribbean. Any thoughts?"

Tyler put his hand to his chin and paced back and forth a few times. As he was doing so, Sean joined the group. "What's up guys? You calling an audible on the play?" Sean asked. Ryan explained the situation.

"Ok, yea that's a problem. Anyone got any ideas?" Sean asked and Ryan pointed to Tyler who was still pacing.

Tyler joined them in the corner. "Maxwell is right. We can't send a technician to a moving ship. We'd probably get close but if we missed, well that wouldn't be good. I think the best we can do is send someone to the cruise line office, find out the next docking location, and take care of it while the ship is in port." Tyler half-smiled and kind of shrugged.

"And who do we send?" Maxwell asked. "It will need to be off the books, so to speak."

Without hesitation, Tyler said, "Timothy. Timothy Whitmore. He's a good technician and is always looking for opportunities to travel. We tell him it's a time sensitive project and needs to be done quickly. He can find out the port location, travel to that time and GPS coordinate and get it done quickly. Probably a few hours, if he leaves soon."

Sean interjected, "Um, just out of curiosity, what needs to be done exactly? I mean, does he use a laser or something?"

"Not exactly," Tyler answered. "He just needs to get close to the person in question and run a pre-programmed scan over the person's head. It's completely painless and takes about 20 seconds."

"Well, he doesn't need to do it on everyone," Ryan said, "just our four parents and my older siblings. They are the only ones that are involved in this. Oh, and my little brother. It would be nice if he didn't remember being kidnapped."

"Is Timothy here?" Maxwell asked.

"He's on call, always," Tyler said, "we can call him now and get him on his way. He'll be thrilled."

"Ok. Ryan, write down the names of everyone he needs to contact. We'll get him going before we go to Darius' office," Maxwell said as Ryan grabbed a piece of paper.

As he wrote, Ryan asked, "How will he find them on the ship?"

"Timothy is very resourceful," Tyler answered. "Don't worry, he'll find them."

Chapter 85

Maxwell and Tyler sat outside Darius' office not saying anything to each other. They had just spoken with Timothy and, as Tyler predicted, he was more than willing to get the job done. He was gone before they arrived at Darius' office.

Maxwell leaned towards Tyler, "let me do the talking." Tyler nodded his head.

Darius' secretary said, "Mr. Ramsey will see you now." She pushed a button and his open door appeared. Maxwell and Tyler entered the office and walked directly toward Darius' desk. For the first time, Maxwell didn't even notice the massive sail boat that hung from the ceiling but walked directly underneath it.

"Well, Tyler, good work! You said you would find Maxwell and you did. Please come sit down gentlemen, Would you like a brandy?" Darius said much too nicely which made both men nervous.

Darius walked around his desk toward his bar and poured three snifters of brandy. Darius took his glass and walked back to his desk. Maxwell and Tyler each took their glass and moved to the front of their boss's desk and sat down. This was not what Maxwell had expected. Something was very wrong here.

Darius sat down, took out three coasters and placed them on his desk. All three men set their glasses down. Darius sat down, leaned back and stared at the two handlers.

'Here we go again,' Tyler thought.

"Gentlemen, I have a problem," Darius began. "I got a call from my observation team earlier this afternoon and was told that our current contest has completed. Imagine my surprise!?!

The most important experiment we have ever performed and it's over. I was also told that there was no audio or video surveillance. Nothing. No data," Darius slowly rose, walked around his desk and behind the two seated men. He placed one hand on each of their shoulders and bent down and whispered, "what the holy fuck happened?" Darius rose and walked back to his chair and sat down.

Tyler was well aware of what happened last time he said 'I don't know' so he kept his mouth shut.

Maxwell had another idea. He cleared his throat. "Sir, with all due respect, that isn't our only problem." Tyler's eyes slightly widened and he half turned his head to look at Maxwell.

"Do tell, Maxwell. What problem could possibly be worse than missing the entire showdown of our most important contest ever?" Darius leaned forward to hear the older man's reply.

"Well, sir, we have no idea the whereabouts of two of our contestants. Their tracking data is offline and frankly, they have simply disappeared," Maxwell wasn't sure if this was the right path to take but at least it didn't result in the violent outburst that Tyler had experienced.

"To be honest, my friend, I couldn't give two shits where Ryan White and Sean Jensen are. In time, we will find them and deal with them accordingly. Tyler's team is either dead or in jail from what I've been told. I really don't care what happens with our contestants," Darius replied, confirming Maxwell's suspicions.

"Okay, well the reason I didn't immediately report to your office was I was attempting to locate my team. But now that I know that is not in my purview any longer, Tyler and I will stay through the night and work with the engineering team to determine what happened to the surveillance. Tyler and I have spoken at length about what happened and we have not been able to find a reason for the failure. We know it wasn't anything we did and the contestants certainly couldn't do anything. It must have come from an outside sabotage," Maxwell couldn't believe he was allowed to say so much before being screamed at. His fingers were literally crossed in his lap.

Darius didn't say anything. Just sat back in his chair and stared ahead. Maxwell could tell he wasn't directly looking at them. He was looking sort of through them.

Darius rose again from his chair and slowly walked across his office and stopped at the globe in the middle of the room. He slowly spun the globe, stopped it, and slowly spun it again. Without looking back at the two men in front of his desk, Darius said "I'm not sure what to believe, Maxwell. You said you had nothing to do with this? Frankly I believe you. I mean, why would you?" He turned around and walked back toward his desk.

"You and my father shared the vision, right? Why would you deliberately ruin one of our most important ventures to date?" He again bent down near Maxwell's ear and whispered, "you wouldn't do that, would you Maxwell?"

"Of course not, Mr. Ramsey," Maxwell answered.

"OF COURSE NOT, MR. RAMSEY," Darius repeated animatedly and sat down.

"And what about you, Tyler, would you deliberately sabotage a contest?" Darius asked a shuddering Tyler.

"Of course not, sir," Tyler eked out.

"Of course not." Darius picked up his glass and took a rather large gulp of brandy.

"I tell you what I'm gonna do. I am going to give you, my security team, and my crack engineering squad exactly 24 hours to find out what happened. You will lead the investigation Maxwell," Darius' eyes got very narrow, "and if you fail, you will not live the see hour 25. You're dismissed," Darius picked up his brandy and turned in his chair. Maxwell and Tyler slowly got up and walked out.

"I can't believe we're still breathing," Tyler said as soon as they were out of the secretary's earshot.

"We have a lot of work to do," Maxwell said.

"Yea, I know, we have to come up with a reason why this happened," Tyler agreed.

"You don't understand, Tyler. We're not going to come up with a reason why this happened. We're going to stop Darius and destroy the time travel system," Maxwell replied.

"Oh, no," was all Tyler could muster.

Chapter 86

Bill White slowly opened his eyes. He looked at the ceiling but it was wrong somehow. He looked over and saw his wife sleeping next to him. As he was trying to get his bearings, there was a knock on the door. Bill sat up suddenly. This was not his room. Then he remembered, they had all come on a cruise. But, why?

He stumbled up, grabbed a pair of shorts and approached the door.

"Who is it," he asked.

"Your daughter," Jessica answered. Bill opened the door as his wife was putting on a robe and coming up behind him.

"What's wrong, dear?" Ryan's mom asked. Jessica entered their room.

"Mom, dad, why are we on this cruise ship?" Jessica asked somewhat flustered. "I mean, it's great that we're here, but John and I have been racking our brains trying to remember why we did this?"

"Well," Bill started, "it's because we…um…we always wanted to take a cruise…well this is just stupid. Liz, help me out. I'm still waking up I guess. I can't really remember why we are on this cruise."

"Well we wouldn't have just come on a cruise for no reason," Liz said. "Let's just get everyone together at breakfast and talk about it."

"Fine, we'll meet you there," Jessica said and left.

After eating and sending the little ones off to the pool, the two families gathered together. Linda and Sean Sr., Liz and Bill White, John and Jessica, and Debbie.

"So," Bill began with a smile, "anyone had any grand recollections during breakfast?"

"Nope," Jessica said. "And, oh by the way, where the hell is Ryan?"

"Oh my goodness!!" Liz cried as she looked around the room. "Where is Ryan?!?"

"Ok, ok, just calm down," Bill said. "I'm sure if Ryan isn't here, he had a good reason. The weird thing is why we can't remember why we came. What's the last thing you remember, Jessica?"

"I remember we were at your house for dinner and we had some family meeting but I can't remember for what," she said.

"I remember that too," Sean Sr. said. "Obviously we were talking about this cruise. Remember, Bill, you and I were kicking this idea around a few months ago."

"Yea, I do remember that," Bill replied. "Maybe we just enjoy the rest of the cruise and not worry about why we came?"

"I'm good with that," Debbie said. "I'm going to get some sun."

"Alright, it's weird, but okay," Jessica said as she got up and left.

"Are we losing our minds, Bill?" Liz asked.

"I sure hope not. It is weird though. Oh well, let's enjoy ourselves while we're here," Bill said with a smile.

Chapter 87

"Oh crap. Sean get over here," Ryan whispered as they heard someone at the door. Sean sat next to Ryan on the couch. Ryan flipped the VCD on and the two disappeared.

"What do you mean we're going to stop Darius?" Tyler asked as they entered the office. Maxwell looked around his office and quickly in his bathroom. When he walked out, Ryan turned off the VCD.

"Very stealthy, Ryan," Maxwell remarked.

"What's going on Maxwell?" Tyler asked.

"I told you. We're going to stop Darius and destroy the travel department," Maxwell said confidently. "You know as well as I do what he's been doing. This whole Institute is a fraud. It's just a front for him and his rich friends to play their sick games."

"I know, but what can we possibly do? Darius has an army of security," Tyler asked and sat down at the other end of the couch.

"Darius employs an army of security. Except for a few, I'm not sure they are all 100% loyal to him. At least I hope not," Maxwell said as he sat down at his desk.

"Whatever we do," he continued, "we have to figure it out tonight. Darius has given Tyler and me only 24 hours to come up with an explanation of what happened at the memorial. Plus, if we all agree on my plan, I don't want anyone else in the Institute when it happens."

Ryan stood up. "When what happens, Max? What is your plan?"

Maxwell began clearing his desk. "Just let me talk for a minute without interrupting and then you can ask questions. Okay?" Maxwell asked as he pulled out a blank sheet of paper and a pencil.

Chapter 88

Darius tapped his ear three times. His personal code for his secretary, Mary Bainbridge. "Mary, get me Bruce Holstetter."

"I'm sorry sir, Mr. Holstetter has left for the day," Mary replied.

"I don't care if he's in Hawaii on vacation! I want Bruce in my office within the hour!" Darius bellowed.

Within 20 minutes, Bruce Holstetter was entering Darius' office, a little out of breath. It was lucky he lived relatively close to work. He had just started reading his granddaughter a story when Mary called. But if Darius Ramsey wants to see you, you drop everything and run. "You wanted to see me, sir?"

Darius had been drinking a consistent stream of brandy and was a little more relaxed. "Yes, Bruce, thank you for coming in after hours," Darius said quite politely.

"It is no trouble sir. How may I be of service?"

"Bruce, I'm sure you have heard that there was a bit of a mix-up in surveillance earlier today involving our current experiment?" Darius asked.

"Yes, sir. I heard something about that. Although I was told security was not to get involved at this stage," Bruce explained.

"Yes, yes, I am not upset with you Bruce," Darius assured the head of security, "but I do have an assignment for you that is a security matter. It would seem that two of our contestants have gone missing."

"That's most distressing, sir. Who is their handler? I will get with them immediately and pull their tracking data," Bruce was about to tap his ear.

"No, wait," Darius stopped him. "I want you to find these two contestants without involving their handler. At least for the time being. That is possible, correct?" Darius asked.

"Yes, sir. We will need to alter the protocols in the tracking system. It's not a difficult process, but it takes a little time to fully calibrate," Bruce explained.

"How much time," Darius probed.

"At this time of night, the load on the system is low. I would estimate 90 minutes for a complete reset. All I need is the names of the contestants and their handler. Just the handler's name, of course. We will not need to contact the handler, per your instruction."

"Very good, Bruce," Darius said approvingly, "their names are Ryan White and Sean Jensen. And their handler is Maxwell Sanderson."

Bruce turned to leave.

"And Bruce," Darius called after him, "when you find them, bring all three directly to my office. And I don't need to tell you to keep this between you and me, for now."

"Of course, sir," Bruce said as he turned and left. His granddaughter would not be hearing the rest of the story tonight.

Chapter 89

"You're out of your mind, old man," Ryan said as Maxwell finished explaining his plan. "Yea, you might get Darius that way, but you're going to kill the rest of us as well."

"I think I would have to agree with Master White, uh, Ryan," Tyler said. "Gilderene is extremely unstable if removed from the containment pods."

Gilderene is a compound formulated by mixing Trinitrotoluene (TNT) with Gilda, a naturally occurring compound that was discovered around 2075 in a Russian mountain range. It was named Gilda due to its golden color. Around 2105, shortly after founding the Institute, Alexander Ramsey, while mining for gold on the company's land, came upon a very large bed of Gilda. It was found that Gilda burned very hot and for long periods of time but was difficult to ignite. The Institute engineers began experimenting and finalized on a combination of Gilda with TNT. It burned at an extremely high temperature but produced little to no emissions. Therefore, it could be used to power the Institute and not alert authorities. It was estimated that the bed of Gilda that Alexander discovered could power the Institute for at least 500 years. The engineers called it Gilderene. A mix of Gilda and Toluene, the base material for TNT. Although TNT is relatively stable, Gilderene exhibited unstable behavior during storage. Portable storage pods were developed to keep the fuel stable during storage but easily accessible for continuous use.

Maxwell was quiet for a moment. Then he said, "What about the mini-pods used in the North Expansion Project? There are still hundreds of them just sitting below Level 1."

"Yea, but… well, those aren't…uh…hmmm," Tyler stammered, "actually, we could theoretically move the Gilderene in the mini-pods."

"What do you mean 'theoretically'?" Maxwell asked. "That is what they were made for."

Ryan and Sean were lost. "Could one of you clue us in on what the hell you're talking about? I thought you said this Gilderene, or whatever it's called, is highly explosive?" Ryan asked.

"Yes, that is exactly what I said Ryan," Maxwell answered. Maxwell gave Ryan and Sean a short history lesson on Gilderene.

Afterward, Sean spoke up. "So this Gilderene is stable as long as it stays in these mini-pods? How do we use it to destroy the time travel system if it's so stable? And how the hell do we blow up half the Institute without killing ourselves in the process?"

Tyler spoke up rather enthusiastically, "that's easy, the mini-pods weren't only used for storage. They were also used for injection. Each mini-pod has a release mechanism that is activated by the injection system. If we can figure out a way to activate the release remotely, we don't need to be anywhere near the pod when it opens. Plus, it will be easier to contain the fire to a localized area." Tyler smiled as though he had won the Nobel Prize.

Nobody spoke for several minutes. Finally, Ryan spoke up, "I have a question. Let's say we are successful in destroying your time machine. How do Sean and I get back? Where is the consciousness transfer system? Isn't it part of the travel department?"

"No, it's not," Maxwell said. "The consciousness transfer system is located on a completely different string element. But it is in the same wing, relatively close to the travel department. Maybe 100 feet."

Ryan and Sean exchanged a concerned look.

"The good news," Tyler interjected, "is within that 100 feet there are two cement walls on either side of a rather large garden area. Each cement wall is 14" thick and hardened to earthquake standards. The question, I suppose, is will they withstand a 3500-degree Celsius fire?"

Ryan stood up. "Okay, let's do it. Like you said, Max, we really have no choice. If we don't destroy Darius' time machine, he'll just hunt us down in any time period and kill us. Probably our families too, just for kicks. Where did you say these mini-pods are?"

Chapter 90

"Wait a second," Sean spoke up. "What about the problem of opening these pods once they're in place and, more importantly, when we're not standing next to them? Plus, how do we light the suckers?"

"Lighting them won't be a problem," Tyler said. "We can use a lightning stick. We use them all the time to remotely trigger less volatile liquids in the field. As for the release, I might have an idea but it involves bringing someone else into our little terrorist cell."

"Who are you thinking of? And I don't like being called a terrorist. This is all for a good cause," Maxwell asked.

"That was a joke, albeit a bad one," Tyler replied. "As for who I am thinking of, Margie Greenspan. She is definitely not a fan of Darius ever since he publicly accused her of theft last year. Plus, she is working the late shift in the environmental section right now."

"So, how can Margie help us?" Maxwell asked. Maxwell had known Margie and her husband for years. Her husband was killed in a hiking accident a few years back and Margie was seriously injured. Maxwell had helped her through her recovery.

"Margie and Tom, her husband, worked on the North Expansion Project before it shut down. Tom was the explosives expert but Margie helped to design the mini-pods for containment. I think she'll help us, Maxwell. But it needs to be you who asks her. You know her much better than I do, ever since the accident," Tyler said and briefly explained the hiking accident and her long recovery to Ryan and Sean.

Maxwell thought for a moment. He hated to bring others into this but they definitely needed her help if they had any hope of success.

"Alright, Tyler and I will go talk to Margie. You two stay here and keep that VCD close," Maxwell said and he and Tyler left the office.

The environment section was one building away from Maxwell's office. As he and Tyler made their way, they noticed several security guards but nothing unusual. Nobody gave them a second look as they passed. There certainly didn't seem to be any noticeable increase in personnel.

They arrived at Margie's office and knocked. "Come in," a female voice said. Maxwell and Tyler entered.

"Maxwell!!" Margie said excitedly and stood to hug her friend. "Hello, Tyler, how are you?" Tyler shook her hand.

"Fine Margie, how are you?" he said.

"I'm good. So why did the top two field agents in the company decide to grace me with their presence?" Margie asked as she sat back down. "Please sit down," she motioned to the chairs.

"Margie," Maxwell started, "have you heard what's going on in the experimental section?"

"Yes, something about a major surveillance failure? We get a lot of gossip down here. Lots of theories," she chuckled. "From what I hear, Darius is quite upset, poor baby," and wrinkled her nose in disgust. "Serves his privileged ass right. The man thinks he lives in a perfect little world. He needs to know not everything goes as planned."

"Well, Tyler and I have been put in charge of finding out what went wrong. But," Maxwell paused, "we have uncovered some information that will probably come as quite a shock."

"Oh good, more gossip," she pulled herself closer to her desk in anticipation.

Maxwell had a very serious look on his face which Margie noticed and her smile disappeared.

"Margie, this isn't gossip, and it's very troubling and serious. Frankly, you are the only one we feel we can trust," Maxwell said. He then stood, walked to the door, and locked it.

"What's going on, Max?" she asked with an even more concerned look on her face. Besides Ryan and Sean, Margie was the only other person who called him Max.

"Margie, I'm going to trust that you will keep what I'm about to tell you confidential. It's absolutely critical that nobody else gets this information. It's literally a matter of life and death."

"Okay, I promise," Margie said and sat quietly.

Maxwell then took the next 20 minutes explaining everything from beginning to end. All the factual information as well as their suppositions based on fact. He also informed her of their plan to destroy the travel department. When Maxwell was finished, tears were streaming down Margie's face. She felt sick to her stomach and picked up a glass of water with shaking hands.

"I feel like throwing up," she said and took a sip of water.

Maxwell knew this would be a shock to her system. All he could hope for was that she was strong enough to compose herself and get through it.

"Margie, I am deeply, deeply sorry for laying this all on you at once like this. I know it is difficult to hear," Maxwell said.

Margie cleared her throat. "Oh, I don't know. I find out that my boss is a terrorist and has systematically been killing people for sport. Oh, and not to mention, everything I've been working on for the last 17 years has been for absolutely nothing. Yea, you could say it's a little difficult to process."

Tyler chimed in. "Margie, everything Maxwell has told you is absolutely true. But I want you to know that your work has not been for nothing. The environmental breakthroughs you and your team have achieved are real and extremely valuable to mankind. Please don't let Darius' failures cause you to think that what you do isn't worthwhile. It absolutely is," Tyler felt a little out of place but thought she should know how he felt.

"Thank you, Tyler. I know. We have a great group of people here, and I like to think we have done good work," she had finally stopped crying.

"You absolutely have, Margie," Maxwell agreed with his colleague.

"So Max, I can't say I appreciate you telling me all this. But what is it that I can do to help?" Margie asked as she refilled her glass.

"When we came up with a plan to stop Darius and destroy his time travel capabilities, the most important thing and the first we thought of was that we didn't want anyone else to get hurt. Everyone working here means a lot to Tyler and to me. We want to make sure we limit any damage to the travel section. So we are considering using Gilderene," Maxwell said. He had not yet told her specifics of their plan on HOW they were going to destroy the travel system.

"Gilderene!?!? Do you know how unstable that compound is? You'll never get it from the containment pods to the travel section! You'll blow yourselves up!" Margie replied vehemently.

"You're quite right," Maxwell said, "that's why we want to use the mini-pods."

Margie was silent. She began to speak but stopped herself. Finally, she spoke.

"Well, they are portable and easy to fill and transport. A full mini-pod only weighs about 25 lbs. But how will you remotely release the Gilderene? It probably won't spontaneously ignite, but there is definitely a possibility that it will," she explained.

"You're exactly right, Margie," Maxwell said, "and that is where we need your help. You worked with mini-pods on the North Expansion Project. Do you have any ideas on how we can remotely release the material once we're far enough away?"

Margie sat down and put her fingers on her forehead in thought. "Hmmm, I wonder if it would work," she said quietly.

"If what would work," Tyler asked.

Margie stood and walked to her filing cabinet. "About halfway through that project, we had an area of forestation we needed to clear. We couldn't get large enough equipment in place before the snow fell. So we did a controlled burn. We didn't use Gilderene, of course, but we used the mini-pods filled with napalm. Obviously, we couldn't just pour it out and light it. Napalm burns at 1200 Celsius and it sticks to you so there was no easy way to hand deliver it," she shuffled through her files as she spoke. "So we came up with a release mechanism that was radio-controlled. I know, old school. But it worked and we created quite a bonfire," she pulled a folder from the cabinet. "Here it is," she said and handed the folder to Maxwell. Maxwell studied the drawings and sighed, "Yes, this would definitely work, but from the looks of it, it will take weeks to build." He handed it to Tyler, his more technically-minded partner.

"Yes, it would," Margie said with a smile, "unless there were some already built."

Chapter 91

Margie led Maxwell and Tyler down some hallways and tunnels even Maxwell was unfamiliar with. "Where are you taking us, Margie?" he asked.

"The excess equipment from the Expansion Project is stored in Annex T," she said as they walked briskly but not too fast to raise any suspicion.

"Annex T?" Tyler asked. "I've never heard of Annex T. I thought I knew everything about this place."

"Annex T isn't exactly a fun place to be. It is filled with napalm and other things that go boom. We call it Annex T for TNT, which by the way there is plenty of," Margie explained. Tyler looked at Maxwell, who just shrugged his shoulders and tried to keep pace with the younger engineer. Finally, they arrived at a large door with Annex T handwritten on it.

"Here we are," Margie said and was about to punch in the code when she pulled her hand away.

"What's wrong," Maxwell asked.

"Damn, I forgot," Margie said, "this door is alarmed in security. There's no surveillance but if we open this door, the guys upstairs will definitely know."

"Is there another way out besides the way we came in?" Maxwell asked.

"Yea, we just keep heading down this hallway, and there's a stairwell at the end that leads to the west garden," Margie said.

"Well, if I've been accurately tracking our path down here, security will come from the way we came. How long do you think it will take to grab four of your radio release mechanisms?

Even if they run down here, which I doubt, it will probably take security at least 4-5 minutes to get here," Maxwell asked.

"That depends," Margie said, "on how much 'stuff' is in there and how well it's marked."

"If we don't get those release devices, we're back to square one," Tyler stated the obvious.

"Alright," Maxwell said, "let's give it a shot. Tyler, keep an eye on your watch. We leave at 4 minutes whether we've found them or not."

"Okay, timer set," Tyler clicked his watch.

Margie punched in the code, and the door opened with a whoosh, indicating the positive pressure inside the room. All three walked in. There was a strong odor, kind of like fertilizer mixed with ammonia. Margie felt along the wall and clicked the light on. The room was good sized but not huge. There were four rows of shelves on each side with a main walkway down the middle. The shelves were 3' high, the top shelf being slightly out of reach, even for Maxwell. "Okay, you take that side. We'll start on this side," Maxwell pointed. They started down the aisles. Margie shouted out, "Remember, look for either RR-315 or RR-815." Maxwell had made his way down one side of shelves in his aisle and hadn't seen anything remotely close to the numbers Margie had yelled out.

"2 minutes," Tyler shouted out.

"Keep looking," Maxwell shouted back.

Maxwell almost ran into Margie as they both reached the end of their respective aisles. "Maybe they're not he..." Margie started to say.

"Found it," Tyler bellowed from the other side of the room. Margie and Maxwell ran over. Tyler was pulling down a plastic bin marked RR-815. He ripped off the packing tape and pulled the top off. It was empty! "Holy crap," Tyler said dejectedly.

"Wait, look behind it. Another bin marked RR-815," Margie pointed. Tyler jumped up on the first shelf and reached as far as he could but couldn't get his fingers on the bin. Maxwell looked around and spotted a small 3' ladder at the end of the aisle. He ran and grabbed it. "We're out of time, guys," Tyler alerted them. "Coming up on 4 minutes."

Maxwell just hoped they sent their most out-of-shape security guard to check the alarm. He grabbed the bin after stepping on the ladder and pulled it down. It felt heavy, which was a good sign, he thought. They ripped off the top, and there were several smaller boxes stacked neatly in stacks of 4. Tyler grabbed four of the units and asked

"Margie, is this all we need?"

"That's it," she said, and they hurriedly put the bins back and ran toward the door. As they turned off the light and quietly shut the door, they heard footsteps and voices emanating from the way they had come. They quickly ran down the hallway away from the security guards.

"Whew, that was close," Margie said when suddenly Maxwell put his hand up. They all stopped to listen. There were footsteps coming from up ahead. They were trapped!

Chapter 92

"What could possibly be taking them so long," Ryan asked nobody in particular.

"No idea. What has it been? 90 minutes?" Sean asked.

"Yea, I think so," Ryan said and sat down hard on the couch.

Suddenly, there were footsteps and voices coming from outside the door. Sean sat down quickly next to Ryan, who flipped on the VCD. The couch suddenly looked empty.

The door opened, and two security guards walked in. "Where do you think he is?" one of the guards asked the other.

"No idea. Why are we supposed to find this guy anyway?" asked the second guard.

"I don't know. I learned a long time ago not to ask questions when Bruce gives an order."

"I hear that. Check the bathroom, then let's get out of here," the first guard went towards the bathroom. The second guard walked toward the couch. "Why does everyone get a couch in their office and we get a piece of shit futon," the second guard sat down on the couch. His left shoulder was inches from Sean's shoulder. Both boys held their breath.

"And, it's damn comfortable. Maybe we stay here and relax for a while. He raised his legs and began to swing them over on the rest of the couch. Right on top of Sean and Ryan!

"Get real," the first guard said and smacked his smaller partner on the back of the head. "You wanna keep your job?" The second guard groaned and stood up. All he had to do was look a little left and notice the couch cushions were pushed down on the other side of the couch. But luckily, he missed it.

The first guard dropped a note on Maxwell's desk and they walked out and flipped off the light as they left.

"Good freaking crap," Sean said and stood up. Ryan looked white as a ghost. "Where the hell is Maxwell?" was all he could say.

"In here," Margie whispered as she punched a code in on the door to their left. They ducked inside and held their breath. They waited until the footsteps passed, then Margie cracked open the door.

"Let's go," Maxwell said. The three of them half jogged and half ran the rest of the way down the corridor, trying to keep as silent as possible. They reached the stairwell and hurried up to the next level. There was a doorway that led outside to the west garden. Once outside, they slowed their pace, although it didn't appear anyone was around. They walked to the far side of the courtyard and entered another door that led to the administrative offices. The bad part about their current position was that they would need to pass by Darius' office on their way to Maxwell's. The only option would be going all the way around the building to the front, where security was certain to be stationed.

They slowly walked toward Mary Bainbridge's desk. Mary looked to be intently going over some files in a folder. They stuck to the far wall and walked at a normal pace past her desk. She never even looked up, much to Maxwell's relief. Unfortunately, they were not completely unnoticed.

Darius tapped his ear twice, a code he had recently changed for his head of security.

"Mr. Holstetter, please send two security personnel to Maxwell Sanderson's office and bring him to my office," Darius instructed.

"Right away, sir," Bruce responded.

A couple of minutes after Bruce relayed the order, he received the reply that Maxwell was not in his office.

Bruce called Mary Bainbridge and asked her to relay the message to Darius that Maxwell was not in his office. The fewer times he had to speak directly to his boss, the better.

Maxwell peeked around the corner again. The door to his office was still open and the light was on. The two security guards had entered just seconds before Maxwell, Tyler, and Margie had arrived. Now they were huddled down the hallway, waiting to see if Ryan and Sean would be discovered. Maxwell peeked again and jerked his head back. "They're coming," he whispered and shooed Margie and Tyler into the alcove next to the water fountain. The two security guards walked by and disappeared around the corner. Maxwell led the other two towards his office and walked in. But kept the main light off.

"Ryan?" Maxwell whispered for no apparent reason.

"Right here, Max," Ryan came out of the bathroom. "So what the hell took you so long? We almost got sat on by a fat security guard."

"I know. We saw the whole thing. Darius must be up to something if he's trying to find me," Maxwell said, sounding exhausted.

"I thought we had 24 hours," Tyler questioned. "Here's a note for you," he said and handed it to Maxwell. It read:

"Darius Ramsey has requested you report to his office immediately upon receipt."

"Damn, I wonder what the hell he wants?" Maxwell asked.

"What are you going to do?" Margie asked.

"At this point, I'm going to do as I'm told. If I don't, he'll get more suspicious," Maxwell said. "I'll be right back," he said and walked toward the door.

"Do you want me to come along?" Tyler asked.

Maxwell thought for a moment. "No, I'll see what he wants and let you know." He walked out the door.

Chapter 93

"Mr. Ramsey will see you now," Mary said to Maxwell, who was waiting patiently. He felt like a puppy about to be disciplined for soiling the carpet. He was so sick of this shit, he thought as he walked into his boss's office.

"You wanted to see me, sir?" Maxwell said as he crossed around the hanging sailboat.

"Ah, Maxwell, yes, I wanted to get an update on your investigation. I trust you are uncovering a wealth of valuable information?" Darius said as Maxwell sat down.

"The investigation is proceeding. We are currently focusing on the element strings, looking to identify any anomalies," Maxwell said.

"Oh, element strings. I see. And is that all you've been doing?" Darius asked. Suddenly Maxwell got the feeling Darius knew something.

"Well, we've only had a few hours, and that seemed like the most reasonable place to start," Maxwell answered.

"I see. Yes, of course, that makes perfect sense. I'm just curious why I saw on my monitor a few minutes ago, you walking past my office with Ms. Greenspan from Environmental and Mr. Tyler carrying several boxes. Could you enlighten me as to how this helps in your element string analysis?" Darius asked.

Maxwell wasn't sure what to say. Monitor? Darius had always strictly forbidden surveillance anywhere near his office. How did he see us walking by? He had to think quickly.

"Margie, sir? She isn't...she isn't part of the investigation. Tyler and I just ran into her on her way back to her office, and we were helping her carry the equipment she had. It wasn't heavy but we thought we'd help her out," Maxwell silently held his breath.

"I see. And if I asked Ms. Greenspan to join us, she would certainly corroborate your story, I assume?" Darius asked.

"Of course," was all Maxwell could say.

"Maxwell, you were a good friend of my father's, so I am obligated to give you every benefit of the doubt but believe me, I do have doubts about your dedication to this investigation. Why would you suppose I feel that way, Maxwell?" Darius asked with every bit of belittling emphasis he intended.

"I don't really know, sir. Both Tyler and I are very intent on finding out what happened and how it happened. We both understand the gravity of the situation," Maxwell replied.

"I see. Well, I certainly hope you find what you are intently looking for," Darius said, somewhat mocking Maxwell's use of the word 'intent.' "I wouldn't want anything unsavory to happen to either of you if you fail. You can go now," Darius swiveled in his chair away from Maxwell. Maxwell got up and walked out. 'Something unsavory might happen to you, Mr. Ramsey,' Maxwell thought as he walked back toward his office.

As he walked, a general announcement sounded in his internal communication device:

"Marjorie Greenspan, please report to Mr. Ramsey's office immediately."

Luckily, Maxwell caught Margie as she was leaving his office. "Crap, Max, what does he want to talk to me about?" Margie asked as Maxwell approached her.

"Don't worry. He just wants to know why you were walking with us past his office. As far as I can tell, he doesn't know anything about Annex T. I told him we ran into you and were helping you carry your equipment. He didn't ask, so I didn't say what the equipment was. Just stick to that story, and you should be fine," Maxwell placed his hand on Margie's shoulder. "Again, Margie, I'm sorry for pulling you into this."

Margie put her hand on top of Maxwell's. "I'm not sorry," she said with a half smile and continued walking toward Darius' office.

Maxwell got back to his office and walked inside.

"So, how did it go?" Tyler asked. "You know, they just paged Margie to Darius' office."

"Yes, I know. I just spoke with her. I'm glad I caught her. Darius has put surveillance in and around his office. He saw us walking with Margie and wanted to know why. I told him we just ran into her and were helping her carry some equipment," Maxwell sat at his desk with a groan.

"Surveillance?" Tyler asked. "He was always against that. He never wanted anyone knowing what he did in there."

"I know," Maxwell agreed. "But for whatever reason, he now has eyes anywhere near his office. He was also asking about our investigation. I told him we were focusing on the element strings. I think he bought it. Pretty sure he was just trying to scare me."

"Well, it's working," Tyler said.

"So, how is it going with the radio release devices?" Maxwell asked. "Does Margie think they will work?"

"They should. We just need to get our hands on 4 mini-pods filled with Gilderene," Sean said.

"Tyler, how many release mechanisms did you carry out of there?" Maxwell asked.

"I grabbed six in case a couple of them were damaged," Tyler answered.

"Good. We need to get 5 mini-pods filled with Gilderene. I have something else I want to burn," Maxwell said.

Chapter 94

"Mr. Ramsey will see you now," Mary said to Margie. Margie rose and walked into Darius' office. It had been a while since she had been in his office. She looked up at the massive sailboat that hung from the ceiling. She suddenly felt very small.

"Ah, Ms. Greenspan, please come in and sit down. Would you like a drink? I know you're on the clock but I won't tell if you don't," Darius said with a smile.

"Uh, yes sir, thank you, sir," Margie said, and Darius handed her a brandy. She took a small sip. Never in her life had she tasted something so wonderful. The alcohol sold at the marketplace tasted like rat urine in comparison.

"So, how are things down in environmental," Darius asked as he sat down.

"Fine, sir. Thank you for asking," Margie answered dutifully.

"I know you and your team are doing wonderful things. Just wonderful. I have been so busy I haven't had a chance to come down and visit with you," Darius said, still smiling.

"Well, that's fine, sir. I know you have a lot going on. I wouldn't want to distract you," Margie said, growing ever more nervous with every passing minute.

"No, it wouldn't be a distraction. I'll make it a point to come by very soon."

"Thank you, sir. That would be great. I'm sure the team would appreciate it," Margie took another small sip.

"Well, I'll get to the point," Darius said as he rose from his chair and came around the desk and sat in the chair next to

Margie. Uncomfortably close. "I was wondering, Marjorie, have you seen Maxwell Sanderson lately?"

"Maxwell? Yes, I saw him earlier this evening. I haven't seen him for some time. So it was nice to catch up," she took another small sip.

"Yes, I was speaking with Maxwell earlier, and he told me he had run into you. I know you two built a very close relationship during your recovery period from your accident. So, what did you talk about?" Darius stood up and walked toward the globe in the middle of the room.

Margie turned slightly in his direction. "Um, nothing much. Just catching up. I asked him about his work. I've always been interested in field work," Margie hoped she hadn't gone too far.

"His work, you say? Yes, he is one of our top handlers. Did he say anything about his current assignment?" Darius asked.

Margie couldn't believe Darius was being this direct. But she was willing to play along. "Uh, he mentioned that he and Tyler were conducting an investigation into a recent surveillance failure. I had heard about it. You know, through the grapevine. It sounds like a significant system failure. I'm sorry," Margie took another sip.

"Yes, it was most disappointing. Is that all he said about his work?" Darius was slowly spinning the globe.

"Uh, yes. The rest of the time, we talked about Tyler's date last week," in a fake way she chuckled and took another sip.

Darius stopped the globe abruptly with his hand. "Well, I won't keep you from your duties, Marjorie. Please let your team know I will be down soon for a visit. I'd really like to know about all the wonderful accomplishments you're making," Darius walked back to Margie and took her glass. He walked to his desk and sat down.

"I will tell them. Thank you for the drink, sir," Margie said as she walked toward the door. She felt like running but figured that might not be the best idea. After she walked past Mary's desk, she noticed she was visibly shaking. Maxwell was right. Darius was not the same man that hired her so many years ago. Once out of Mary's sight, she broke into a jog toward Maxwell's office.

Chapter 95

Margie knocked on Maxwell's door but didn't wait for anyone to open it. She came in and sat down on the couch. "That man is pure evil," she said as she kicked off her heels.

"The fact that you're here leads me to believe that it at least went well?" Maxwell asked.

"Define well. He basically grilled me on what you and I talked about. I told him we discussed the investigation…"

"What? Why did you tell him that?" Tyler blurted out.

"No, that's good," Maxwell said. "If she hadn't said that, he'd be even more suspicious."

"I told him I had heard, through the grapevine of office gossip, that there had been a surveillance failure. Which is true. Everyone knows. I told him the rest of the time, we discussed Tyler's love life. Sorry, Tyler. I couldn't think of anything else to say."

"That's fine," Tyler said. "It would be nice if I had a love life."

"So where are we at?" Margie straightened up, "if you haven't figured it out by now, I'm in 100%."

"We need to get the mini-pods filled with Gilderene. We figure we need at least five," Sean said from across the room.

"Five?" Margie asked. "You guys know that one or two would probably be sufficient."

"We don't want to leave anything to chance," Ryan added. "Margie, just curious, how big are these mini-pods?"

Margie held out her hands about 12" apart. "Probably a foot long and maybe 4" in diameter. They're cylindrical. Completely full, they probably weigh 25-30 lbs."

Tyler pulled out a piece of paper he had been doodling on since Margie had left. "I drew up an idea of how to combine the lightning stick with the radio release device. I think we want to have the lightning stick activated as soon as the release device is activated. That way, there won't be any delay in the ignition," he handed the paper to Margie.

She studied it for about a minute.

"This should work, but you're going to want to switch these two connectors," she pointed to the drawing and handed it back to Tyler.

As Tyler was reviewing the design with Margie, Maxwell walked over to where Ryan and Sean were standing.

"I just got a digital alert, something akin to your text message, from Timothy," Maxwell said as he sat down on the couch. "It would appear that he was successful in erasing your family's memories. No doubt they were scratching their heads as to why they were on a ship in the middle of the Caribbean."

"Well, that's better than them having a full memory of this circus from Hell. I'm sure it will all dissipate over time. Please thank Timothy for both of us," Sean said, and Ryan agreed.

Maxwell stood back up and walked toward Margie and Tyler. "So, you two engineers think we're ready?" Maxwell asked.

"The plan is ready," Tyler said. "but the execution of that plan still concerns me."

"What are your main concerns?" Maxwell asked and sat at his desk with the design in front of him. "Looks to me like this should work."

"Oh, it will work," Margie said. "As Tyler said, the mechanics are sound. But with all the increased security and everyone on 'alert,' so to speak, it's going to be tough to get five of the pods filled and placed in the server room. It's 12:30am, and people will start arriving in about 5 hours."

"Okay, so as I asked before, but nobody answered, where are these mini-pods?" Sean asked.

"They're kind of spread out all over, but there are at least five down in Annex 2 with the main containment pods. I was down there a couple weeks ago and saw several of them stacked up. We can also fill them at that location," Margie said.

"How long will it take to fill 5 pods?" Tyler asked.

"Not long. Maybe 2-3 minutes. It's all automated and sets up quickly," Margie replied.

"So, how safe is it to fill the pods?" Ryan asked.

"Actually, it's fail-safe. The pods are designed with a seal at the injection point that prevents any Gilderene from getting out during the filling process. As I said, it's all automated. Once the lid Tyler and I designed is put on, it pierces the seal, and the Gilderene will leak out quite quickly once it is remotely opened. Like I said before, the mechanics are sound," Margie said with a proud smile. Her smile then disappeared. "Again, I'm worried how we get to, and inside, Annex 2. That door is alarmed, and there is video surveillance in both directions leading to the door."

"Have none of you ever watched an action movie from the 1980s?" Ryan asked. "We obviously need a diversion.

Something to occupy security so they aren't all watching the surveillance cameras."

"Well, a mini-pod of Gilderene would work nicely," Margie said.

"Uh, yeah, but that's the problem we're trying to solve," Sean replied.

"You didn't let me finish. We don't use Gilderene. We use Napalm and we don't need a mini-pod."

"Ok, you have our attention. Please explain," Maxwell said with interest.

"I have Napalm in my lab. Not a lot, but there's enough. We use it in very small amounts for some of our environmental impact studies. Napalm is very stable by itself. But we could put a small amount in a container, mix in a little fuel, top it off with a lightning stick and it would make a nice little bomb. Nothing too destructive but enough to get everyone's attention."

Maxwell paced back and forth for a few seconds, deep in thought. "How much Napalm do you have?" he finally asked.

"Like I said, not much, but it burns very hot, and it's hard to put out with standard fire extinguishers," Margie answered.

"You guys still use fire extinguishers?" Ryan asked. "I thought you would have come up with some high-tech anti-flame laser or something."

"Some things never change," Tyler answered.

"Okay, so say we make this little Napalm bomb. Where do we put it?" Sean asked.

"I know where I'd like to put it, but I don't really see any way to do it," Maxwell said.

"And where is that?" Tyler asked.

"There is one thing in this Institute that I hate more than anything else. I've hated it from day one."

A small smile appeared on Tyler's face. "I know what it is," he said.

"What?" Margie and Ryan asked at the same time.

Maxwell looked up. "That damn sailboat."

Chapter 96

"What sailboat," Ryan asked.

Maxwell began to speak, but Tyler put up his hand. "Allow me," he said.

"Years ago, long after Alexander was killed and Darius took over as Director, he brought in a massive sailboat. A full-size, completely sea-worthy sailboat. He had the contractors build his office big enough to hang the boat from the ceiling on cables. Don't ask me how they did it but it must have cost a fortune. In order to get to his desk, you have to either walk directly beneath it or hug the wall."

"I hug the wall," Maxwell said. "I trust the engineers, but I've had nightmares of that thing falling on me."

"Well, as cool as that would be to burn up his sailboat, I think you're right that it would be a little difficult with him sitting at his desk," Sean said from the couch.

"Who says he has to be at his desk?" Margie asked.

"The man goes from his office to his helicopter to his home and back again. He basically lives in his office. He very rarely goes anywhere else. Especially lately," Maxwell sighed.

"His helicopter," Ryan said from the corner of the room and everyone turned his way.

"We'll blow up his helicopter! Okay, it's not his sailboat but it is something he cares about."

"There's surveillance out there," Tyler reminded everyone.

"We've got the VCD, and it only takes one person to place the container near it," Ryan replied. "Three of us get as close to

Annex 2 as possible and one person places the container. We set off the bomb, wait a few seconds for the security to scramble, and we get in and fill the mini-pods and get the hell out of there. It will burn for a while, and we might even have time to place the mini-pods in the server room."

Nobody spoke. Maxwell started to but stopped.

"I'll do it," Tyler said boldly. "Every time I hear that damn thing wind up, it irks me."

"Okay," Maxwell said, "but we need more VCDs. Tyler, can you get your hands on a couple more? They don't last very long, but I have a feeling we may need them."

"Yea, we can stop by the field office on the way to Margie's lab. I should be able to get a few. But we need to remember if two VCDs are used in close proximity to each other, the light bending effect gets a little hinky. If two of you are using them at the same time, stay at least 5' or so apart from each other," Tyler warned.

Maxwell turned to Ryan and Sean. "You two need to stay out of sight. I can explain why we're walking the halls but I can't explain you two. Stay here while we go get what we need from Margie's office."

Maxwell, Margie, and Tyler walked out of the office, leaving Ryan and Sean alone.

Sean sat down on the couch and sighed. "This has been quite the ride, dude."

Ryan sat in Maxwell's desk chair. "No doubt. Seems like a million years ago before all this started. It's still hard for me to believe it's real. I'm just freakin' tired." He put his head down on the desk.

Sean sat silent for a few minutes, then said, "So you think we'll actually get out of this and get back home?"

Ryan didn't respond, he just breathed hard as he slept.

Sean put his head back on the couch and closed his eyes. He was asleep in less than a minute.

Ryan was back in his living room, sitting on the couch, watching Colton and Jackson open up presents piled under the Christmas tree. Michele sat next to him. She leaned over, kissed him on the cheek and whispered in his ear, 'I love you Ry...'

Wham!! The door to Maxwell's office exploded inward as four security guards with rifles burst in. "Don't fucking move!!" one of them yelled.

Both Sean and Ryan froze in place, disoriented from being awoken so suddenly and slowly put their hands up. The four guards entered further into the office and surrounded them, guns pointed at their heads. Behind them, a man walked slowly into the office with his hands behind his back and smiled.

"Gentlemen, so nice to finally meet you. My name is Darius Ramsey."

"Bring them," Darius said as he exited the office.

Chapter 97

"How much do you think we need?" Maxwell asked Margie as she carefully lifted the container of Napalm.

"I'm not really sure. We don't need to actually blow up the helicopter. Just ignite it. The onboard fuel will do the rest." Margie scooped out about two cups of a gelatinous liquid and poured it into a glass container. She then poured a little clear fuel on top, placed the small lightning stick inside, and sealed the container.

"Tyler, you will need to place this near the back of the helicopter directly underneath. When the lightning stick lights, this will explode and cover the surface of the helicopter. This stuff burns at about 1200 degrees Celsius, so it won't be long before the whole thing will explode. In any event, it will certainly get everyone's attention," Margie handed the container to Tyler, who took it very gingerly.

Suddenly, there was a lot of commotion going on outside Margie's office. She poked her head out. "Steve, what's going on?" she asked one of her lead technicians.

"They caught those two contestants," Steve said, somewhat out of breath. "Larry saw them being led to Darius' office." Margie closed the door.

Maxwell was pacing.

"Holy crap," Tyler said under his breath.

"Max, what're we gonna do?" Margie asked. Maxwell continued to pace.

"Nothing," he said. "We stick to the plan. But with one minor change. Tyler, get moving and plant that device under the helicopter. Then you and Margie get your asses down to Annex 2. Keep the remote detonator close. In exactly 20 minutes, blow it. Wait a few seconds, then get those mini-pods filled and placed in the server room as we planned. But don't blow them until we meet in the west garden."

"What's the minor change"? Margie asked.

"I'm going to Darius' office."

Chapter 98

Sean looked over at Ryan as they were pushed and shoved along the hallway. Ryan was just staring ahead. Sean could actually see the wheels turning in his head.

"Sit!" one of the guards said and pointed to two chairs that were lining the window by what looked like a reception desk. Both boys took a seat.

They watched as the one who called himself Darius walked right through the wall and disappeared. Ryan looked at Sean with eyebrows raised.

"You seem exceedingly calm," Sean whispered.

"Actually, I'm terrified beyond the capacity for rational thought," Ryan replied.

Sean eked out a smile at his friend's ability to quote Ghostbusters at a time like this.

"Well, if you're Egon, that makes me Dr. Venkman. But need I remind you we don't have our proton packs?"

Ryan and Sean had each seen Ghostbusters at least 100 times. They both knew it by heart.

"Yea, well, hopefully, Maxwell has something up his sleeve?" Ryan said quietly.

"Why don't you ask him?" Sean said and looked down the hallway. Maxwell was headed right toward them. He slowed down somewhat at the sight of the automatic rifles the guards held.

"I need to see Mr. Ramsey immediately," Maxwell said as he approached the guards.

"Sorry, Mr. Sanderson, we were told nobody is to be let in until Mr. Ramse..."

"Let him in," Darius said. Neither Ryan nor Sean could tell where his voice came from.

Maxwell pushed past the guards and walked through the wall.

"Ah, Maxwell, do come in. I can honestly say I did not expect you so soon. Have a seat. Would you like a drink?" Darius walked towards the bar.

"Yes, please," Maxwell said but did not sit down.

"As I'm sure you noticed on your way in, we were fortunate enough to find Mr. White and Mr. Jensen," Darius said as he dropped two ice cubes into each glass.

"What's your plan, Darius? Those two boys did everything we asked of them and deserve to be sent home," Maxwell figured he would at least try the civil approach.

"HOME?!!" Darius picked up one of the glasses and threw it directly at Maxwell as hard as he could. Luckily, Darius wasn't exactly a starting pitcher for the Yankees. The glass missed by at least 3 feet and crashed into the wall behind Maxwell.

"Not only will they never be sent home, they will pay the ultimate price for ruining my production!! And if I were you, MAX, I'd worry more about what is going to happen to you and your little buddy Tyler!!" Darius drew a knife from his back pocket and started to move toward Maxwell when Maxwell pulled out a stun gun from his pocket and fired it directly into Darius' chest. It was set to medium but still blew Darius back a few feet, and he fell to the ground like a rag doll, completely unconscious. The stun guns of this era (called immobilizers) were not like those of the 21st century. There were no wires with barbs, just a targeted burst of energy that didn't rely on contact with flesh.

Maxwell turned and quickly looked toward the door. Nobody had heard anything. He looked at his watch, 3 minutes to go. He grabbed Darius under his armpits and dragged him over to his chair. With a little effort, he was able to get Darius into a sitting position and turned him away from his desk as though he was looking out the window. Maxwell seriously considered taking Darius' knife and slitting his throat. 'Later,' he thought. He quickly looked around the room for something to tie him up with, but Darius' office was like a museum. Nothing out of place and nothing to tie him with. Maxwell looked under his desk and noticed what looked like an orb pushed back in the corner. That was odd, he thought. Orbs were closely tracked and monitored. Why would Darius have a travel orb in his office? Oh well, Maxwell thought. It won't do him any good in a half hour or so. Then he noticed Darius' shoes. 'Better than nothing, I suppose,' Maxwell thought as he pulled the laces out and tied Darius' wrists to the chair. He knew it wouldn't hold him for long, but he was hoping he wouldn't need very long. He looked at his watch for 30 seconds. Maxwell moved close to the door and waited. 10-9-8-7, Maxwell glanced at Darius. No movement. 3-2-1. Maxwell closed his eyes and tensed for the explosion. Nothing happened. 'Dammit, Tyler, what the he...?"

BOOM!!! The entire building shook. Maxwell waited two seconds and ran full speed through the door with the intention of bowling over at least one guard. As he flew through the door, Ryan and Sean were standing over the guards with their guns pointed at them. Maxwell smiled. "Well done, gentlemen. Use their restraints and drag them into the office.

The fire alarm was blaring so loud it was difficult to hear. Once Ryan and Sean had dragged the security guards into

Darius' office, Maxwell pulled out his stun gun again. "Sorry, lads, but this will hurt," and he pulled the trigger twice, once for each guard. He felt bad for having to do it. He knew each of the guards personally and had nothing against them, except for the fact they were loyal to Darius and needed to be silenced, at least temporarily. Maxwell knew they would be fine, albeit with a horrendous headache for a couple of days.

Maxwell hurried out of the office just in time. CRACK!! The wire supports holding the massive sailboat to the ceiling gave way, and the entire ship crashed to the floor, splintering into a million pieces and spewing dust and debris throughout the office. Maxwell could see enough to know the security guards did not get crushed, but he could not see to Darius' desk. There was no time to check.

Maxwell, Ryan, and Sean ran down the hallway toward the west garden.

Chapter 99

"This is the last one," Margie said as she handed the final mini-pod filled with Gilderene to Tyler.

"Place it next to that server there," Margie pointed and backed up toward the door.

Immediately following the initial blast at the helicopter, Margie and Tyler had immediately entered Annex 2 and filled the mini-pods. They had then taken the 5 mini-pods to the time travel department and snuck in using a VCD. They were almost run over twice by security running toward the blast. And carrying 5 mini-pods and staying hidden within the VCD perimeter was not an easy task. But Ryan's idea of a diversion worked as planned.

"All set. Let's get the hell out of here," Tyler exhaled loudly as they both ran toward the exit to the west garden.

Once outside, they looked over to where the helicopter pad was and could only see a mass amount of thick black smoke rising quickly. "Damn, girl, how much napalm did you use?" Tyler asked as they headed toward a darkened portion of the garden.

"Apparently, more than I neede..." BOOM!! Another massive explosion from the direction of the helicopter pad.

"There goes the fuel tank," Margie said as she shook her head. The noise from the explosion was deafening.

"Well, that worked," Maxwell said from behind Margie and Tyler.

"Holy shit!" Tyler wheeled around. "How the crap did you sneak up on us?"

"Not too hard with all the fireworks," Ryan said as he came out of the shadows.

"Master White! I mean, Ryan. Good to see you. Is Sean with you?" Tyler asked.

"Right here," Sean said and stood next to Ryan.

"Well, if everyone is up to speed on who's here, let's finish this," Maxwell said as they all walked toward the far edge of the garden.

"Sean, Ryan, this is where we part ways," Maxwell said. "Tyler is going to take you to the Consciousness Transfer Section and send you on your way. All I can say is it's been..."

Suddenly the entire garden area lit up with huge floodlights. Every corner of the expanse was fully lit. No sooner than the lights came on, automatic gunfire rang out. Bullets whizzed by their heads and exploded into the ground around them. All 5 instinctively ducked and ran for cover to a small brick wall that gave some protection. The shots had come from the other side of the garden, maybe 70 yards away. Ryan slowly raised his head and looked over the wall. Nobody was visible but instantly bullets smashed into the bricks just inches from his face.

"Tyler," Maxwell winced as he spoke. "Take Ryan, Sean, and Margie around this far end and get to the CTS and get them home. Margie, you keep running and don't stop."

Margie reached down to Maxwell's side that he was holding. "Good Lord, Maxwell. You've been shot!" She ripped off the lower half of her shirt and pressed it to the wound.

"Nevermind," Maxwell blurted out. "I will hold them off as best I can with my immobilizer."

Ryan knelt down. "We can't leave you here, Maxwell."

A small smile formed on Maxwell's face, hearing Ryan use his full name.

"You can and you will," Maxwell said calmly. "Or all this will be for nothing! There's no time for goodbyes. Get moving now!"

Tyler grabbed Ryan and tried to pull him, but the smaller man barely budged him.

"Go!" Maxwell growled.

Ryan stood to a crouch, and the four of them ran toward the far end of the garden that led back toward the building.

Once they were out of sight, Maxwell crawled as best he could to the edge of the wall and peeked around the corner. At least a dozen security guards were within about 20 yards of his position with weapons drawn. Maxwell took a deep breath, stood to his full 6' 6," and aimed and fired his immobilizer. The blast took about 5 of the guards out but several remained. No less than 20 rounds immediately ripped through Maxwell Sanderson's body. He fell with a groan and his final breath.

At the sound of the gunfire, Ryan tried to turn and run back. Sean stopped him with full force. "He's gone, dude! You go back, and it's suicide." They kept moving toward an employee's entrance that was rarely used.

"Margie, keep going down this path and get to your car. Drive away and don't come back until I call you," Tyler pointed in the direction of the front of the building.

Margie looked at Ryan and Sean. "Good luck, fellas. It's been, well, interesting to know you." She ran down the path and out of sight.

Tyler led Sean and Ryan inside the building, down a couple of hallways, and to a door labeled CTS (Consciousness Transfer Section). The halls were eerily quiet. Their 'distraction' had apparently worked. Everyone that wasn't out trying to kill them in the garden was obviously out fighting the helicopter fire.

Once inside the CTS, Tyler strapped Ryan and Sean into what could best be described as a standing gurney.

"You ready?" Tyler asked, still out of breath.

"Wait," Sean stopped him. "Tyler, what's going to happen to this place? What's going to happen to you?"

Tyler stooped up as tall as he could. "Master Jensen. Master White. It has been an honor working with you. I will deal with my destiny. You deal with yours." Tyler reached around the back of the panel next to the gurneys and pushed a red button. The button then turned green, and he pushed it again. Ryan and Sean's bodies went completely limp and lifeless. They slowly disappeared to be automatically sent back to 1982 with their previous consciousnesses in place.

'One last thing,' Tyler thought to himself. He reached into his jacket pocket and took out a rather large square box that looked like a homemade science experiment. He knelt down, covered his ears as best he could, and pushed the button.

The impact was more than Tyler had prepared for. It was more like a violent earthquake than an explosion. The CTS where Tyler was kneeling wasn't destroyed but the outside wall facing the garden was heavily damaged, and all the power in the building went out. Tyler slowly stood and, as quickly as possible, made his way out to the parking lot and drove away. As he drove, tears streamed down his face as he thought about his lost friend. Internally, he vowed never to return. But never is a long time.

Security guards and other institute personnel were scrambling to dig through the nightmare that Darius' office had become. When they finally reached his desk, Darius was nowhere to be found. Just two shoelaces lying on the floor next to his chair.

Chapter 100

Ryan slowly opened his eyes. It was dark, but he could barely make out the patterns in the ceiling. Many nights, he and his wife had laid back and looked up at the ceiling above their bed. They could make out figures like a duck and a ballet girl dancing and what looked like an alien face. Ryan's eyes slowly adjusted, and he realized he was looking at that ceiling again. Inch by inch, Ryan turned his head to the side. Michele's face was, without a doubt, the most beautiful sight he had ever seen. He raised his hands to his stomach. A nice little roll of fat jiggled under his grasp. He'd never been so happy to feel his out-of-shape body. And just to be sure, he put his hand on top of his head. Yep, head shaved. It was over!

He glanced at his nightstand clock; 4:57 am. Needless to say, he wasn't going back to sleep. He quietly got out of bed and checked on both his kids. Sound asleep as if nothing had happened. Because he supposed nothing had happened. To them at least. He moved to his office and began typing. He wrote straight for over an hour, everything he could remember.

Then the phone rang. It was 7:30 am. "Ryan?" Sean said, whispering for some reason.

"Sean, I think we need to talk?"

"Ya think? I'm coming over."

Ryan had decided to hold off with details to his wife until he and Sean had talked. He tried as best he could to act normally as he helped get the kids ready for school. Michele said she had an early appointment, so she left with the kids just as Sean pulled in. Sean waved at them as they pulled out of the driveway.

Sean walked in to find Ryan sitting at the island in his kitchen, just staring out the window.

"Dude, what the Hell?" Sean said as he sat down next to Ryan.

"Yea, I'm not sure what to think. I mean, we know it all happened. But nobody will ever believe us," Ryan said and sipped his orange juice.

"I know. I just spent the last hour and a half writing everything down so I don't forget," Sean said and opened the fridge to get some juice.

"I did the exact same thing. But somehow, I really don't think we're going to forget."

Just then, the doorbell rang. When Ryan opened the door, a young girl about 7 years old was standing there. It was Katy Newman from a few houses down the street.

"Hi, Katy. What can I do for you?" Ryan asked.

"Hi, Mr. White. I have a letter for you. A really nice man gave me five whole dollars to bring it to you." Katy handed the letter to Ryan.

Ryan took the letter. On the front, it just said, "To Ryan White and Sean Jensen." A chill ran up Ryan's back. "Thank you, Katy. You run on home now, okay?"

Ryan took the letter into the kitchen. "Check it out," he said and handed the letter to Sean. It was a normal size envelope with what felt like one piece of paper inside. Sean slowly slid his finger along the seal, pulled out the paper, and unfolded it. This is what was written on the page:

Good Morning Master White and Master Jensen.

It's my turn now.

Get ready to play!

-Darius Ramsey-

Ryan looked at Sean. "Ah shit!!" they both said in unison.

To Be Continued...

www.ingramcontent.com/pod-product-compliance
Lightning Source LLC
Chambersburg PA
CBHW050957180726
48291CB00006B/1862